Adrian Mourby

Adrian Mourby is a freelance writer, broadcaster and journalist, well known to *Radio 4* listeners as the creator of *What Ever Happened To . . . ?* and SILKIES – *Single Income, Lots of Kids*. He lives in Cardiff with his family, and is working on his second novel.

18/8

SCEPTRE

We Think the World of Him

ADRIAN MOURBY

SCEPTRE

Copyright © 1995 Adrian Mourby

First published in 1995 by Hodder and Stoughton
A division of Hodder Headline PLC
A Sceptre Paperback Original

The right of Adrian Mourby to be identified as the Author of
the Work has been asserted by him in accordance with the
Copyright, Designs and Patents Act 1988.

10 9 8 7 6 5 4 3 2 1

A CIP catalogue record for this book is available from
the British Library.

ISBN 0 340 64920 8

Typeset by Palimpsest Book Production Limited,
Polmont, Stirlingshire
Printed and bound in Great Britain by
Cox & Wyman Ltd, Reading, Berkshire

Hodder and Stoughton
A division of Hodder Headline PLC
338 Euston Road
London NW1 3BH

Before I wrote a novel I never understood why men wrote:

To my wife without whose help, love and encouragement this book would not have been written.

Acknowledgements

∫

My thanks to Angus and Jane West, Chris & Louisa Wilson, Anthony Whitworth and Phil Humphreys for their assistance.

To Carolyn Mays and Sarah Lutyens for setting this book up without even a lunch and to all the Pontcanna Mums.

Introduction

Losing his job did wonders for Duncan's sex life. Suddenly he felt released from all the restraints that office life imposes on existence. Duncan Lewis was no longer someone who had to be up by a certain time, and out by a certain time and in by a certain time. He was now someone who could lie in bed as long as he wanted, and make love to his wife for as long as she wanted.

Fortunately, Jane Lewis worked part time, and so routine hardly inhibited her either. One morning, after the girls had gone into school, Duncan and Jane had suddenly decided at the breakfast table that they would, then and there – and they did. After all, what was there to stop them? All things were possible and the cleaning lady never arrived before eleven-thirty.

Cut loose from timetables and other people's expectations of a provincial architect, Duncan experimented with life. He walked slowly one morning to Jacobs, the delicatessen and flower store. Another morning he stopped and played football with a small boy who was practising against some garage doors. The small boy was unimpressed, but Duncan – who had not played football for over twenty years, and then only under duress – found the experience profound.

'I've just played football with a small boy,' he told his wife as he joined her at the breakfast table.

'Did you win?' asked Jane, who had been kept waiting too long for the bread rolls.

'I mean,' said Duncan, who wasn't entirely sure what he did mean any more, 'I mean that it's never occurred to me before how much there is to do in the day if you're not having to clock on.'

Seeing Jane looking at him sceptically, Duncan stumbled on to explain that he had been hit by the sheer enormity of choice. He could get up, or not get up. He could fetch bread rolls from Jacobs, or he could get on a plane to Tunisia. Anything was possible now that he wasn't expected to go into work every morning. As he thawed out from the initial shock of redundancy, Duncan was finding himself wandering around in a warm daze of Infinite Possibility. He liked it.

Jane Lewis was a sensible woman, fond of her husband and still very defensive of him. She felt that Duncan's being thrown out of his post of associate architect at the age of thirty-eight was unjust. She wanted him to look positively on this new phase of their lives, but at the same time she did not want to be still sitting breadless at the breakfast table when he phoned in from North Africa.

Someone had to get a grasp on their lives.

In purely practical terms, money was not an immediate problem. Duncan had been given a reasonable lump sum by Howard The Louse, senior partner in Louse, Louse & Tosser (as Jane had recently renamed them), and Jane earned a fair amount drafting leases and wills for her old firm of solicitors. More worrying were their long-term prospects: Duncan was an unemployed architect, in a country that was building less and less and which – when it really had to build – seemed to prefer not to use architects at all, if possible.

Thus it was that on one particular January morning – after Duncan had spent a very interesting fifteen minutes discussing with the young lady at Jacobs how you get yeast to rise successfully; and after he had stopped on his way back to admire a late-Victorian fire hydrant he'd never noticed before, and *just* as he was about to grow amorous over the breakfast table again – Jane had said, 'Duncan, this has really got to stop.'

Duncan's first reaction was to assume this was the morning that Mrs R. the cleaning lady came early, and he knew that in Jane's family it was considered bad form to be caught *in flagrante* by the domestics. But no, Jane was addressing wider subjects: Life, the Future, Money.

'I don't want to be the boring one,' she began as Duncan's arm circled her waist, 'but we can't go on like this. There are pensions, and mortgage repayments and insurance premiums to think about.'

In Duncan's opinion he had spent the last fifteen years conscientiously thinking about little else, and at that moment he was far more interested in what was to be found inside Jane's towelling robe. Besides which, there was a large dark pit called *What Am I Going To Do With The Rest Of My Life?* that he had been ostentatiously refusing to look into ever since his job disappeared from underneath him. He knew it was there. He had expected to fall headlong and screaming into it, as soon as the door of Louse & Tosser slammed to behind him – but somehow he had been wafted away to a world of warm tranquillity, where Howard's ego, and salary cuts, and the grim prospects facing architects everywhere no longer impinged. He didn't quite know what he was doing there; he knew it couldn't last. But he was making the most of this unexpected holiday.

'Our outgoings are currently approximately twice our income,' Jane said. 'Which means that either we reduce our lifestyle drastically or one of us goes out to work full time.'

Duncan sighed.

'So I'm going to see Tony this afternoon,' Jane said. 'Is that OK?'

This news came totally and most pleasantly out of the blue. Talking to Big Fat Tony always betokened one thing in the Lewis household: Jane was going to try and get preferential treatment from her patron and former employer. Jane's record being unbroken at that stage (be it to get a salaried partnership, to withdraw from a salaried partnership, to work part time or to work part time from home), the announcement could only mean one thing. Jane was planning to go back to work.

'Do you mind?' Duncan asked.

'I was thinking of doing something different,' she replied.

'But going back to work . . .' Duncan let these words hang in the air.

'My turn,' said Jane generously, making it sound as simple and positive as possible.

In the kitchen of No. 11 Katrin Street, Duncan Lewis kissed his wife and headed for the washing up. But inside his own spiritual landscape he headed back to the beach. It was going to be another lovely day.

Duncan had no plans for the rest of his life. He was after all still coming to terms with who he was. He used to be an architect. But less than a month ago he had been told he wouldn't be one of the architects paid by Howard Losen any more. Did that mean he was no longer an architect? Was he perhaps a former architect? It seemed to Duncan that until he had a grasp of his own identity there was no point in making plans. Who would he be making them for?

However, after a few days of unstructured home life, Duncan was beginning to feel a resurgence of the old instinct to influence his surroundings. He collected up all the spices and arranged them in a rack. He gathered all the framed photos that had accumulated or fallen over in different parts of the house, and displayed them on a shelf in the upstairs drawing room. To Jane these little acts of domestic introspection were signs that Duncan was thawing out. She watched him but didn't comment.

So while Duncan was keeping his mind off the Dark Pit by lining up books in ascending order and matching pyjama tops to long lost-bottoms, his wife went down to the Cardiff Marina to see Big Fat Tony.

The redevelopment of Cardiff Bay was only one-third completed, which meant that restored bonded warehouses and pseudo-restored bonded warehouses huddled together, isolated amid flattened demolition sites. The few executive car parks with their reproduction balustraded gateposts looked as if they had been drawn in by an optimistic planner. In this world, where anything was possible because so little had actually *happened*, worked Tony Morgan-Jones, a senior partner in the ancient Cardiff firm of Follet Pryce.

Big Fat Tony was pleased as ever to see Jane Lewis, and his big pale eyes could not disguise the fact. Tony had a liking for most women, but Jane had been one of his first protégées. She had a special pedestal in Tony's personal pantheon.

'And how is Duncan?' Tony asked, setting a chair for Jane to sit on. Big Fat Tony always asked his young ladies about their husbands or boyfriends. 'Is he bearing up with all this silly business?'

It didn't surprise Jane that Tony knew all about Duncan's redundancy. Tony was one of those people to whom gossip gravitated. Not only did he make it his job to know what was going on, he positively enjoyed his job. Besides which he had probably already seen the recently updated Losen & Prosser notepaper, a little white label pasted over Duncan's name.

Tony's office was on the first floor of Bosun's Chambers, one of the few genuine converted bonded warehouses on the redeveloped wharf. It was a location about which Tony's fellow senior partners had given him no choice. The rebuilt interior of Bosun's gleamed and shone, and grew pot plants to the height of rain forests. Tony on the other hand was built on Victorian proportions. The folds of his double chin rolled seamlessly into the folds of his waistcoat. He was a man who needed old oak and tobacco stains about him.

Checking Jane was comfortable and well provided with coffee and biscuits, Tony eased himself into a hi-tech metal armchair opposite her. It constricted his bulk like a chromium corset.

Jane put down her coffee and gave it to him straight, which was how Tony liked it. 'I think I may need to ask for your help, Tony.'

Tony's limpid eyes grew a little moister. He always let it be known that Mrs Jane Lewis knew exactly how to handle him, and he loved it. He knew that she knew how he always responded to the direct emotional appeal. All that was left for him was to savour the moment. Tony could find it in him to like most women, but he particularly admired the sheer length of Jane Lewis. Height was a rare commodity in the part of Wales that Tony came from, but Jane wasn't just tall: she had long hair and long legs, and managed to move both in a way that delighted him. She also had a determined thrust to her jaw that inspired clients and left Tony feeling buoyed up for the day.

Half an hour, two cups of coffee and several biscuits later, Jane emerged with what she wanted. Like everything in life it hadn't come quite as she'd expected, but Tony had delivered. All she had to worry about now was Duncan.

'Tony's offered me a full-time job in the main office,' Jane told him as he put the finishing touches to the girls' bunk beds. Duncan was pleased to hear the news but preoccupied by one matching pillowcase that had eluded him.

'There is one snag,' Jane continued. 'I'd have to start on Monday.'

'Most jobs start on Monday,' said Duncan, trying to be helpful.

Jane grew exasperated. '*This* Monday coming,' she explained. 'Four day's time. Could you cope with that?'

This seemed an odd question. Why should he not cope? All that Jane going out to work full time involved was taking over full responsibility for the house and children. 'No problem,' he replied. 'You leave it all to me.'

And it was as simple as that – except that it wasn't. Jane believed they had coped, thanks to Tony. And coping was what mattered because that was what life was about. Coping with domestic and professional difficulties meant that she and Duncan were still left with time to savour the little moments that make living worth while. But this little moment was shorter than either of them expected because they were interrupted by Mrs R. downstairs who put her foot through a loose pane in the conservatory and simultaneously fused the vacuum cleaner. So while Jane took the cleaning lady home, Duncan swept up the glass, put the vacuum cleaner somewhere convenient to await the purchase of 5 amp fuses, and walked down to pick up the girls from school.

Because Jane always coped so well in the short term, she and Duncan never got round to that 'How will this affect the rest of our domestic life?' conversation, which was a shame because everything started to change almost straight away, before they realised it could and would and had.

Someone Who Isn't Duncan

Of course Duncan had been to the school before. The twins were eight years old now, and in their four years at Fulwood Road Infants & Junior, Duncan had been to three Christmas plays and two Summer concerts. He'd also attended what seemed like numerous parents' evenings when earnest thyroid young women or bored fat elderly women had told him time and time again that Alice and Ellen were 'somewhere in the middle there'. Regardless of the conviction with which the message was given, its import remained the same: Alice and Ellen had started school exhibiting all the signs one might expect from five-year-old girls, and in the years that followed they had proved themselves, in sequence, to be exactly what might be expected of six-, seven- and, most recently, eight-year-olds.

To Duncan his daughters' position in the dead centre of a developmental curve seemed exactly what he too would have expected. Having found himself, simultaneously, the father of two children he had always assumed that if they *both* did something at roughly the same time, then that was probably what nature expected of a child that age.

So the fact that Alice and Ellen were no brighter, no more competent, socially aware or manually dexterous than the average eight-year-old accorded exactly with Duncan's expectations.

Jane, on the other hand, worried greatly about her children. She couldn't help feeling that all the effort that had gone into their nurturing and bringing forth should have resulted in something drastically more – or even drastically less – than two averagely talented, reasonably adjusted eight-year-olds.

'Is there something wrong with them?' she had asked Duncan more than once.

'They're just ordinary little girls,' he'd replied.

'But should they be?' Jane persisted. As far as she could see there was no one particularly normal in her family, and both Duncan's parents had been perfectly potty.

'Perhaps all the oddity from both families has sort of cancelled itself out,' Duncan suggested, and they got into an argument about whether he was being facetious.

'You can't shrug everything off with a joke,' Jane insisted.

'I wasn't joking,' Duncan replied, and to prove it he pointed out that Jane wasn't laughing.

'I often don't laugh at your jokes,' she retorted.

The girls didn't laugh at Duncan's jokes either. He had reached an age in their eyes when he was capable of embarrassing them. In Duncan's eyes it was them who had reached the age, but they insisted it was him.

'And there are two of us,' said Alice.

'Outvoted again,' said Duncan as he stood at the school gate.

The gate at Fulwood Road was only a notional portal, as the old Victorian wrought iron barrier had rusted off and never been replaced. The school gap would have been a more appropriate term. It was here, sandwiched in with all the mothers in padded anoraks, that Duncan met with his daughters and their disapproval. The point of contention that particular day was that Alice and Ellen always had to walk home when several of their friends were picked up in cars.

'It's really embarrassing,' Alice said.

'What isn't?' said Duncan.

'Why can't you pick us up in the car *sometime*?' asked Ellen who, of the two, was more moderate in her strictures and demands.

'Because,' said Duncan, 'the nearest parking to Fulwood Road is Meirion Street and Meirion Street is next to Katrin Street and I am not going to drive our car just round the corner to save you a walk of a hundred yards.'

'Are you being facetious?' asked Ellen, who had cottoned on to this word recently.

'No,' Duncan said, 'I am being *reasonable*.'

'Why are you dressed like that?' asked Alice suddenly. Duncan had thrown on an old Barbour jacket when he set off for the school. It had seemed an unremarkable choice to him; a fairly neutral item of clothing for someone of his milieu: useful when on site and practical given that it actually improved in appearance when coated with dust.

'You look as if you're going to work,' Ellen replied when Duncan tried to fathom the basis of their objection.

'I might be,' said Duncan, hoping not to get on to the subject of his redundancy. It was something the girls had accepted as a temporary and unimportant blip in their lives.

'None of the other mums dress like that,' Ellen continued.

'Well, I'm not a mum,' Duncan pointed out. 'In case you hadn't noticed.'

But there, of course, was the rub. Duncan was dressed for the school gate like a man who has called by on his way back from work. Duncan was not a house father. Was it possible that the semiotics of the Barbour were giving the lie to his proclaimed acceptance of a life without work?

Duncan and the girls walked along in silence for a while, or at least as near to silence as the distant roar of cars on Cathedral Road would allow them. Then Alice returned to the attack.

'If you picked us up in the car, Tristram Davis wouldn't be staring at us.'

Duncan was quite thrown by this rebuke. Then he noticed an orderly convoy of boys walking home on the other side of the road. One of the four was indeed looking at Alice and Ellen. He was a tall boy with long blond hair. Alice stuck her tongue out at him. Duncan was shocked, but the boy seemed unsurprised.

Duncan's attention was drawn by the woman heading up this little squadron. She was hardly any taller than Tristram, but by her age Duncan assumed this must be the mother. She had a pretty doll-like face and walked ahead with an air of self-conscious devotion, holding the hands of her two younger boys. For the last fifteen years Duncan's nine-to-five existence had been spent looking at men and occasionally at their secretaries. A woman's face at three in the afternoon was something of a novelty, certainly one that was not plugged into a computer screen or a telephone. This face reminded Duncan of a print he had once seen of a missionary's wife striding, head held high, out of the camp of some hungry cannibal. This woman's imperial virtue had clearly caused the captor to lose his appetite, because her route was unobstructed.

Like her hand-tinted forbear this diminutive Fulwood Road matriarch was setting a good pace, and her two smallest children were having to work hard to keep up. Behind the first pair came Tristram and another boy, nearer eleven, with shorter dark hair. The four children kept in close formation behind their mother. Viewed in convoy, they reminded Duncan less of a band of Victorian Christians than a flotilla of tugs bobbing around an ocean-going liner as she returned to port, although the tug called Tristram clearly wasn't keeping his eye on the shipping lanes. There was a palpable clang as Tristram collided with a lamppost.

'Typical,' said Alice.

'He's such a wet,' said Ellen.

Duncan felt rather alarmed that his family group had been the cause of Tristram's shipwreck, and he crossed the road without further thought.

'Oh *no*,' said Alice and Ellen in unison.

When Duncan reached the Davis family, Tristram was standing up again and being addressed by his mother in serious but compassionate tones.

'How many fingers am I holding up now, Tris?'

'Three,' mumbled the boy, who was clearly not enjoying the numerical ministrations of his mother.

'Speak up, Tris. I know it's a nuisance, darling, but I have to decide if we've got to take you back to Casualty again, and you know how that will delay getting everyone's supper and Daddy will wonder where we've all gone.'

'I'm all right. Honestly I am,' said Tristram uncomfortably.

Duncan had been standing there a while by this time, and he felt he ought to speak now or be in danger of appearing a ghoulish bystander. Tristram's mother seemed not to have registered his presence in the slightest.

'Is he OK?' Duncan asked.

The woman turned and looked at him. The look was surprised and intense. Laura Davis was noticeably shorter than Duncan, but she still managed to give the impression that she was gazing down at him and his mud hut from the summits of Evangelical Certitude. 'I'm sorry?' she asked. The inquisition was so utter, her expression so shocked by his intrusion, that Duncan didn't know quite where to begin. Should he explain that he witnessed Tristram's collision, or that he was a parent at the same school, or that he was of the human species and currently resident in the neighbourhood?

'I think . . .' Duncan began. 'I think my daughters may have distracted your son.'

As if to substantiate this hypothesis, Duncan glanced over to where Alice and Ellen were waiting on the opposite pavement. They must have understood something of what was being said because both cringed, self-consciously and theatrically, Alice putting her hands over her eyes and Ellen putting hers over her ears. They looked like two very embarrassed eight-year-old monkeys.

Laura looked across at the girls and then at Duncan and finally at Tristram. 'Oh no,' she said. 'No. I don't think so.' And with that, she took her two youngest by the hands again and moved off. Tristram and his brother were caught up in her slipstream and bobbed off after her.

Duncan was quite staggered. He realised that somehow he must have committed a gaffe. He walked back across the road.

'You're telling me,' said Duncan. 'Who is that woman?'

'Mum says she's OK when you get to know her,' Ellen replied. 'She's Laura Davis and she's married to a very old man.'

'He was probably quite young before she started on him,' Duncan muttered.

When they got home, Jane was very pleased to see the girls. Duncan watched as she gave them big hugs and exclaimed how huge they were getting. She was clearly worried about going back to work full time.

'Have you told them?' she asked as they prepared the

girls' supper together. Alice and Ellen were watching TV upstairs.

'No. I thought you'd want to,' Duncan replied. Jane looked suddenly close to tears, and Duncan hugged her.

'You're only working down the road, Ju Ju,' he said in a reassuring voice.

'They're so *young*,' Jane mused, gazing at a half-chopped carrot in her hand.

"They're older than me,' Duncan replied and then, to try and cheer her up, he thought he'd tell her the story of Tristram Davis.

'Do you know I met someone ruder than your mother today?'

'That's Laura Davis,' said Jane. 'The girls told me. Don't worry, she's quite human underneath.'

Duncan kissed her. He loved her very much at that moment.

'That's what you said about your mother,' he reminded her.

All the same, he couldn't help thinking that fetching and taking the girls to school every day wasn't going to be quite so easy if the shipping lanes were littered with dreadnoughts like Laura Davis.

The next day was Friday and the dummy run. The great unanswered question that had hung over them since Tony's substantial bombshell had burst was whether Duncan could single-handedly get Alice and Ellen into school by nine o'clock. Duncan had often helped out. Indeed, since he became a gentleman of leisure he had done the occasional walking in, but mainly so he could call by at Jacobs on his way back – but this was different. This morning – and every other morning in the immediate future – Jane wouldn't be forcing the girls to dress and quelling arguments over who wore what. And Jane wouldn't be getting the girls downstairs, around the breakfast table and fed. Jane wouldn't be lining them up with lunch boxes, project money, lavatory roll holders (for which Mr Harper seemed to have an infinite need), sandwiches and break, all ready for Duncan to collect.

In fact, as Jane lay in bed that Friday morning under strict instructions not to impede the wonderful way Duncan was going to cope, she couldn't help feeling that driving down to the docks was going to be a doddle by comparison.

Duncan burst in to the bedroom. 'Hats,' he said. 'They need hats.'

'Why do they need hats?' asked Jane.

'Don't worry about it. You're not here.' Duncan climbed up to look on top of the wardrobe. 'They need *bee-keeper*'s hats,' he said, digging around in some old hat boxes and sneezing at the inevitable swirl of dust.

'We haven't got bee-keeping hats,' Jane told him as she got out of bed.

'Get back into bed!' said Duncan. 'I am coping.'

'But if you want me to help—' Jane began.

'I do not want you to help. I am talking to myself!' Duncan shouted and off he went, muttering about why eight-year-old girls would need bee-keeping hats at this time of the morning.

Jane could hear the girls downstairs, shouting that they were going to be late, and Duncan swearing at them that any sensible child who needed a bee-keeping hat first thing Friday morning would normally look the bloody thing out Thursday night.

Suddenly Jane remembered. She ran to the top of the stairs. 'In the dressing up box!' she shouted over the banister. 'They made them on Sunday with the lace from Mrs R!'

The girls were certainly convinced this was right.

'In the dressing-up box Dad!'

'We made them on Sunday!'

Duncan reappeared from the cellar steps. 'Well go and get them!' he growled. The girls took flight to find the dressing-up box. Jane, one floor up, caught Duncan's eye, one floor down.

'*You*,' said Duncan,' are not here. I am coping magnificently.'

The walk to school was a little faster than Alice and Ellen would have liked, but Duncan was determined to get them in on time. To speed matters up he carried their school rucksacks, the lunch boxes and of course the bee-keeping hats which, it turned out, looked like two of Jane's very old Laura Ashley summer hats with bits of uneven gauze taped round the rim. It was an irregular and uncomfortable pile of bric-à-brac to be transporting at any speed. But to be stepping out down Meirion Street and Fulwood Road in the company of two skipping eight-year-olds, while piled high with such paraphernalia, was absurd and uncomfortable. Duncan sincerely hoped that no one from the office would be driving past.

They reached the gate with what seemed like seconds to spare. The naughty boys who every morning climbed into the sandpit and refused to come out were just being herded by Mrs Lin into the entrance marked INFANTS, and Alice and Ellen flew into school behind them, the gauze fluttering from their hats.

Duncan did not feel entirely at home at the school gate, he had to admit that. It was a world predominantly inhabited by women and a few men with beards who probably made their own bread. Duncan had no urge to linger. He wished he had a mobile phone on which he could be seen talking to clients in Turin or Los Angeles. He turned round, ready to head back, only to find his way barred by Laura Davis who was talking to a woman with blonde ringlets and clothes that had clearly been bought to help tribal workshops from all round the world. By rights this woman should have been Tristram's mother, because she looked very like him – but that was one of life's pointless little coincidences. Duncan knew, to his cost, that Tristram's mother was the small pale matriarch with bright little eyes and neat auburn hair who was standing very close to Afghan Workshop woman and telling her in a loud clear voice that of course she was the ideal person for the job, whatever job that was.

'I don't know . . .' said Afghan wistfully. 'I think they wanted a Welsh speaker.'

'Well you speak Welsh, don't you?' Laura asked.

'Gwyn speaks it,' her friend replied, 'I sort of . . . listen.'

Duncan felt this conversation was none of his business and he made to bypass the women by crossing to the pavement opposite, but at that moment the Third World Consumer kissed her friend on the cheek and moved off, blocking his path with her shoulder and leaving him face to face with Laura.

'Oh hello,' she said in a cheery, noncommittal voice. Duncan wasn't quite sure whether she remembered who he was, so he just smiled in a weakly all-purpose kind of way that could be taken as a response, had she genuinely addressed him, or polite indifference – even indigestion – if she hadn't.

The pavement was still quite blocked by mothers who were trying to turn themselves and their pushchairs and their younger children and dogs round without actually ending up in Fulwood Road itself, so Duncan found he hadn't moved on more than half a pace before Laura continued in her ringing voice, 'We didn't take Tris to the hospital. I was in two minds but fortunately he didn't even have a bump this morning. Small bruise the size of a penny, but that's nothing unusual for him.'

Duncan looked round to see if Laura was talking to

anyone else but, no, he seemed to be the only one in her range.

'His father has a tendency to bump into things, but then he's so clever. I can only hope Tris is heading the same way, can't I?'

Now this was a direct question, so Duncan felt he had to answer. He muttered 'Yes' as casually as he could, just in case some hidden interlocutor loomed over his shoulder and staked his or her claim on this conversation. But no one emerged to challenge him.

'We haven't been properly introduced, have we?' said Laura. She stopped and peered up at his face. Maybe she was short sighted. 'I'm Laura Leighton Davis. You're Duncan Lewis, aren't you? I do think it's wonderful the way you look after those girls.' And with a single footstep she seemed to open up a path in the crowd of milling mums for them to pass through. The cannibals withdrew on both sides, or was it the local shipping making way for this busy little corvette? Duncan followed, for want of any other route, and Laura walked him all the way to the top of Meirion Street.

'We go in different directions now,' said Laura. 'So nice to talk to you.' And she was gone.

'I've just met that woman again,' Duncan said as he arrived at the breakfast table.

'Did you get any bread?' asked Jane who had come down to find him.

'She's very odd, you know. Told me all about her father and how he used to walk her to school, and how good it was to see men taking an interest in their children. She knew ever such a lot about us.'

'Did you get any bread?' Jane asked again. She had been going to suggest they took their hot rolls up to the bedroom, this being her last morning before full-time work.

Duncan's face registered that bread had completely

slipped his mind. 'I'm so sorry.'

'Never mind,' said Jane. 'There's plenty in the freezer.'

Soon after that a taxi arrived with files that Tony Morgan-Jones was delighted to offload on to Jane. She had been sorry that a perfect opportunity had been lost because of the time it took to defrost something from the ice box, but studying the new case load soon took her mind off hot rolls and the marriage bed. It wasn't long before the kitchen table was stacked with piles of paper and Duncan's wife was muttering 'Bloody Tony' in a way that took him back, with perverse nostalgia, to the early days of their marriage.

On Saturday morning Jane Lewis woke with the conflicting desires to talk to someone who wasn't Duncan and to make a big fuss of her family. The problem was that seeking out someone who wasn't Duncan meant briefly abandoning her family. There was no way that Alice and Ellen could be described as someone who wasn't Duncan, not because they resembled him so closely, but because, by definition, someone who wasn't Duncan was someone who would listen to Jane talk about herself. Whereas the girls' idea of a conversation these days was a list of complaints about how very awful it was to be eight years old.

Ordinarily Jane's need to talk about herself could be assuaged by talking to her husband, but there always came a time when she knew she had to escape from him. Duncan used to find this worrying. When they were first married he assumed that Jane must harbour dreadful thoughts about him that could only be voiced to others; whereas Jane maintained that even if all she was saying was that Duncan was the best husband in the world, there would have to come a time when she just had to say it to someone else.

'You're everywhere,' she would tell him. 'You're huge and omnipresent.'

To Duncan, who was only just six feet tall and relatively slim for someone with such a sedentary lifestyle, this seemed a curious accusation. In the early days of their joint identity he had put it down to the influence of Jane's family, who existed in a state of perpetual recrimination. But after the children were born he came to recognise that there was something about his very presence that would suddenly irritate Jane beyond endurance.

'It's not just you,' she would say. 'It's the girls and this house.'

'Now the house really is big,' Duncan had said. 'I'll grant you that.'

So on Saturday morning, when Jane Lewis kicked off the bedclothes in a sudden and angry way, Duncan knew what was coming.

'I'm sorry, Dunc. I've just got to get out.'

'What about me?' said Duncan, who was clinging on to his narrow raft of duvet and trying to maintain the wonderful body heat that had, until a moment ago, been wafting around him.

'What about you?' said Jane.

'I've had the girls all week,' Duncan pointed out. 'I need some time to myself as well.'

Jane was full of indignation. 'You have not had the girls all week,' she replied as she pulled on some track suit bottoms. 'You've had the girls on Thursday afternoon and twice on Friday. That is not having the girls all week!' Jane put on a sports bra. 'I should know, Duncan, I have had the girls all week in my time. I have had the girls all week *for weeks and months on end*!'

The girls came in. 'It isn't easy for us either,' said Alice.

Katrin Street was one of a number of respectable terraces that shuffled sideways on to Pontcanna Fields rather than overlooking the parklands directly. Here and there, gateways breached the great stone walls that had once kept the park private for the Marquis of Bute, and it was through one of these that Jane ran.

The proximity of Katrin Street to Pontcanna Fields had always acted as a release valve during their marriage.

Once Jane had skirted the camper van park, she knew she had six miles ahead of her. She could head north to Llandaff or south to the city gates, then circle back and return along the Taff embankment.

Thinking about Tony Morgan-Jones and how he was clearly handing her something massively complicated – and no wonder he wanted her to start on Monday – Jane found she had reached the National Sports Centre already. She dodged the early-morning fathers, who were parking their cars and thinking they'd done pretty well to be out with the boys by eight o'clock, and pounded on. Her left arm was aching. She pumped it back and forth to stimulate the circulation, poking an imaginary Tony in his porky ribs.

By the time she reached the gates that let on to Castle Street, Jane had finally convinced herself that Alice and Ellen's teachers told *most* of the parents that their children were 'in the middle there', and that this phrase was simply a convenient disguise for the fact that these lazy women didn't want to perceive any individuality in the classroom.

Doubling back along the river bank, she turned her attention to Howard Losen of Louse, Louse & Tosser, who was forcibly being reminded of the fact that Duncan was by far the only original talent in that second-rate partnership. And the only reason Howard had pushed Duncan out was that Dic Lloyd was married to his cousin, and he'd been to school with Dic's brother, and when it came down to it, Howard would protect Dic. And Dic would protect Howard because they were Welsh and they'd always look after each other first. Jane was so angry, and she was angry with Duncan too for just letting it happen. 'You just let it happen,' she told him as her heels thudded down on the uneven river bank.

Duncan. Big daft lovable Duncan with his mop of mousy hair that always needed cutting and his dark eyes that could look sensitive or confused by turns. Duncan, who padded around in a quiet distracted way, not even noticing when people were plotting against him. Stupid, stupid Duncan!

She stopped suddenly, breathless, before it was time to turn back towards Katrin Street. Her eyes were streaming, whether with the cold early-morning air or the anger she didn't know. She bent double and watched the black shallow water of the Taff trickle away towards the sea. Banks of weed and abandoned beer crates grew where the waters flowed too low.

A man with a dog came past. The kind of man out with a dog first thing who always discovers the murder victim. Jane got up and walked back. She'd lost the energy to run. She'd got too angry. She hadn't got it out of her system. Bugger.

She walked through the wet grass back towards Pontcanna. Who could she go and see at nine o'clock in the morning? All her friends with families would be ministering to their children and all her friends without children would be ministering to their men. Jane couldn't think of anyone in Pontcanna who was suitably and reliably single. Even Siân, who was half divorced, might well be in bed with Roger 'for old times sake'. It had been known to happen.

Of course there was always Elaine, who invariably insisted that you must 'call round any time' but who might well look aghast if you arrived without having rung in advance, preferably the day before. Elaine used to be Jane's personnel officer and she could be marvellous in a crisis. She just needed ample warning that one was on its way. Jane had spent some good evenings with Elaine and a wine bottle, but she knew that you didn't drop in on her, least of all at nine on a Saturday morning.

Jane reached the gates that led back to Katrin Street. It wasn't fair to try Holly because Holly was already baby-sitting for them tonight. She wondered about her friend Binny, who was good in a crisis and even better at creating one. Binny Barnes' stormy relationship with the dubious Flyn was always in a state of incipient disintegration, and she found no difficulty at all in taking on board other people's problems. But it was at Binny's that Jane and Duncan were having dinner that evening – (providing the Barnes' quasi-marriage was holding up). To turn up now would make Jane seem too greedy of Binny's chaotic attention span.

Jane reached the front of No. 11 with the realisation that normally, when she got to this stage of her run, she no longer actually needed to see the somebody who was not Duncan. The exertion had normally worked its magic by now. She let herself in. The smell of the house hit her as it always did after a run. It was a comfortable but stale smell, with overtones of Indian carpet and old yoghurt.

Duncan was in the kitchen probing the deep freeze for something that might be bread in its cryogenic form.

'Do you want me to go to Jacobs?' Jane asked.

Duncan, deafened by the grinding sounds echoing up from their ice box, hadn't heard her arrive. As he turned to face her, Jane added that she'd given up on her intention to breakfast elsewhere. 'Saturday's not a good day for most people.'

'You're telling me,' Duncan replied. 'Alice has retired to her bed already.'

During Jane's absence Alice had drawn Duncan's attention to his shortcomings as a parent. With the backing of Ellen, she had pointed out that now they, the girls, had discussed the business of Jane going back to work, they were on the whole not in favour of it.

'They don't seem to think I'm even up to the job of taking them to school,' Duncan reported.

Jane looked at him with a mixture of wry amusement and compassion.' What did you say?' she asked.

'I read them the Riot Act about being spoilt little whatsits, and how sometimes things have to happen differently from what we expect,' he replied. 'At which point Alice said I had ruined her day and she stalked off to bed. Nel's gone to look after her.'

'I'm sorry,' said Jane.

'I'm sorry too. Must be partly my fault. They're only half your children.' Duncan returned a disappointing plastic bag to the ice box with finality. 'Although I do sometimes think Alice is directly descended from your mother with no input from me whatsoever.'

Or me, thought Jane.

She closed the freezer door. 'Why don't you go to Jacobs and chat up the girl with overactive yeast, and I'll see what I can do to talk Alice down,' she suggested.

Duncan liked that. It seemed like a good example of taking from each according to his ability. Jane, having been a girl, had a head start when it came to defusing that emotional time-bomb called Alice, and he, having been a boy, was well suited to admiring the young women who served at the deli and cut-flower store.

Jane's friend Binny lived in an even bigger house than Duncan and Jane, but with considerably less furniture. About the time that their son was born, Binny had spent all her capital on the house itself and on eradicating every possible form of infestation, which meant that floorboards, joists, even whole walls had been pulled up, stripped back and hacked down. It was an aberrant form of the nesting instinct, Duncan thought. Binny wanted to bring Josh into a world without disease, dampness or dry rot. In fact, she'd pretty well brought him into a world without furniture, for there was very little left to spend once the house in Ebenezer Street had been proofed against all malaise. Eating at Ebenezer Street was a spartan affair, using trestle tables with old school chairs, relieved, if that was the word, by copious supplies of alcohol that Flyn's relatives shipped over for him from Galway.

It had to be said however that Binny's dinner parties – when they actually occurred – were done with panâche. Binny threw dinner parties the way some people threw paint at walls. Her County Sligo family had once been wealthy and had entertained Yeats on two occasions. The instinct to round up a random selection of interesting characters and ply them with whatever food was to hand remained with Binny, although her house lacked both the servants and even the heating of Sligo.

On this particular Saturday Binny had invited two single friends who, it turned out, were both in the throes of divorce. Nick was silver-haired and fifty, and happy to tell all comers that his sex drive was undiminished by a particularly vicious settlement. Audrey was in her early thirties, small, and far less forthcoming about the miseries of divorce. Both knew Binny from sending their children to The Abbey, a local private school where Josh, Binny and Flyn's hyperactive son, ran around a lot.

Old Nick was clearly out for a good night, and exclaimed that he couldn't believe his luck at finding three women whom he fancied in the same room. That's what I call living dangerously, thought Duncan. Jane had been known not to respond well to gallantry. But Nick got the measure of her quickly and was soon explaining that he was basically harmless. Flyn kept everyone's glasses cruelly topped up, and at one stage Duncan, already under the influence, was nominated to see if he could remedy Binny's blocked sink with a plunger. It was the kind of occupational hazard that came with being an architect. Even a redundant one like Duncan. There followed a period of prolonged hilarity while Binny and Nick watched Duncan produce a series of convoluted farting noises from the old sink.

'I have just the same problem myself,' chuckled Nick before a shower of old coffee grains suddenly spurted up over the draining board. Binny and Nick seemed to find this enormously funny, so Duncan left them to it. Binny was one of those people who couldn't just enjoy herself; she had to have a Good Time, which activity seemed to involve holding on to people and laughing a lot. How she was ever quiet enough to have told Jane all the dreadful things about Flyn – things that Jane had inevitably reported back to Duncan – he could not imagine.

Back at the front of this long empty house Duncan found Jane and Audrey clustered round two portable heaters and talking earnestly in the chill drawing room. Guessing that Jane had finally found someone who wasn't him, Duncan retreated upstairs to find the bathroom and wash the coffee grains off his hands. On the landing he found Flyn, who was coming down from the loft with several bottles of whiskey. Flyn was not the kind of man to hang around in a room when two women were clearly talking to each other.

'Hello Duncan,' he said.

'How's things?' said Duncan, for want of something better.

'She misses Galway,' said Flyn, shaking his head. 'I'm a terrible man for bringing her over here.'

And with that Flyn and his bottles passed on their way. Duncan was surprised at this exchange. Binny's complaints were well known among Jane's friends. They centred on the various absences of Flyn – who had never even offered to marry her – from the family home. Nothing had ever been said about her frustrated desire to return to Flyn's relatives in Galway. How little we really understand each other, Duncan thought as he peered into the bathroom mirror. He was feeling vaguely profound, which was always a sure sign of having drunk too much and eaten too little.

Fortunately the sound of a gong and much laughter erupted from down below. Binny and Nick were taking it in turns to strike the very heirloom that had once summoned Mr Yeats to log fires and vintage port in County Sligo. Jane and Audrey came out of the drawing room like apparitions, white-faced spectres of moral sententiousness. Duncan guessed that men had been having a bad time of it in there. He had serious doubts about what was to follow. On the one hand Old Nick and Binny were clearly bent on finding everything hilarious, while Jane and Audrey might well take the world to task at any moment. In between these two camps were himself and Flyn who, on the basis of their one exchange so far, were not likely to keep the conversation sparkling.

However, Duncan need not have worried. Binny, with some daring, sat Nick between Audrey and Jane and he immediately set to work charming them both. Flyn was kept busy serving and Binny devoted her energies to probing Duncan about his plans to become a house parent. To his surprise Duncan found that, under the encouragement of Binny's glittering teeth and eyes, he was able to turn the recent domestic upheavals into something for everyone's amusement.

'I was nominated for a retraining course,' he told her.

'How interesting,' said Binny, who clearly wasn't concentrating on the answer to her own question.

'I was nominated once,' said Old Nick, 'to be screwed in the County Court.'

'Ah you're a terrible man,' said Flyn to no one in particular as he prowled around the table.

'What was the retraining for?' asked Audrey, who at least was still in the conversation.

'They seemed to think I should become a new man and spend more time baking bread.'

Jane and Binny laughed.

Audrey ventured a joke. 'I'm looking for a new man if you see any going spare.'

'I'm going spare!' laughed Nick, and Binny tried to hit him.

Duncan watched Jane shaking her long hair and laughing at Nick and Binny's tussle. It was strange observing her from the perspective of several glasses of wine. Something out of joint in his brain made it seem as if he was seeing her for the first time. How strange that he was married to this grown-up woman with her dark eyebrows and long nose and beautiful hair. She looked so admirable, so capable, so well preserved for her eight years with children and eleven years with him. Jane Lewis did not look like the kind of woman whose husband was, as of this year, unemployed.

Nevertheless, something in the pit of Duncan's stomach gnawed at him. Here he was, seemingly at home with all these people, who were not as funny as they thought but regular people none the less – yet was it not true that someone paid Flyn to fly to Brussels on a regular basis? And hadn't someone paid Nick for his business and set him up in luxurious early retirement? Someone even paid poor Audrey as their PA. But who paid Duncan? Was he an interloper in this world of marital disharmony and financial stability?

Somewhere between the second and third courses Binny noticed that she had coffee grains all over her amazing red dress and went upstairs to change. Jane went to join her after a while, and they talked at length about each other's problems. While this was happening, Flyn forgot about the dessert entirely and poured himself, Nick and

Duncan several large whiskeys before turning bellicose about modern architecture. Duncan refused to be drawn, and announced that one of the things he had most happily given up when he was made redundant was having to defend post modernism and 60s brutalism. He then got up and zig-zagged his way to the drawing room where he promptly fell asleep.

Meanwhile Audrey, having declined the whiskey, climbed on to Nick's knee and began remonstrating with him about the fact that his BMW took up two of the parents' parking spaces at The Abbey every morning. 'It's so big,' she kept saying. Nick laughed quite a lot, but began to find Audrey heavy and the room very quiet. Flyn, who often went through an aggressive phase when he drank whiskey, got up suddenly and threatened to make coffee.

The evening ended with Duncan asleep at one end of the house and Flyn asleep in the kitchen. Audrey was crying on Nick's lap while Jane and Binny cleared away.

'No one's had any strawberry mousse,' said Binny in sudden moral outrage.

'It's been a great evening,' Jane told her generously.

Duncan woke up as the taxi pulled up in Katrin Street. For a moment he had the wild belief that he had been kidnapped in the middle of a dinner party and was being taken back to wherever the ransom note was being prepared. Jane was paying the taxi driver. She had a large bowl of strawberry mousse on her lap.

'Did I fall asleep?' Duncan asked.

'I told everyone you were under a lot of pressure at the moment,' said Jane.

Duncan felt less good when he got out of the taxi. He went straight into the kitchen where the woman called Holly was wrapped in a blanket. Duncan opened the fridge door without speaking and stood there, hanging on it, trying to remember what a carton of orange juice looked like.

'See you on Monday,' Holly said quietly as she left.

Duncan looked up at the person his wife was talking to, and then remembered that he had seen their baby-sitter before. She was the woman in Afghan clothing that Laura Davis had been talking to on Friday. Outside the school gate she'd looked like a bundle of ideologically sound rags, but this evening she looked suddenly very beautiful, like the PreRaphaelite Ophelia – tired by long empty hours of baby-sitting, and about to drown under a sea of duvets and thermal jackets – but beautiful nevertheless.

He really hadn't noticed before.

'Good night,' Holly whispered to Jane.

'Is it me . . .' said Duncan when Jane came back from seeing her out. 'Is it me or is she very beautiful?'

'It certainly isn't you,' Jane said. 'You have great charm, Dunc, but you are not what anyone would call beautiful.' She was spooning some of the strawberry mousse into a dish. It made for a tasty midnight feast.

Duncan stood up to aim for the stairs. 'Am I drunk?' he asked his wife.

'You'll find out tomorrow,' she told him.

Actually he found out at half past six, having opened his eyelids very slowly just in case his brain started to rattle inside its cranium but, no, he was fine. He sat up in bed. He still felt fine. He swallowed. Slight dryness in the throat but, no, basically fine. Duncan patted his stomach appreciatively. 'Well done,' he told it.

It was one of those dreadful damp wintery Cardiff Sundays when the buildings and trees dripped cold moisture all day. Even the Sunday papers arrived limp with the grey dew that hung over Pontcanna. Cardiff had a hangover even if Duncan didn't.

Somewhere the other side of Cathedral Road he could imagine Flyn and Binny waking up in that ice-cold house of theirs, and he rather wished he couldn't. And where was Nick? Was he with Audrey? Come to think of it perhaps he was with Binny. Duncan had been married to Jane for ten years and not had sex with anyone else for eleven. He'd rather forgotten the sexual mores attendant on dinner parties for the single person like Nick. Were you expected to seduce your dinner partner? Or even your hostess, for that matter? Duncan turned these ideas over in his head. These were questions that he hadn't even considered in so many years as a conscientious husband and associate architect.

Jane stirred beside him.

'I was thinking about seduction,' he said abstractly.

'Do me a favour,' said Jane, who had a hangover. There was no justice in the world.

In Meirion Street Laura Leighton Davis was already up and cooking breakfast. Every Sunday morning at eight, Laura's husband took their sons swimming. By nine they were usually back. Laura had only recently allowed all four boys to go to the leisure centre. The youngest, Mawmaw (short for Mordred), had been desperate to go for weeks but Laura had a rule that her boys had to be able to put on all their own clothes (apart from shoes) before they were allowed to go swimming with Gerald.

'It's not fair on Daddy otherwise,' she used to say. 'Don't forget he's older than other people's Daddies.'

Laura had lots of rules. Laura's house in Meirion Street was run according to rules, and these rules were justified in many ways. 'Because we live on an academic's salary' was one cause for constraint. 'Because Mummy is a woman and has different needs' was another. Or, 'Because Mummy and Daddy need some time on their own together'.

But a regular pretext for prohibiting anything was 'Because our Daddy is older than other people's Daddies'. And for this undisputable reason Laura always had to know when she should expect her family back.

'And that's why you have to be able to put on your own clothes, Mawmaw,' she explained to her youngest son. 'Because I need to know that if you're not back on time it's because something has happened to Daddy, *not* because he's having to get all my lovely boys dressed.'

'But why you need to know something's happened?' asked Mordred, who had more of his mother's spirit about him than the other boys.

'Because I need to know to ring for an ambulance, don't I?' said Laura happily, and she took her husband's hand in hers. 'Poor Daddy isn't as young as other people's Daddies.'

That particular Sunday morning the Davis family only just made it back to breakfast in time, and then only because Gawain had helped Gerald get Mordred dressed at the leisure centre.

'Not a word. Any of us,' said Gerald. The boys all nodded. 'Your mother is a wonderful person and we don't want to disappoint her.'

When they got back, Tristram gave Laura the flowers and Gerald handed over the Sunday papers. 'Breakfast's on the table,' said Laura. 'I've already had mine. Mind if I take a peek at the Educational Supplement?'

This was pretty well what Laura always said some time between nine and nine-thirty on a Sunday morning.

Laura went through to the front parlour where was housed an absolutely enormous Victorian sofa with bolsters the size of doric columns. Laura loved this sofa. She had inherited it from Gerald's mother and gone to classes to restore it. Whatever representatives of the British Empire had commissioned Laura's settee, they must have taken tea with monumental guests because Laura's little legs hardly reached the floor. This was one of the reasons why Laura allowed herself to kick off her sensible shoes and curl up in amongst the cushions. She had thirty minutes until the boys and Gerald had eaten every last mouthful and stacked the dishwasher.

Laura turned to an article that suggested fathers should take a more active role in their children's education. She nodded. How like Duncan Lewis, she thought. He really was an excellent father.

2 ∫

Too Far Down The Road Already

Jane Lewis' first day back at full-time work had a strange, calm quality about it which reminded her of that dangerous stillness to be found at the eye of a storm. As she drove down to the docks, the traffic on Lower Cathedral Road seemed to part and let her through. When she arrived at Follet Pryce there was none of the fabled congestion in the neat grass-trimmed and balustraded car park, and when she entered the new premises no one in particular seemed to be about except a very quietly spoken receptionist who didn't know who Jane was, and who wasn't expecting her, but who insisted out of embarrassment that she waited in Tony's office.

The whole experience was rather like starting a new school on the day before everyone else returns. For Jane, who had never worked at the dockland offices before, it was doubly like beginning at a new school. Which was her room, and where were the loos?

Jane remembered Follets when they were in the old St Mary Street offices, where every room seemed to be up or down a flight of stairs and the photocopier could only be reached by going back down to reception. Here every room led off the deep, plant-lined glass atrium. You could stand in reception and see whether there was a light on in each and every office – and there were photocopiers on every floor.

Whenever Jane had been to see Tony before, cups of coffee, tea and sherry used to appear from nowhere. Jane therefore had no idea where she was supposed to get a coffee from while she waited. She wandered back out of Tony's office into the leafy atrium and leant over the highly polished chromium staircase.

'Excuse me,' she started to say to the receptionist, but her voice echoed so loudly that the poor woman jumped. 'My God, what was that?' Jane whispered.

'It's an acoustic boom,' hissed the secretary. 'They've had experts in with baffle boards, but they can't work out what causes it. Everyone has to be very quiet when we're not actually in the offices.'

Jane could see that Follet Pryce was going to be a different kind of experience. She asked, as quietly as possible, how she might get a cup of coffee. The secretary indicated a drinks machine set into a small brick recess at the far end of the gantry.

'You're OK there,' she whispered. 'They say the old brickwork absorbs the sound. That's where everyone goes to let off steam and have a natter.'

Four miles away in Pontcanna, Duncan was not having the problems he had encountered on Friday. The girls had been grilled on Sunday evening about what they needed, and everything had been laid out in the kitchen ready. This didn't stop Alice complaining that her legs were tired and couldn't she have a lift to school.

'No,' said Duncan

'Why not?'

'Because Jane's taken the car,' Duncan explained.

'Why don't we have two cars any more?'

'Because we don't need two cars.'

'I need two cars,' said Alice.

'No you don't, you need a good kicking,' Duncan told her. And Alice told him people who kicked children could be arrested these days. Ellen agreed. They'd heard about it in school.

'Out!' shouted Duncan, pointing to the front door in a semblance of rage.

Waiting to cross Cathedral Road, Duncan realised he was on the look out for that Holly woman. He had a great curiosity to find out if she was really as beautiful as the PreRaphaelite vision of Saturday evening.

'Do you know Holly Williams?' he asked. The girls didn't.

'She's somebody's mum,' Duncan added. The girls couldn't think of anyone in their class with a mum called Holly Williams.

'She's a friend of Laura Davis,' he explained.

The girls were quite definite that there was no one in their class who had a mum like that. It was impossible. Of course, with so many sons Laura must have friends with children in just about every year at Fulwood Road. It was therefore quite possible that Holly and Laura knew each other through Mrs Lin's class, or Mrs Evans', or even Mrs Parker's – but Duncan had his doubts. Whenever the girls were that emphatic they were usually completely wrong. Alice and Ellen were usually definite in inverse proportion to their sense of conviction. When they were genuinely and confidently in possession of the facts, they were often diffident and plagued with manufactured doubt.

'I *think* I know,' Ellen would say, 'but I am only eight.' Even when the question related to her favourite foods or whether it was raining outside, Ellen could be the voice of morbid scepticism and Alice would pick up on this. But in matters of uncertainty the girls blustered.

They were just about to step out into Cathedral Road when a tall white Mitsubishi jeep accelerated over the crossing. Duncan grabbed Alice and Ellen as the vehicle, with its passenger list of one overdressed mother and one dumpy daughter in maroon school uniform, sped past in elevated repose.

'Snotgobs!' said Alice in world-weary despair.

'What?' said Duncan.

'Kids from The Abbey,' Alice explained. 'We call them Snotgobs.'

'Why do you call them Snotgobs?' Duncan asked. He was rather shocked at this eruption of class hatred.

'Because they're different from us,' said Ellen, who of the two was the more analytical.

Duncan saw his children across the road safely. 'But it's such a horrible word.'

'Well they're horrible kids,' said Alice.

'How do you know?'

'Josh is horrible and he goes to The Abbey,' Ellen suggested.

'Josh is horrible because his parents are totally bound up in themselves and their house is a mess,' said Duncan.

'Our house is a mess,' said Ellen. 'We're not horrible.'

Duncan didn't want to argue with that, although he was tempted to on both counts.

'Look, there are the Britto boys,' Alice exclaimed, pointing. Duncan was rather worried about what epithet he might hear applied to the Brittos, but the general view of the girls was that the Britto Boys, currently to be found walking on the pavement opposite, were OK or even lush. In fact, Duncan discovered, Alice and Ellen had decided to marry the Britto Boys. The only problem was who should have the younger one. It soon dawned on Duncan that the chief attraction of the smartly dressed pair of toughs opposite was that they came in a pack of two and were therefore numerically compatible with Alice and Ellen.

'You know you don't have to marry when you grow up,' he pointed out. It occurred to Duncan that while he was *in loco Jane* he should continue to represent some of her views.

'Yes, yes,' said Alice impatiently.

'I'm just saying you don't have to.'

'You and Mum got married,' Ellen pointed out.

'Yes,' said Duncan.' Because we wanted to.'

'Well we want to as well,' said Alice with finality. They had evidently had enough of Jane preaching disembourgeoisment.

Duncan was struck by the sulky young woman accompanying the Britto Boys. She was considerably younger than any of the other Fulwood Road mums, and was dressed in the kind of tight-fitting skirt that, sadly, had not been around young women of that age when Duncan had.

'Is that their mum?' he asked. There might after all be advantages in marrying one's daughters to the Britto family.

'No, that's the Swiss Cheese,' said Alice. 'Their mum's too important. She doesn't come to the school. Ever.'

At Follet Pryce the chromium-polished atrium was beginning to fill up with quietly spoken solicitors and secretaries who asked each other in hushed tones what kind of weekend it had been. Down below, a red-faced junior partner was complaining in quiet but heated tones about somebody having taken his parking space, but even he was careful not raise his voice.

From her sipping position by the drinks machine, Jane could hear the salaried partner giving his choleric description of the offending vehicle – hers, she assumed. But no way was she going to own up in these acoustics.

A young man bounded in to the alcove and started talking to her. 'Bloody awful day, but never mind, probably get worse.' He pushed coins into the cold drinks machine with what Jane took to be unnecessary force, then banged his fist on one of the buttons. A can of Coke shot out at such speed she guessed it was in fear for its life.

Jane was expecting the young man to look up and realise he was talking to a stranger but no, he seemed to be expecting her.

'Hi. I'm David,' he said. 'Your first day back,' he informed her, ripping back the ringpull on his can.

Jane felt she had to regain some of the advantage here. 'My first day here. I used to work at the St Mary Street offices,' she explained.

'Before my time,' said David.

'That's right,' said Jane. This was her first challenge in the world of working adults, and she was determined not to apologise for having been out earning her living while this David person was still at school. But the jovial young man didn't seem intent on scoring points.

'Before old Bernard went mad, eh?' he added in a gloomy footnote to the company history.

'I presume so,' agreed Jane.

She wasn't aware that Bernard Pryce had gone mad. He had certainly been unpleasant a lot of the time Jane had been working for Follet Pryce, but that was nothing unusual in a solicitor's office.

'Ace fucking cuckoo,' David laughed. Then he looked rather embarrassed. 'Tony isn't in today,' he announced abruptly. This was something of a surprise to Jane but in David's opinion it didn't really matter because he'd been working to Tony on this one, and anything she wasn't sure of he could help out with. And then it dawned on Jane that not only had Big Fat Tony given her a monster conveyance to sort; he'd also passed her his junior.

Bastard.

*   *   *

The rest of Duncan's day went better than Jane's. He had got Alice and Ellen into school in good time, having checked not only that they had all the daft impedimenta that Mr Harper regularly demanded, but that they knew they had it, and knew *where* they had it.

He glimpsed round at the school gates for Holly Williams, but she was nowhere to be seen. The entrance to Fulwood Road School was a narrow alley between two houses, and this morning it seemed clogged with grandparents. While Duncan was not the most observant of men he had already noticed that the age range at the gate varied according to income. The working classes from Canton occupied the extreme edges of the age spectrum: young women who looked too young to be parents, and older women who looked too young to be grandparents. In between were the middle classes from Pontcanna who, on the whole, looked too old to be the mums and dads of such little ones.

The only exception was the Swiss Cheese, who walked dutifully and slowly up to the gate with her mind in another world (and, presumably, another language), and then retraced her steps in exactly the same attitude of detachment. The Cheese released the Britto boys rather in the way an aeroplane releases a pair of gliders: one moment they were there and nothing to do with her; the next moment they were gone and nothing to do with her.

Duncan found himself watching the return flight of the Cheese when a voice nearby broke in on his distraction.

'Yes . . .' He knew straight away that it was Laura Davis. 'I know what you're thinking. The deportment is extraordinary. Did you see that film about mating habits on BBC2?'

Duncan felt he ought to break in to Laura's peregrination, partly to say hello but also because he was worried the Swiss Cheese might still be in earshot.

'It's all to do with the hips,' Laura continued. 'Don't you

think? That kind of walk projects them forward to emphasise childbearing potential. You can see it on the catwalk.'

There was something interesting in what Laura was
saying, and the Cheese had now sauntered sulkily out of
earshot, but Duncan still felt a bit embarrassed.

'According to the chap on television, some tribes actually
paint circles on their hips to draw attention to the movement. And of course we shouldn't forget the farthingale
was quite racy in its time.'

'How's Tristram?' Duncan asked.

Laura seemed not to have heard the question. 'Not *really*
your type though, is she?'

Duncan was rather thrown by that. How did Laura
Leighton Davis know his type? But when he looked round
at her porcelain face, Duncan could see that she was smiling
up at him. This was a tease.

'Come on, I'll walk you home,' she said. 'Keep you on
the straight and narrow.'

There was something strange and yet companionable
about Laura. She seemed to pick up conversations where
you had left them previously, as if no period of time had
elapsed since. And it was flattering to Duncan to realise that
she had been thinking about something he'd said on their
Friday walk, and had even found out who Miles Davis was
over the weekend

'Tris was very impressed the way you rescued your girls
from that Mitsubishi,' said Laura, switching subjects with
a speed to which Duncan was growing accustomed. The
Davises had evidently witnessed that incident at the top
of Cathedral Road. 'Of course, the boys' father is so much
older,' she explained matter-of-factly. 'They do tend to
admire agility in men of your age.'

'How old is your husband?' Duncan asked. He didn't
often manage a question that directly to Laura, but this
one scored an immediate response.

'He'll be sixty in two years' time. We're just hoping the university don't retire him prematurely. He's quite brilliant in his field but most of the other heads of department are ten, fifteen years younger. They've moved in some awful little manager to help him, you know.'

Laura's description of the career and prospects of Gerald lasted all the way to the top of Meirion Street. Gerald, it seemed, had been a loyal number two during the stormy tenure of Professor Erikson, 'a difficult man'. When Erikson left, Gerald had deputised for him, but the chair had not passed to Gerald.

'Rumour has it that they were looking for new blood,' Laura said with an important air that suggested all Cardiff had been rife with speculation over Gerald's expected promotion. But it seemed that none of the blood on offer was youthful enough to satisfy the University of Wales, and so the chair was left vacant with Dr Gerald Davis as acting head of department.

'It was a very bad time for us,' said Laura, her white doll's face growing patches of pink indignation. 'Mawmaw was only one, Tristram had cracked a rib when he fell off the garden swing and Gawain failed his cycling proficiency. But you know, I think it brought us all closer together.'

Duncan had to admit to a growing fondness for Laura. She was clearly one of those women who felt things strongly, and he had always been a sucker for such women. His own view on the world was so much more muddied. Eleven years ago Jane Beale had impressed him with her sudden bursts of technicolour anger, her passion, physical and emotional. Now it seemed that Laura Leighton Davis was made of similar stuff. Maybe the ingredients were different – Duncan couldn't imagine Laura throwing things around the house or storming off to breakfast with friends – but the pressure at which they were cooked was similar. You didn't have to know Laura for long to realise that she was deeply committed to a small range of things that were her constant preoccupation. Education was one. Her sons – collectively – was another. And Gerald was a third.

'It was a great blow for the boys too,' Laura continued as they reached the junction of Meirion and Fulwood. 'We had always hoped to send them to The Abbey one day, but on Gerald's salary it isn't possible, not to send all four. Had he been given the chair that would have made a difference. We could probably have managed it.'

'You agree with The Abbey then?' Duncan asked. Jane, having gone to boarding school, was a committed state-sector parent.

'Well, the class sizes are half those at Fulwood Road,' Laura replied. 'Poor Mrs Evans and Mr Harper and dear Mrs Parker do their best, but even they say that with classes half the size they could do so much better.'

Duncan was getting interested in this conversation. He had a mental image of the fun that might arise if you put Jane and Laura together for eight rounds. 'You don't think it's wrong then, to use your money to buy your children an education?'

Laura looked at him with that look of sharp surprise he had encountered when they first met. 'Oh no,' she said, in a very quiet and definite way. 'No. What is more important that you would spend you money on? What is more important than your children's education? We have gone without a lot of things in our time and I haven't resented any of it.

They had stopped walking, but the conversation continued with Laura staring into the middle distance of Meirion Street.

'Of course one day we'll have Grandpa Leighton's money,' she said wistfully. 'But I think that may come too late for Gawain and Tristram.'

And at that point she switched subjects to the election of a new parent governor. Laura had strong views on the candidates and wanted to know if Duncan thought the Iranian widow who was 'so admirable in many respects' was soft on the national curriculum.

Duncan knew very little about the curriculum, the role of parent governors, or even who the admirable widow was, so he made a point of remembering that he had to call in for some yeast at Jacobs. 'I'm going to try and bake Jane some bread,' he told Laura.

'You are wonderful,' she told him, smiling her approval, and went on her way.

Duncan didn't quite know why Laura seemed to think so well of him, or whether that remark might have been another tease, but it was very difficult to resist somebody else's good opinion, especially when it was expressed with such conviction. As he crossed over to Cathedral Road, he couldn't help feeling buoyed up and genuinely well disposed towards Laura Davis. It was only when he got to Jacobs that he realised that in none of his conversations with Laura had she ever mentioned Jane. And on reflection that was odd, because Laura knew Jane, and one thing Duncan had noticed when he talked to other women from Jane's baby-sitting circle was that they'd always make frequent reference to Jane, almost as if she was an absent member of the conversation.

There was no doubt that Laura was different.

At Follet Pryce, Jane had already formed the same impression of her new employers, and she was forming it again as she and David started to look at the work Tony had bequeathed her. Among it was a massive and highly complicated conveyance to do with the dockland development, consisting of bundles and bundles of documents. Every time Jane asked David something he'd go off to his office or to

Mair Lloyd's office and come back with more bundles. This wasn't odd in itself; what was strange was David's reaction when Jane kicked off her shoes and padded round the disorganised spread of paperwork and finally said to him, 'We need a bigger office. Is there a conference room?'

'Ye . . . es,' replied David, as if this was a trick question that needed careful handling.

'Well, can we get it for the rest of the day?' Jane asked.

David's head bobbed from side to side in little movements that suggested he was thinking about all the ramifications of such a request. 'Ye . . . es,' he said again in that same cautious, conditional way. Jane asked him what the problem was. David explained that they'd have to go through Mair, who was a legal executive working for Tony, as all the booking of facilities was done through the execs now.

'Then let's ask Mair,' said Jane, who remembered Mair Lloyd as someone reasonable, friendly and efficient.

'Well, Mair has to get partner agreement,' said David awkwardly.

Jane looked at him as if he was speaking nonsense, which to her ears he most certainly was. 'Partner agreement to use a board room?'

'All facilities, excluding stationery and refreshments up to five pounds, have to be booked through two of the partners,' David told her, trying to disassociate himself as far as possible from the words he was speaking. 'I told you the place was ace fucking cuckoo.'

Jane really hadn't intended to come in like a new broom. This was just a temporary job. But then she hadn't expected quite so many cobwebs. 'OK,' she said slowly.' So why don't we ask Mair to book a conference room?'

'Well, she can do that,' David told her, 'but it's got to be signed by Bernard and one other partner other than Tony – as we're working for Tony – and Bernard's not here.'

Even in Jane's day, Bernard's absences from the St Mary Street office had been legendary. So she suggested that surely this fact must have been anticipated when such a Byzantine system was introduced. Wasn't somebody deputised to sign for Bernard, otherwise the place would grind to a halt? 'Oh yes. Bernard's secretary can sign for him,' said David. 'But she and Mair aren't speaking to each other. Haven't for months.'

Jane was beginning to feel that she was the only sane person in the building. 'OK. If Mair fills in the booking form, I'll take it Bernard's secretary.'

David shook his head.

'Why not?' demanded Jane.

'All facilities are booked at secretary or executive level. Assistant solicitors and partners aren't allowed to book facilities. Look,' said David, in response to the look he was getting from Jane, 'I didn't invent this system, all I'm trying to do is explain. You can get into real deep shit around here at the moment—'

Jane had put her shoes back on. 'Come on,' she said, gathering up a pile of files. 'You bring that pile. We'll come back for the rest later.' With David in tow, she clattered along the chromium gantry to the little office Mair shared with a very tall silent woman called Marjorie and some posters of little fluffy animals.

'Hello Jane,' said Mair, as Jane put her pile of files down on her desk. Mair Lloyd was a rather vacant looking woman in early middle age, whose main features seemed to be a pair of glasses and a smile drawn in peach lipstick. Without these artificial aids, Mair Lloyd might well not have had a face at all, just a pair of dark little eyes set into a blank white expanse of skin.

'Hello David,' she said in exactly the same gentle sing-song. Mair was giving them both her welcoming smile.

'We've got a problem in Tony's office with all this stuff,'

Jane began, as if David had told her nothing. 'I need space. Can you be a love and book us a conference room or board room or something, Mair? Don't mind what it is long as we can have it now or my arms are going to drop off!' Jane kept the tone light, friendly, one mate to another.

'Well,' said Mair, casting a glance at David. 'I'll do what I can.' She looked at Jane's files as if seeking the inspiration to answer such a conundrum. 'The only problem is Bernard's away, you see.'

'But Bernard's always away,' Jane riposted with deliberate cheerfulness.

Mair looked at Jane's files again. 'If we moved some of the furniture out of Tony's office . . .' she began to suggest.

'No, I want a big room, not a small one with no furniture.' Jane replied.

Mair looked lost. Jane caught herself about to say, 'I'm not asking you to build one, Mair, just book one,' but she held her tongue.

'I could ask someone in Bernard's office if they'd sign for him,' Mair conceded.

'Great!' said Jane, picking up her files as if the business was now sorted.

'Only I don't like to do that while Tony is away.'

'Why not?' Jane asked.

Mair looked at David and then at the files and finally at tall silent Marjorie, who was listening but not participating in the discussion. 'It is *difficult* . . .' she said with the same dying fall.

Jane waited. As far as she was concerned Mair still had not answered her question. Maybe Mair expected her to take a cue from all this prevarication and leave the subject alone, but she did not intend to do any such thing.

'I *could* speak to Bernard's office . . .' said Mair.

'Great,' said Jane for a second time.

'Only I'd rather not,' Mair said, speaking in capital letters. This was Mair laying it on the line.

'Well I'd rather you did,' said Jane. 'Because otherwise we're not going to get anywhere with this case. Now, which room can we have?'

Mair breathed heavily, and then with precise movements took out a piece of paper and filled it in and asked Jane with studied politeness to sign the sheet. She then walked out with the air of one who is only coping because she has always prided herself on taking a superhuman professional approach to her work.

Jane suggested that she and David retire to the drinks machine while they waited. Once ensconced, she expected him to laugh at the absurdity of what they had just witnessed, but all he did was slam coins in to the machine and mutter, 'Ace bloody fucking cuckoo.'

To Jane, as an outsider, it all seemed ridiculous, but she could see that David was genuinely bothered.

'This place,' he said. 'You're either with Bernard or with Tony. You must know that. And Mair's on Tony's side. I mean she's taken it really to heart.' He nursed his unopened Coke unhappily.

Jane tried to sound reasonable, but she wondered how reason would sound in this environment. 'David, we've still got a job to do. Clients don't give a monkey's about feuds between legal execs and secretaries. They pay us for getting the job done.'

Poor David no longer looked the cocky young man she'd met that morning. 'You wait till you've been here a few days,' he warned her.

The whole business of getting into a conference room and carrying files through under the silent, watchful gaze of Reception took so long that Jane completely forgot to ring Duncan and check that all had gone well. In fact it wasn't until one-thirty that she remembered, in a flood of guilt, that she had two eight-year-old daughters. She found a phone in the dark, heavily carpeted conference room and pulled up one of the white leather chairs.

Between the corporate bunker in which Jane was eating her sandwich and the steaming kitchen in which Duncan was cleaning there seemed to be no common ground. It was like two worlds colliding. Duncan had been having trouble getting the yeast to rise in a loaf he was baking, but he was very pleased with an idea that Norman the blacksmith had come up with for their conservatory. Norman was supposed to be renewing some of the old ironwork, and he'd unexpectedly called when Duncan was looking again at the pane of glass which Mrs R. had broken last week.

Jane couldn't understand what Duncan was talking about at first. She wanted to know if he'd got the girls into school OK and if they had been happy with the new regime. She would also have liked to tell him about how mad Follet Pryce seemed, given that David was out of the room.

For all Duncan's faults, Jane relied on his sense of the absurd. Duncan alone could confirm to her that Follet Pryce was laughable. He might be short on the necessary dedication to corporate life – indeed, Jane had told him this all through their marriage – but he was definitely the person to be with when you'd had enough of it yourself.

This Duncan though, this Duncan on the telephone – he seemed absurd. What had fallen dough and cantilevered conservatories got to do with life, the girls and Jane's job? Duncan, for his part, felt rather hurt that Jane showed no interest in what he'd been doing all morning.

'Oh for goodness sake, buy some ready baked from Jacobs!' Jane exploded. 'And don't forget to pick up the girls.'

'You don't have to remind me,' Duncan growled back. 'That is my job.'

And the phones went down.

Two minutes later, somewhere down in the docks and somewhere up in Pontcanna, Jane and Duncan felt sorry. She remembered that poor Duncan was still adjusting to the trauma of rejection. She had to accept that he wouldn't always behave reasonably. And he was feeling guilty that there was poor Jane going out to work to keep them all, and if she wanted to ring up and be quite unreasonable to him then he had to accept that. He resolved to cook her a really nice supper.

So intent was Duncan on the recipe books for the supper he had in mind that he was late picking up the girls and very unpopular indeed. And so intent was Jane on inculcating David's enthusiasm for this mammoth conveyance that when he suggested they adjourned for a drink in the hotel bar opposite she really couldn't pour cold water on that day's little victories.

Consequently, when Jane did get home the girls were in a double state of virtuous indignation. Jane had planned to apologise to all for her late return, kiss the girls goodnight and if possible send out for a pizza while she looked through some of the piles that David had given her. Instead she had the disapproval of her daughters to face. Firstly she had abandoned them to be looked after by Duncan when they had made it clear on Saturday that they weren't confident about this arrangement, and now they had been proved right because Duncan had marooned them at school for fifteen minutes, which was so embarrassing with that awful Mrs Lin wanting to get off home herself and giving them looks all the time. And finally, to crown it all, their mother had stayed out all night drinking.

'I have not stayed out all night drinking,' said Jane firmly. She felt this one had to be quashed now or else the story would be all round Fulwood Road tomorrow. 'I went for one glass of white wine and spring water with a colleague, which is what working people do. It's what Dad used to do when he was working.'

'But Dad's a man!' cried Alice. Both girls had worked themselves up to the verge of tears.

'Sex has nothing to do with it,' said Jane, raising a finger. 'If working men can go for drinks so can working women.'

Duncan hung around on the threshold of their bedroom. He didn't feel he should add that Dad had never much enjoyed going for a drink with the boys. He had already had his carpeting from Alice and Ellen. He didn't want to complicate Jane's.

'It's early days,' Jane told the girls as she tucked them in.

'It's early days,' Jane told Duncan when she came downstairs. 'But we must get our act together.'

Duncan agreed. Jane offered to ring out for a pizza. Duncan told her he'd cooked a wonderful meal, most of which had turned out not bad at all.

'Thank you,' said Jane putting her arms around him and hugging him by the sink.

'Can't promise three courses every night,' Duncan replied.

'I mean thank you for not reproaching me for being back late as soon as I came in through the door,' Jane told him.

'I'm saving that for later,' said Duncan. He held on to her and she held on to him and they both felt that it was all somehow very difficult, more difficult than they had expected.

'We'll manage it,' Jane told him.

It was the same kitchen that last week had seen Jane and Duncan, in the face of Infinite Possibility, thrash around on the kitchen table like a pair of teenagers. This evening sex seemed like another world.

*   *   *

Tuesday was very much like Monday, except that Mair now made no pretence of supporting Jane. She did what she had to do silently or with compressed lips or with little blips of speech. 'Very well', 'As you wish', and 'Yes' – a dangerous word which she actually managed to pronounce as if double-underlined with a dangerous and drawn-out hissing sound at the end.

David grew in confidence as he got to grips with the work. Jane on the other hand began to see how very complicated it all was, and she wished that Big Fat Tony would come back. Her team's morale wasn't everything. She needed to know what was going on from the man who was employing her.

Duncan made a point of being on time to collect the girls on Tuesday afternoon, and actually arrived early. Isolated from the anonymous wedge of parents, he found himself looking round for Ophelia or for Laura Leighton Davis. He had grown used to her already and rather missed the sound of that voice, so clear and precise above the murmur of mums and grannies.

Alice and Ellen's class was usually the last to arrive at the gates, as Mr Harper was obliged to escort them in crocodile fashion past the large hole that Welsh Water had dug and cordoned off for no discernible reason. This meant that the three other Davis boys had usually gathered waiting for Tristram long before Alice and Ellen emerged. This afternoon, Duncan could see Mawmaw and Gawain and the one who came between Tristram and Mawmaw but who never seemed to get a mention in Laura's accounts of family life. The three boys were waiting with a tall elderly man in a tweed jacket who could easily have been one of the Fulwood Road grandfathers. This had to be Poor Gerald. He was surely too young to be Grandpa Leighton, whose demise promised so much to the boys' private sector chances.

Duncan couldn't help but make a study of Dr Gerald Davis. He had a very big gentle way about him, like a thin grey elephant inclining forward to take Mawmaw's hand in his trunk. From time to time Gerald dipped down further to say something to Gawain or the anonymous one. He even swayed a bit on his feet like a circus elephant. Duncan wondered whether he ought to go forward and introduce himself. But as what? Gerald quite possibly had no idea that his wife talked to Duncan and walked him back to 'keep him on the straight and narrow'.

Tristram arrived behind Mr Harper and tripping along somewhat ahead of the girls. He saw Duncan and made a good mime of the steering wheel of a Mitsubishi being wrenched from side to side to avoid Duncan and the girls. Tris then completed the performance by giving Duncan the thumbs up. To Duncan, who knew little about boys of that age, Tristram seemed a really nice lad. Gerald turned instinctively to see who his son was gesturing to, but before he and Duncan could make contact Duncan found that Holly Williams had swum into his line of vision.

As soon as he recognised the many layers of multi-coloured clothing and long blonde hair, Duncan remembered the question that had puzzled him on Sunday. Was this the cold looking bundle of rags or the beautiful baby-sitter?

Holly was talking to him. She had a very quiet voice, or maybe she just chose to speak quietly. '. . . bit of a hole . . . wonder if Jane, or indeed, you could.'

No, she wasn't beautiful, although she might once have been.

Duncan had missed what it was Holly was talking about. 'I'm sorry?' he asked.

She had wonderful blue eyes, or eyes that must once have been wonderful but which perhaps had grown a little too pale. And she had wonderful ringleted hair too, just like one of those PreRaphaelite masochists. The colour looked genuine, but it was wispy. It must have been truly something before she'd had it permed too often. '. . . late notice I know but you did say . . .' Holly murmured. Duncan had missed it again.

Her face was so pale but not as Laura's was pale. All around Holly's eyes the skin had crinkled up, which made her look tired. And of course Laura's white face was in sharp contrast to her striking auburn hair, whereas Holly was too anaemic. White skin, pale eyes, faded hair. She was like a wraith, the ghost of someone who had been very beautiful in her youth but from whom all colour had been drained.

Duncan realised Holly was expecting an answer from him.

And of course with all these clothes she looked like a refugee, whereas on Saturday night she'd seemed quite elegant with her blankets falling about her. Guinevere, that's who she reminded him of – not poor drowned, lifeless Ophelia but Guinevere, beautiful and compromised.

But what the hell had she been saying to him? Fortunately the girls arrived at this point.

'Hello, Alice and Ellen,' said Holly.

'Hello!' they chorused in great friendliness. Duncan was surprised how free of awkwardness his daughters seemed. It was like coming across them as a stranger might. *What nice daughters you have, Duncan*. They looked like miniature Janes, tall, rosy cheeked, really rather definite about everything. Duncan even noticed that their hair had grown long and had grown ribbons that tied it back like Jane's.

'Bit of a nuisance then is it?' asked Holly.

Duncan gazed vacantly at her then decided to come clean. 'I'm sorry. I didn't quite get that.' He pointed to his ear. 'Fluid on the ear drum I think.' It seemed rude to suggest that Holly spoke too quietly.

'It doesn't matter if it's a sort of nuisance,' said Holly.
'No, no,' Duncan insisted. 'Really, I didn't hear you.'
'Dad's going deaf,' said Ellen helpfully.
'No he isn't,' Alice retorted.

Duncan hoped Holly would repeat herself before Alice announced,' I can't hear what she's saying either.' He knew what was in Alice's mind.

'Is it possible that Jane or perhaps you could baby-sit for us tomorrow night?' asked Holly.

Duncan had said he'd check with Jane about sitting. Several years ago Jane had joined this reciprocal system where she sat for tokens which she could then use to hire another parent to sit in when she and Duncan went out. As neither of them had family in Cardiff, it was an ideal solution to the baby-sitting problem.

Duncan had never taken much notice of the workings of this system, except he knew that from time to time Jane would disappear with body warmers and large paperback books to sit in other people's houses, and that whenever he and Jane went out, one of the interesting side issues to the evening would be the identity of the sitter Jane had arranged. Sometimes Duncan would have a chat to the woman in question while Jane was saying goodnight to the girls. It was one of the few times that he actually spoke to other mothers, and he always found it rather reassuring that they seemed to display the same obsessions and irrationalities as Jane.

Of course, that was in the days when he had a job. Nowadays Duncan seemed to meet mothers wherever he went.

When conversation turned after supper that evening to Holly's request, Jane surprised Duncan by saying, 'It's up to you, but don't keep her waiting. She'll need to know.'

'Why's it up to me?'

'*Duncan,*' Jane replied.

Saying his name in that way usually meant only one thing. The answer to Duncan's question was obvious for all but him to see.

'Oh, you mean it's up to me whether *I* want to sit.'

Duncan was piecing the thought together. It genuinely hadn't registered with him that he was now the one to set off into the night with thermal underwear and reading matter at the ready.

'Well, I did the sitting while you were working,' said Jane.

'Yes, you did,' Duncan admitted. And indeed there had been the occasion, once, when he'd let the baby-sitter in and found it to be a small curly-haired microbiologist called Mervyn who had come in with a pile of scientific papers, sat down at the kitchen table and got straight back down to work.

Duncan had always regarded such men as rather odd. Rather as he regarded men who baked their own bread as rather odd. But then he had tried baking bread recently. So why not? After Binny's lengthy binge on Saturday they did need the tokens. There were of course a few things to sort out, like what time Jane would finish work tomorrow and what time Jane would finish having a drink with David tomorrow and was there a danger that Jane might go on for a Chinese meal afterwards?

'Piss off, Duncan,' Jane said in a matter-of-fact sort of way as she began to arrange a pile of papers along the kitchen table.

Duncan had noticed that since returning to full-time work Jane was enjoying his playful sense of irony less.

Duncan rang Holly, assuming that he would not be able to hear a word she said, but on the telephone she was quite audible and, thanks to the amplification, he was able to detect a very pleasing cadence in her voice. Holly's voice had a very soothing quality, like tiny waves breaking effortlessly on the sea shore.

'Hi,' she said.

'That's great,' she said.

'See you at eight,' she said. 'Love to Jane.'

Duncan could almost feel himself drifting off to sleep, washed on the shores of that great lake where Guinevere and her ladies embarked, through the mists of time, with the body of Arthur.

'Wonderful voice,' he told Jane. 'She sounds so relaxed.'

'She doesn't go out to work,' Jane replied with due significance.

Duncan pointed out that Jane had always told him it was far more difficult to run a home than work in some office. Jane gave him one of her looks. She had a lot to do. Big Fat Tony was supposed to be back in the office tomorrow and she wanted to be sufficiently on top of the paperwork to be able to ask him all the right questions and tell him off in a knowledgeable sort of way. She had a feeling Tony might not be hanging around for long.

At half-past one in the morning Duncan found himself awake, very very definitely awake. He'd had an image of himself never working again. It was an odd sensation because it hadn't been what you might describe as a dream. It was like a shaft of knowledge that had pierced his brain in the night. He had woken in a state of panic.

'So?' he tried to say to himself. 'You didn't like working, not for most of the time. The clients were awful and your colleagues worse. You used to get into a bad mood on Sunday afternoons. The last two days of any holiday were always ruined by the prospect of going back to work. Take your time. There's no rush.' That had been what Jane had said to him, after all. He was supposed to be seeing this as an opportunity to rethink his life, not a mad scramble to get back into any kind of paid employment.

Duncan realised it was the baby-sitting for Holly Williams that was bothering him. For no particular reason it was a watershed. Was he going down a road from which he might never come back? He looked around their bedroom. The street lamp outside broke in through a chink in the dark double velvet curtains. The narrow band of light which shone across their room illuminated so many objects, so many possessions. How did they ever get to afford so much stuff?

Duncan shuddered and cuddled up to Jane. She was curled away from him and so he stretched his body in an arc around hers. He lifted her arm and tried to cup his hand over her breast, but something instinctively defensive stirred in her and she flattened herself face down on the bed. Jane, at a level that was not even aware it was Jane, had no time for being woken up by the likes of Duncan. She, was preserving herself for the battle tomorrow. It was tiresome but inevitable.

3

Duncan, This has Got to Stop

Tony Morgan-Jones had enjoyed three days with one of his most demanding clients who would only discuss business at the golf course in St David's. This was a burden that Tony bore without complaint but also, annoyingly, without telling anybody where he was. Consequently, on his return Big Fat Tony found himself besieged by secretaries and assistant solicitors, and the secretaries of his partners, and a particularly unhappy legal executive who wanted to come and tell him she was *not happy*.

Tony could have guessed just by looking at Mair Lloyd that she was not happy, but he duly promised to hear the full story at eleven o'clock. First, however, he had to see how Jane Lewis was getting on, because it was unforgivable of him not to have been around when she first arrived.

'You'll find a way of forgiving yourself, you old bugger,' Jane thought when Tony had concluded his little speech. But she didn't say it.

'Now come and sit down and tell me how it's been going,' said Tony, drawing up a chair. They were in the low dark conference room together, and Tony had settled himself by the row of black ash tables down which Jane had parcelled out thirty-two files.

Jane slung herself into an armchair and gave it to him straight. The whole conveyance was a tangled mess because Tony's clients, Gooderson Marine, were trying to develop some of the most curiously owned bits of dockland.

'The site is ripe for redevelopment, but there are all sorts of problems here and to be honest I don't think anyone's ever really thought about them.'

In Jane's view there was a very real danger that if she didn't act soon Gooderson might well lose to other bidders land that was vital to the marina development. But at the same time, if Jane secured that land ahead of other, separately owned strips, Gooderson might end up owning disconnected bits of dockland that were of no use to them

'It's chicken and egg,' said Jane, pulling her shoes back on as she concluded her polemic. 'They need to get the chicken and the egg simultaneously.'

Tony looked up at her in affectionate admiration. She was a wonderful woman, and it was impressive that she had proved beyond doubt in two days what he had suspected within half an hour of looking at the papers.

'I think I need to talk to the client,' Jane concluded.

Tony nodded. 'You should speak to Miles Mihash,' he suggested. 'He's great fun. We'll have him in for lunch.'

'I don't want us to do lunch,' said Jane, waving her hands at the bundles of paper behind her. 'I want to get someone in here, the right person, and take them item by item through what we're doing to clarify the instructions.'

But Tony was already imagining Miles Mihash being very impressed by Jane; he could visualise Miles enjoying the way she swept her long mane of hair round and back over her shoulder as she started on the next point of discussion, that jut of her chin, the stern rebuke of those dark eyebrows and the gleam in her eyes when she pinned him down, intellectually speaking . . .

'I'm sure you'd like Miles,' he persisted.

He didn't really know why he played these little games with Jane, but it had always been a part of their professional relationship. He would behave in a feckless way and she would tell him off. She would give it to him straight – which gave her the sense of being in charge – and he would let her bully him into what he was going to do in any case, or into what he now realised was the best course of action.

'Tony, for God's sake!' Jane said. Even that was part of the ritual: these little blasphemies that she only used with him. Tony's background was Port Talbot fundamentalist stock. He had even contemplated training for the Ministry at one particularly perverse stage in his life. Even now he got a particular frisson from blasphemy, especially when it was Jane who took the Lord's name in vain.

'Whatever you say, Mrs Lewis,' said Tony Morgan-Jones, throwing up his hands. 'Now – coffee.'

It was the final part of their ritualised combat which Jane well remembered from her days as an assistant and as a salaried partner. These little set-tos always ended up with tea or coffee or sometimes a glass of sherry. Jane was usually pretty thirsty by the time she was calling upon God or, on some occasions, more foul-mouthed deities to aid her case. But this meant that Tony usually had five or ten minutes to savour the sight of Jane Lewis simmering down. He had missed her.

'Now,' he said leaning forward to pour, 'how's Duncan? Is he bearing up?'

Jane emerged ten minutes later with the go-ahead to do everything she wanted, but she felt tired. These silly sessions with Tony were always so taxing. She hated the way he gratuitously avoided the issue. So much energy had to go into simply getting him to focus on the matter in hand as he deliberately changed the subject, trivialised what she was saying or behaved in a plainly irresponsible manner.

As she went upstairs Jane caught sight of Mair Lloyd checking over the balcony to see if Tony had come out yet. Mair disappeared back into her office when their eyes met. Jane went along the chromium gantry and kicked the drinks machine.

David came in and joined her. He was checking that all was well.

'Yes,' said Jane before David had said a word.

'And Mair?' David asked.

'We discussed Mair,' she said. For indeed they had over coffee. 'And Tony's going to talk to her and I'm going to talk to her. Oh this *place*!'

'Ace fucking cuckoo,' said David with a grin. He liked Jane; he was enjoying working with her but he had been worried that she was going to rock the boat. Tony's people had to stick together whatever happened.

Seeing that she was still looking bothered, David suggested they had lunch in the hotel's wine bar that day.

'Why does everybody want to get me out to lunch?' Jane demanded of the drinks machine. Then she laughed. 'OK. But half an hour maximum. And no drink tonight. I've got to get back as soon as we finish. My husband's going out this evening.'

'You're too good to him,' said David, who had an image of Jane rushing back to facilitate Duncan's social life.

'Oh no I'm not,' Jane replied.

Duncan was worried. The baby-sitting for Holly Williams had grown in his mind into an expedition redolent with pitfalls. What if the Williams children didn't like him? What if they became hysterical, or ill, or accused him of molesting them? He had done some research with the girls, having discovered (of course) that his children did know the Williams two. The boy was younger than them and a friend of that other Davis boy – the one who wasn't Tristram, Mordred or Gawain. The girl was older than Alice and Ellen. The only explanation Duncan's daughters had for having strenuously denied this association yesterday was that they did know an awful lot of people and it was difficult to remember them all.

'We're really quite popular these days,' Ellen explained with a voice full of responsibility.

On Jane's baby-sitting list it transpired that Holly's off-spring were called Buddug (pronounced Bithig) and Siôn (pronounced Shaun). To Duncan's Anglo-Saxon ear a name like Buddug was truly alarming, and his tongue went dysfunctional as soon as he tried to pronounce it. Why Holly had opted for a name that would be greeted with incomprehension as soon as her daughter got within earshot of the Severn Bridge Duncan couldn't imagine. He and Jane, like many of their friends, had looked into books of Welsh names when they realised they were having Welsh children, but in the end they had chosen familiar English names which had an optional Welsh form. 'They can always be Alis and Elin when they're older,' Jane had decided.

But Buddug and Siôn were a different proposition altogether. Perhaps they were Welsh speaking? It was strange to think that soft spoken, vaguely West Country Holly Williams could have Welsh-speaking children, but you didn't normally choose names like that unless your children were able to back up their Welsh credentials with the Language of Heaven. Duncan could foresee himself battling with two hysterical children who were accusing him of child abuse in a language he didn't begin to understand.

'What are Siôn and Buddug *like*?' he asked the girls nonchalantly as they walked back that afternoon.

'They argue all the time,' Alice announced.

'Who with?' asked Duncan, alarmed.

'Each other.'

It was a relief to Duncan to think that even if Siôn and Bithwhatsit were going to spend the evening screaming in hysterical Welsh, at least it would be at each other and not at him.

When Duncan actually turned up at Holly's house that Wednesday evening, equipped with a large amount of reading matter, several videos and a blanket, he was surprised to find the door opened by a plump ten-year-old girl who did not look as if she had been interrupted in the act of raining Celtic imprecations on her sibling.

'Hello,' she said in a quiet but friendly way. 'Are you Duncan?'

'Yes,' said Duncan. 'And you must be Bith . . .' He let the name taper out.

'Buddug, yes,' she said helpfully. 'Holly's just on her way down and I'm reading Siôn a story.' Before she disappeared back upstairs. Duncan noticed Buddug was already in a dressing gown, Good. In fact, so far not so bad at all.

Holly and Gwyn Williams lived in another Edwardian stone terrace, but one narrower than Duncan's. Pontcanna was built on a series of gradations falling back from Cathedral Road and Cardiff city centre. The further you were from either, the smaller the house.

There were no old bell pulls or dressing rooms to be discovered in Pontcanna Terrace. This was a straightforward turn of the century three-bedroom teachers' street, still occupied today by the teaching profession, plus a few young doctors who were aiming at better things in a few years' time.

Duncan had wondered if Holly might be a teacher. She looked as if she might be good with little children, but

Jane was adamant that Holly didn't have a job. She did some vague kind of good work, but it was almost definitely unpaid. Gwyn Williams was musical and played in several orchestras – but Jane, being not at all musical, couldn't say which.

Duncan wandered into the breakfast room, taking in the telltale signs of his new surroundings: the sunglasses on a bust of Wagner that loomed at the top of a built-in, pine-stripped dresser; the large rainbow painted by a combination of adults and children on the chimney breast; a framed tapestry that read 'Holi a Gwyn', with the date of their wedding given in Welsh underneath. The whole place had a deeply lived in, but paradoxically unfinished feel to it.

Holly walked in, carrying some children's clothing and looking very elegant in a long knitted dress, waistcoat and cardigan. She had long boots on under the dress and Duncan guessed they were probably fleece lined. She was taking no chances with the temperature that evening.

'Hello Duncan,' she whispered, and came across the breakfast room to kiss him on the cheek. Surprised, Duncan remembered that Holly had also kissed Jane, she even kissed Laura at the school gates. Holly was a kissing kind of person. Another telltale sign.

'Gwyn's in the bath,' she said. 'Shall I sort of . . . show you where everything is?' 'Everything' turned out to be the location of tea, coffee, biscuits, television and lavatory. Duncan remembered Jane giving baby-sitters a similar tour of their house.

Holly Williams seemed to flow through 27 Pontcanna Terrace like some ethereal being, abstractedly picking up and putting down discarded clothes, books and toys as she went. By the time they got to the first floor she had started to explain where the children's bedroom was to be found, but she meandered within seconds to talking about how she and Gwyn had been thinking of building on and how she didn't like the way these Edwardian houses had the meanest rooms towards the garden.

Duncan was beginning to realise that his own wife was a very straightforward kind of person to discuss things with. Laura Davis kept a small range of topics constantly on the boil, and seemed to expect you to be up to date with her own thinking. And this Holly seemed to merge one thought with another so seamlessly that you began talking about a ten-year-old girl's need for privacy at the bottom of the stairs, only to find that you were discussing the gradations of room sequences in Edwardian architecture and the English class system two minutes later on the landing.

Holly had by now absent-mindedly shed all the things she had tidied on her way upstairs. She was trying to explain how Architecture was a very male sort of thing, and how there was this house in Devon designed by women. The plan of the house was round (and therefore non-hierarchical), and the only way that Holly could demonstrate this was by making slow circular gestures with her hands. Each time she came to the idea of Female as sharing and enveloping, her voice got quieter, as if she was less and less sure this was the best way to explain her thoughts. Duncan leaned in to try and hear better and Holly, noticing that his head was inclined conspiratorially towards hers, also leaned forward so that by the time she had got on to the fact that Siôn actually liked playing with his sister's toys and that it was good for him to explore his feminine side, they were virtually huddled together on the landing and Duncan could smell the planet-friendly soap with which she must have washed her neck.

At that moment the bathroom door opened in a flood of light and a short stocky man with a lot of body hair and a maroon towel around his midriff came out.

'Hello!' said the small man with gusto. Duncan jumped

backwards. Had the situations been reversed and he, Duncan, had emerged half naked to find a strange man head to head with Jane, he might have felt embarrassed or outraged, but Gwyn Williams was too intent on movement to notice what was going on.

'Good of you to help us out,' he exclaimed, shaking Duncan's hand in a fierce grip. 'All my fault. Damn socials eh? There's plenty of beer in the fridge, isn't there Holly? Offer him one will you love?'

And with that, Gwyn Williams had passed into the front bedroom. Duncan could see only too well where Buddug got her shape from. How cruel to be the daughter of such a mother and take after her father.

'Would you like a beer? Or a glass of wine?' asked Holly. Duncan wondered whether he was allowed to drink while sitting. He didn't want to be drunk in charge of two children, but if the parents offered, why not?

'Yes please,' he said, but Holly's thoughts had already moved on.

'I thought if we could sort of widen the landing rather than create another bedroom,' said Holly, indicating the space she had in mind. 'Then we would have more territory in common.'

Duncan decided that Holly had already forgotten the beer.

'When the children were younger we all slept in the same bed. It was such a . . . such a positive thing . . . I miss that.'

Duncan could think of nothing worse than sharing a bed with the girls. It seemed that Gwyn had put his foot down when Buddug was six. In Duncan's opinion Gwyn had been remarkably forbearing. 'Perhaps we should have had more children but . . . it sort of didn't happen,' said Holly.

Yes, thought Duncan, conception must be a bit tricky with a bed full of kids.

'You're so lucky having twins,' said Holly. 'The possibilities must be limitless.'

'Oh, I don't know,' said Duncan. 'The reality can be a bit of a fag. They gang up on you.'

Holly smiled abstractly at him. Presumably she yearned to be ganged up on. 'Our two lead such separate lives. They don't even argue.'

Normally Duncan would have assumed that this was once again his daughters getting the facts all round their necks, but this evening he wasn't so sure. Maybe they knew Siôn and Buddug better. Holly had a conspicuous detachment from the world around her.

When she led him back downstairs, Duncan asked where they were going that evening.

'Oh this thing of Gwyn's,' Holly said as she looked into the fridge. 'It's a Welsh National Opera thing or National Orchestra of Wales do or the Something Philharmonic. Probably.' She emerged from the fridge but it was with a flask of ready-diluted orange juice. 'This is for Siôn,' she said. 'If he wakes up. Do you find boys wake more often in the evening than girls? Or is that being sexist? I never know. Oh, of course, you've only got girls. Must be fascinating.'

Duncan realised that his beer had disappeared off the agenda entirely.

At about eight-thirty Jane Lewis decided she should check how Duncan was getting on. At first she got through to a bilingual answering machine, but when she said, 'Duncan it's Jane – can you pick the phone up?' he did.

Although Holly and Gwyn had been gone for an hour this was the first moment Duncan had had to himself. Almost as soon as his parents had left Siôn, a thickset little seven-year-old, had come down and talked to him for half an hour about Lego and what he was having for his birthday.

Duncan was keen to get on with boys. He had when he was thirty years younger, and he now wondered whether he might have lost the knack. But Siôn made it easy. There were things he wanted to say, things one chap told another about specifications and compatible sets and upgrades that sounded familiar to Duncan. The terminology was different but the aspiration was unchanged. Siôn had got some and he needed more. Much as Duncan used to have some but never enough.

Holly had left instructions that the children's light was to go off at eight o'clock. The instruction was, by her standards, an edict. 'Eight o'clock-ish,' she had said. So at eight precisely Duncan was about to say, 'Come on Siôn, time for bed,' when Buddug came into the breakfast room and ordered him back upstairs. Siôn went without a word.

'Thanks,' said Buddug over her shoulder. 'I needed a bit of time to myself. Hope he wasn't a nuisance.'

Duncan had been impressed by the young girl's show of authority, but rather peeved to find that he was not only working for Holly and Gwyn but for Buddug Williams too. What dreadful self-possession would Alice and Ellen have acquired by the age of ten? Duncan said as much to Jane when they compared notes. Things didn't sound too bad at Duncan's end, so Jane said she was going to bed to think about Tony Morgan-Jones.

'Rather you than me,' said Duncan.

As the evening progressed into night, Duncan was surprised how uncomfortable he felt in someone else's house. There wasn't anywhere that felt like his place in this house and yet he felt he ought to feel at home. He wasn't a guest here after all. He got up and prowled around in the kitchen that smelt of sweaty cats. He found a packet of digestive biscuits laid out with the coffee and ate several, along with a handful of raisins, in an attempt to settle himself. Then he looked at Holly's notice board and read the grisly details about the campaign to release several political prisoners, to which Holly had added her name, and he counted the number of tokens collected by Miss B.M. Williams of 27 Pontcanna Terrace, Cardiff, Wales towards an inflatable pink plastic cat.

After about an hour of staking out the territory like a bear newly arrived in this neck of the woods, Duncan found he could settle to his book after all. It was the autobiographical account of a city executive who had given up everything at the age of forty and begun his life again somewhere exotic where all the women had breasts like melons.

Jane had bought the book for Duncan the day he told her that he wasn't going to fight Howard the Louse over redundancy. There was a fiercely loyal dedication that she had written in the front. Duncan didn't particularly identify with this fellow, who had gone from a highly successful career in marketing to a highly successful career in marketing himself as the man who had given up a career in marketing, but it was good to try and actually read a book after all these years of architectural journals.

He had just reached the bit where, a year later, our hero's former employers travelled out to the melon groves and begged him to return to work, when Siôn came downstairs looking very bleary eyed. He cast a glance at Duncan and pottered to the fridge for his drink. This was now a different Siôn. A not-quite-awake Siôn.

'You're Alice and Ellen's Dad,' he said with the kind of stray belligerence that drunks sometimes fall into.

'That's right,' Duncan replied.

'They're all right,' said Siôn. Duncan replied that he thought they probably were.

'Only, they don't half argue,' Siôn cautioned. 'Something terrible. Tris Davis said Mr Harper had to move them.'

And with that he teetered back to bed. Duncan decided that none of this child evidence stuff was worth pursuing and settled back to his book, when he heard the central heating go off. In an end terrace like Holly and Gwyn's, even if he hadn't heard the sudden silence, he would certainly have soon guessed what had happened from the cold that bit within minutes.

The next hour was spent intermittently looking for the central heating boiler which, now it was silent, defied discovery.

At ten to twelve the front door mercifully banged and Duncan woke to hear Gwyn making his way towards the kitchen.

'Christ, this place is like a tomb!' Gwyn flung open the breakfast room door.

'You need a whisky,' he declared. 'And so do I. Holly, this place is freezing! Didn't she tell you where the controls were?'

Gwyn busied himself with three glasses, poured one each, and disappeared again.

Duncan was still waking up while this was going on. By the time he was fully in command of all his faculties he had a glass of single malt in his hand and so did Holly, who was sitting on the kitchen table with her own coat, and Gwyn's coat, draped around her shoulders. She was watching him and sipping thoughtfully.

'Where's Gwyn?' Duncan asked.

Holly nodded towards the ceiling. 'He doesn't drink socially at home. It's a family sort of thing with him. We never have people to dinner. We always take them to restaurants,' she explained.

'Really?' asked Duncan.

'Yes . . .' said Holly, feeling her way through the implications. 'It means you can't be spontaneous and just offer someone a meal, you know . . . Gwyn does like to be hospitable but he can't drink while others are around, not in his own house, you see.'

Duncan felt he ought to be collecting his tokens and going, but Holly seemed to have found her voice. She started asking him about Jane and their relationship and were they happy, and before Duncan knew where he was he was telling her about his feelings of guilt, his admiration for Jane and his own frustration and sense of inadequacy.

Holly slid off the table and came to sit down on the floor in front of him. It seemed a very mediaeval thing to do, as if she were indeed Guinevere and he a visiting warrior lord being entertained by this attentive handmaiden. She refilled his chalice while the once and future king of Pontcanna Terrace brooded on his whisky upstairs.

'You are a *good* man,' she told him, as if goodness was a peculiar attribute that he might not be familiar with but which she had the special instinct to discern.

'No I'm not,' said Duncan. 'I'm under-ambitious and easily satisfied.'

Holly thought that ambition was masculine. Duncan, in her opinion, was relaxed and centred.

'Jane says I make jokes because I'm too detached,' Duncan replied, full of sudden gloom. 'My humour is the humour of detachment. I find things funny because really I think I'm above everything.'

That was one of Jane's views. Duncan didn't think he thought he was above everything, but he asked Holly if she thought he thought it. 'After all,' he continued when Holly took too long considering this conundrum. 'After all, I should be out there fighting for my family instead of sending Jane down the docks to work.'

'Marriage is . . . it's a sort of . . . partnership,' said Holly at last. 'And you can only have a partnership of equals. You can't be everything Jane needs and she can't be everything you need.'

Duncan nodded. It was getting increasingly difficult to articulate his words this late in the evening and this deep into the whisky bottle, but he had a go. 'It's just that I'm more not everything she needs ... than she's not everything I need,' he explained.

Holly nodded. It was a deep sort of thing. She was about to think that particular idea through again but she had not allowed for the effect that whisky invariably had on Duncan. When she next looked up from her position on the rush matting he was asleep.

'This has got to stop,' Jane Lewis said, sitting Duncan down on the bed. Duncan was surprised to be there. The last thing he remembered was waking up in a taxi convinced that he had been kidnapped while baby-sitting for Holly and Gwyn Williams. 'Holly rang me,' Jane explained. 'She said you'd fallen asleep and should she cover you up for the night or send you home in a taxi.' She was pulling off Duncan's shoes. 'I asked her "Has he been drinking whisky?" "Yes" she said.'

'One glass!' Duncan protested. 'Gwyn gave me one glass and ... Holly gave me another. OK, two glasses!'

Jane lowered her eyebrows and looked at Duncan the way she sometimes looked at Tony Morgan-Jones. 'Duncan, I can't keep telling people you're under a lot of stress,' she told him, more in anger than in sorrow. 'And besides, I don't want to be getting up at one o'clock in the morning to let you in when you've been out carousing.'

Carousing was not how Duncan would have put it, but at one o'clock in the morning he was willing to let that pass. He wanted to go to sleep. If there was going to be an argument it could wait till the next day.

In the morning Duncan woke to find his digestive system had once again responded surprisingly well to the challenge of double single malts. He also woke slowly to realise that

Jane was lying on top of him and kissing his ear. 'Am I forgiven?' he asked through the thick layers of hair that inevitably spread across his face when Jane became amorous.

'Holly said you looked ever so sweet,' Jane told him as she took an increasingly active and intrusive interest in his body, 'asleep in the chair like that. I think Holly fancies you.'

Indeed, while Duncan had been sleeping Jane's anger and irritation had been replaced by the memory of Holly Williams on the telephone speaking very fondly of the sleeping Duncan. And now that Jane had that same sleeping Duncan beside her she had begun to find him attractive too.

A similar thing had happened when one of the secretaries at Follet Pryce's Whitchurch office had kept telling Jane how fortunate she was to have a husband like Duncan. Jane found she couldn't help nightly interposing her body between Duncan and his would-be admirer. It had been a memorable phase in their sex life, unbeknownst to the prim little secretary who might well have been shocked to know that she was the inspiration for such feats of passion.

Twice during the night Jane had tried to wake Duncan. He had a duty to her because she was now unable to sleep and they had a traditional cure for that, but Duncan had been proof against any overtures. Thirty-five per cent proof in fact.

In the morning Jane had woken them with enough time. However, just as Duncan began to realise what was going on the heavy thump of Alice and Ellen heading down the landing was audible.

Jane rebuttoned her pyjama jacket and gave Duncan a quick consolatory kiss.

'Another time,' he suggested.

*   *   *

Laura and Holly were standing together at the school gate as Duncan dropped the girls off. Laura was looking at Duncan as Holly spoke to her. Laura's small face registered concern. Why today of all days did Holly have to turn up to school? Duncan wondered. He felt sure that Laura Leighton Davis had to be a teetotaller of the most moral and disapproving kind.

'Duncan . . .' said Laura significantly as he drew level.

'How are you?' asked Holly.

'Fine,' replied Duncan cheerily.

'We're worried about you,' Laura told him.

Duncan reiterated that he was fine, really fine. 'Sorry,' he said to Holly.

'No, it's not your fault,' Laura insisted. 'Gerald went through a similar phase.' Duncan tried to explain that it wasn't a phase, it was whisky.

'Well of course,' Laura replied. 'Gerald developed a terrible allergy to gin just after they failed to offer him the chair. You've got be careful.'

'I just won't drink so much,' said Duncan. That seemed the obvious answer.

Laura disagreed. Allergies didn't work like that and Duncan had to accept the fact that he had developed an allergy to alcohol.

'It's a very male thing to ignore symptoms,' Holly chimed in her gentle monotone.

Duncan had always been told by Jane that actually it was a very male thing to complain loudly about the slightest thing wrong with you, but he didn't venture to quote her.

Laura took Duncan's arm and led him back to Fulwood Road. 'Now Duncan,' she said. 'You must take care of yourself. That's what we think, isn't it Holly?'

Holly, who was walking on the other side of Duncan, nodded.

'We think you're coping marvellously, we really do,'

Laura continued. 'But that doesn't mean you have to pretend to be invulnerable.'

'An allergic reaction when you are stressed is quite normal,' Holly added. 'It's nothing to be ashamed of . . .'

'You may be wonderful but you don't have to be Superman,' Laura declared.

They left him at the top of Fulwood Road. Laura reminded Duncan about the forthcoming parents' night, and how they really had got to make up their minds about the Iranian widow, before she turned off to the right and Holly to the left. As he carried on past Meirion Street, Duncan wondered whether it was better to be regarded as a piss artist or an allergy victim. On the whole he preferred Jane's analysis. At least he got a slap on the wrists and nearly rogered the next morning. Laura's cotton-wool compassion held the prospect of being very stifling.

Duncan turned down Cathedral Road and decided to give Jacobs a miss that morning. Norman the Blacksmith was supposed to be coming at nine to look at the conservatory again, and they had to talk. Duncan fell to wondering about Holly again. Since ceasing to work he had spent a lot of time thinking about sex, and Jane's words that morning held out dangerous impossibilities.

Last night he'd started off thinking that Holly Williams would be attractive if she didn't so obviously look like someone who had been even more attractive when she was younger. Then he had come to the conclusion that Holly would be attractive if she actually engaged with other people. What Duncan liked about Jane, and about Laura Davis for that matter, was that you knew they were listening to you, even if they were about to disagree or tell you you were an allergenic old boozer. But Holly was never quite there. She could sit on the kitchen table and elicit confessions from you late at night, she could kneel down in front of you like a whispering Arthurian handmaiden proffering mead and sympathy, and yet you never quite knew if she was hearing anything you said. Jane said Holly fancied him but he could equally believe that Holly didn't even know his name.

Duncan was wary of women like Holly Williams. He had thought he was in love with that type more than once. They were like quicksand, these fey women. The surface was unclear, and before you knew where you were you were in too deep. And they were nowhere to be seen.

Crossing Cathedral Road, Duncan was nearly run over by that same top-heavy white Mitsubishi as it made its return journey down into Cardiff. Duncan was sure it was the same vehicle, the same blowsy woman at the wheel.

There were a lot of women about these days.

From the top of Follet Pryce's bonded warehouse you could look back into the circular grey mass of Cardiff and the surrounding pale green hills that hemmed it in. Or you could look down the still waters of Atlantic Wharf to the dockland development and the bleary white Bristol Channel beyond. It was an ideal vantage point to see where all the money was coming from and where it was going. Not that anyone from Follets ever took the chill wet air from that rooftop position. Once inside the hothouse below they locked themselves into their offices, their alliances and hatreds.

Jane Lewis had been nice to Mair that morning. Aware of the fact that she had clearly put Tony's exec's nose out of joint, she had made a mental note to do something about it once she was getting on top of the Gooderson conveyance. She'd also discussed the nose job with Tony and had found out a bit more of the background.

It seemed that when Bernard and Tony had had their big set-to, Bernard's secretary and Mair, who had always been good friends, had a big argument in the car park. Although both Bernard and Tony came out to calm things down (it was one of those rare days when both were actually in) things were said that could never be unsaid.

'Well, you'll have to move one of them,' Jane told Tony, remembering that Follets had satellite offices, little suburban Siberias in Whitchurch and Penylan, for just such eventualities.

'Yes, but I can't afford to lose Mair,' said Tony. 'And Bernard's being difficult.'

In short, there was stalemate. Not Jane's long-term problem, she hoped, but a definite short-term irritant.

Armed with all this backstory, Jane went in on Thursday with some flowers for Mair. 'We never said hello properly did we?' she said, offering the bunch.

Mair breathed in and took her time putting down her pen. She seemed to begin to speak a number of times. Big Marjorie watched silently from her desk opposite while Jane's flowers stayed proffered across Mair's blotter and pot of coloured pens. Eventually Mair's blank face found voice.

'I must say, Jane, I'm glad Tony has talked to you, because I have always prided myself on my loyalty to this company . . .'

Jane decided to count to ten.

'I've always given my best and I think that other people know I've given my best.'

Jane got to ten very quickly. 'Mair, these flowers are to say let's be friends. That's all.'

Conflicting emotions seemed to fight within Mair Lloyd. At least part of her wanted to tell Jane to stick her flowers. After all she, Mair, had been with Tony for many years. Girls like Jane Lewis came and went. Sometimes they came back, but they knew nothing about loyalty as Mair knew about loyalty. Jane Lewis had no right to barge in and order her around. But another part of her wanted Tony's faction to be strong and united – and this was the part that won out.

'For Tony's sake I am willing to put matters aside,' she said with a massive dignity, heavily laced with reproach. She had not forgiven, she would not forget, but she had put an end to the hostilities. Hoo-bloody-ray, thought Jane as Mair accepted the flowers, commenting, for the sake of form, that they were lovely.

Duncan was also having problems with the staff, but in his case it was old Mrs R. who was still offering to pay for the broken pane of glass.

Louisa Radzinowicz looked as Polish a peasant as her name sounded, but in fact she was born Evans, within flooding distance of the River Taff. In 1942, as a Cardiff munitions girl of nineteen, she had married a Polish air mechanic who had told her he was an Air Force pilot. He also told her his name was something very like Radzinowicz and that he had property in Poland where his family were counts. As well as his rather curious surname, Jerzy gave to Louisa Evans a jewelled necklace of his mother's and told her that one day he would give her wardrobes of furs, ancestral plate and cut-glass drinking sets.

Five years later, when Count Radzinowicz ran off, Mrs R. discovered that her war hero had never flown and that his duelling scar was the result of an accident with a lawn mower at the factory where he worked before the German invasion of Danzig. She also discovered that his main possessions in Poland were a wife and two children. But Mrs Radzinowicz kept the curious Polish name that no one could pronounce, which meant that half a century later she tended to answer to Mrs R. wherever she cleaned.

Now in her seventies, Mrs R. had grown slow, stiff and round. She would easily have fitted into some queue in an East European market. It was as if, before he left her, Jerzy Radzinowicz's last gift had been to bequeath Louisa Evans his nationality.

Mrs R. had arrived in Katrin Street as Duncan was in the conservatory with Norman the Blacksmith. Norman worked to his own timetable and he often called in to look at Duncan's conservatory and make a few sketches on the back of an envelope. Jane had always found this particularly irritating, as Norman would let it be known that he wouldn't say no to a cup of tea even though she was trying to work herself. And to make matters worse, despite all the cups of tea and all the recycled envelopes Norman didn't ever do anything and the old conservatory continued to leak.

That very week Jane had drawn up a list of economies and Norman's name was on the list. Although she was getting well enough paid for being dropped in the shit by Big Fat Tony, Jane had to admit that her full-time salary was not going to equal what Duncan had brought in, particularly when that sum had always been supplemented by her own bits of part-time work.

'I think we should put the conservatory on the back boiler,' Jane had suggested. Duncan had agreed, although he refused to demolish his way out of the problem like some of their neighbours. However, Duncan did have an economy of his own to propose. He would take over some of Mrs R.'s duties in the short term, reducing her cleaning days at Katrin Street from three to two.

'But we only pay her peanuts,' Jane argued.

'So we'll save peanuts,' said Duncan. 'Every peanut counts. You ask a monkey.'

By one of those irritating coincidences to which their clearing lady was somehow often a party, Mrs R. turned up, having thought it over, convinced she must pay for the broken pane of glass in their conservatory door, just as Norman was telling Duncan that he'd had some time come free and he'd actually now made the struts for the new conservatory roof. And he'd bring them round at the front end of next week.

With Mrs R. trying pathetically to pass a five-pound note in through the empty window pane on one side of him and Norman measuring up on the other side of him, Duncan felt that this was not a good time to announce economies on the domestic front. In the circumstances he hoped that Jane would forgive him and he chickened out of laying both of them off.

'I was outnumbered,' he insisted, trying to make a joke of it over supper that evening. Jane's mind was elsewhere. Duncan had forgotten how effectively she could cut off from him when work impinged. 'So what do I do?' he asked.

Jane pushed her plate away. 'You must do what you think best,' she said abstractedly.

'Hey – I'm not a client,' Duncan replied, pushing her plate back at her.

Jane didn't seem to be listening. 'I'm going to ring Tony,' she said and got up.

'Excuse me,' said Duncan. 'I used to have a job and yet I think we managed conversations over supper.'

'No we didn't,' said Jane, walking towards the phone. 'You used to tell me how much you hated what you did, and everyone you worked with, and I used to listen.'

Duncan was stunned. Jane stopped in her tracks, also looking startled. 'Sorry,' she said. She hadn't meant to say that, she'd never even thought it as such, but now it was said there did seem to be a sort of sense to it. It was a reproach that had been hovering in the air, unspoken for many months, years perhaps – but it was unspoken no more.

'Oh,' said Duncan, treading water. 'Wasn't I even vaguely entertaining?'

Jane did not wish to be cruel. 'Yes you were,' she replied '*Very* vaguely at times. I'm sorry, Duncan, I didn't mean to have a go at you. It's just that I've got a lot on my mind. What is it you wanted to talk about?'

'Well . . .' said Duncan, going to the first item on his agenda. 'It's parents' evening tomorrow at six. There was a note in the girls' bags. Do you want me to go? Do you want me to get a baby-sitter so we can both go?'

Jane breathed in and out as if respiration would help calm her sense of irritation. 'I'll try and make it,' she said.

'So I'd better go?' he replied.

Jane searched around for a way of explaining the situation. 'Look, if I had asked you that question a few months ago what would you have said?'

Duncan thought. 'I suppose I'd've said, "You do what you think is necessary and I'll make it if I can".'

'Right,' said Jane. 'Well that's what I'm saying.'

Duncan felt peeved that he was being rebuked for consulting his own wife. 'You're the one who's always so concerned about parents' evening,' he reminded her.

'Yes, but I'm the one who's bloody working tomorrow!' Jane pointed out.

It was the first time since his redundancy that Jane had drawn that distinction. Duncan felt quite hurt. To be fair, Jane had bent over backwards to put a positive gloss on their current situation. *He* had been a provider for years and he had earned the right to take time out and rethink. That was the view she had put to him and that was the view he had accepted. What reproaches he felt were self generated. He had not thought of it in terms of Jane Bloody Working Tomorrow.

'OK,' he said, backing off. 'I'll go. I'll be there. It's OK. It's not a problem.'

But it was.

4

Disney on a Sunday Afternoon

Jane Lewis definitely felt under pressure at the moment. Follet Pryce loomed very large in her emotional life, too large, in fact. Her journeys home on those dark winter nights were never easy. She realised she was a traffic hazard after a day's pussyfooting round the Follet feuds. Jane just knew she had to take up squash or badminton again, and soon. The need to hit something hard was growing every time she left that building, and she would rather it was not one of her family or another car.

Yet it was good to be working again, to have phone calls fielded for her, to have cups of tea and coffee brought, to have people asking her opinion – and seeming to value it when they got it. It was good to have a place in the world, to be considered important again. In short, Jane found that Follets offered all those things that she and her women friends had missed since giving up work.

Eight years ago at coffee mornings in Pontcanna, Canton and Llandaff, Jane had joined in the laments for lost independence and lost status. Yet even as an overburdened, breast-feeding mother of twins she had occasionally paused to wonder whether the grown-up delights of office life were illusory, whether she and her fellow new mums were idealising the life before children.

She had started working again when Alice and Ellen were three and in nursery. One day's teaching law at the Poly every week had been something neither she, her students nor the girls had particularly enjoyed, so Jane spent some time in Follet's Whitchurch office once the girls were at school. Tony installed her grandly as if she were his representative on earth, but Jane found the childcare arrangements a nightmare, and she persuaded Tony to let her move to drafting leases and wills from home. This fitted in well with the school holidays, the various illnesses and the Inset days when, out of the blue, the school would declare itself a child-free zone for staff training. It also brought in a reasonable sum. But even if she put in five days a week from nine-thirty, to three, Jane never quite felt that working from home accorded her the same status as that enjoyed by her friends who went in to an office each day.

However, the work in Follets' main office was everything Jane believed she had missed. It was a challenge and it was grown-up. The problem was the people who worked there. They were far from grown-up. While the feud between Bernard and Tony continued, Follets was ever so slightly out of control. Partners abnegated collective responsibility and behaved like children, and juniors appropriated what responsibility they could to themselves.

Of course it didn't look like that to anyone who walked in hoping to get a will drawn up, house conveyed or marital partner financially ruined, but Jane could see the telltale signs of an organisation that was a danger to itself: assistant solicitors signing the post; bills going out too late; costs being rounded up in a cavalier way; and all the time the silence of that atrium, as up above people crossed to each other's offices and conspired. For within Follets there were many factions.

To Jane, whose priorities were to earn enough money for her family and yet still get to see them, these feuds and gross pettinesses loomed far too large in her life. By Friday lunchtime she was longing for the weekend. She wanted to cook, to read the girls stories, to walk by the sea and to make love to Duncan. The last thing she wanted was to be told that Miles Mihash was coming over for drinks at six-thirty.

'Why six-thirty?' she asked.

'I thought you'd be pleased, Mrs Lewis,' Tony replied with that crestfallen look that he always manufactured if anyone gainsayed him. 'You said you didn't want to do lunch yet.'

'It's my first week full-time in seven years,' Jane complained.

Tony offered to put him off, but Jane was determined not to use special pleading so soon after her return to work, and moreover she just knew she couldn't take the obsessive solicitude she would get from Tony were she to suggest there were problems at home.

'Anyway, you'll like Miles,' Tony reminded her.

'Clients I always like,' Jane replied.

Fortunately Jane did like Miles. He was a small moustachioed American of Czech descent who was very funny about how he, a New Jersey middle-European Jew, came to be fronting a Welsh maritime project on this scale.

'I think they wanted someone who absolutely nobody trusted,' he said. 'And all the English were busy.'

Miles also understood Jane's reservations about the conveyance, and suggested that they booked two and a half hours first thing next week to go through all thirty-two files.

'What if we don't finish?' asked Jane, who suspected that

if Tony liked him Miles must be deeply superficial at some level she hadn't yet plumbed.

'If we don't finish we book some more time but, to be on the safe side, prioritise,' Miles replied. 'Hit me with your biggest problem first. There's nothing I like better than a triple whammy Monday morning.' Then, realising that Jane had children, and it was well gone seven, he insisted they broke up the meeting so she could get back.

Miles escorted Jane down to the car park as Tony kept a satisfied eye on them from the gantry. 'How about dinner sometime?' he asked.

Jane reiterated her view that this project needed a rigorous plod through the files before any kind of lunch was in order.

'I wasn't talking about lunch,' said Miles as they got to Jane's car. 'I meant dinner. You and me.'

Jane was surprised; more than surprised, she was slightly shocked. 'I'm married,' she said. 'Those children we were talking about have a father and I'm still married to him.'

'You keep it that way,' said Miles, without any sense of irony or disappointment. 'I've got two lots of kids with different former Mrs Mihashes. Nice meeting you, Jane.'

It was the most complete and courteous back-off that Jane had ever encountered. Miles got into his low on the ground, heavy on the expense account German-looking automobile and drove off. Jane sat for a moment in her rather dog-eared Volvo saloon and thought, 'I've just been asked out by an American in a sportscar.' Later, as she skirted the city centre, she thought about all those abandoned Mrs Mihashes, and little Mihashes, and felt sad to think that in Miles' world you assumed that a middle-aged woman with children was probably divorced.

It should have been an ideal time for her to return to Katrin Street and count those blessings, but things had happened in the meantime. Duncan was quietly solicitous.

He even took her coat and offered her a drink. After so much Brecon Water, Jane had her mind on a glass of Friday wine, but it was Duncan taking her coat that made her twig something.

It was just like the time after New Year when he came home from that interview with the Louse and put his arms round her without speaking. Then it was the redundancy; what was it this time?

Duncan suggested she go and say goodnight to the girls first.

'Are they all right?' Jane asked.

Duncan said yes because, he thought to himself, maybe they were. He could explain things properly when she got down.

That Friday had started well enough for Duncan, although the girls were more than normally reluctant to go to school. Once Alice had understood there was no option they had got up and dressed, breakfasted and lined up in the hall in record time. Duncan checked they had all the usual paraphernalia plus the egg boxes which were Mr Harper's latest curious demand on the family dustbin.

Approaching the school gate, however, Duncan realised they were distinctly late because the Swiss Cheese was already draggng her fertile hips back up Fulwood Road and Laura was standing very close to the Iranian widow and saying goodbye, with many last-minute footnotes to what must have been a pretty detailed conversation. And if Holly Williams had been there she had certainly gone by now.

Left on his own to walk back, Duncan felt himself invaded by that awful challenge to his identity that Jane had touched on two nights ago. *She* was someone who was bloody working today. Who was he? He had no particular wish to be an architect of the kind he had been for Howard

Losen, but neither did he wish to be a redundant architect. He wanted an identity that gave him confidence. Coping wonderfully, as Laura Davis saw it, was not enough. Whatever she actually meant, Duncan was pretty certain it was some kind of consolation prize Laura was offering. He could be a house husband and father of course, but was that what he wanted?

What if secretaries from the office saw him plodding to school every morning? 'I saw that Nice Mr Lewis yesterday . . . walking in the street with his children.'

Never!

He must do something. But what? Duncan didn't want to become an architect again just so people from the office wouldn't pity him.

Fortunately, that morning Duncan had set himself the task of Socks, and this was bound to cheer him up. His recent spate of spring cleaning had unearthed much stray footwear behind the radiators, at the bottom of wardrobes, under the roll-top bath and even above the pelmet in one of the bedrooms.

By the time he was preparing (and simultaneously eating) lunch, Duncan could take private consolation from his work that morning. He had started supper, had another go at baking bread, cleaned the oven when this became necessary, and taken non-scratch cleaner to all the work surfaces. He was also able to reflect with a certain amount of pleasure that first thing this morning there had been nine fewer working pairs of socks in this house than there were now. One could continually create little islands of order out of domestic chaos.

The afternoon had seen a hurried visit from Norman the Blacksmith who seemed sorry not to find Jane in, although Duncan had explained the new domestic arrangements several times already. He seemed to be doing that over and over again these days. Norman was keen to explain that if you want quality work you got to pay for it, and preferably in cash, but today Duncan was not up to Norman's bluster. When he tried to hint that the conservatory had slipped down their list of priorities, and Norman seemed not to hear, Duncan just left it at that.

However, there was genuine pleasure in the three o'clock walk down to school during an uncommon and very welcome burst of sunshine which signalled a brief clearance in the general moist miasma under which Cardiff dripped that February.

Gerald Davis was picking up his boys and he waved to Duncan, a slow vague gesture of recognition like a circus elephant who thinks it is time to lift its trunk and perform but is not quite clear about the cue. Holly was not around. Duncan did feel slightly disappointed at reaching the weekend without a sight of her. Wondering if he found Mrs Holly Williams attractive was one of the little intellectual exercises Duncan had set himself, and the days when he did certainly had a lift to them. She was his hobby.

At six o'clock Duncan left the girls with Laura while he went to the parents' evening. He had hastily rung the Davis family at half-past four, having realised that he had done nothing to arrange someone to look after Alice and Ellen. Laura had spent a long time considering his request and taken him laboriously through her deliberations, but she assented with a kind reproach.

'You should have asked me yesterday, Duncan. You can't always cope alone, you know.'

At the parents' evening Duncan found himself in a small queue of two seated opposite a nature table which looked as if it had been newly assembled that day.

Fulwood Road School was an unfortunate mixture of old and new-but-rapidly-ageing buildings. It had none of the sense of order of the purpose-built schools Duncan had helped design over in Gwent. Fulwood's answer to the lack of apparent order was to stick posters and word processor generated graphics over every available interior wall space.

'*Where We Live!*' one sign announced, over an aerial photo of West Cardiff for which the previous headmaster had been heavily criticised. The picture offended no one's political sensibilities (there were many at Fulwood Road), but rumours did get around that Mr Roberts used school funds to buy himself a flying lesson in order to take the shot. Even Duncan had got to hear about that.

'*Who We Are!*' read another, over a press photo of an evenly balanced group of smiling black, white and yellow children, although you would be hard pressed to find the Cardiff Chinese at this school. Their offspring went *en masse* elsewhere.

'*What We Do!*' Duncan turned to this one with particular interest when he noticed Gwyn Williams come out of Mr Harper's classroom, appearing to wipe the sweat off his brow.

Gwyn also noticed Duncan. 'Hello there,' he said. 'Little bugger! Pulled all the bad boys in first, is it!' And with that he was gone at a pace. Having only met Gwyn in his own house Duncan hadn't really noticed what acceleration this man was capable of over a distance. He seemed to bound down the hallway causing posters to flap in the slipstream.

Duncan had been sitting next to a very stern-looking woman with very thick, heavy-rimmed glasses with whom he had not bothered to attempt a conversation. She wore a tight-fitting, aggressively belted mackintosh which seemed to heave with indignation each time she breathed. The classroom door opened again and Mr Harper beckoned her in. Poor sod, thought Duncan. One word of criticism and that mum was going to explode.

He was just going to look again to try and work out what it was *We Do!* when a thin woman with sunglasses and spiky hair walked in, looked around, swore and stubbed out her cigarette on the nature table. The spiky woman coughed a smoker's cough, swore again, took off her glasses and caught sight of Duncan where he was sitting.

'Oh God,' she said, in an accent that surprised Duncan with its twang of fashionable London, 'sorry – didn't see you there. Thought I was all on my own. Thank Christ I didn't fart.'

Duncan was uncertain about replying to this verbal torrent, so he just smiled.

The woman continued. 'God, I hate this place. Am I in the right bit? Jeremy Harper?'

'That's right,' said Duncan, nodding to the door.

The woman sat down a few chairs from Duncan and put her dark glasses back on and her feet up. Then she took them down. 'Usually my husband comes to these things, seeing as he sent the kids here, but the bastard's got an emergency. Six o'clock I ask you! My body clock's expecting G and T, not pep talks from Jeremy Bear.' She looked over her glasses at him. 'Sorry. I talk too much when I'm nervous. Hate this place. Hate it. Sorry, have I offended you? You're not the headmaster or something are you?'

Duncan insisted he wasn't offended. Or the headmaster. Actually he was wondering when he was going to climb aboard this particular conversation or whether the spiky woman even wanted him to.

'I'm Kit Sinclair,' she told him.

'Duncan Lewis,' said Duncan, offering his hand.

'Oh, you've got the twins,' the woman exclaimed, ignoring Duncan's gesture. 'My eldest is in their class. Ben Britto. I suppose round here I'm Mrs Britto,' she said with an exaggerated Cardiff accent. 'God, the Bastard would love that.'

Duncan caught up. 'Your au pair brings the boys to school,' he said. 'I've seen her.'

'That's about all she does,' Kit replied, taking out a cigarette packet. 'She's out till three most mornings, the tart. She takes the boys in at half-past eight and sleeps most of the day till it's time to collect them. I ought to get rid of her but I'm not going to leave myself stranded.' She sought a lighter in the biggest handbag Duncan had ever seen. 'I told the bastard that if he sent them here I was not going to be responsible for getting them into school or collecting them. Of course he's impossibly important now, so he's paying for the tart. I told him it'll cost him, and it does. It's the only way to get through to him sometimes. Bastard.'

Duncan had never met anyone quite like Kit before, although some of Jane's London friends used to be like this a few years ago – but not very often. It took a lot of nervous energy to be like this. That Kit Sinclair was the mother of the Britto boys seemed extraordinary. She looked more like the kind of person that any sensible mother of the Britto boys would warn them about. She was fashionably dressed in tight clothing that emphasised how uncommonly thin she was. The darkness of her clothes showed up the while pallor of her gamine face which gave her the aura of a naughty pixie. That the pixie was decked out in flame-red lipstick only added to the alarming impression that Kit Sinclair was the most demonic of elfen folk and quite possibly a punk vampire. This was not the way most people came to parents' evenings.

'I suppose I shouldn't smoke,' she declared, lighting her cigarette. 'D'you want one?' Duncan declined. She was perhaps a little old to be dressed in such a startling manner.

'What do *you* do?' Kit was clearly ill at ease with silence. That question seemd to crop up a lot these days. Duncan still hadn't worked out how to answer it.

'I used to be an architect,' he admitted.

Kit was interested. 'That's good. I used to be a journalist. Medical mainly. Some fashion. Odd combination, but there you go. Of course, that was before the bastard dragged me off to this place. God, I hate Cardiff – do you?' She didn't pause for an answer. 'Are you looking for work?' she said suddenly. 'Only we're thinking of building a conservatory. I'm trying to ruin the bastard. Come round and run up some huge bills.' She smiled at him. 'Only joking,' she added. 'Seriously though, we are looking for an architect.'

Duncan told her, modestly, that there were specialist companies working in Cardiff. Kit wasn't interested in specialist companies. 'I want something *designed*, not a pile of UPVC windows stuck on top of each other.'

Duncan nodded. Kit warmed to her theme. 'I don't want something tacked on, I want to bring light into the house,' she explained. 'Look, will you come and look at what I'm thinking of, and tell me if I'm mad?'

'Sure,' said Duncan. He was, theoretically, in the free-lance market now, although having Kit for a client sounded like trouble. An enthusiastic client was one thing, an imaginative client could be helpful, but a visionary was something else. Kit fumbled in her bag for a card. The door opened and Jeremy Harper ushered out the heavily suppressed woman in thick glasses. Nothing that had been said seemed to have eased the pressure that was boiling away beneath that tightly belted bosom.

'Mr and Mrs Lewis?' said Jeremy Harper. Kit looked at him in total surprise and then convulsed in silent laughter.

'This is my friend Mrs Britto,' said Duncan, getting up.

Kit was still laughing as he was ushered in.

Duncan had been to many parents' evenings but he realised that this was his first with a man. All those interviews had blurred into one all-purpose conversation during which the teachers would insist happily that Alice and Ellen were 'in the middle there somewhere', and Jane would try and get a more detailed response.

Duncan had always felt such sessions were a waste of time. Like sending corporate Christmas cards, nothing of import ever attached to this time-consuming activity. If there was something that genuinely needed saying there were proper channels open. The parents' evening was a classic piece of noncommunication which neither side felt confident to abandon just in case it meant something to the other.

This tolerant but blasé frame of mind had meant that it took a while for him to catch up. This serious but kindly man was not saying that Alice and Ellen were in the middle, but something quite different.

'Can you repeat that?' Duncan asked.

Jeremy Harper was not a young man although he was new to teaching. He spoke with cautious authority and real compassion. He must have assumed that Duncan was annoyed by what he had just heard, because his remarks were now prefaced by a helpful preamble. 'Before I came to Fulwood I encountered something very similar to this on teaching practice. We had a pair of twins very like Alice and Ellen. They always sat together and worked together, and when they gave their work in it was understandably identical – but then, when one of them was ill for a while, we found that the other made huge strides in her work. She really demonstrated that she was a very bright little girl. However, when her twin came back, she reverted to the same much slower pace.'

Duncan interrupted. 'But neither of them has been ill.' He was trying to get a purchase on this.

'Yes but since they've been separated—'

'Separated?' echoed Duncan.

'For talking in class,' Jeremy Harper explained. 'Since they've been separated, and it's only been a matter of two weeks, Ellen's classwork has improved drastically. Her homework is still identical to Alice's but her classwork is really very good indeed.'

'And Alice?' Duncan asked, dreading the answer before he'd even asked the question.

After what genuinely seemed an age Jeremy Harper replied. 'I have to say there are problems.'

At that moment Duncan simply felt a range of despairs. Despair that Alice was educationally subnormal and despair that Ellen's development had been irretrievably damaged by helping her. For the rest of the interview Jeremy Bear (as Duncan couldn't help thinking of him) was very keen to rebuild Duncan's confidence. He was obviously concerned, but not so concerned that Duncan found it difficult to trust his judgement.

In fact, by the end of the interview Duncan was feeling pleased that the girls had Jeremy Bear as their teacher.

'Will you stop saying that,' Jane snapped. 'His name is Harper.'

She looked very worried, as if the basis on which she viewed the sane universe had suddenly collapsed. Her reaction was immediate. Alice was at risk. She must give up work immediately to help her.

Duncan tried to calm her down.

'Yes, but what do we do?' she asked.

'Mr Harper thinks they should be put in separate classes,' said Duncan.

Jane looked horrified. 'They've never been in separate classes,' she declared.

'As a way of finding out the extent of the problem, Ju,' said Duncan. 'Even as a way of finding out if there *is* a problem.'

'Well of course there's a problem,' said Jane, staring at the table.

'Not necessarily,' said Duncan, trying to remember exactly how it had been told to him. 'It might be that because Nel has been willing to help Alice Alice hasn't really bothered. But that once she's on her own she'll make the effort and catch up. In a few months' time there may be no difference between them.'

Jane disagreed. Duncan had told her that Ellen would soon be streets ahead if she was cut free from Alice. So even if Alice did catch up to where Ellen was now, Ellen would no longer be there.

Duncan agreed but he tried to look on the bright side. 'At least we'll have one bright daughter and one averagely bright daughter,' he suggested.

Jane became distressed at the thought that her children would grow apart when a joint sense of identity had always been so important to them.

'But that was bound to happen sometime,' Duncan argued.

'But the school is deciding, this Mr Harper is deciding, when it will happen,' Jane argued back.

Duncan insisted that Harper wanted them to think about what he was proposing. Just think about it. That had been the tenor of his last words to Duncan. That he and Jane should talk it over and come back and see him before anything else was done.

Duncan had left the interview stunned but recovering. He had no recollection whether that Kit woman was still waiting outside the classroom. The next thing he remembered was turning up at Laura's red-brick house to collect the girls. Laura had opened the door to him and taken him straight into the front parlour where she'd asked him what the matter was.

Realising his need to talk, Laura had sent Gerald down to the school and told Gawain to bath Mordred. Fortunately the girls were reading in Tristram's bedroom. Gerald had come past the parlour door on his way out and waved a gentle, trunk-like arm at Duncan where he sat on Laura's huge recovered sofa. Then Gawain came past, leading Mawmaw. Duncan had been aware that he was causing a disruption in Laura's house but he didn't yet have the energy to get up and go.

Laura had brought tea in a large pot. 'Tristram's showing Alice and Ellen Gerald's train track now,' she said, closing the door. 'They'll be happy for hours up there.'

Laura had been marvellous. Perhaps with just a hint of self-awareness, she had been calm and very reassuring. She told Duncan how she and Gerald had had lots of worries with Arthur (the third son whose name never seemed to appear on Laura's litany), and in fact it turned out in the course of the conversation that each of the Davis boys had specific learning difficulties, none of which Duncan had ever heard of. And yet all but Arthur were achieving excellent results at Fulwood Road.

'Of course at The Abbey they might be scholarship material,' Laura had said, tucking her feet underneath her. 'But I've told Grandpa Leighton that we will not touch his money while he is still alive.'

But that was the only occasion that Laura dwelt on her own concerns. The rest of the time she had been enormously positive, and she did seem to know a great deal about education. By the time she went upstairs to find the girls and Tristram, Duncan had felt much more positive about the whole business.

A confidence that was unfortunately completely out of tune with Jane's reaction.

'Have you told the girls?' she asked.

'Of course not,' Duncan replied.

'I've got to give up work,' said Jane for the second time. 'They need me.'

'I don't see that having no money is going to help,' said Duncan.

Jane didn't like him for saying that. She didn't like him for suggesting that she went and talked to Laura Davis either. 'It's nothing to do with Laura,' she said. 'Why did you talk to her about it anyway?'

Duncan apologised. He could see the way Jane's mind was going. This whole experience had been between Duncan and the teacher, and between Duncan and Laura Davis. 'I just wish I could help you make sense of it the way they helped me,' he said.

'Maybe there isn't any sense to it!' said Jane miserably.

It was not a good evening. They discussed options, every option under the sun. Maybe they should think of moving schools. Perhaps smaller classes would help.

'That means The Abbey,' said Duncan.

'No it doesn't,' said Jane, who disliked him for assuming that money could solve their problems, particularly when they had none to spare. Then she remembered that if Duncan was still working they might at least have had the option, and then she disliked him even more for making her blame him which she had never intended to do.

'Perhaps we should think of moving out of Cardiff?' Jane suggested. 'Somewhere with better schools.'

'Or perhaps I should get a job,' said Duncan, reading her mind.

'We could always move to an area which makes it easier for you to get a job.'

'There aren't areas where architects can get jobs,' Duncan insisted.

They passed a gloomy evening considering every idea that might help the girls, and decided in the end that

Jane should spend a lot of time with Alice that weekend and that Duncan would compensate with Ellen, and then they'd go and see Mr Harper next week. To extend the list of possibilities, Duncan agreed that he would now start actively looking for a job, but Jane accepted his reservations that the problem with Alice and Ellen was unlikely to be linked to his redundancy. It might have been going on for years.

Nevertheless, when they went to bed Duncan did feel like a pretty useless father and Jane did feel like a dreadfully neglectful mother. And both of them thought that they had perhaps taken advantage of how remarkably self-sufficient the girls had always been. Jane was also angry that Duncan had spent so much time talking to Laura about this problem when she should have been the first to know. They kissed getting into bed and curled in opposite directions, then clung to each other briefly before falling asleep.

On Saturday morning in Pontcanna, Laura was up early getting Gerald breakfast in bed which was his treat on Saturdays; Gwyn was up early taking his son Siôn for a brisk and indirectly punitive walk into town; and Jane Lewis was running in Pontcanna Fields to the alarm of several people out walking dogs. Holly Williams was hiding from the morning chill, as ever, in a deep hot bath, while her large daughter sat and talked about her problems and Holly said 'Mm'; Duncan was in bed having woken with a depressingly exact memory of all that was currently besetting him and Jane. Kit Sinclair was not in her bed, but sleeping off the previous night on a camp bed in what she called her office. Kit had returned in a taxi at three in the morning. Her usual routine was not to wake anyone by attempting the stairs but just to crash out in a box room next to the hall. At midnight, Barry Britto had gone down and put a large sleeping bag on Kit's camp bed in anticipation of her return, and it was inside this that he found his wife the next morning.

'Come along, darling,' he said, lifting her with gentle irony.

The Davis boys had Bogey-jobs on Saturday morning – unrewarding household chores that had to be done by somebody, 'because the Bogeyman never did them'. Gerald also had his Bogey-job. Laura had told him this wasn't necessary but Gerald was always in an excellent mood after breakfast in bed. So Laura helped Mordred and Gerald helped Arthur who needed a bit more assistance than the others, while up above Gawain and Tristram worked at their own tasks which took place on separate floors because otherwise Bogey-jobs degenerated into Gawain's favourite game of lunging at Tristram's genitals.

The Lewis girls watched television until Duncan got them breakfast and Jane came back full of energetic optimism.

'Right,' she said. 'We're going to do something today. We're going to have fun.'

'Can't we have fun *and* watch the telly?' asked Alice because Jane had just switched it off.

'You're so funny Ali!' Jane cried, giving her daughter a great big affirmatory cuddle.

Jane's first idea was for everyone to go round to Binny's or Elaine's for coffee, but Duncan suspected this would prove an excuse for Jane to talk to someone who wasn't Duncan and the girls seemed to get wind of this too. Then she suggested the Folk Museum at St Fagan's to which there was general roar of disapproval. (Alice and Ellen had done the folk museum as a school project several years running and they had never enjoyed going back since.)

'The docks!' said Jane. 'We could have coffee at the Norwegian Church.'

'The docks are smelly,' replied Alice.

'The docks are not smelly,' replied Duncan. 'Cardiff Bay

Development have spent millions in order to prove you wrong. I read about it last week.'

Jane glanced up at Duncan. This was no time to be facetious.

'How about the sea?' Jane asked. 'We could go the Light House and take a picnic.'

'It isn't really the sea,' said Ellen. 'It's only the Bristol Channel.'

Alice told her to shut up because she was a silly Nelly.

'Well what do you want to do?' Jane asked Alice. Duncan thought all this consultation a bit overdone considering how foul and unfair Alice had just been to Ellen, but Jane was determined to bring her daughter out. Alice's view was that if they couldn't watch telly (which Jane said was not an option) then she would like to walk into town and have coffee or lunch in Garlands.

'What a lovely idea!' said Jane.

Duncan had his doubts about how much approval of Alice was going to be good for the family as a whole, but he could see the very admirable intentions that lay behind Jane's actions. She was going to give Alice all that she needed. Even if it meant sitting up all night and going without food and drink, Jane was going to go on approving of Alice.

During the walk into town Jane and Alice played chasing games through the park while Ellen walked through the long grass with Duncan, complaining that her nose was too flat.

'It's impossible for your nose to be too flat at the age of eight,' Duncan replied. 'Who knows where your nose is going to end up by the time you stop growing?'

This wasn't what Ellen wanted to hear.

'I like your nose,' said Duncan, hoping that might be better received.

'What about Ben Britto?' Ellen asked.

Duncan had to own up. He had no idea if Ben Britto liked her nose, but did that really matter at her age?

'You don't understand girls, do you?' Ellen told him.

Duncan tried apologising. He felt that Ellen's relationship with her features should not be mediated by Ben Britto who, even if he was only one-tenth as batty as his mother, should not be allowed to pronounce judgement on the nose, eyes, teeth, or any other salient feature of his daughter.

Just as Ellen was about to complain that nobody liked her, and that even Mum preferred Alice, Alice chose to involve Ellen in a game of catch and tickle that seemed to be all giggling and improvised rules. The two girls ran ahead and Jane retired.

'Ellen was feeling left out,' Duncan warned her.

'We're both going to have to work at it,' said Jane. She took his hand and squeezed it. 'We'll make it work,' she told him.

Duncan squeezed back. Watching their two daughters run healthily and happily down the mile-long arcade of tall trees that led into Cardiff he could not help but feel that things would work out all right.

'How about getting some fish from the market?' Jane suggested.' And you could do that wonderful thing you do . . .'

'And then later you can do that wonderful thing *you* do . . .' said Duncan, who was bothered that they hadn't had sex for over a week now.

'I'm not feeling very sexual at the moment,' Jane replied as if she'd only just noticed. She tried to look sorry, but loss of appetite is not one of those things you can genuinely mourn while the loss is continuing. 'They have that effect on me,' she said, nodding at the distant girls.

'I hope they don't have that effect on their boyfriends,' Duncan observed.

Jane took his arm. 'But I do love you and we are coping aren't we?'

Duncan agreed. They were coping, but it was a weekend with awkward edges. In the past he and Jane had indulged themselves on winter Saturdays. Tea in front of an open fire in the upstairs drawing room, a glass of wine while the girls had their bath, the lengthy preparation of a meal together, talking over the food, and watching a late-night film or video until sleep or sex interposed. Saturdays drifted seamlessly by. They were a celebration of the life Jane and Duncan had built together.

But this Saturday nothing happened easily. Alice declared she wasn't having a bath and Jane let her off. Then, when it was time to cook supper, most of the ingredients were missing because neither Jane nor Duncan had been to the shops that week, and so they settled for something simpler – and Jane read an article from that morning's paper while they ate.

The article was alarming and seemed to interpret what Duncan would have described as personality traits as symptoms of a syndrome which led to educational underachievement. The weekend papers seemed to run these features constantly but this was the first time Jane had taken them seriously.

She read the symptoms to Duncan twice: 'Uncooperative, high self-regard, indolent but verbally articulate. Well, doesn't that sound like Alice?'

'It sounds like most eight-year-old girls,' Duncan replied.

Not surprisingly, he ended up watching the late-night movie on his own.

On Sunday morning the grey air over Pontcanna hung latent with rain but undecided. Jane declared that she really had to do some work, and so Duncan took the girls to St Fagan's despite their protests. The National Folk Museum opened its many acres at ten o'clock on a Sunday, and Duncan usually found other fathers there on similar missions. This was one of the few amenities available so early in the day, and after a Saturday-night dinner party Duncan often stood in line with the other dads, watching their children on the hugely popular climbing frame which was, ironically, the one edifice at St Fagan's that had not been disassembled in some distant part of Wales and painstakingly reconstructed by craftsmen.

Duncan saw Flyn with a hangover keeping a not very close eye on Josh. Flyn nodded darkly at Duncan in a way that discouraged conversation. Flyn wanted to be left alone with the pain in his head and the dryness in his throat. Despite their professed aversion to Snotgobs the girls made a big fuss of little Josh, and when Duncan asked if they would mind if he went to look at the old farmhouses they waved him off cheerily.

At lunchtime the lack of basic food in the house became even more apparent, so Jane suggested to Duncan that after their baked beans he went to Sainsbury's or Tesco's in the car while she listened to Alice reading.

'You'll go with Dad, won't you?' she asked Ellen.

'Shopping?' said Ellen with uncharacteristic alarm.

'You could help me,' said Duncan in a kind but patronising tone.

'You'll probably need helping,' said Ellen. Helping someone who needed help was no fun.

'We can have tea in the café . . .' Duncan hinted.

Ellen capitulated.

The shopping came to £150.89, which was rather more than Duncan had expected. Jane had said get the basics. Duncan wasn't quite sure what these were when he saw the rows of shelving stretching into infinity. So he bought most things that he knew they used, including just about every vegetable, plus strawberries and a large tub of cream because Ellen claimed she had never eaten strawberries and cream. He also bought red and white wine and, as there was an offer on double purchases, he bought two bottles of champagne and some cans of cider. They also bought rather a lot of ice cream which Ellen insisted was 'basics', and an exotic dessert which might cheer them all up. At the last moment Ellen grabbed four ripe avocado pears because she knew Jane liked them and, although Duncan didn't, he thought it a nice gesture.

Taking the two trolleys back to the car Duncan began to feel that he might have exceeded his brief. He was sure that when Jane shopped the Access bill never showed triple figures for food.

'Do you still want to go to the café?' he asked Ellen. Strip-lit fast food outlets weren't his favourite venue, and he had spotted one of the Louse & Tosser secretaries preceding them inside. (Duncan could already hear the gossip in his head: 'Guess who I saw getting in the week-end shopping? That nice Mr Lewis!' *'Never!'* 'Who'd have thought it, eh?')

The fact that he had shopped with Jane most weeks throughout his working life had never bothered him before. Previously it hadn't mattered. Now it seemed to be proof that he hadn't gone straight out from Tossers and got a better job. Bloody stupid. Bloody stupid. Duncan was angry to feel he was defining himself in terms of Howard's decision to make him redundant.

'Could we go and see Tristram?' Ellen asked.

Duncan was surprised. 'I thought Tristram was a drip,' he told her. But it seemed Ellen wanted to play with Gerald's train set again. Duncan couldn't see why not. Jane and Alice wouldn't be expecting them back for a while yet and Laura was, despite appearances to the contrary, a sane person. She approved of Duncan anyway.

Laura and Gerald Davis lived halfway down Meirion Street in an old red-bricked semi dwarfed by a roof of truly gargantuan proportions. The half-glazed door was opened by Tristram and Gawain who stood there for a moment awaiting Duncan's salutation.

'Hi,' said Duncan. 'Is Laura in?' He didn't quite feel that he knew Gerald well enough yet to use his name.

'Mum and Dad are in bed,' said Gawain in a dull but direct way.

'Oh,' said Duncan, 'Are they unwell?'

'No,' said Gawain. 'They always go to bed on Sunday afternoons.'

'We're watching Walt Disney,' said Tristram in a friendly way. *The Sword In The Stone.*'

'You can come in and wait if you like,' Gawain suggested.

'Well . . .' Duncan began, but Ellen had already made her way towards the back room where Mordred and Arthur were watching the screen with uncommon interest.

'Budge up, Maws,' said Gawain, lifting the four-year-old on to his lap so Duncan could sit down. The Davis' back room was much more basic than the parlour where Duncan had sat on Friday. The walls were scrubbed white, the floor was lino and the furniture was what Gerald and Laura had when they were first married – which wasn't much because his first wife took everything. Duncan knew this already.

What he didn't know until now was that Laura and Gerald Davis retired to bed every Sunday afternoon while their children were allowed to watch Disney films on the video. Duncan couldn't really imagine either highly organised little Laura or the great crumbling form of Gerald Davis reaching the heights of passion somewhere upstairs in Meirion Street, but that was certainly one interpretation of Gawain's words at the doorstep. If this was an accidental and innocent quotation of the popular euphemism then what Gawain had said was very funny, but if his words bore out the other interpretation then Duncan felt he really shouldn't be here.

After ten minutes the film ended and some trailers came up on screen. Gawain picked up Mordred and put him on the floor. He wandered out to the hallway and shouted upstairs, 'Mum, Dad! Film's finished.'

The video cassette came to its end after a lot of blank tape snarled across the head. Mordred was now sitting on Ellen's lap. He grew very excited when the TV set jumped channels automatically and up came HTV.

'I like HTV, do you, Duncan?' Mordred asked in a piercing little voice.

'Oh yes,' said Duncan, who had no real opinion on the subject.

'Mum, Dad! Duncan's here!' Gawain shouted up the stairs.

'I like the advots, don't you?' Mordred announced.

'Mum, Dad, Mawmaw's watching the adverts!' shouted Gawain.

Almost immediately Duncan heard footsteps coming lightly but firmly down the stairs. Laura entered in a swirl of expensive kimono and switched off the TV. The boys didn't protest. It was a fair cop.

'Hello Duncan, hello Ellen,' said Laura, going to the sink to fill a kettle. Duncan only caught a glimpse of eye contact with Laura, but he knew straight away that his first assumption had, incongruously and extraordinarily, been right. Laura had that look about her; the bright eyes, the flushed cheeks, the delighted way her bare feet moved across the lino, enjoying its touch.

Little Laura Leighton Davis had been upstairs making love with her husband while Duncan and the boys watched Walt Disney in the back room.

'Hello Duncan,' said Gerald, who was also in a dressing gown and also looking somewhat pleased with life in his paisley pyjamas. He shook Duncan's hand. 'The boys are just taking your girl here up to see the trains, is that OK?'

'Lush!' cried Ellen, and all the boys and Gerald and Ellen were gone.

Left alone with Laura, Duncan genuinely didn't know what to say. He didn't want to appear coy and pretend that he didn't know what he had walked in on but, at the same time, Laura was such a proper person he didn't quite know how you should raise the subject with her. Laura, though, was calmly emphatic that there was no problem.

'I've always felt that with four growing boys in the house you can't disguise the fact that their mother and father need time together on their own,' she announced as the kettle boiled. 'Lapsang or Earl Grey?'

Duncan opted for the latter.

'After all, Gawain is nearly eleven and, really, what kind of example is it to grab a few minutes if the children oversleep? Or stay up late waiting for the last of them to nod off? It makes sex furtive doesn't it?' She stirred the teapot with a flourish. 'And so much less fulfilling,' she concluded with a smile. 'Don't you think?'

Duncan and Ellen arrived back just as it was getting dark and a drizzle was settling in. Carrying the shopping in from Katrin Street seemed to take ages. At first Jane was delighted to see them and very positive about Alice helping Ellen bring it all in. Jane was also very jolly about how much shopping they had done and what busy bees they had been, but she was horrified to find how much ice cream Duncan had bought, particularly as much of it had begun to melt while the car was parked outside Laura's house.

And she really felt that there was a danger so much salad and vegetables might go off before they could eat it, and strawberries cost a fortune this time of year; and when she discovered four ripe avocado pears which would need to be eaten in the next two days (and she was the only person who liked them) Jane was not happy – and as for two bottles of champagne . . .

'They were on offer,' Duncan said.

'We got one free,' Ellen added, trying to be helpful and sensing an argument brewing.

'No, we got five per cent off each for buying two,' Duncan tried to explain.

'How much did all this *cost*!' Jane suddenly demanded from the overburdened kitchen table.

Duncan told her approximately £150.89. The exact figure was etched on his conscience.

'You useless man!' Jane said, looking at him as if she had no idea what could be done with the melted ice cream, the overripe avocados or Duncan for that matter.

'And you haven't got any salt, have you? £150 on champagne and ice cream and you haven't even got any salt!'

'We got dishwasher salt,' said Ellen, who was looking very worried and responsible by this stage.

'How can I go out to work if you can't even do the shopping?' said Jane.

Duncan was suddenly pricked by this. He grabbed the dishwasher salt because it was to hand and could be waved to make a point. 'Listen!' he said. 'I did my best. It may not be much – OK, in fact it's pretty useless, but you tell me I've got to get on with things and not ask your opinion on everything.'

'No I don't!' said Jane.

'Either I'm allowed to have a go or I'm not!' He banged the dishwasher salt on the table.

'I'm sorry,' said Jane.

'And!' said Duncan, running out of steam in mid indignation. 'And!'

Jane was looking at him sadly, and the girls had their arms around each other and were sobbing.

'Stop it!' cried Alice.

So they did. They stopped it and all embraced together.

Duncan went to bed early that night. It was rare for him to turn in before Jane but she had work to do and they'd just spent two hours going through lists of what he had to do and what she had to do and what they had to do together.

He lay in bed and thought of Laura Davis and Gerald. He would never have imagined that of them. Other people were full of surprises. What did people think of him and Jane? What did he?

5

Doing Something For Duncan & Jane

Bond-Kyle Avenue was one of the more unusual street names in Cardiff, but one look at Kit's card meant that Duncan could date her house before he even saw it. When those first great tunnels of Edwardian stone terraces were being thrown up across Pontcanna, roads were named after Welsh saints and Old Testament prophets, but by the time the gaps between Pontcanna and Llandaff village were being turned into housing, the councillors had run out of saints and started naming the streets after themselves.

The road to which Alderman Bond-Kyle had donated his name consisted of double-fronted interwar semis with large flat lawns to the front and back and ample parking space in all directions. This was Cardiff Garden Suburb.

As Duncan walked up from Pontcanna the roofs got progressively lower, the houses got wider and the air grew clearer.

Kit opened the door a few inches and Duncan saw one eye blink at him over the security chain.

'Oh it's you,' she said in surprise. Duncan had rung that

morning (and been told to call any time after ten-thirty), but she still seemed not to be expecting him.

'Come in,' she said, and an exhalation of smoke drifted over the double chain and out into the chill morning air.

Kit's house was well protected with security devices. It took a while for her to admit Duncan into the wide wooden hall. He tried to look as if he wasn't taking a professional interest in these surroundings but he couldn't help it. The curious thing was that although Kit was still dressed as the punk momma Duncan had met at parents' evening, the house in which she was living was very respectably restored. A lot of money had been spent returning this particular sub Lutyens 1925 semi to its original spacious charm. The walls were replastered and flawlessly white. The stair-rods and banisters had been accurately and expensively renewed, and the woodblock floor looked as if it had come out of an art gallery.

Kit saw Duncan taking it all in. 'Well, if you're going to live in the most boring house in Cardiff you may as well do it properly,' she said.

In the kitchen Duncan found that Kit had been having coffee with the Swiss au pair.

'You know Gabriele don't you?' Kit said with a wave in her direction. 'Put some more coffee on will you, G? There's a sweet.'

Gabriele slid silently off the stool on which she had been parked. Duncan watched her legs extend slowly to the ground. His wife had nice legs but Gabriele's seemed to start higher up than everyone else's.

Kit showed him round the kitchen which was spacious, very clean, very cream and white, very much not Kit Sinclair. In these surroundings she stood out like an ink blot on a pristine sheet of white paper.

Of course what Duncan didn't know, but would soon learn, was that when Kit knew he was coming she had changed out of the white tracksuit in which she normally breakfasted and spent twenty minutes painting her face that particular deathly hue. Nobody ever met Kit by chance. They met the person that Kit had chosen to be.

The Cheese known as Gabriele called to them in a very French accent and said that coffee was boiled and she would go and tidy the boys' rooms. Kit thanked her and guided them over to the breakfast bar.

'I don't get it,' said Duncan. 'This kitchen goes all the way across the back of the house. Where d'you want to put a conservatory?'

'In the roof,' said Kit, making ostentatious gestures, the cigarette fluttering between her fingers. 'I want to take the back of the roof off and glass it over.'

Duncan was impressed by her style. He was amused by the extravagance. He enjoyed the challenge of Kit but he was wary of trespassing on other people's dreams. 'I don't know whether you'd get planning permission,' he cautioned. 'You back on to the conservation area here.'

Kit shook her head. 'Don't worry about that,' she replied. 'My fellah's one of them.'

'Your fellah?' Duncan asked.

'My husband, the bastard, the ball and chain', Kit explained. 'He's from round here. They think the sun shines out of his arse. Welsh you see.'

Duncan had had some dealings with the City Council and he knew that growing up in the same street as a committee chairman could have its advantages at times, but it didn't normally override planning regulations.

'You tell me if it's practical,' said Kit, 'Barry will sort out the rest.'

'It would be expensive,' Duncan warned her.

'He'll sort that out too,' said Kit with sublime confidence.

*   *   *

Laura and Holly were at an NCT coffee morning in Elaine's house. The Pontcanna National Childbirth Trust were a broad church although Holly's Gwyn referred to them collectively as The Memsahibs or English Middle Class Mums-in-Exile. Gwyn avoided all contact with their meal evenings and chose not to think about who or what they discussed at their covens. Nevertheless, he had been heard to predict that the two likeliest topics of conversation would be how their husbands were too Welsh and Cardiff so insufficiently English.

But this morning Siân Roberts was asking Binny what she should do about Roger, who still wouldn't give up his key and who these days was ending up in her bed far too frequently for a man who had left her, and Laura Davis was in the kitchen telling Holly about how poor Duncan was so worried for his daughters.

'I think Duncan has a very female side,' said Holly quietly, almost secretly. 'And he isn't finding it easy to bring that out at the moment.'

'But he's a wonderful father,' Laura insisted.

Holly nodded emphatically. She didn't have any particular view on that subject, but she did believe in making way when other people had strong feelings. Holly's concept of debate was a very positive one. All fresh ideas should be added to the sum total of group consciousness so that eventually there would accumulate a great mass of convictions held in common, and hopefully none of them would actually cancel each other out. It was possible, of course, for Duncan to be a good father in a feminine way. After all, why should the term 'father' betoken the masculinity?

Binny joined the conversation briefly as she pursued her mid-morning craving for extra coffee. 'D'you know he hasn't taken her out in weeks,' she said, refilling Elaine's kettle.

The Barnes' dinner party was now all of two weeks ago, and Binny had forgotten most of what happened that night except for the mousse that no one ate and the chat she had had with Jane in her ice-cold bedroom. To be fair to Jane she had only been offering sympathy that night. Binny had been moaning on that Flyn hadn't taken her anywhere since a Christmas skiing trip that they could ill afford, and Jane had commiserated by adding, lightly, that she and Duncan hadn't been out for a meal since the one to celebrate his redundancy, which was no more than four weeks ago. Jane had intended the analogy to leave Binny feeling less hard done by, but in Binny's mind this passing statement of solidarity had become a lament. Duncan was neglecting Jane.

'Well . . .' said Laura judiciously.

'Yes . . .' said Holly.

'He does have a lot to worry about at the moment,' said Laura.

'Yes,' said Holly.

Binny, sensing that their conversation was not going to turn in the direction of Flyn's iniquities, went back to the living room where someone had just brought in a new baby.

'I think we must find some way of showing our support for Duncan, don't you?' Laura decided, opening a fresh packet of biscuits.

'Yes,' said Holly, who had no idea what Laura had in mind. It sounded a bit like remembering him in their prayers, but Holly thought that any man who was striving to get in touch with his feminine side did need encouragement and support.

Duncan had spent a very interesting morning with Kit who, once she got going on a subject, seemed unstoppable. This morning she was giving him her views on architecture, which bordered at times on the totalitarian but were very well informed. She had magazines and cutting in her office, and a small tidy room next to the stairs stacked with papers and dominated incongruously by a camp bed.

Kit's view, which she could illustrate with photographs clipped from various sources, was that owners should not be given any choice in the outward appearance of their house, as this was something that the rest of the world had to look at. Exteriors should be the preserve of experts who would be briefed to ensure that all façades were easy on the eye. 'I don't want to know about other people's taste as I walk down the road. I want anonymity,' she declaimed from the first-floor balcony. 'If I choose to come inside your house then I want to know something about you, but I don't want your taste rammed down my throat as I go to work!'

'Yes, but which experts?' Duncan asked. 'How do you decide who's to decide?'

Kit became more extravagant, which was her way when she stumbled into previously unexplored territory. 'Elect them or appoint them, and then if they get it wrong kick the fuckers out. Shoot them!' She laughed.

'And what about people who will want to use their husband's influence to get round all these new regulations?' Duncan asked, chancing his arm at reproach.

Kit got the message. 'Shoot them too,' she declared. 'Christ, is that the time?'

It was a quarter past twelve. Duncan assumed he was getting his marching orders.

'Drinkies,' said Kit with a grin, and she led him back downstairs to the kitchen where Gabriele was preparing an intricate salad.

'You'll stay to lunch, won't you?' Kit asked, making her way to the fridge. It wasn't exactly a question but, as it happened, he had nothing in his diary that needed doing that morning. 'Geegee and I get so tired of looking at each other,' she said fetching out three bottles, two of wine and one of mineral water.

At the breakfast bar she paused for a rethink. 'Or would you prefer whisky?' she asked.

'No thanks,' said Duncan.

Laura Davis had also had a busy lunchtime. Now she had gathered Mawmaw, Gawain and Arthur to her and was just waiting for Mr Harper to arrive with Tris when she saw Duncan walking up to the gate with that Swiss au pair girl. Laura was surprised. She felt she knew Duncan well, although they had only met within the last few weeks. Laura Davis acknowledged and understood that married men continued to find other women attractive; this was a natural thing, as natural as what Gawain got up to underneath his sheets. What mattered was that this impulse was treated responsibly. Sheets should be washed and Duncan should restrict himself to married women who would not misinterpret his attentions.

Duncan and the Cheese joined Laura. Duncan always walked slowly but Laura noticed he was slower on his feet than usual. He smiled at her, rather foolishly Laura thought.

'Hello Duncan!' yelled Mordred.

'Hiya Mawmaw,' said Duncan, 'Laura, you know Gabriele don't you?'

Laura looked into Gabriele's face as if to check on this curious assertion of his. She was not the kind of person to express such a view but she did think that the girl's look of blasé indifference was positively smug that afternoon. And as for what she and Holly had decided about that concert, well Duncan could just wait.

From Duncan's point of view Laura seemed to be staring at Gabriele in a manner that bordered on the hostile. He felt the need to explain. 'I've been to lunch with Kit Britto; Gabriele looks after her boys.'

Ah well, thought Laura, that explains it. It also explained the way that Duncan was talking. His speech was not slurred but it came out haltingly, rather as if he was working hard at a language in which he was almost fluent but where the speech rhythms still occasionally defeated him.

'Are you feeling all right?' she asked kindly, with sympathy at the ready.

'Fine,' said Duncan, determined not to get on to the subject of his infamous allergy.

He was not a good drinker, especially in the afternoon. Two large glasses of admittedly very good Australian white wine had made him feel tired, whereas Kit had polished off the bottle and started on another without seeming to feel any ill effects.

It had been a strange lunch party. Despite the laziness of which Kit had been accusing her, Gabriele had virtually waited upon them and eaten in silence. More strange still, Kit had taken only two lettuce leaves from the salad bowl when the meal started and seemed to have both of them left when it finished.

Kit had talked a lot about her own career which had somehow been blighted by Barry the Bastard, her husband and a very high flier in local medical circles, out of whose rectum the Cardiff sun was repeatedly said to shine. Kit had been a journalist in London and she knew that she was wasted in Wales. When Duncan asked her if she did any writing now she claimed that she wouldn't take the kind of work she was offered locally, but she did hint darkly that she made some money by immoral means so that she wasn't totally dependent on the Bastard.

'What means?' Duncan asked.

'That's my sordid secret,' Kit said with a puckish grin.

It was nearly a quarter to three when Duncan noticed the time. Kit insisted that Gabriele would pick up his daughters for him but Duncan was sure they wouldn't go off with a stranger.

'Quite right,' said Kit. 'You've got to teach them the world's a nasty, manky little place.'

Duncan suggested that he and Kit walk down together, but Kit was adamant that she never collected the boys. 'Besides, the tart's got to do something to earn her keep.'

Although Gabriele wasn't in the room, Duncan felt he had to stick up for her even in the mildest of terms. 'She seems to be very busy to me,' he suggested.

Kit looked at Duncan as if he was trying to spoil her game and he realised that in the four hours he had been talking to Kit she had been nothing but critical. Much of what she had said was very funny, or very true, but she had spoken in defence of nothing and no one. Kit was very enthusiastic about her own ideas about journalism, architecture, fashion and medicine, but these enthusiasms were all illustrated by attacking what existed.

'I'd better go,' he said.

Kit had pulled an address book out from her enormous handbag. 'What's your woman's name?' she asked. 'Your wife . . . you are married aren't you?' 'Yes,' said Duncan. 'Jane.'

Kit wrote this down. 'D'you think I'll like her?'

Duncan paused. He was intrigued by the question. It wasn't one he'd heard before.

'*I* do,' he replied, hoping that a joke might avoid having to decide.

'Yes, but men are such useless judges of character,' Kit told him. She wrote down *Jane* in her large address book. 'Still, she chose you as a husband so she wasn't daft. I think I might invite her to lunch.'

'You could invite us both to lunch,' Duncan suggested.

'You've just had lunch!' Kit retorted. 'Now bugger off and play house husbands. Geegee will run you down.'

And with that she went to find Gabriele. Duncan felt a bit uncertain on his feet. It was in part the effects of that exchange but also of standing up so quickly after two glasses of wine. As he gathered up his coat Duncan wondered whether Kit's rudeness was in fact a form of initiation. Until she could bad-mouth you the aquaintance was formal. Had he passed a test perhaps? And would Jane?

Kit had left Duncan at the door and asked him to give her a ring about the conservatory idea. She didn't come outside. Kit didn't like to venture out during the day if she could possibly avoid it. Once Duncan had left she went upstairs to shower and change into something suitable for welcoming home her boys.

Gabriele had been provided with a very small car for her fetching and carrying. Duncan found the greatest of difficulties getting his legs folded into it, which gave rise to the surprising realisation that his legs were actually longer than hers. As they drove to Fulwood Road he sat for a while puzzling at this fact and realising that any glasses of wine at lunch time were, pathetically, not a good thing for him.

After a while he decided to engage Gabriele in conversation by asking her which part of Switzerland she came from.

'Neuchâtel,' she said, keeping her eyes firmly on what was for her the wrong side of the road.

'Where's that near?' asked Duncan, who had a less than basic knowledge of Switzerland.

Gabriele had looked rather put out to hear that question yet again. 'It isn't near anywhere, it is . . . near Neuchâtel,' she'd said with finality.

As they turned down the hill into Cathedral Road Duncan tried another approach. 'Do you like working for Mrs Britto?' he asked.

Gabriele had shrugged, although there was little room for such a movement in her car. Duncan assumed that he was getting no more out of her on the subject, but more she had.

'She is a better lady than you think,' It sounded as if Gabriele was formulating these thoughts for the first time in English, so Duncan tried to gaze at her encouragingly. 'Always everything is *fuckbloodythisthat*, but she is a very kind lady and I think she does not like people to know that. If I thought she was just *fuckbloodythisthat* I do not stay with her.'

Duncan recounted his meeting with Kit to Jane later that evening as he cleared the take-away pizza boxes. He also told her about Laura's hostility to Gabriele at the school gate.

'She's probably jealous,' said Jane who was drinking her coffee and staring at the latest pile of papers to have reached the Lewis kitchen table.

'Why should she be jealous?' asked Duncan.

'Because you're her friend,' Jane told him. 'You know what it's like going to school, being best friends and all that.'

Duncan cast a glance at Jane to check that she was teasing him. 'Even so . . .' he said. 'It's odd. I hardly know her.'

'You walk to school with her, you go round and pour out your problems to her, you talk to her about . . . what was it?'

'The Miles Davis Trio,' said Duncan.

'Well, there you are!' Jane laughed. 'You'll be lending her your LPs next, Dunc.'

It seemed to be the first time Jane had laughed since Jeremy Harper's bombshell. Duncan was pleased that she was less tense, but he felt rather protective of Laura Davis. He was glad now that he hadn't told Jane about calling in at Merion Street when Laura and Gerald were in bed. At first he'd kept quiet because Jane was sufficiently annoyed with him that day over the shopping and he didn't want to exacerbate things by disclosing that he'd been for another heart to heart with the woman who had heard Jeremy Harper's news before Jane. But then not having told Jane took on the status of an odd, uncharacteristic thing to have happened – and so, of course, telling Jane gained dire significance because it would also mean telling her that he had chosen originally *not* to tell her something. And so it became easier for Duncan to continue not telling Jane. And now that Jane had chosen to find Laura amusing, Duncan decided then and there that he didn't want the Davis sex life laughed at – and so there would, after all this time, be something in his life that Jane would not be told.

He poured himself another glass of wine and suddenly decided there were too many women in his life. The girls with their problems, the highly focused Laura Davis, the completely unfocused (if possibly desirable) Holly Williams, and now Jane with her little digs at Laura. Duncan experienced what was for him the uncharacteristic desire to spend his days working back in the world of men.

He had been given an open invitation to have a drink with two of the assitant architects at Louse & Tosser who were getting out to set up on their own. Richard and Geraint were pleasant enough fellows in a rather dull sort of way, and they seemed to like him. Duncan had been tempted to find some excuse, but now he thought, 'Yes – why the hell not?' On certain days there was something to be said for good-hearted dullness. A good uncomplicated chat with a good uncomplicated chap could have a simple therapeutic effect like drinking water after too many liqueurs. A chap had no hidden agendas. A chap wanted to know if you could make money out of it or shag it or, failing that, could you drive it quickly round and round and frighten people? Chaps started off like that at a very early age, like Siôn Williams, and they didn't change much for the rest of their lives. Whereas girls just got deeper and deeper until you were completely lost and out of your depth.

'This Kit Sinclair,' Jane began, apropos of nothing and deciding to have her glass refilled, 'D'you think we should invite her to dinner?'

'Why?' asked Duncan, who was still in his male bonding mode. 'I think she's inviting you to lunch.'

'Yes, but if we get her to dinner maybe you can get her to ask you to design her conservatory thing!' said Jane. 'Really Duncan, you are not one for the main chance.'

They fell to discussing what a main chance might be in architecture. The opinion Duncan expressed to Jane was that he would be unlikely to make much on the plans for Kit's conservatory, however extravagant her ideas. Jane's view was that it sounded to her like the kind of project that could get him noticed. To which Duncan's counter view was that it sounded like the kind of project that wouldn't even get built, given its proximity to the conservation area.

Jane was getting irritated by Duncan's lack of drive. When he was younger he used to be so keen. She didn't say it but she was dearly beginning to wish he would gather some momentum. All that her husband was capable of at the moment was alternating bouts of domesticity and worry. His career seemed to be shipwrecked and all he wanted to do was tread water and tidy the flotsam.

Jane most definitely did not say that either. She was determined not to reproach Duncan even when he most patently deserved it.

With Jane suppressing her feelings and Duncan resolving on secrets and machismo, the atmosphere in Katrin Street grew cool – not hostile, but the domestic warmth definitely chilled. Both were aware of this, but neither felt able to rekindle the affection incipient when Jane had laughed about Laura and Miles Davis. Duncan was disappointed because it had been two weeks now since they had had sex, and for them this was unusual. Jane was disappointed too because she was looking for the right moment when she could talk to Duncan about his career and the mood had seemed positive earlier on.

'Bugger,' they both thought.

In Meirion Street, Gerald Davis was in the back room sewing name tags into Mordred's new sports kit while Radio 3 played on his ancient transistor radio. Laura had been round all the bedrooms checking on sleeping boys and abandoned toys. On her way down she called into the bathroom to check that stocks were not diminished among her copious supply of sanitary towels and tampons. Her period was due the next day.

Returning to the back room to make up the boys' morning drinks, Laura saw Gerald put down the needle and squeeze his tired eyes.

'You are wonderful,' she said, kissing his thinning hair.

'All done,' said Gerald.

'Do you know what?' Laura asked him.

'What?'

'Somehow it feels like . . . Sunday afternoon to me,' she rested her head against his.

'Yes . . .' said Gerald appreciatively. 'You know, I think it does.'

In Bond-Kyle Avenue, Barry Britto was watching *Newsnight* when the front door banged open and shut. Kit, in a red plastic raincoat and PVC boots, opened the door to the TV room.

'Hello, you old Bastard!' she called jovially.

Barry looked up from the deep leather settee. 'You're back soon,' he said.

'And I'm stone cold sober,' Kit added. 'There's a turn up for the books.'

*　　*　　*

Jane Lewis was seeing Mr Harper on Tuesday evening, and had left Duncan to sort out who would look after the girls so he could come along too. Duncan now carried his old Louse & Tosser company diary around with him to make lists and, that morning, ARRANGE SITTER had been double asterisked over breakfast. Jane was pleased to see that Duncan was using his initiative around the house more. In fact, in many respects having him at home was a very good thing. The place had never looked more inviting to live in. Even the bathroom soaps were attractively stacked and the spare toilet rolls had been formed into a pyramid in the airing cupboard.

But Jane was also worried that Duncan was becoming fulfilled by loading the tumble drier, folding away pullovers and trying to bake bread. However good he became at it, that wasn't why she had married him. So far, though, the yeast from Jacob's Deli had not risen sufficiently to the challenge of Duncan's baking and this gave Jane hope that his New Man phase would pass.

She was feeling more settled at work now. Her Monday-morning session with Miles Mihash had gone well and, when they ran out of time, he didn't suggest reconvening in a month, as Tony might, but booked himself back in for first thing Tuesday morning.

'I like working with you, Jane,' Miles said as they hit eleven.

'I like working with you,' said Jane. They had shifted virtually everything now and she had just sent David out to chase the coffees.

'How about dinner?' Miles suggested.

Jane, who was looking for her shoes under one of the tables, paused, surprised. 'I thought I'd told you I'm married,' she said.

'So you did,' Miles replied, neither brazen nor coy.

'But you don't believe me?' Jane asked.

'My mistake,' said Miles with a smile.

'Why don't you come round to dinner with *us*?' Jane asked him. It was a challenge, yet it was thrown out in all innocence.

Miles looked surprised but took it on the chin. 'Great idea,' he said. They were into a game of bluff. Jane had expected Miles to demur but he simply took out his diary. 'I'm going to be in Swansea all next month. let's make it before then, shall we?'

Now Jane was on the spot – and her diary was upstairs. 'Fine,' she said.

'The Saturday after this is free,' said Miles.

'Fine,' said Jane.

Miles wrote in his diary. 'What time do you want to say?'

'Eight?'

'Eight it is,' said Miles. 'I'll look forward to it, Jane.'

Jane was struggling to catch up. 'Anything you don't eat?' she asked.

'Not so far,' Miles told her.

David came in with a cafétière.

'David!' Jane said all of a sudden. 'Why don't you come to dinner Saturday week?'

'You've done what?' Duncan asked. It was lunchtime at Katrin Street, and he had had a difficult morning trying to put Norman the Blacksmith off. He'd left Norman to see to the oven which was belching fumes of carbonated dough, and now the phone had rung and it was his wife asking if they could have her colleagues to dinner!

Duncan's immediate reaction was disbelief that Jane wanted him to cook a three-course meal for the entire staff of Follets.

'You don't have to do it all, Dunc. Just the shopping and the starters.'

He calmed down. 'Who else is coming?'

Jane explained that it would be this very funny American and David. She hadn't thought to ask if either of them would be bringing someone. At that point a frightening crash from the conservatory curtailed their conversation.

Norman was standing beneath a large broken piece of rusted Edwardian ironwork with little shards of broken glass around him and a hole in the glass roof above.

'I knew that would happen,' he said, shaking his head.

It had been only moments before that Duncan had all but convinced Norman that they really couldn't afford to have the new roof installed, so could Norman just effect repairs in the struts and Duncan would buy some glass to replace the cracked and leaking pane? Then the forgotten bread had incinerated and the phone had rung.

'I just *knew* it,' said Norman shaking his head and avoiding eye contact with Duncan by gazing at the glass-strewn floor. So why did you bloody do it? Duncan thought, but he didn't ask. What was the point? There was now a large, unsupported and dangerous section of the Lewis conservatory which was going to have to come down – and once it was down the choice would be to demolish the entire structure or rebuild with Norman's sodding cantilevers.

Duncan left Norman to make the damage safe, binned the blackened lump of what was once almost bread and took the lunch he had been making upstairs, away from the noise and smoke. The hugely irritating thing was that he knew if Jane had been at home, and not him, Norman would not have dared effect that nifty bit of demolition. Jane would have been able to tell Norman very clearly as soon as he arrived that he was stood down from his conservatory duties and, because Jane had something in her manner frighteningly reminiscent of mad old Mrs Beale, her mother, Norman would not have dared pull a sneaky one like that. It had been just the same when Duncan was on site as an architect. The foreman would become his friend and they'd get on fine until Duncan had to read the riot act, and then suddenly no one would seem to be listening.

On occasions like that Duncan usually had the choice of lying down and being walked over or of reasserting the authority he should never have lost by growing hysterical.

This was not a good day. Duncan cleared a space in the upstairs drawing room and sat there with his salad. From downstairs he could hear the sounds of glass cracking and metal bending. He wished that Norman would just go.

And what was the matter with Jane at the moment? Inviting her firm over for meals and badgering him to invite Kit Sinclair for meals. Anyone would think Jane had gone back to work just for the purpose of eating!

Laura and Holly met by the school gate early that day. The two women had known each other for many years via the NCT, the baby-sitting circle and the school, but until now they had never been close friends.

Laura liked Holly and admired her visual style enormously. Laura's sense of the visual had never run to anything more ambitious than recovering her mother-in-law's Victorian sofa, but she did appreciate how well Holly could draw and make floats for the carnival and Christmas cards. At times Laura wished that Holly would make more of herself and work harder with her children. With such talented parents, Buddug and Siôn ought to do so well . . . but that was not Laura's business and she was not the kind of person to express such a view.

Holly liked Laura too. She enjoyed looking at the clear-cut lines of her neatly cropped auburn hair. There never seemed one strand out of place, whereas none of Holly's seemed to have ever had a place to be in. Holly admired the decisive way that Laura walked and the lustre of her eyes, but she knew that Gwyn thought Laura the very worst kind of Englishwoman. Holly herself tended not to judge people unless they were openly hostile to her, and very few people were ever that because Holly's quiet solicitude disarmed almost everyone, with the exception of a few motorists (all men).

But today Laura and Holly had a lot in common. They had hatched a plan and, like a pair of schoolgirls, were enjoying going over the details. Laura had reserved two tickets for a jazz concert at St David's Hall, Holly had cleared with Gwyn that she could baby-sit, and now all that remained was for Duncan to be told that he was taking Jane out on Friday.

'Duncan and Jane' had become a little project for Holly and Laura. Both felt that Duncan needed their support in taking on the domestic responsibilities and especially those girls. Laura knew how difficult girls could be and how much they needed a good father. Holly agreed. All Buddug wanted to do was *talk*, whereas Siôn at least had his Lego.

Holly Williams saw in Duncan the kind of man that she sometimes wished Gwyn might be. She preferred men who acknowledged doubt and the multifaceted nature of existence. Men like her aromatherapist, whom Holly liked very much because he was so unsure about what was actually wrong with her. Totally baffled. If anything, Holly was happier in the company of such men rather than Gwyn. Gwyn had become very certain about everything in his thirties.

As for Laura Davis, she liked Duncan because he was a good father and reminded her somewhat of dear Grandpa Leighton in his earlier days. If Laura saw anything else in Duncan she did not acknowledge it. Laura was a woman who made up her mind very easily, and on her second sighting of Duncan Lewis she had decided that she liked and approved of him. She wasn't so sure about Jane but the important thing was that Duncan and Jane stayed together.

'Marriage is so important,' said Laura.

'Yes,' said Holly, even more quietly than usual. Holly did not share Laura's view of marriage but she knew it certainly had huge consequences. 'And Jane is so lovely,' said Holly.

Laura looked at Holly because, if the truth be told, she didn't share her view of Jane. Laura had Jane Lewis pigeon-holed as a career woman who was lucky to have someone like Duncan. 'Lovely' was not the first word Laura would have chosen to describe her.

But Holly was a great fan of Jane's. Not only did Holly enjoy looking at her, but Jane actually asked her things. Holly seemed to have the kind of face to which people only ever told things, particularly her family – they never stopped. It was so nice to have someone listening to you for a change.

But Laura and Holly were agreed on one thing: what mattered was that Duncan and Jane remained happy and happily married.

'Ah, *Duncan*!' said Laura.

Jane's meeting with Jeremy Harper that evening went well. He seemed prepared for the kind of state that she was in, which was fortunate because Jane wasn't.

She had left Follets early, but nevertheless drove with considerable panâche to get to the school in time. She had managed to park the Volvo in a very tight space and marched into Fulwood Road like a solicitor going about her business, but one look into Jeremy Harper's clear grey eyes and she instantly touched base with the other Jane Lewis, the one who was going to be an anxious mother to her dying day.

When Mr Harper asked her if she'd like to sit down,

Jane found herself thanking him in a tiny voice. And when she looked around the classroom and saw the pinned up pictures of *Dan's Mummy* and *Lewin's Mummy* and *My House*, her eyes filled with tears. All these little lives that promised so much. All these blighted souls. These *children*! Probably not one of them was without some incipient learning difficulty, some deep emotional problem, some dreadful parents who ignored them and went out to work all day.

But Jeremy Harper was wonderful. He soon took her through the background, as he understood it, to the way twins could develop educationally. He talked about bringing Alice on without holding Ellen back, and Jane's confidence in him grew and grew. He so clearly cared about her children.

'Of course I may be wrong. I am relatively new to all this,' he explained. Jane didn't think he was at all wrong but she was intrigued by this statement, so Harper explained that he had come into teaching from industry.

'How wonderful to retrain for something you clearly enjoy,' Jane said, adding that for the past year she had been thinking of retraining herself. And then she told him the full story, that her husband had lost his job and so she'd gone back to work in a world to which she no longer belonged and that it was hard. She felt she was having to prove herself as a solicitor and as a mother, and now the girls were having problems it seemed like a judgement on her for abandoning them.

'It really isn't,' said Jeremy Harper. 'Whatever else is the cause I can assure you that this situation – I don't even think we should call it a problem – this situation has been developing slowly. Probably over years.'

Jane had always relied on her women friends when things upset her. Only once before had she poured out everything to a stranger and that was when her mother had suddenly got worse and blamed Jane for all her difficulties.

Twelve years ago Jane Beale had met a Roman Catholic priest at Llanthony Abbey and talked to him for hours, sitting on the ragged wall that kept the cattle from grazing the ruins. That was like this.

'I'm very sorry,' she said at length, wiping an eye.

'Not at all,' said Jeremy Bear kindly. 'It's very useful to know the background.' He had his own reasons for wanting to go soon, but he hoped that Jane was about to find her own conclusion to what she wanted to say.

She, stood up. 'Right, well, I'll tell Duncan you're keeping them in the same class but separated to see how things go.' Jeremy nodded and stood to say goodbye. It was only at that moment that Jane realised Duncan hadn't turned up after all. He said he'd be there. Why wasn't he?

At three-thirty Duncan had been somewhat surprised by the news that Holly and Laura had arranged for him and Jane to go out on Friday. It was very nice for Laura to say, 'We thought you needed a break,' but it had rather thrown him, to the extent that he completely forgot about asking one of them to have the girls at six o'clock. And when he remembered at five it seemed insensitive to ring either Holly or Laura to ask more favours. He had a look at the baby-sitting list which he had pinned up on the recently streamlined notice board. None of these names meant much to him except Elaine, who needed much more than an hour's notice if she was going to be wonderful in a crisis, and Binny, who, apart from the night of the dinner party, had always treated him with disdain as if, as a man, he must be one of the swine who had led Flyn astray.

There was of course his new friend Kit Britto/Sinclair, but she was unpredictable and in any case Jane might take him to task for asking baby-sitting favours of a potential client.

Duncan asked Ellen if she'd mind coming into school while he saw Mr Bear. Ellen didn't, but Alice, from the room next door, most certainly did. In the end Duncan decided that he shouldn't make a big issue of getting to the meeting or else the girls might start to suspect something.

Jane was away for ages. It was half-past six and Duncan was receiving complaints about the beans on toast being made from bread he'd baked when Jane walked in. Duncan could tell she was much happier but he got his apologies in nevertheless. She hugged him in a strong and meaningful way and said it was going to be OK in the end, she was sure of that. While Jane was being updated on the latest vicissitudes visited on the average sensitive eight-year-old Duncan got her a cup of tea. And after the twins had gone to bed Jane told him how wonderful Jeremy Harper was and went through the post.

'Laura and Holly press-ganged me today,' Duncan said.

'You must be careful about married women, Dunc,' Jane replied, opening the Access bill. 'They're very susceptible to men who make their own bread.'

'Not the way I bake it,' he joked. Jane was about to join in the banter when her face fell at the sight of their Access bill. Duncan asked what the matter was.

'I thought we were cutting down,' she said, and showed him the four figure sum which was not noticeably less than their usual monthly score.

Duncan tried to think of what the bright side might be. 'You'll be paid by Follets by the time we have to settle that, won't you?'

'Yes, but *this is* about what I'm going to be *getting* after tax,' Jane reminded him, pointing at the paper. 'It leaves us nothing to actually live on. I thought we were cutting down,' she repeated.

'We are cutting down,' said Duncan although no immediate examples of economy sprang to mind. He hadn't even managed to shave a day off Mrs R.'s weekly cleaning bill yet.

'We're going to have to dip into your redundancy again,' Jane informed him.

Duncan felt depressed; Jane felt depressed. Duncan's redundancy money had been designated a cushion against any future hard times, but they looked set to loot its stuffing every month.

'But you're not earning that much less than I was getting at Tossers . . .' Duncan told her, hoping that logic would discover untapped funds.

'Yes, but I was adding to that,' Jane reminded him. 'I was easily making six thousand pounds a year, even when I was working from home – so although we've gained my full-time income we've lost my part-time income, which means, all in all, we're easily eight to ten thousand pounds a year worse off. This is the kind of bill we were paying when we were pulling in an extra eight hundred a month!'

It sounded monstrous, as if a great weight of debt was going to drag them precipitately to the bottom of the sea. Duncan's redundancy cheque was no longer a cushion – it looked more like a lifeboat that was leaking steadily month by month. Cautiously, Duncan cleared away the uneaten salad to make sure it could all be recycled for tomorrow's lunch.

'What shall we do?' he asked.

'Well,' said Jane, imagining she was dealing with a client and keeping very calm because that was the only way to help. 'Well . . . we need to work out how much of the redundancy we *absolutely* must keep. How far we can continue to dip into it. Then we divide what's left over by the monthly shortfall, and that will tell us . . .'

'Tell us what?' asked Duncan.

'Tell us how long you have off,' Jane explained. 'How long you've got to think it all through. How long we can last before you need to get a job.'

They did the calculation twice, using Duncan's lap top and

checking it on the calculator Jane had brought back with her from Follets. The alarming news was that if Duncan didn't generate a source of income within the next four months they would have to start drawing on what Jane designated as emergency funds only.

'And by emergency funds I mean what we live on if one or both of us is too ill to work,' Jane told him.

Duncan nodded. He knew all right.

Not surprisingly, Duncan didn't get round to telling Jane that night how Laura and Holly had arranged for him to take her out. He didn't mention the fact that Norman had started work on their £4,000 conservatory extension either. She would notice in the morning. What he did do was sit up in bed and write out a list of all the companies he knew and who he thought might like him. It wasn't a very long list, particularly when he crossed off the firm run by Alice's godfather because it would be unfair to approach them. And it was an even shorter list once he crossed off two more companies that he just couldn't imagine himself liking, however much they loved him. A drink with them, yes, but nine till seven, eight, *nine* in the evening . . . ?

'I'm sorry,' he said to Jane as he switched off the bedside lamp.

'I'm sorry,' said Jane, then she added, 'Dunc . . . if I told Tony I was interested in staying on, I might be able to squeeze another few thousand a year out of him.'

'But are you interested?' Duncan asked.

'I might be,' Jane lied, because she knew if she told the truth Duncan would say that no one should put up with a job he or she didn't like. He'd done that too long himself.

'There's the Britto boys' mother and her conservatory,' Jane reminded him.

'I'll give her a ring,' Duncan said.

'Invite her to dinner!'

'We're supposed to be on an economy drive,' Duncan protested.

'OK,' said Jane. 'Invite her with David and Miles, Saturday week.'

Duncan sighed. He hated business meals, particularly in his own home. Neither he nor Jane operated well in those circumstances, although Jane at least made an effort. But the time was coming for an effort. It was effort now or a sinking lifeboat in four months' time.

Jane snuggled up to him. 'You know you are a very good architect,' she told him.

'I'm OK,' said Duncan.

'You used to have some really bright, original ideas,' Jane insisted.

'No. They just seemed original to me,' he replied. 'I thought they were original but they weren't. I'm just an OK architect. That's all you have to be. You don't have to be brilliant to make a living.'

Duncan's reticence upset Jane. She was convinced that he was deliberately underselling himself.

She moved close to his ear. 'When we first met you used to tell me wonderful things about turning buildings inside out and how the space between buildings was more interesting than the buildings themselves.'

'I was trying to impress you,' he said.

This just made Jane angry. 'Don't, Duncan. Don't undersell yourself all the time!' she whispered, passionate with her concern and gripping him.

Duncan felt trapped. 'Please!' he almost shouted, turning to her. 'Look, Jane, I am willing to find another job – as an architect or as something else – I know that is important, but you must let *me* decide how good I am. I can't go around telling people my wife thinks I'm a genius!'

Jane turned away rather than get upset.

Duncan sighed again and turned away from her. 'I'm sorry,' he said.

Gwyn and Holly Williams had been to a Ukrainian folk evening where the visiting orchestra got out its traditional instruments and its sentimentality for the benefit of their hosts. The night had concluded with an impressive rendition of 'God Bless The Preence Of Wales', which the visitors had assumed would please their hosts.

'Bit like playing "Stars and Stripes Forever" in Hiroshima,' Gwyn had commented to Howie from the horns. It was the kind of joke that Holly didn't like. Holly believed that jokes were often based in cruelty, particularly Gwyn's. Holly didn't understand why it was that men needed jokes to enjoy themselves.

In the taxi on the way back, Gwyn noticed that his wife seemed to have developed a fascination for street lamps. She gazed out of the window and hardly heard a word he was saying. Occasionally she would turn her head and smile at him, a brief snapshot of a smile that would fade away as soon as it flashed.

'You all right, Hol?' Gwyn asked, plunging his arm into the folds of Holly's voluminous cloak in the hope of finding a shoulder to embrace.

Again the smile, extinguished as soon as it began.

'What's the matter, my lovely?' Gwyn asked, trying to draw her to him.

'I was just thinking . . .' said Holly in her most wistful whisper, '. . . how when we were young we used to go to concerts together. Do you remember?' She dropped her head towards him. Gwyn kissed the small bit of forehead that was visible between Holly's cloak, scarf and long ringleted hair. 'We don't do that any more, do we?' she asked.

'Well,' said Gwyn, 'bit of a bloody busman's holiday for

me, Holly. Seeing as I'm usually playing twice a week. Is that what's really up, love?'

Holly snuggled up against him but she wasn't feeling fond. She was like a cat making a fuss of its owner. She was giving Gwyn his due. If she appeared to be purring maybe he'd let her alone. What Holly really didn't want was for Gwyn to be bothering about her. He was such a botherer. She needed space to think her own thoughts, and sometimes she could actually find that space inside Gwyn's arms because he'd got her then. The pursuit was over. He wasn't trying to discover what was going on inside her head any more. Recently she'd even found that space once or twice while they were making love. There had been a time when Holly had wanted her lover to be lost in his own enjoyment because she wanted to be everything he needed from life, but these days she wanted it because the more Gwyn enjoyed himself the more she was alone. She so needed that. To escape to that place where no one else could be.

Holly thought about Duncan and Jane and was pleased that Laura had organised Friday evening for them. Holly missed the thing that she called romance. She wanted to feel her own way towards people and feel them reaching out towards her. She didn't want to be pursued and jostled and grabbed, talked to and held on to. She liked the idea that Duncan and Jane could rebuild slowly, tentatively, on Friday. It would be like when she and Gwyn, and several other students in her group, used to go to concerts in the Brangwen Hall, and she could feel from four seats away that he had been looking at her. He had been so shy then. He'd gained such confidence since . . .

Duncan and Jane. It must be a wonderful evening.

6

Some Not Quite Wonderful
Evenings

It nearly wasn't an evening at all. Jane's first reaction to
the news of their night out came fast on her reaction to
the news that Norman had embarked on the conservatory,
and she was about as enthusiastic. Had it not been for Holly
being to hand, the idea of a concert at St David's Hall might
well have been thrown out as soon as Jane was acquainted
with it.

'We're so pleased,' said Holly, kissing Jane. 'Duncan's
been working so hard and you've been working so hard.
You deserve a night out.'

In fact the revelation had only come about at all because
Holly had been looking after the girls that afternoon while
Duncan went to meet some people. In the midst of everything else, Duncan had entirely forgotten about Laura and
Holly's concert until he came home at seven o'clock to
discover Siôn chasing Buddug, Alice and Ellen, and Holly
and Jane in the half-demolished conservatory discussing
who Jacques Loussier was.

Jane Lewis was not a great one for music; economies

were much more her thing that week – but Holly saved the day.

However, it was Laura who saved the night itself, as Holly discovered late on Friday that Gwyn was playing in *Turandot* at the New Theatre – and so, with Gerald's permission, Laura turned out to baby-sit. Jane had been all for calling it off. After all, Duncan's friends had arranged for Duncan to take her to Duncan's kind of evening. Why didn't Duncan just go with Laura if she thought he was so wonderful? But Jane acquiesced.

Surprisingly, the concert was very good if you liked that kind of thing, which Duncan on the whole did and which Jane discovered she could once Duncan had bought champagne at the interval. Jane could enjoy most things after two glasses of champagne. By the time they were coming out and Duncan suggested going on to Le Monde, she was no longer office fatigued or grumpy but game for anything.

Laura had been very well prepared for her baby-sitting duties. She had arrived in corduroy hiking trousers and a peaked cap, to eliminate heat loss, and she had told Jane and Duncan that she would stay up till midnight and then, if they weren't back by one, she would go to sleep in one of the spare rooms. This seemed to given them carte blanche for a night out, and so they climbed the expensive sawdust-strewn steps of Le Monde in eager anticipation.

Cardiff's Le Monde was a dark and noisy restaurant at the best of times, but on a Friday evening its heady mixture of moneyed clients, handsome waiters and young women in non-existent dresses clamouring round the bar made a surefire aperitif for sex. The atmosphere buzzed with it, and Duncan and Jane found themselves heading home in a taxi after only two courses.

As he got out into the night air in Katrin Street, Duncan was aware that he had drunk well over half a bottle of wine on top of their champagne, and so he kissed Jane and sent her ahead to relieve Laura while he paid off the taxi.

'Hi Laura!' he shouted from the stairs, and crept up to the bathroom. He really didn't want Jane getting a lecture on her husband's allergic tendencies.

Duncan went into the bathroom feeling distinctly sexual. It was Friday night and all over Cardiff men were having it off with women like those he and Jane had been watching in Le Monde. He cleaned his teeth, drank a lot of water and then ran a bath. Why not? There was nothing like warm water to make you aware of the sensuous potential of every inch of skin. Besides which, they hadn't done it in the bath for ages.

Meanwhile, downstairs, Jane had given Laura her tokens, actually thanked her for arranging all this and started talking about the girls and Mr Harper. Twenty minutes later, Duncan had got fed up of feeling sultry on his own and wandered into their bedroom. From below he could hear Jane and Laura discussing education. To his surprise they seemed to be agreeing with each other loudly.

Duncan got into bed. Before his bath he had even put the electric blanket on, and so he now snuggled naked under the warm duvet. He decided not to switch off the blanket so that Jane would also experience the pleasure of a very warm and welcoming bed. He really didn't want her resorting to pyjamas that night.

How much later Duncan woke up he was not certain, but he was very hot and uncomfortable. The pores on his back, opened by a warm bath and cooked by the electric blanket, were actually beginning to sting. He hopped round the room scratching and wondering where the hell Jane was. Opening the bedroom door he found that the landing light was still on, so he thought better of striding round the house naked, shouting 'Jane!' like some urban Tarzan and put on his towelling robe. This was a fortunate decision because down in the kitchen he found Laura and Jane *still* engrossed in the subject of schoools.

'Anyone coming to bed?' he asked with a hint of irony.

Laura looked at Jane. 'Oh, I think you,' she said, as if making the choice for them.

Jane laughed. She really thought that was very funny.

It was decided that Laura should not get a taxi to travel back the six hundred yards to the other side of Cathedral Road and, in the circumstances, it was also decided that Duncan should not get dressed and walk her back – so Jane made up a spare bed for Laura and they talked a bit longer in the back room.

At something like half-past one in the morning, Duncan was aware of Jane clambering into bed in a pair of thick winter pyjamas.

'Laura really is very interesting,' she told Duncan. Duncan made a noise to tell her he'd heard but didn't want to wake up for any more. 'She's been reading this book on developmental variations amongst twins.'

'I'm tired,' mumbled Duncan, and so Jane postponed that particular conversation.

Before he fell asleep Duncan reflected on the fact that Laura Leighton Davis had a knack of ruining their sex life. Whether she made Jane too angry, or made Jane too happy, or kept him talking at the school gate when Jane was waiting in bed for their last mid-morning tumble before Follets, Laura was not good news. What was it with Laura and sex?

Actually sex was very important to Laura Davis.

Duncan knew something of how Gerald and Laura passed Sunday afternoons, but he knew this curious fact out of context. Laura was one of the more idiosyncratic Fulwood Road mothers, and one who led an active sex life. Those were the facts. But this Sunday afternoon business might have been a form of eccentricity or an aberration or even a Leighton family tradition for all that Duncan knew.

However, anyone who had heard Laura talk in somewhat reverential, and occasionally passionate terms about her courtship with Dr Gerald Davis would have divined that sex had played an important role in the course that Laura Leighton's life had taken twenty years ago.

Laura always maintained that although Gerald was married when they met she had done nothing to 'endanger' his marriage to the unsuitable Bridge. Of course she would have preferred to say that Gerald was already divorced when they met but this was not, alas, true. It was during Laura's first year at St David's University College, Lampeter that she had noticed Gerald Davis, a sympathetic admissions tutor in the less than impressive German department. At the time poor Gerald was still going through hell with his notorious wife, who was often to be found in the Students Union bar and who, during Laura's second term, actually moved in with one of his third-year students out in Tregaron Bog.

Dr Gerald Davis was a tall shuffling figure even twenty years ago. Laura used to see him walking to lectures with his large head swinging from side to side as he thought through the daily round of administrative problems. Laura, as a first year Modern Languages student, conceived of a very strong affection for Gerald Davis even before she was attracted to him. The man was something of a laughing stock amongst the language students, but in Laura's eyes poor Gerald Davis was somebody deserving of a good wife long before she wanted that wife to be herself.

Laura had sympathy for outsiders. In her first year at Lampeter the eighteen-year-old Laura Mary Leighton had found herself becoming marginalised from mainstream student life as one of the girls who belonged to the Christian Union, an oddly assorted group of fundamentalists, would-be clergymen and would-be clergy wives who campaigned ceaselessly against the chaplain and the Theology Department. Laura had joined the CU on the advice of her vicar in Goring-on-Thames. His views had been very important to her when she was in the sixth form, but by the beginning of her summer term in the isolated Welsh University village of Lampeter, Laura felt herself out of sympathy with the Christian Union's wholly negative and frequently vindictive agenda. Besides, by the summer term Laura had met Gerald.

Her relationships with boys had until that stage been unsatisfactory for all parties concerned. During her teens Laura had suspected that she might well enjoy sex but she had never considered the possibility of sleeping with anyone before University. At college Laura believed it was possible – and acceptable – to have sex, but the boys she met behaved as if they thought it obligatory, and Laura disappointed a number of young men. Returning to the college for its summer term (known perversely at Lampeter as the Easter term), Laura had decided to give up thinking about relationships altogether until her Part One exams were over.

But on the Sunday before term started, just after Mr Leighton had dropped her off, Laura had met poor Gerald Davis in Conti's Cafe and they began to talk in that narrow, unmodernised little espresso bar. An hour later they emerged into the bright sunlight of Lampeter's High Street and walked down to the river because both had discovered they were going to the Co-op Superstore for biscuits.

They stood in the warmth of the early evening and watched the shallow Teifi flow under Pont Steffan bridge for another hour and talked again, and by the time that Gerald remembered neither of them had actually bought biscuits yet, Laura was quite in love with him. As they shopped in the wide bright aisles of Lampeter's Co-op, Laura felt as though they were shopping together, man and wife, and she had decided that she would stand by Dr Gerald Davis whatever was being said about him on campus and whatever his awful wife was doing to humiliate him. Falling in love with a married man was not the kind of thing that Laura would normally have countenanced, but Gerald's notorious wife had forfeited much of the respect Laura would otherwise have accorded her.

Gerald had walked Laura back to her hall of residence, a tall sentry box of girls' study bedrooms set amongst even taller trees, and she had told him that she very much wanted to invite him in but in the circumstances she didn't think that was sensible. However she would come and see him in the Arts Block during lecture hours if he wanted her to. Dr Davis was rather thrown by this speech, delivered with that same emphatic school girl candour and vocal clarity so characteristic of the Laura that Duncan was to know twenty years later. But Gerald was also attracted to the diminutive figure before him and he made a good effort of inviting her to coffee during his free period the next morning.

What followed was a period of blissful and wild frustration that lasted through May and into a very difficult June.

The next day Laura Leighton, trying hard not to dress too differently but nevertheless quite transformed, called at Gerald's office in the German Department. It was five past eleven and Gerald already feared that she was not coming. But Laura did arrive in the long, strip-lit corridor with a large pile of books that gave the impression that she was going to consult Dr Davis on every aspect of German literature.

Unable actually to knock on the door without first putting down the books, and being short-sighted at the best of times, Laura stumbled. Gerald, hearing a noise outside his office, and fearing another of Bridge's scenes, went to open the door and was confronted by Laura rising gracefully up from the floor like Botticelli's vision of Spring. She was wearing a long flowing dress, as was then the fashion, and seemed to be not much taller when she had finished standing up.

Gerald shyly invited her in without a word and Laura picked up her books. He offered to help her with them and they ended up carrying the pile between them like removal men. Gerald guided them to a large chair where the books could be put down and was going to offer to make the coffee (as indeed was Laura), when both of them were suddenly unable to resist any longer the unbearable temptation to plunge into each others arms and kiss. It was as if they had been held apart all their lives and nothing but a pile of books stood between them now. The impulse was overwhelming and all of Goethe went flying.

Laura Leighton at eighteen had never experienced any-thing like that kiss (neither to be honest had Gerald at thirty-eight), and they could have easily and enthusiasti-cally dispensed with Laura's virginity on the spot. But after what seemed like an eternity of near ecstasy which had left Gerald's papers in considerable disarray, Laura's prudence and iron resolve intervened and she broke from him. She needed to see his face.

To this day Laura's memory was that when she looked at Gerald after that epic kiss, what she saw was the face of the only man she would ever love. It was as simple and as enormous as that.

She swallowed twice and wiped her mouth. 'I can never be your mistress,' she told him without hesita-tion, but added, lest he misinterpret her, 'I love you too much.' Laura had no idea what was happening to her except that it was clearly something that was meant to happen.

Those words marked a watershed in Dr Gerald Davis' life. Before he met Laura, Gerry Davis had only been a visitor in the world of academic Bohemia. He had never belonged, although he'd attended the occasional low-key orgy organised by his colleagues. Laura Leighton's candid refusal to consummate the extraordinary passion of their last twenty-four hours was the most sexually charged moment in Gerald's life (despite his wife's claim to have studied under several erotic Indian masters). But her solemn words also confirmed to poor Gerald that the kind of woman he'd been looking for when he was eighteen and when he was twenty-eight he had finally found when he was thirty-eight and virtually given up.

'I will get a divorce,' he replied and kissed her fingers, the tiniest whitest fingers. 'And then I will marry you.'

Little Laura Mary Leighton, assistant treasurer of the Christian Union, secretary of the newly formed German Society and first-year modern languages student, was engaged to a man twenty years her senior the day after meeting him by chance in Conti's Cafe.

At first, Gerald and Laura kept quiet about their relationship because neither wanted to provoke the wrath of Bridge upon the other. Gerald wanted to shield Laura from the dreadful world he and his wife had been dragged down into, and Laura wanted to shield Gerald from his wife's vindictiveness. She had no doubt that she could stand up to Bridgette Davis if it came to it; Gerald's love made her feel absurdly strong.

They dared not meet daily in a place as small as Lampeter, and were discreet when they did, but the Christian Union found out within two weeks of the start of term and Laura was denounced *in absentia* at one of their prayer meetings.

Gerald was as good as his word and went to a solicitor in Carmarthen to initiate divorce proceedings the following Saturday. He had chosen a firm out of Lampeter in the hope that any squabbles or public brawling of the kind he anticipated would not be witnessed by the students. That evening he and Laura went out to dinner on the sea coast and watched the summer sunset, but Gerald dropped Laura off some yards from the college campus as he was always to do for the next six weeks.

Laura went to chapel on the following Sunday, and then wrote to her father telling him that she was engaged and asking for his blessing. She received a telegram as soon as the post hit Goring, as did the College Principal, demanding that *nothing whatever* must happen, although the Principal had no idea what it was that Grandpa Leighton actually expected him to intervene in. Gerald was taken to task by his head of department, and when Bridge had done a bit of nosing around he had a very unpleasant visit from his estranged wife during which she made several disparaging remarks about Laura, in particular about her age, inexperience and boyish figure. Dr Davis was provoked beyond even his legendary endurance, and he squashed a tomato into his wife's face and bundled her out of the door.

There followed a period of unreality when Laura and Gerald lived in two worlds. In one, Laura was struggling to revise while being ostracised for alleged adultery by her former friends and receiving tearful phone calls from her mother on the payphone. In this world Gerald also suffered. Despite the fact that liaisons between staff and students were far from unusual, it seemed to be Gerald's lot alone to receive dark looks from his head of department. Bridge even threatened an assault charge. But there was another world in which they lived. No longer able to meet in Gerald's office, Laura and her fiancé used to drive in his old Morris Minor to Falcondale Lake or Pencarreg Mountain late at night and watch the midsummer stars. Gerald would bring sleeping bags, on the off chance, and once or twice Laura curled up on the back seat while Gerald took the front with his legs hanging out of the window.

No wonder people talked.

In her imagination Laura still liked to think that this innocent, childlike courtship continued until Gerald's divorce came through, but Bridge was proving difficult. One night she smashed Gerald's windows; another time she followed Laura across campus in the twilight, but never addressed her, even when Laura turned to face her on the Arts block bridge. The pressure on Gerald and Laura grew. Gerald was encouraged to apply for a sideways move within the University that might take him and either of his 'wives' to Swansea or Cardiff, or even Bangor. And Laura stopped revising entirely to write letter after letter to her parents and brothers and extended family, even to the vicar of Goring-on-Thames, in the hope that someone would understand.

Then, unexpectedly, one morning Gerald received a solicitor's letter from a local firm which advised him that their client, Mrs Bridgette Davis, did not intend to contest the divorce as long as she could have the house. Gerald ran into college with the letter in his hand and found Laura coming out from breakfast in the glass-fronted refectory.

Under the gaze of two hundred Alpen-chewing students, Gerald Davis and Laura Leighton, a full fourteen inches difference in height between them, walked hand in hand down to the brook dividing the halls of residence from the main campus, and crossed the bridge. Gerald had never been to Laura's room before, but he noticed none of the details of posters and books and toys that might have told him so much about his future wife, for Gerald and Laura were planning the rest of their lives.

Folded up together (somehow) on Laura's narrow bed, they discussed weddings and names of children, religion and whether there was life after death, then the talking stopped because they had to kiss. And in kissing they realised, as if some primeval switch had been thrown, that all they wanted in the world was each other, passionately, desperately, and that clothes were a total encumbrance. Such was Laura's haste that she lost two buttons from her cuff and never found one of them.

Afterwards Gerald watched the tears well up in Laura's eyes and assumed that she was crying because they had not waited until they were married. Laura shook her head. She was moved by so many emotions that words did not come easily, and so tears flowed instead.

Laura had been delighted to find that sex was as wonderful as she had thought it might be. She was suffused with a love for Gerald that was even greater than before, and she was so relieved, so marvellously relieved. She felt that all the tension of this extraordinary summer term had evaporated. And yet she *had* broken one of her rules: Gerald was still married to someone else. But this was also very moving to Laura. She had been humbled by giving in to sex. Laura Leighton had always prided herself on the standards and rules she had set for herself. The family had called her Mary Poppins from an early age. And now Poppins had been laid low – but what a way to be laid.

'We must do this a lot,' she whispered to Gerald, and kissed him over and over again.

'You're not sorry we didn't wait?' he asked. Gerald hadn't actually realised until they were making love that Laura had been a virgin. It all made so much more sense to him now.

'If I could put the clock back to this morning,' said Laura, pausing, 'I would still have done this. I wouldn't have missed it for the world.'

They lay naked in her room all morning, making love while the cleaners thumped huge vacuum cleaners up and down the stairs. Eventually it became uncomfortable for Laura, and Gerald realised he had failed to take two seminars. When he had gone clattering down the stairs Laura took a bath, dressed and changed the sheets on her bed. Then she sat at her desk, put on her glasses and looked into the mirror lost in thought. Who was this person that had once been her? She had changed. Not just because she had had sex – Laura expected that. What she hadn't expected was that she had changed because she now knew that she was not able to keep to the high standards she had always set herself, and while part of her was disappointed, part of her was actually relieved. Laura never forgot that lost button from her cuff.

Saturday morning in the Davis' Pontcanna household found Gerald's breakfast in bed being served by a woman in corduroy trousers and a peaked cap. Laura had told Jane Lewis that she would pop off back to Meirion Street first thing and not to worry if she had left before they woke.

'You don't know how long you've got, do you?' she had said to Jane as they made up the spare bed. For Laura, the thought of being widowed had been a continual preoccupation during her marriage and she claimed to value every day with Gerald. 'You're very lucky to have Duncan,' she said.

Jane felt she ought to agree. After all, he did have his good points.

'No, I mean it,' Laura insisted. 'Duncan's got years ahead of him.'

As well as his comparative longevity, Duncan Lewis also had going for him the ability to command a reasonable salary, if the conditions were right. He and his wife agreed on this. Of course, *when* Duncan was going to command it again was another matter. However, he was doing his bit. The day that Holly had looked after Alice and Ellen he had been out to talk to some former colleagues about their plan to set up in partnership. Within half an hour of arriving at Buffs Wine Bar, Duncan was sure that he did not want to go in with Richard and Geraint, but he was interested by their suggestion that they all meet for lunch with CPM, a company that specialised in finding venture capital from various agencies, with a rumoured golden touch when it came to the Welsh Development Agency.

The following Tuesday, Duncan accomplished by half-past-twelve all that was required of him domestically, including finding Alice's swimming kit, and took the bus into Cardiff. Buses were another new thing to him. When he'd been working he'd relied on his company car and taxis. The first time Duncan got on an orange No. 25 bus after giving back the Sierra, he'd caught himself saying 'Number eleven Katrin Street' to a bemused driver. But he had grown to like buses. You could change your perspective on familiar vistas by sitting on the top deck. Buildings looked different. You could also see into people's gardens and into their bedrooms, like the fabled window cleaners of old.

Duncan caught himself thinking about sex again. It really was becoming a preoccupation of his, fuelled by a growing sense of frustration. Somehow every night he was busy getting everything ready for the girls tomorrow, or Jane was busy, or they'd bickered over something, or they were just too tired. Duncan had even thought about sex the previous Sunday afternoon, and had actually suggested the girls watch a video while he and Jane discussed what to do with the attic in Katrin Street, but Jane had been more interested in taking them all off to St Fagan's for a healthy walk.

Quite why sex had become so important him since his work left him he was unsure. Maybe it was displacement activity, he thought, as he watched a very dark-haired Welsh gypsy-looking girl coming up on to the top deck. All that architectural creativity finding another outlet? Or maybe it was a reaction to losing his identity. Was he trying to find himself in the orgasmic moment? he wondered as his bus crossed the Taff and rows and rows of naughty hotel bedrooms passed by. Or maybe he'd just forgotten how much he enjoyed it, just as Jane was beginning to forget how much she enjoyed it.

Not that working for Tossers had been creative in any sense – other than Howard's accountancy. Maybe it was just a priapic reaction to freedom. Duncan even found himself thinking about sex when he found Geraint and Richard in Champers, the bodega-style wine bar directly below Le Monde. The only time he actually stopped thinking about it was when he went inside and realised that Geraint and Richard were in the company of a blonde woman who seemed vaguely familiar but definitely not his type.

'This is Carolyn Parry Morris,' Geraint said. This Carolyn person was very well turned out, but overmade-up and overcompressed in Duncan's view. She seemed to have no neck, and all three vital statistics occurred within the same twelve inches of her body. It was on occasions like this that Jane used to point out to Duncan that he was no oil painting. Duncan could mentally hear his wife ticking him off as he shook the rings on Carolyn's hand.

Carolyn Parry Morris apologised for the fact that Caedfael wasn't able to be there, which was a shame, as Duncan's main reason for letting himself be lured into this pseudo-Spanish barbecue house was the expectation of meeting the brains behind CPM, the fabled Welsh Mr Big.

They took their seats round a table plastered with black paint and screened from the rest of the clientele by a wrought iron grill (Spanish style), and knotted timbers (Tudor style). Compared with Richard and Geraint, Duncan felt pleasantly underdressed in his cord trousers, expensive sweatshirt and big cardigan. If anyone who felt sorry for Duncan Lewis happened to see him in Champers with that Carolyn Parry-Whatsit, they'd see that he was well enough off and hardly making the running for another job.

Carolyn, it seemed, was being bought lunch by Geraint and Richard because she could tell them all they needed to know about what she could do to facilitate the free flow of funds from a number of bodies who relied heavily on her brother's advice. Duncan had soon switched off from this patter, but the news that this Carolyn woman was the sister and not the wife of Mr Big rekindled Duncan's interest. Was Mr Big as dumpy as she?

The food came sizzling hot in black metal dishes but without garnishes, much to Carolyn's dismay. Geraint hopped off eagerly in search of garnish, which expedition held up the conversation.

'You're not saying much,' Carolyn said, turning to Duncan.

'I'm all ears,' he joked.

'Duncan's much brighter than he pretends,' said Richard, who had been Duncan's assistant at one stage. 'He's the best I've worked with.'

'I thought Geraint was the best you've worked with,' Carolyn said archly.

'That was when Geraint was sitting opposite him,' said Duncan.

Richard looked embarrassed for a moment. Poor guy, thought Duncan, he wants this so much. Carolyn Parry Morris put down her glass and smiled at Duncan. He could see that these were just boys to her.

Duncan told Jane about the lunch. 'It makes me so glad I'm out of that world,' he concluded.

'Are you?' Jane asked

'Well, I'm not going to take just any job,' Duncan replied.

'*Yet*,' said Jane.

'OK, not for the next three months,' said Duncan.

The rest of the week began to show that a pattern was emerging from the realignment of their lives. Duncan moved the girls around, fed them, got feedback from the teacher, talked to Laura, talked to Jane, thought about his career, came to no decision, felt guilty and went to bed before getting up to move around and feed the girls again. Jane went in to Follets and kept her head down to avoid conspirators, got out of Follets for lunch, came home as soon as was politic and played silly buggers with Tony when it was necessary. Even the girls seemed more settled. They accepted the fiction that they had been moved apart in class for talking too much, and so the walk to and from school became an opportunity for catching up on all the imagined gossip. Duncan's role became that simply of escort, combining his skills as traffic warden and sheepdog and leaving him time to get lost in his own thoughts.

There were big things to think about in his life. In the first place he still had to decide what he was going to do with the rest of it, and in the short term he had Jane's dinner party to prepare for and a financial damage limitation exercise to effect on the conservatory.

But life did seem to be settling into a pattern.

Then one night Duncan had a dream about Holly Williams. It was a curious, almost non-narrative dream in which he was in Holly's kitchen and she was offering him a choice of relishes in different whisky bottles, and then they were swimming together beneath the waters of some bright aquamarine ocean, in search of the Holy Grail, and their bodies were drawing closer and closer, hers as white as some shimmering fish.

Duncan woke up highly aroused and tried to wake Jane. She was half asleep but realised what was happening and kicked off her pyjama trousers in mute agreement. It seemed an age since Duncan and Jane had done this and both wanted to, but it was all wrong, nothing felt right. They were doing what they usually did and yet neither of them was turned on by it. Duncan persisted for some time and then gave up.

'I'm sorry,' he said.

'I'm sorry too,' said Jane, who was feeling rather sore and fully awake now.

'Not like us,' Duncan said into the pillow.

'Maybe we're out of practice,' Jane said, hugging him to her.

'We need a break,' Duncan said.

'What from?' Jane asked, hoping he wasn't going to say 'each other'.

'Cardiff,' said Duncan.

Jane agreed. It was probably the damp, the unrelieved neo-gothic streets, the bilingual road signs.

Duncan sniggered. 'At least we can still have a laugh,' he muttered.

Holly Wiliams had not been dreaming about Duncan that evening.

Gwyn had gone with the orchestra to Oxford for three nights and Holly had the house to herself once the children were in bed. Holly in the emptiness of Pontcanna Terrace was not the same wistfully inaudible Holly from Fulwood Road. At first she sat and listened to the silence of the house. She even turned off the central heating so the house was completely quiet and then she listened as the psychic echoes of Gwyn died away. It wasn't enough to know that Gwyn was not there; the house had to recognise that he was gone, that he wouldn't be back that night. Then the energy returned to Holly and she'd celebrate in a spree of tidying and polishing and ordering. One night she sorted all Siôn's Lego into twelve different plastic boxes. Another time she moved the front room furniture round and rewired the stereo so that the speakers now faced the wall which supported their sofa.

This night Holly had been cleaning windows and the hall mirror. At half-past eleven she poured herself a glass of whisky and wondered about the tour of Japan that Gwyn might be offered. She would love to accompany the orchestra to Japan and find out more about Buddhism, but equally good for Holly's karma was three weeks in a house without Gwyn. Holly thought these thoughts but never expressed them. For this reason she'd never had to address the question of something being wrong with her marriage. Had she talked to someone like Jane Lewis, she might have ended up considering if it was significant that Gwyn's wife looked forward to her husband's absences. Maybe Gwyn's wife didn't like Gwyn? But Holly, inside her own head, didn't pose such questions. Gwyn was Gwyn and she didn't judge him for that. Everyone had to be someone.

Up in Bond-Kyle Avenue Kit had made it up to the front door and chosen to lean face flat against it rather than get her keys out. Barry Britto was just coming down the stairs with Kit's sleeping bag when he saw her features pressed up against the frosted glass, the condensation from her breath rising like a white stain.

'Good evening?' he asked, taking her coat and smelling the stale cigarette smoke.

'Couldn't even give it away tonight,' said Kit, weaving cautiously into the TV room.

'Shall I make up the office?' asked Barry, holding up Kit's sleeping bag.

'No,' said Kit, falling the length of the white leather sofa.

'Coffee? Tea? Bed pan?' asked Barry.

'Can you take me upstairs?' she asked, lifting her arms. Barry picked her up. For all his gentleness and mannered self-control, Barry had been a ferocious rugby player in his London days. Lifting Kit was like lifting a tray of sandwiches.

'My hero,' said Kit as he carried her upstairs.

'Glad to be of service,' said Barry.

Kit gave him a big smile. 'Bazza,' she said, 'I think your luck may be in tonight. You dirty little devil.'

In Oxford, Gwyn Williams had been for a drink with some of the brass section and two violinists. Good old '*Turdandot*' always left him with a considerable thirst, particularly the end of Act Three, which Howie had marked in pencil on the score as a 'Ten Pint Job'. Puccini clearly knew that there was nothing the brass and horns liked better than a good blow before the final curtain and then straight down the pub. The entire horn section had been signalling to each other during the sixteen-bars rest at 42 and one of the trumpet players had mimed siphoning beer out of his valves.

The only problem was, as Howie endlessly pointed out, the beer in Oxford was twice the price of Brains. Gwyn found Howie's parochialism boring when they were in Cardiff, but once across the Severn Bridge Gwyn also missed his Brains Dark and all it stood for. At eleven o'clock in Cardiff Gwyn could pack up, walk round the castle, over the Taff and up Sophia Gardens, and be back home by half-past. The walk helped him calm down, particularly after Wagner.

But as it was eleven o'clock in Oxford, Gwyn was stuck in The Welsh Pony with Howie who was remarking with enthusiasm that after a blow like that the first pint never touches the sides. In theory, Gwyn could get in the car and be back in Cardiff by one, then drive back down tomorrow. But he'd had his two pints now and he always got the feeling that Holly didn't like surprises like that. She was never unfriendly, but sometimes . . . Gwyn didn't know what it was. Some times he felt such a stranger. He'd asked Merryl the harpist if women like surprises. Merryl usually came along to the pub but would sit on her own reading. Merryl said it depended what the surprise was. That was the kind of answer you got from women. Never pin them down.

Gwyn loved Holly very much. He missed her when he went away but he was aware that something was wrong. If she was in a room and he came in, after a while she'd move out. Now that wasn't normal. Not straight away, mind, but always after a while. She still did things for him, got the meals, tidied the room where he practised, but when he talked to her she didn't seem to listen. Maybe it was the menopause. Gwyn knew women went funny, but Holi was only forty-two.

He bought a bottle over the counter and walked back to his digs. This would be his decelerator. God, women were funny things. Look at Turandot – had all her suitors killed. It was the first time Gwyn had thought about an opera plot for years. Plots went on above his head, literally. Plots were people thumping about and singing up on the stage while he blew or rested. But Turandot was an odd one and no mistake. And Calaf won her love in the end – how? The thing about Turandot was that at least you knew where you were with a woman who was trying to kill you. God knew where you were with Holly sometimes.

Gwyn used his key and bounded up to bed. Bloody funny things, women.

On Thursday Duncan began to panic about this dinner party of Jane's. He wanted to get one course done in advance. He needed to feel he had achieved something towards it. On the way back from school that morning he'd talked to Laura about his intention to do quails eggs, but for her food was something of a blind spot. She knew a lot about the nutritional side of it and she knew how much to buy for hungry boys of which she seemed to have four, five if you included Gerald, but dinner parties were not her kind of thing.

'We never entertain,' she said. 'Gerald takes the department out from time to time but I only go if it's wives and
girlfriends, which is rare these days.'

Actually, in her early days as Mrs Dr Davis, Laura had
worked very hard at giving dinner parties. Having failed
her Part One exams 'because of the difficulties we were
having with Gerald's ex-wife,' Laura had left Lampeter
and followed Gerald to Cardiff where he'd been offered the
sideways move into a slightly better German department.

Laura's parents were very distressed that their bright
little daughter had thrown up the chance of becoming a
teacher, and Laura's mother was particularly upset when
Laura admitted that she was planning to live with Gerald
until his divorce came through.

'But Mummy, we have slept together now,' Laura had
said, very red in the face but determined to have the
truth acknowledged. The truth about Gerald and her was
very important to Laura. Mrs Leighton had collapsed in
more tears.

Eventually Gerald and Grandpa Leighton had gone for
a long walk along the Thames and discussed what was to
be done. A compromise was agreed by which Laura could
go to Cardiff as long as she had her own flat, which the
Leightons would pay for. Grandpa Leighton had been going
to say that he didn't want to know what his daughter got
up to when she was with Gerald as long as she had her
own flat, but when he met the big shambling form of
Dr Davis it was clear that this man was not deserving of
such bluster. Laura and Gerald were married in January
the following year and Grandpa Leighton and Laura's two
younger brothers officially helped her move from the little,
underoccupied flat in Cathays. As a peace offering Laura
and Gerald actually went round beforehand and moved in
some things for the Leighton boys to move out.

For the next few years Laura had thrown herself into

Gerald's career, attending departmental, collegiate and University parties and, although several of the academic's wives remarked that it was odd being drawn out in conversation by a girl of twenty-one, especially one who looked even younger, there was no doubt that Laura was a great help in getting Gerald the post of deputy to the perennially absent Professor Erikson.

'When Gerald failed to get the chair I'm afraid we rather retired from social life,' said Laura sadly and nobly, as if it was Cardiff's loss. 'Besides, on an academics' salary one can't entertain that much.'

All in all Laura did not feel that she could be much of a help to Duncan's dinner party, and unfortunately that week she was having to take Mordred to his 'testicle man' at the Heath Hospital so it wouldn't be easy to have the girls while Duncan experimented with quails.

The day of the dinner itself, Duncan was busy before Jane got back from her run. Norman the Blacksmith had been told to be round at ten to diminish and make safe the damage he was doing to the conservatory so that Duncan could serve drinks in there, and the girls had been told to tidy their bedroom.

'But no one's going to be going into our bedroom!' Alice protested.

'Someone might walk in by mistake looking for the lavatory,' Duncan replied.

'Well that's their fault,' said Alice.

'Yes, but it'll be your fault if the place is such a mess they think they've found the lavatory,' Duncan explained. He was not a man to be crossed that morning and logic of all things was not going to be allowed to defeat him.

Alice and Ellen complained to Jane that Dad had said their bedroom looked like a lavatory.

'Only from certain angles,' Jane had conceded. She was on Duncan's side in this one. The girls went off in a huff and sat and talked in their room all morning about what they were going to do when they left home.

Jane came up and hugged Duncan while he was doing things to carrots and leeks.

'You don't have to do it all you know,' she said.

'I am a little marvel,' Duncan insisted.

'I may have to go to Swansea next week,' Jane began in a cautious voice.

'These things happen,' he commiserated, chopping away. 'Think of the poor sods who have to live there all the time.'

'I mean I may have to stay overnight,' Jane continued, wanting to talk this through. 'Tony told me yesterday.'

'You mean you may be going to stay the night in a Swansea Hotel with Big Fat Tony?'

'Yes, perhaps two,' Jane replied.

Duncan laughed. 'I am not jealous. Oh dear!' He laughed again. 'Don't worry!'

'David and Miles would be coming as well,' Jane added.

'What is this?' Duncan asked. 'The Jane Lewis Appreciation Society's Seaside AGM?'

'I'm just telling you in case it comes up tonight. It's not even definite yet. I didn't want you to hear it being discussed before I'd asked you if you could cope.'

'Oh, I can cope,' said Duncan, adding, 'I just hope you can.'

Jane dug him in the ribs. 'That's not funny. I don't want to be stuck in some naff hotel with Tony and Miles and David.'

'I thought you liked Miles. Isn't he supposed to be funny?'

She thumped him again. 'Why are you being so aggressive?' she demanded.

'I am not being aggressive!' he protested. 'You're the one who keeps hitting me. I am just being funny. Like Miles. Now, where is bloody Norman?'

At midday Jane took over to do the main course and Duncan decided to paint one wall of the conservatory a temporary light blue to cover up some of the damage that Norman had inflicted while removing his props. The girls were offered a pound each to help. Ellen negotiated two and they settled on five if the bedroom was tidied as well. Jane objected that the smell would ruin everything, but Duncan had some paint that dried quickly and odourlessly which contractors relied on for the morning of official openings. Alice and Ellen had a good time sloshing away the afternoon while rain hammered down on Norman's patched-up roof.

At four o'clock they had tea in the upstairs drawing room in front of the fire and Jane began to panic about who was actually coming. Miles, she was pretty certain, was coming alone. Duncan was pretty certain of that too. 'If he's really after you he won't be bringing the future Mrs Miles Whatsit the Third, will he?' Duncan explained.

David was bringing his wife, which was a complete surprise to Jane who assumed that young men like David didn't settle down till their mid thirties. But in fact David, now thirty, had been married since he was twenty-eight.

'The best ones always go first,' he'd explained to Jane.

As for Kit Sinclair, she had told Duncan that the Bastard was in a conference near Paris helping to save the world so, in theory, that meant an equal number of men and women.

'Not that it matters,' Jane conceded as she poured some more tea. 'It's a dinner party, not an orgy.'

'Yes. That can wait till Swansea,' Duncan agreed.

Jane glared at him. 'You are being very unpleasant,' she said. 'Why?'

'I don't think he was being unpleasant,' said Ellen.

'Why do you keep having a go at me?'

'I don't think he was having a go,' said Ellen.

'I'm sorry,' said Duncan, realising that his Swansea tease hadn't been considered funny the first time round.

'Just because you don't want to work doesn't mean I can't take mine seriously,' Jane told him. That hadn't come out quite as she intended, but she was feeling that Duncan was definitely mocking her for some abstruse reason and she believed in retaliation.

They got into an argument about whether Duncan was supporting Jane psychologically and whether Duncan realised that Jane didn't want to be working but somebody had to. And was Duncan really supposed to be so thick he hadn't worked that out? Alice turned up the volume on the TV pointedly.

Jane went and had a bath while Duncan laid the table, a project that could easily take him an hour. When Jane came down the entire dining room was lit by candles and there was a slightly surreal blue glow coming from the conservatory. He is so talented, Jane thought. He could be a such a good architect. But she didn't mention it. Her high opinion of Duncan's abilities had been crossed off the agenda.

The girls went upstairs for their bath when Jane got changed. Quite why Alice had got contractor's blue paint all the way up her arm while Ellen escaped scot free Jane had no idea. Mr Harper had warned her about seeing every difference as significant.

Jane changed into a dress Duncan had bought at her request for Christmas but which she had forgotten in all the upheaval of January's redundancy. It was something long with a slit skirt.

'Not at all like a solicitor,' said Duncan proudly when Jane came down.

'Or a Mum,' said Alice with a certain ambivalence. The girls had been allowed to stay up to look at the guests. They liked to see Jane looking wonderful, but they were always wary that she might be distracted by her appearance and get ideas about not being their mother first and foremost.

David arrived with an expensive bottle of sherry which he'd chilled specially in the hope of being offered some. He also brought with him Bronagh (pronounced Brawnya), who was surprisingly fat and Scottish, and quiet, and unfortunately dressed.

'Are you a solicitor?' Jane asked.

'No, I work at The Heath,' said Bronagh sadly.

'What'll you have to drink?' Duncan asked to follow the silence that followed this doleful announcement.

'Just an orange juice,' said Bronagh, adding to her woes the fact that she was driving.

'Men,' said Jane in a positive aren't-they-dreadful-but-we-love-them-really sort of way, but Bronagh didn't rise to the bait.

David launched in to talking about the day's rugby, but Duncan hadn't even realised that Wales had been playing France and so they skipped quickly on to the subject of the conservatory roof. Some water had edged its way between the overlaid panes of glass in Norman's patch-up job, and David wondered how long it would be before it started to drip through. It was not the kind of conversation that architects – even former architects – enjoyed.

'We've got a place by the sea,' said David cheerfully. 'Leaks like a sieve!'

'Really?' Duncan said to Bronagh, who was sitting in isolation because Jane had popped back to the kitchen.

'Yes,' said Bronagh, as if all that leaking water weighed heavily upon her.

Duncan went to fix the drinks, leaving David and Bronagh to gaze silently up at the conservatory roof. Duncan asked Jane whether he should spike Bronagh's drink because she looked like hard work.

'She's only twenty-seven,' Jane said, trying to be kind. 'We forget what it's like.'

'You were standing up in court defending murderers when you were twenty-seven,' Duncan replied.

'Motorists,' said Jane. Her heart also sank at the thought of Bronagh, but she felt as hostess it was her job to bring out the best in her guests, not slag them off in the kitchen. Bronagh was probably feeling a bit out of her depth amongst all these grown-up professionals.

Fortunately, by the time Duncan went back to the conservatory the girls had found Bronagh and were admiring her shoes, which looked to Duncan like patent leather hiking boots peeping out from under a totally shapeless long woollen dress. But Bronagh seemed happier talking to them.

Next to arrive was Miles with two bottles, one red one white, plus a single red rose in a phial which he asked Duncan's permission to present to Jane.

'You can give her a whole bunch if you like,' said Duncan generously.

Miles suggested Jane should put the rose in her hair. Jane decided a vase would be more appropriate and went back into the kitchen.

'Duncan, your wife won't wear my present,' Miles shouted as he followed her.

Duncan arrived in the kitchen with Bronagh and David's empty glasses. 'She's wearing mine,' he replied, which provoked Miles into more gallantry towards Jane, and praise of Duncan's taste in wives and dresses. Jane noticed that Duncan and Miles had struck up a banter that sounded simply foolish to her, but she could tell that they were delineating territory. Miles was probing good humouredly to see where Duncan would draw the line, and Duncan was declaring certain areas acceptable within the bounds of humour. They were like two lions who had decided that this territory, marked out by nonsense and badinage, could be held in common.

'I'm asking her just for this evening,' said Miles.

'He's asking you just for this evening,' echoed Duncan.

'I can't wear a rose in my hair. I'm a middle-aged solicitor,' Jane said.

'That's not what you look like,' said Miles.

Jane caught sight of herself in the mirror. No, that wasn't what she looked like. Maybe people weren't middle aged at thirty-seven any more. Maybe small amusing American Jews knew about that kind of thing.

'*Vase*,' she said firmly, but she couldn't help enjoying the attention.

While Jane introduced Miles to Bronagh, and the girls suddenly went all shy, Duncan went to put the porch light on to help Kit locate number 11. As he approached the door he heard a muttering sound coming from the other side. A voice, quite low but probably female, was repeating over and over *shitbuggerfuck, shitbuggerfuck*. Duncan's first reaction was that this must be someone with an aerosol trying to work out what word, from their limited repertoire, to spray on his wall, but when he opened the door he found Kit, cigarette in hand, caught in mid mutter.

'Hi,' she said with a big public smile. 'Just doing my exercises.'

Duncan's face must have registered that he didn't understand.

'Something the Bastard taught me. If I'm worried I'm going to embarrass people I get all the words out first before I go in. Stops me saying 'fuck' all the time. Oh Christ, I'm already saying it. Shit!'

Duncan laughed. 'It doesn't matter, I don't think anyone here's going to mind.'

'But you've got kids,' said Kit. She was clearly quite nervous. 'I never swear in front of my boys.'

'I think the girls have just gone to bed,' Duncan said reassuringly, taking her coat. She was dressed in a white trouser-suit, to his surprise, and seemed to have aquired a tan. But what really threw Duncan was Kit's lack of composure.

'Look, I'm really sorry, I should have brought some bottles but I clean forgot.'

'That's OK,' said Duncan. He'd laid in extra supplies with a view to Kit's lunchtime level of consumption.

'I'll send you a crate of something tomorrow,' Kit continued.

'It doesn't matter.'

'Barry will bring it round,' Kit told him.

Duncan was surprised and asked if Barry was back from Paris.

'Oh yes, got back this morning. Seems they saved the planet yesterday and caught an early plane home first thing.'

'Is he coming then?' Duncan asked, looking towards the door. 'Oh no,' said Kit. 'I gave Geegee the night off. Told him he can do the baby-sitting. Serves him right, the Bastard. Christ I need drinkies!'

Kit was very friendly to everyone, but especially nice to Jane. She seemed to know a lot about the clothes Jane was wearing, recognising makes and labels and being altogether very positive. Duncan wondered if she was self-consciously playing the perfect dinner guest. Kit quickly established that she knew most of the people Miles knew, through Barry, and was gracious to David. She apologised to Bronagh for her cigarette as soon as she saw her, but she didn't stop smoking – which was either a deft move calculated, Duncan thought, to label Bronagh as 'one of those people who objects to my ciggie but stuff you, baby,' or a mammoth want of practical tact.

Duncan noticed with a certain satisfaction that he had

to keep Kit's gin and tonic topped up more often than anyone else's. He felt rather proud and proprietorial about Kit. Jane might have invited David and Miles, but Kit was his contribution to the evening.

The candlelit dining room was greatly admired and Miles explained that Duncan could earn a living in New York just setting people's tables. Duncan wanted to avoid the subject of jobs altogether so he made some joke about how his travel costs might make working over there prohibitively expensive.

David and Kit drank a great deal and Kit began to drop the occasional expletive into her conversation as if she was warming up or testing the water. Duncan looked at Jane being chatted to by Miles and wondered when it was he was supposed to have done his conservatory sales pitch to Kit. Somewhere between her fourth gin and her first bottle of wine perhaps. But that was long gone.

Kit tried being nice to Bronagh but it was clearly an effort.

'Where do you work?'

'At The Heath,' said Bronagh dolefully

'All those fucking doctors!' roared Kit. 'Don't you hate them? I used to be a medical journalist. Medical and fashion, bit of an odd combination but that's how it turned out, but, Christ, the doctors! Such randy little buggers. The old ones are the worst!'

Kit had discovered the launch she needed to tell a story about when she'd last gone out to dinner with Barry. 'Nothing but doctors and doctor's wives. The entire table. Most of them in private practice too, unlike bloody Barry.' She was warming to her subject. 'And I spent all night sitting next to this fat old fart who did plastic surgery, you know, shifting women's tits around and cutting bits off their fannies with a bacon slicer, and he kept looking at me, this fart, sideways on . . .' She gestured to the flatness of her chest and David laughed. Duncan saw Bronagh look at David but David didn't and neither did Kit. 'So anyway, by this time I'd had a few and I'd really tried to behave, but he was really beginning to get to me and so I said to him, "I know what you're thinking, you dirty little devil. I may have flat tits but I've got bloody enormous nipples, isn't that right Bazza?" At which point, you can imagine, everything went very quiet and I could see Barry, as ever, talking to the Secretary of State for Something Medical, I don't know . . .'

Kit's story ran out of steam, but not before David had enjoyed it enormously. Miles was laughing generously too. Bronagh smiled. Duncan wondered whether she was politically out of sympathy with Kit or just plain embarrassed.

Miles started on a story about a couple he knew who bought each other plastic surgery every year for their birthdays.

'Great idea,' said David, enthusiastically draining his glass and probably not intending any disrespect to Bronagh, but she caught the implication. Duncan could see it in her face. He found himself watching to see if there might be a flashpoint soon. He felt detached and interested in the idea of a blazing marital row over his table. God, why was he becoming a spectator on life?

Jane changed the subject to Swansea and Tony's forthcoming visit with David and her to Miles' Swansea office, but although her steering had avoided the plastic surgery pitfall it wasn't able to stop the conversation veering out of control on to the vexed subject of Wales. Many years ago Jane had tried to ban Wales entirely from their dinner parties. Concepts of nationhood, failures of nationhood, the North–South divide, the thorny language issue, the hostility towards England – all these matters were never resolved and could genuinely divide dinner guests.

'The Welsh are just randy little sods,' said Kit, who had

reached the stage when her husband's nationality was like a red rag and that was her contribution to the nation's debate.

'I don't think you can generalise,' said Miles.

Was this a whiff of political correctness or a joke? Duncan wondered.

'I'm Welsh,' said David, who was born in Newport although he had only recently returned to Wales.

'I rest my case,' Kit declared, grinning.

'Are you saying I'm a sandy little—' David began amid an outburst of laughter from Miles, Kit and Duncan. David, realising the effect of his spoonerism, continued as if it was a joke. 'Are you saying I'm a sandy little rod? Am I a sandy little rod?' he asked Bronagh. 'Am I, Bron?'

Bronagh sighed something quietly that might have been 'Oh that's enough, Dave,' but no one could tell.

'Come on,' David insisted, too drunk to realise he was being boring, 'We rods have our self-respect . . .'

'Coffee!' said Jane suddenly.

Miles, who Duncan realised wasn't at all drunk, galloped to the rescue. 'Correct me if I'm wrong, David, but under British law a wife cannot be required to testify against her husband,' he pointed out.

David made a show of collapsing in laughter. 'Good point!' he bellowed to the man he saluted as his friend.

'My husband's a randy sod anyway,' said Kit, pouring herself another glass of wine. 'And he's Welsh and they think the sun shines out of his arse.'

Believing that the conversation was now on to safer ground, Jane started to clear away. Duncan joined her in the kitchen and set about making coffee.

'She's quite something,' said Jane.

'Kit or Bronagh?' Duncan asked.

'Your friend,' Jane replied.

'I don't know,' said Duncan. 'I think Bronagh could pack

a mean punch.' He kissed Jane on the back of her head. She kissed him back.

'I hope tonight you're not going to have too much to drink and fall asleep,' she said, and then she kissed him full on the mouth.

'I hope I'm not going to either,' said Duncan, running his hand up the slit in her skirt. They had forgotten the aphrodisiac effect of food and wine and other people talking about sex over dinner. They had forgotten it and were now pleasantly surprised.

Another surprise was Miles who wandered in with some plates. 'Can anyone tell me where the bathroom is?' he asked. Jane and Duncan moved apart but not too quickly. It was their house, their dinner party, their marriage after all.

Duncan had planned for them to have coffee in the upstairs drawing room but he'd forgotten to light the fire, so while Jane and Bronagh finished clearing the table, and David and Kit finished all the bottles, he nipped upstairs. Duncan was just going into the drawing room when he heard the sound of muffled crying from the far end of the landing. Alice was sitting outside her bedroom looking very red-faced and upset.

Duncan went down to see her, realising as the concern hit him that he had had a bit to drink. His mind was racing ahead of him; something was wrong, why did it take so long to get to her? God he'd had too much to drink, this was awful.

'Daddy, I don't feel very well,' said Alice simply and pathetically. She was indeed very hot. Duncan asked her if she'd like some Calpol or a drink.

'Hey, little lady,' said Miles, bending down behind them. 'You've got some great spots there.'

Duncan hadn't noticed but Alice had a great rash of blotches all the way up her right arm across her neck and down the other arm too.

'I'll get Jane, shall I?' Miles suggested calmly.

Jane was all deep concern. She hitched up her long skirt and looked into Alice's eyes with effusive, calm love and then up at Duncan with desperate worry. Anything that struck at her daughters struck at the very core of Jane. 'Have you got a temperature, Ali love? Duncan, will you look at Nel?'

Duncan checked on the sleeping Ellen while Jane looked after Alice in the bathroom. Ellen seemed fine. When Duncan got back Jane suddenly remembered the fast-drying odourless blue paint that Alice had got up her arm and began to panic.

'Duncan, what was in that paint?' she asked. Oh God, don't let it be his fault.

Duncan said he'd go and look. As he passed downstairs he heard Kit telling David that she would emasculate Barry if he was ever unfaithful to her and that the sod knew this. Duncan found the paint tin in the side yard and, unable to reach a conclusion out in the rain, took it upstairs with him. As he passed through again he saw Bronagh silently watching him, but David was now all ears as Kit explained why she never committed adultery.

'I wouldn't let the Bastard have that over me,' she announced.

When Duncan got back upstairs Jane had taken Alice into the drawing room and put her down on the sofa. Miles was on his mobile phone trying the doctor's emergency number.

'Engaged,' he said.

'What do we do?' Jane asked Duncan. All the time she was trying not to think to herself, 'This wouldn't have happened if I hadn't gone back to work,' but the words kept running in her head. 'Dunc, what do we do?'

'Keep trying and keep her temperature down, I suppose,' said Duncan, looking at the prone form of his daughter.

Children collapsed so quickly, so completely. It left you feeling useless. He tried to think practically. 'Look, do you think someone should tell David and Kit what's going on?'

Jane had completely forgotten they were in the middle of a dinner party.

'I'll go,' said Miles, but at that moment they noticed Bronagh standing lumpily in the doorway. She asked if she could help and Duncan was just about to suggest that she tell David and Kit what was happening when Bronagh explained that she was a doctor and though she hadn't done much paediatrics she'd be happy to have a look at Alice while they were waiting to get through.

All Duncan's preconceptions about the big fat medical secretary fell away as Bronagh quietly examined Alice. She was wonderful. Somehow her silence and solidity seemed now to be more a mark of wisdom than of gaucherie. Jane kept trying to explain about the contractor's paint but Bronagh was pretty certain that this was viral.

'What does that mean?' Jane asked in a sufficient state of guilt and worry to need things spelling out.

'I really don't think she's been poisoned,' Bronagh explained. 'I don't think it's the paint. But that's only my opinion. I think you should take her into the Infirmary. That's going to be the quickest way to get her looked at this time of night.'

Jane said they should ring for a taxi. Miles said he'd drive but then he thought he was over the limit. Bronagh offered to take Duncan down in her car. Jane decided she wanted to go but Duncan knew the Cardiff Royal Infirmary wasn't very pleasant on a Saturday night once the pubs had closed, and so Jane agreed to stay with Ellen.

It was a strange end to a dinner party. They could not disguise the fact that Alice was ill, nor the fact that Bronagh and Duncan were on their way to hospital with her. Jane explained to Kit and David as best she could. Everyone seemed to sober up appropriately, and waited until Bronagh had driven off with Duncan and Alice before realising the time and setting off home.

Jane cleared away a bit and waited for Duncan to ring on the mobile that Miles had very generously lent him.

Miles and Kit and David ordered a taxi which was supposed to drop Kit off first and then take Miles down to his hotel and David out to the coast, but things were so confused in the back of the cramped little cab that they ended up in the city centre before anyone knew what was happening, and all went in for a drink from Miles' minibar.

Bronagh stayed with Duncan and Alice until they were seen by a nurse and young doctor in theatre greens. Bron still didn't talk much, but now Duncan didn't want her to.

Jane went to bed at two o'clock, after Duncan had rung to say that Alice's temperature was down but that they were keeping her in and had given him a chair to sleep on. By this time Jane had cleared, stacked and washed everything. There was no trace of there ever having been a dinner party at Katrin Street.

Kit got a taxi from hotel reception at four o'clock in the morning, because David was asleep on the floor and Miles, after four brandies, just had to hit the sack. Gallantly he'd asked Kit if she'd like to share his bed and Kit told him she had given all that up years ago.

Sunday morning began early for Duncan when the battery on Miles' phone started to beep to indicate that it was giving up the ghost. Duncan checked Alice who seemed fine. Then he checked himself and realised he had never felt so stiff or generally dreadful.

Jane set off in the car at half-past nine with Ellen, who

had slept through all the drama and was looking forward to seeing inside a hospital. For this reason she missed Miles arriving by taxi to collect his car and Barry Britto arriving with a case of wine from Kit. She also missed Bronagh telephoning to ask Jane if she knew where David was. Duncan arrived home with Ellen and a cricked neck to find telephone messages from Kit saying, 'Wonderful evening, hope Alice is OK. Barry's left the wine next door,' from Miles saying, 'Wonderful evening, hope Alice is OK. Left a bunch of roses next door,' and Bronagh saying, 'Miles has brought David back, hope Alice is OK. Oh and thanks for all the food.'

Bronagh didn't say it had been a wonderful evening, and Duncan on the whole tended to agree with her.

7

An Available Man

'Of course, we think the world of him,' said Laura, putting down the teacup.

Jane Lewis felt that it was just her luck, after a busy day at the office, to find that Duncan was not back with Alice, Ellen wasn't home but at Holly's, and Laura had called round to tell her how wonderful Duncan was.

It was not as if Jane hadn't spent most of Sunday sitting with Alice while Duncan stayed home applying Deep Heat cream to his cricked neck. But on Monday morning Jane *had* to be in work. So after much careful negotiation and realignment of Laura's extensive timetables, Duncan dropped Ellen off in Meirion Street at eight-forty so she could be taken in Laura's convoy to school, and then relieved Jane at the Infirmary. Duncan brought with him Jane's work clothes and she'd changed, hot and hospital sticky, in the ladies' lavatory before taking the car into Follets.

Laura had risen to the challenge of helping out the Lewises with great application and deliberation, which made it seem as if she were moving mountains to accommodate one extra person on the walk into school. But she wasn't able to collect Ellen because of Tristram's outpatients, Mordred's recalcitrant genitalia and Arthur's remedials, not to mention a prescription she had to pick up for Gerald. So Holly had been delegated the job, and Ellen and Buddug had disappeared upstairs in Pontcanna Terrace, locked the bedroom door and refused to let Siôn in.

Jane was grateful to Holly and Laura, but what she didn't welcome was Laura calling by as soon as she got back from the office to hand over the various objects Ellen had managed to leave behind during her five-minute sojourn that morning in Meirion Street.

It transpired over tea that, despite Laura's relentless schedules, she always gave herself half an hour off when Gerald came home at six, and she had used this time to walk round to Katrin Street with Ellen's abandoned gym kit, swimming kit and yoghurt pots.

As she poured out a second cup, Jane wondered why Laura couldn't have done something really useful like call in at Pontcanna Street *en route* and actually bring Ellen back with her yoghurt pots, but she was at pains not to display anything but gratitude. Even when Laura started telling her how marvellous it was that Duncan had spent all day in hospital, Jane still smiled on.

'He's such a good father,' Laura continued. 'My boys find him great fun – although, of course, Gerald is marvellous for his age.' A small sigh passed her lips as she lifted the cup. Jane smiled in as enigmatic and noncommittal a manner as she could muster. She was remembering their conversation the night that she and Laura made up the spare bed together. Whatever else Laura saw in Duncan, his relative youth was a clear and signal bonus. Poor old thing, Jane thought. Laura was only a year or so older than her and yet to Jane she sometimes seemed a different generation.

Laura rallied. 'And how is Alice?' she asked.

Alice was fine as it happened. Her temperature had gone down rapidly on Saturday night and by Sunday morning, when Jane had taken over from Duncan, she was wandering round the ward talking to the other patients. Duncan, on the other hand, was making a lot of fuss about not having slept at all in the large padded bedside chair the nurses had provided for him. Jane and Ellen had found him finishing off Alice's breakfast and being attended to by a nurse who said that she had only brought him a cup of tea, and that she wasn't really supposed to be looking after parents at all, but that she had done what she could about his poor neck.

Jane had stayed with Alice all Sunday. Tests were carried out sporadically that seemed to tell the serious young doctors who came round very little indeed, and Jane had begun to campaign about the possibility of being discharged. Alice's rash didn't get any worse, but late on Sunday afternoon her temperature had begun to go up again.

'Mummy, I don't feel well,' she'd said, and clambered up on to Jane's lap. They gave her some more medicine for the temperature and put her back into bed. Jane had rung Duncan. It was clear Alice would not be coming home on Sunday.

But by first thing Monday morning Alice was fine again and it was Jane's turn to have spent a dreadful night on the hospital comfy chair. Unfortunately, on this particular morning Alice had eaten all her breakfast and the nursing staff were very busy because Mr Gee was coming round. The imminent arrival of a consultant meant that no one was the slightest bit interested in the state of Jane's neck muscles, back muscles, leg muscles or indeed her desperate need for a cup of tea. So Jane was not at all impressed when at nine o'clock Duncan had arrived with a tube of Deep Heat cream for her.

'Haven't you got anything I can eat?' she'd asked. Duncan apologised but insisted the cream worked wonders.

'I can't go into the office smelling of that stuff,' Jane had told him, gathering up her work clothes.

'I'm smelling of it,' Duncan replied.

'Yes, but you're not sitting in meetings all day! *You* may be happy to waft around with the fragrance of camel's armpit, Dunc, but it won't go down too well at Follets!'

While Jane had passed Monday feeling as though she'd spent a night under the railway arches, Duncan had read to Alice. And Alice had read to Duncan. And then Duncan had finished his book about the man who gave it all up, while Alice threw her weight around in the play-house that had been provided for children on the mend. The nice nurse who had done something with his neck on Sunday morning recognised him and brought another cup of tea.

'You like it black, don't you?' she'd asked.

'Thank you,' said Duncan, looking up from his book with a smile.

Mr Gee, when he'd finally arrived, was a tall dark man from some distant part of the Mediterranean. He'd seemed surprised at Alice's symptoms and completely incapable of hearing anything Duncan said to him. Mr Gee agreed with the serious young men and women who accompanied him that as long as Alice's rash and high temperature didn't recur she should be allowed home that evening.

'And what about school?' Duncan had asked. Nice as it had been to spend a day nursing Alice, Duncan didn't want a week of it.

'No school this week,' said Mr Gee as if he had read Duncan's mind.

'Yeah! Lush!' cried Alice.

Jane actually arrived to pick them up at six-thirty that evening. Alice wore her dressing gown home as the emblem of convalescence, and she and Ellen sat in the back of the car talking over each other excitedly while Duncan and Jane updated each other in the front.

'They want me to go to Swansea on Thursday,' Jane told Duncan.

'Well it won't make a lot of difference,' said Duncan. 'How long will you be away?'

'We finish last thing Saturday unless there's a breakfast,' she replied.

'Well . . . don't worry,' Duncan reassured her, 'I think I'm going to be at home looking after Alice most of the time, in any case.'

'What if you get an interview or something?' Jane asked.

Duncan thought it unlikely. All he'd done so far was to put in calls to contacts at two big London firms who might possibly give him some pointers. 'I suppose I could always ask Laura or Holly to help out,' he said.

'You ought to have their children back, you know,' Jane told him. 'We ought to offer to reciprocate. Give Laura an afternoon off.'

'Not the Davis boys!' Alice shouted from the back.

'I thought you liked them,' Duncan said over his shoulder. Alice insisted the Davis boys were wet.

'You enjoyed playing with their train set,' Duncan reminded her.

'Only once,' said Alice, which was of course true for her. Duncan wondered whether Ellen had told her about their Sunday afternoon visit. He couldn't see her face in the mirror. Did Ellen have secrets from Alice? And, if so, why that one?

Duncan was about to say something innocent like, 'Ellen's played with it more than once,' something that might flush the whole silly business out into the open, when Jane said, 'Miles really enjoyed Saturday.'

'Really?'

'Yes, it seems they all went on to his hotel afterwards. He made it sound so funny I felt rather left out.' Jane tried to think of the details of Miles' account but there was nothing quotably funny. It had just seemed hilarious when he told her.

'Miles was in the office today?' Duncan asked.

'Yes,' said Jane.

'Is he in your office every day?'

'No,' said Jane.

'It's just that I'm beginning to wonder why you're all going off to Swansea to see him on Thursday when he seems to live in Follets.'

'He's been in three times,' Jane informed him. 'Since I've been there. That's not unusual for a major client.' She made her reply sound completely neutral but inside she was amused. Duncan had actually sounded as if he might be jealous. Jane Lewis had had admirers in the past, but Duncan always manifested indifference. Once, when she'd tackled him on the subject, he had claimed gallantly that he assumed all men fancied her and only took exception to those who seemed not to, but that had sounded too glib. Perhaps, now that Duncan had shared his dining table with Miles, it wasn't so easy to be detached.

When they got home the girls took care of each other while Jane started the grown-ups' supper. Duncan asked if he could have a bath and Jane even offered to bring him a glass of wine while he soaked away the aches and pains of hospital chairs, but Alice and Ellen commandeered the bath and declared they were going to bed early that night, without even watching telly. It seemed like a gift.

'We could both have a bath later . . .' Duncan suggested with his arms around Jane in the empty kitchen.

'I'm too smelly,' said Jane as she cooked.

'That's why people have baths,' Duncan reminded her. 'To make themselves less smelly. I could make you less smelly and you could make me less smelly, and then we could dry each other, and who knows what might happen . . .'

Jane pushed him away but she pushed him away affectionately. 'I've got supper to do and two files to look at. Don't bank on it,' she warned him.

'If I banked on it I'd be in debt by now,' Duncan pointed out.

Jane felt reproached. 'Look, I don't want to go out to work. I don't want to be sitting up till eleven o'clock reading up on all that stuff!'

'I'm not reproaching you,' said Duncan, who could always tell when Jane thought he was reproaching her.

'You *are* reproaching me,' said Jane. 'I can recognise your reproaches a mile off. They are not subtle.'

'All I'm asking,' Duncan began, 'is that, with you disappearing off to Swansea with Miles and David and Tony on Thursday, that you don't forget . . . I asked first.'

Jane swung at him with a ladle. Duncan retreated across the kitchen laughing and offering to concede that he *had* been reproaching, honestly. Jane was half laughing too, but she was also angry and swinging a mean-looking kitchen instrument. It was one of those daft, dangerous moments that had in the past turned their grappling into lust, but at that moment the twins in matching dressing gowns arrived demanding their good-night drinks.

In Meirion Street, Gawain was getting Mordred into his pyjamas while Gerald bathed Tristram and Arthur. Gawain would have his last. He and Tristram no longer shared a bath because too often it degenerated into their favourite game of lunging at each other's genitals, with water flying everywhere. Laura was downstairs filling in her Boys' Diary which was a large book she had kept for the last eleven years, detailing on a day-by-day basis what developmental stage each son had got to. Gawain at eleven was beginning to find the Boys' Diary quite embarrassing and had recently asked if his details could be censored.

'I'm nearly a teenager,' he'd protested.

Seeing her son's genuine embarrassment, Laura had agreed that henceforth Gawain's entries could be written in German so that Tristram, Arthur and Mawmaw wouldn't be able to read what was being committed to paper. She had even brought down a German dictionary from Gerald's office with the intention of keeping it next to the Boys' Diary. This evening however she had been unable to find the German for diarrhoea, the reason being that she didn't know the correct English spelling in the first place.

'Gerald,' Laura called up the stairs in her clear schoolgirl's voice. *'Wie sagt man* DIARRHOEA *auf Deutsch?'*

Gawain glared at his mother from Mordred's bedroom.

'Durchfall, oder Scheisserei,' Gerald shouted back to Gawain's mounting embarrassment. It sounded worse in German.

'Vielen Dank!' called Laura.

Sometimes Gawain hated his parents.

In Pontcanna Terrace Gwyn had just got back from rehearsal. He'd gone straight into the BBC studios from Oxford because the National Orchestra were doing some eight-horn Strauss poem and needed a bumper. He was actually looking forward to seeing his wife and family after three days.

Once inside No. 27, Gwyn caught sight of his recalcitrant son lurking in the telly room.

'Hello Siôn, *sch'mae?*' he asked with gusto. 'What you doing, boy?'

'Nothing,' said Siôn from the pile of Lego below. Ever since Mr Harper had shown Gwyn the drawings he had confiscated in class, Siôn had been wary of spending too much time in his father's company, in case he found he was in trouble again.

'God but it's nice to see you again!' thought Gwyn, but, 'Where's Holly?' is what he said.

'Upstairs lying down.'

'Right!' said Gwyn, bounding up the stairs.

There was a scream as Buddug disappeared back into the bathroom and locked the door.

Gwyn halted on the landing, momentarily thrown. 'Oh, bathnight, is it?' he said to the door.

'Go away!' shouted Buddug.

Gwyn reorientated himself and made his way down the landing to where Holly was lying down in the darkened front bedroom. 'God, there's a sight for sore eyes!' he exclaimed as he caught sight of the reclining form of his wife.

Holly got up to kiss him without a word. Gwyn checked that the bedroom door had swung to behind him and tried to convert the kiss into a prelude to something more amorous. Holly yielded. Gwyn loved the way that Holly yielded.

'I've missed you,' he said, coming up for air, 'every inch of you.'

'Soup's on,' said Holly quietly. 'I left the soup on downstairs.'

'Oh,' said Gwyn, stalling in the embrace. 'Later then?'

'Later,' Holly said, nodding.

It was almost a ritual with them but Gwyn knew that Holly never let him down. Unless it was the wrong time of the month, of course, and that was something she could usually indicate without too much embarrassment on his part. But 'Later' was a sure sign everything was going to be OK.

'Look forward to it,' he said, taking the opportunity to fondle his wife's breasts before releasing her.

'Would you get Siôn up for a bath?' Holly asked, oblivious to the fact she was being aroused by her husband.

*   *   *

'Oh, Saturday's the NCT Meal Evening,' Jane said, looking up from one of her files. She had completely forgotten their social commitments of late. 'What'll you do if I'm not back in time? Will you go on your own?'

'Are you planning not to be back?' Duncan asked from where he was washing those things that wouldn't stack in the dishwasher.

'No,' she said, 'but if I'm not, will you go? Because if you won't go on your own we ought to tell whoever's sitting that it's not definite.'

'Is it *definitely* not definite then, this breakfast thing?' Duncan asked.

'I don't know,' said Jane, getting irritated with him. 'Well,' he replied, closing the washer door with aplomb, 'I will probably go but that's only a probable probable, not a definite probable.'

Jane put down her pen. 'Why are you trying to sound clever?' she asked.

'I didn't realise I was trying,' Duncan countered.

'Well you're certainly not succeeding,' she said. They'd been on like this all evening. Little barbed comments, as if each was suddenly finding the other very annoying but neither was going to admit it.

To be fair to Jane, most of the antagonism was being generated by Duncan. She was merely reacting and adding to it. But to be fair to Duncan he came clean at this point.

'I'm sorry. I'm just feeling very frustrated at the moment, emotionally, professionally and – if I may mention it – sexually.'

Jane was surprised. 'Well I know I've been preoccupied with work,' she said. 'But it's not as if we haven't—'

'Four weeks,' Duncan replied. 'Unless you count the time we gave up.'

'Oh,' said Jane. It did seem a long time if you were

counting. And Duncan obviously was. 'Well, you're not going the right way about it, are you?' she pointed out.

'I tried seducing you earlier.'

'I was cooking!' she complained.

'And now you're working,' said Duncan.

'You used to work late for Tossers,' she reminded him.

'Yes, but I never denied you my body,' he joked. 'Night or day.'

'You were never a mother,' Jane replied. 'It's not so easy when you're a mother. Oh for goodness sake!' she laughed. 'Come here.' She pushed back the two files in front of her and held out her arms.

'Mum, can we have another drink?' asked a voice. It was Ellen.

Laura and Gerald were reading in bed, Gerald sporting his dressing gown over the paisley pyjamas, Laura her kimono over a silk nightdress. Silk was Laura's one luxury. Gerald had bought her a lot of silk on their honeymoon twenty years ago in Paris and he never got round to stopping when the sons came along.

To say that they were reading wasn't quite accurate. Gerald Davis was trying to make head or tail of some new approach to student assessment that seemed to be obsessed with dividing *modules* by *teaching units*, and Laura had her glasses on as she went methodically through her diary. Laura's own diary, unlike her Boys' Diary, was page after page of jobs to be done followed by flocks of ticks to indicate jobs accomplished. It was also a relentless series of accounts and calculations. Page after page, day after day of Laura's attempts to reconcile an academic's salary, the needs of four growing boys, repairs to the house, provision for private education and the demands of Gerald's pension plan. Expenditure was continually being pushed into next month as the unexpected cropped up.

Leafing through to Saturday, she noticed that the NCT Meal Evening was coming up. Laura always made a note of such things, and of church events, appeals for Africa and the like, even though the likelihood of she and Gerald turning up was remote.

'Oh,' she said 'The Meal Evening's on Saturday.'

'Oh,' said Gerald, very happy to be distracted for a moment. Gerald rather liked those Meal Evenings he had been to. A communal supper hosted by so many attractive women in their late thirties and early forties rather suited Gerald Davis.

'Oh . . . we don't want to stir ourselves out on a Saturday night do we?' Laura asked, although it was hardly a question when put like that. 'There'd be the baby-sitter to find. And the food to make. The theme is usually so exotic these days. And of course Mawmaw's still quite young to be left.'

'We'll stay in,' said Gerald, squeezing her knee through the duvet.

Holly was also thinking about the Meal Evening. It was now 'Later' in the Williams' household, and Gwyn had been enjoying himself noisily. Suddenly it was all over. Orgasm in men often reminded Holly of what happened to Siôn's electric toys if you took the batteries out. One moment they were clanging away merrily and the next minute they'd gone completely lifeless.

Gwyn crashed down with an enormous exhalation of breath. Not for nothing was he Welsh National Opera first horn. *'Iesu Mawr,'* he whispered in satisfied blasphemy.

Holly had felt very fond of Gwyn at that moment, but she was also suddenly aware that she couldn't remember whether the theme of Saturday's meal evening was American or South American. There was a very big difference. Nachos and tortillas and whatsits would be very nice, but what would you take if the theme was North American? Hamburgers? Chocolate fudge cake? Maple syrup? Or was maple syrup Canadian? She couldn't remember. Gwyn detatched himself from her with a happy groan. Yes, the Canadian flag had a maple thingy on it, but was maple *syrup* a Canadian or American delicacy? Or perhaps it was both? What other food did Canadians eat?

'What you thinking?' Gwyn asked softly. He had lifted his head from the pillow and was staring at Holly in an amused, sleepy, affectionate way.

'Nothing,' said Holly, putting her arm round him and stroking his hair.

'You and your nothings,' said Gwyn.

Holly stroked his hair.

'That . . . that was all right for you was it?' Gwyn asked with a yawn.

'Mm,' said Holly. She was drifting off now, she knew it, drifting off to that other place. She could hear the wind buffeting the slates on their roof and she was drifting off with the wind. Gwyn started talking, she could hear his voice in the wind, she could recognise the way his voice rose and fell, she could recognise the sound of his questions. And she knew that when she heard that particularly inquisitive rise in his voice all she had to do was make a little noise in her throat.

'Mm.' said Holly.

'You *liked* that?' asked Gwyn, feeling rather pleased with himself. He had worried that he might have been a bit, well, over-intimate. You could never tell, the way Holly kept her eyes closed. 'You did like that?'.

'Mm . . .'

'You're a dark horse, Mrs Williams,' Gwyn told her, kissing her ear. He almost wished that he could start all over again. He most certainly would have, right then and there – but sleep was beginning to overcome him.

'Waffles,' thought Holly. 'Waffles in maple syrup.'

Kit Sinclair hadn't gone out that night. When Barry got home· at seven-thirty the boys were already bathed and waiting in neatly pressed karate-style pyjamas to go through their school work and tell Dad about their day. Normally this was the time when Kit would retire with a cigarette and large gin and tonic to her bathroom. Not even Barry was allowed in Kit's bathroom. It was probably the most expensively decorated room in the house. Anyone who was ever privileged to peep inside was bound to wonder how Barry Britto had afforded it, and Kit would always explain that she cooked the figures so Barry would never know how much it finally cost.

'This is Barry's punishment for bringing me down here. It's also my consolation, my refuge, my Bat Cave where I can change into my secret identity,' Kit would declaim.

But tonight Kit did not retire with her Biggy and her Ciggy. She sat on one of the large white sofas, drink in hand, and watched Barry be the perfect father with his sons. Then she watched as the Bastard took them up to bed, and poured herself another drink.

Gabriele looked in. 'Mrs Kit, are you not going out? I have made the supper for Barry, do you want me to make for you?'

Kit smiled at her, not her puckish grin but her slow, polite, feline smile. 'No thank you, Sweetie.'

She puffed on her cigarette like a cat waiting for its prey.

When Barry came back Kit was listening to the wind bowling down Bastard-Bond-Kyle Avenue, and thinking of pouring herself a third drink.

'Not going out?' Barry asked.

'Can't see the point,' said Kit.

'There isn't one,' said Barry. 'Are you going to sit with me while I eat?'

'High point of my day.' she said, getting up. 'Are you working tonight?'

'I work every night.' Barry said as they went into the kitchen. Kit slumped against the door frame.

'Oh Bazza, please, I don't want to go and get plastered with a load of old tarts,' she moaned. 'I'm fed up of women. The stinky smell of women. The stinky silly tarts.'

'Why don't you do some work then?' Barry suggested.

'I've done some work. I've finished my work. I've been prostituting myself all afternoon, Bazzie. I have been flat on my back. I've even posted it off. Now I want to do something different. And there's nothing to do in this stinky little shithouse of a city!'

Barry knew that whatever he suggested now Kit wouldn't like it. Once or twice she'd been out clubbing with Gabriele but that had only made her feel old. She'd tried concerts and opera and theatre but Kit wasn't good in an audience: she needed the attention of an audience directed towards her. That was why she usually spent her evenings in Le Monde or Portos mingling with women journalists from the South Wales Echo and Western Mail. There were always one or two of those who would get drunk with Kit and listen to her stories. Barry had tried to get Kit involved with the hospital world but she was very reluctant to because she knew that if the University authorities saw too much of her it could cause problems for him at work.

'Can I build a conservatory?' Kit asked suddenly.

'Can I afford for you to build a conservatory?' Barry asked.

'Of course not,' said Kit. 'But I've already ruined you doing this place up. So what's the difference?'

Barry could see that Kit was warming to something – and Kit warming to an enthusiasm, though exhausting and often expensive, could only be for the good. She went off to get some paper and pens from her office under the stairs while Barry seated himself at the table.

'That poncy little architect didn't think I'd get planning permission!' she shouted from down the hall. 'But I'll show him.'

Kit put her head round the kitchen door. 'Bazza, if I get my ponce to do the application, will you bribe some people so I can build it, please?'

Barry laughed.

'Please Barry, please. This is important to me. I'll do all sorts of things for you in return, honest I will, you dirty bugger.'

Barry told her he'd do what he could but it might mean going to dreadful parties and having Wankers, Dossers and Arseholes to dinner.

'You do the bribes and leave the Wankers to me,' said Kit. 'That's what I'm good at.'

Once begun, everybody's week settled down into the pattern of every other week during term-time. Laura walked to and from school twice a day and cycled there and back for Mordred's lunch. Gabriele drove the Britto boys in and out while their mother drew up plans and found out about conservation area regulations. The University of Wales continued to be grateful to Barry and beastly to Gerald.

As Gwyn was back for a few days, the Williamses divided up ferrying Buddug and Siôn between them, but only ever at the last disorganised moment. Over in Katrin Street, Jane started dropping Ellen into school on her way to work because Duncan wasn't supposed to take Alice out, despite the fact that Alice was clearly in the best of health.

Duncan and Laura discussed what was the best thing to do about collecting Ellen from school, and Laura worked out a system whereby Holly would have her on Tuesday, Wednesday and Thursday, and Laura would see what she could do about Friday. Jane would then collect Ellen from Holly's (or possibly Laura's) on her way back from work.

On Wednesday, however, Jane discovered that she had to stay late at work so she would not be able to collect Ellen at a reasonable time. Rather than put Holly to the trouble of bringing Ellen round with Buddug and Siôn in tow, Duncan took the dangerous step of becoming even more beholden to the cleaning lady.

'Would you mind staying on with Alice while I collect Ellen from Pontcanna Terrace, Mrs R.?' he asked.

'Sometimes I wonder what you'd do without me,' said Louisa R. reproachfully from down on the kitchen floor, which was her way of agreeing.

Holly's front door had a very convincing *trompe-l'oeil* reclining cat that she'd painted on it, albeit a rather football-scuffed *trompe*. The door itself was ajar when Duncan arrived. Buddug and Ellen were nowhere to be seen, and Siôn was sitting preoccupied with a pile of Lego in the telly room.

'Holly's out the back,' he said and left it very much at that.

Duncan went through to the breakfast room and kitchen, failed to find Holly, then retraced his steps to try the door into what must once have been the dining room. The room was dark, but Duncan immediately recognised Holly on a chaise longue surrounded by piles of music and brass instruments.

'Oh, hello Duncan,' she said, getting up and making towards where he stood in the doorway. She laid a hand on his arm and kissed him on the cheek.

'Would you like a drink?' she asked, and led them through to the breakfast room.

Duncan was surprised and pleased by that kiss. Of course

he remembered that Holly kissed everyone, but it was still very enjoyable to share that moment of intimacy. Again the question immediately nagged at him. Did he find Holly attractive, and if he did was he going to do anything about it? The way things were going between him and Jane and Jane's work, Duncan was beginning to worry that he'd soon be finding Mrs R. attractive.

'You like whisky, don't you?' Holly said, pouring Duncan a glass.

'Well,' said Duncan, but seeing that Holly was pouring herself one it seemed ungallant to decline.

'The girls are upstairs I think,' said Holly, her voice trailing away. 'Buddug's got some friend to play. She and Ellen seem to be getting on really well. I'm not certain where Buddug went. She may be playing with Siôn.'

'No, Siôn's in your front room,' said Duncan, who was craning in closer to try and catch what Holly was saying.

'Oh well . . .' said Holly. She felt that as long as none of them was actually complaining to her things were probably going well enough.

'How's Gwyn?' Duncan asked. They were standing up in the breakfast room, glasses in hand, like the only two people at a cocktail party.

'Gone to Aberystwyth – or Llandudno, or somewhere up there,' said Holly. 'Three performances. Won't be back till Sunday. Isn't it a bummer?'

Duncan wasn't quite sure what Holly meant. Was North Wales so awful? Wasn't Gwyn up to three concerts these days? Or did Holly miss her husband that badly?

'I'll miss the meal evening,' she added, sweeping some stray strands of hair out of her mouth as she explained the full nature of the bummer. Holly liked meal evenings. She often got to talk to Jane and to Siân Roberts at the meal evening.

'Can't you go on your own?' Duncan asked. People did sometimes.

'Oh, I don't know,' said Holly, 'It'll upset the seating plan or something.'

'This one's a buffet,' Duncan lied, or rather guessed. He was quite surprised at his behaviour, but having to stand so close to Holly in order to hear what she was saying did mean that he was smelling the soap on her neck again, and feeling the folds of whatever loose thing it was she was wearing flap against him.

'Oh, I don't know . . .' said Holly again. 'I usually go with Gwyn even if I never see him for the rest of the evening. Pathetic isn't it?'

'You're not pathetic,' said Duncan, chancing a personal remark.

Holly looked up at him and gave him a brief snapshot of a smile, a smile that wasn't in the eyes. Duncan didn't know whether she was thanking him politely or telling him tactfully to keep his distance. 'Yes I am. Really,' said Holly. 'I want to see people but I don't want to make the effort. No, I *want* to make the effort but it seems hard. It is hard making the effort, isn't it?'

With Jane, Duncan might have pointed out the semi-tautological nature of such a statement, but the agenda here was different. 'It can't be easy with Gwyn . . .' he began to say. What he actually wanted to say was that it couldn't be easy for her to be sociable on her own because Gwyn was so often away on these trips, but the effect of the alcohol suddenly registered in his brain and caused it to miss a beat. In that microsecond of hesitation, no longer than a hiccough, Duncan sounded as if he had said his entire piece, and Holly responded, misinterpreting what he had said completely.

'Yes,' she said, gazing at the skirting board. 'People don't understand, but he just drains me when he's here.'

She turned to look Duncan in the eyes. 'How did you notice?'

Before he could answer Holly was off. She had found her voice by finally finding someone to talk to who understood things that had been boiling away inside her for months, years probably. Everything else she told Duncan was elliptical: that she needed space, she needed to fly, that she was fire and Gwyn was water, that she was paper, he was scissors. Never once did she malign Gwyn or suggest that she didn't love him. Gwyn was Gwyn, and Holly wasn't. 'Sometimes I just need to . . . to fly away on the wind,' she concluded.

Laura Davis had told Holly that Duncan understood women, but she had never dreamt that he might be the one she could tell these thoughts to. 'And you could see all that?' she asked softly. 'I haven't told anyone, but you could see that?'

'Well,' said Duncan, 'yes. I suppose so.'

Holly leant her head against Duncan's shoulder. It was the gesture of one who is resigned to the hopelessness of it all.

Duncan wanted to put his arm round Holly. He genuinely felt sorry for her, but he was also aware that he would never get another chance like this to be wonderful and comforting. Unfortunately, Holly was resting against the shoulder of the arm that he would have lifted to embrace her, and using his other arm would have meant transferring her from one side to the other while simultaneously transferring the whisky glass in the opposite direction. 'Look,' he said, moving his face towards the mass of ringleted hair currently camped on his shoulder. 'Look, I'm going to the meal evening on my own on Saturday. Jane's away. Why don't you come with me?'

Holly stayed on Duncan's shoulder a while longer. He was beginning to think that she hadn't heard him but then she lifted her head, looked up at his face and gave that wry smile again, the smile that wasn't in her eyes. This time Duncan felt sure she had rumbled him.

'Oh Duncan,' she said, 'you are a *good* man.'

Jane Lewis was coming out of the first-floor lavatory at Follets when Mair Lloyd stopped her.

'Oh Jane,' she said breathlessly. 'We've been looking for you *everywhere*.'

'I was in the loo,' said Jane, wondering what was going on.

'David said he didn't know *where* you were.' Mair was enjoying her role as the bearer of dread tidings.

'Well I don't tell David every time I go to the loo,' Jane replied flatly. She was growing used to Mair's melodramatics, which seemed designed to give the impression that she understood the full implications of company matters which Jane, as a temporary employee, would never comprehend.

'What's the matter?'

'There's a Mrs Britto in Reception. She needs to speak to you on a personal matter,' said Mair emphatically.

Jane refused to look ruffled or even interested. She could tell that Mair hoped Mrs Britto was either a plain-clothes policewoman, come to arrest Jane for parking in the junior partner's designated parking space, or better still the mother of Duncan's five illegitimate children come to publicly announce their affair and destroy Jane's marriage.

But of course Mrs Britto was Kit Sinclair, dressed very soberly, as a sober citizen might for visiting one's solicitor, except for the sunglasses, which gave the impression that Kit normally visited her solicitor in Los Angeles.

Jane invited Kit up to her office and Kit apologised for calling in on her at work but she was passing (which wasn't true – Gabriele had driven her down specially). Jane was happy to give Kit ten minutes but thought it only fair to tell her that was all she'd got.

'No problem,' said Kit, taking off her glasses decisively. 'I don't know if your fella's told you, but I want to build a conservatory. Not just a load of UPVC but a fucking big conservatory. Oh—'

'It's all right,' said Jane, laughing at the expression on Kit's face. 'People do use that word round here.'

Kit had just been getting into her stride. She had worked on the idea for two days now and was convinced it was revolutionary. Swearing in Jane's office had not been part of her game plan, so she was briefly rattled and had lost her place.

'I think Duncan has mentioned your conservatory,' Jane prompted, taking on the mantle of agent and wondering what all this was leading up to.

'Well, the fact of the matter is I want to do something that hasn't been done before, and your fella and mine reckon we'd have to square it with the Taffia and, well, I've been using Barry's influence this morning and got some tickets for a corporate hospitality bash at the International, week after next. You know the kind of do – pre-match binge so the rugger buggers can sew up who gets what contracts for the next year or so.'

Jane did know. She retained an interest in the legend of such events. Never having beeen important enough to be invited along, she could well be tempted if Kit was offering.

'So what I've come to ask,' said Kit, 'is if you'd mind me taking your bloke along. You see, I've got two tickets. That's all even Barry can wangle.'

So that was it. Jane wasn't being consulted as Duncan's agent at all. She was being consulted as his wife. Kit Sinclair was asking if Duncan could come out to play.

'Of course he must go,' said Jane.

'I didn't want to ring you at home in case it put you on the spot,' Kit explained.

Jane told her it was fine, absolutely fine. All Kit had to worry about was persuading Duncan to go.

'Yeah, he likes to make out he's above all that,' said Kit with a grin as she got up to go.

On the way back up the clanking metal stairs from Reception, Jane saw David talking to Big Fat Tony on the gantry. Both of them were watching the disappearing figure of Kit. Jane assumed that David was telling Tony all about meeting Kit at her dinner party.

'Hi boys,' she called with a knowing wave. The sound of her voice echoed hugely round the atrium and the poor receptionist jumped.

Later that day, just before their planning meeting, Tony tiptoed into Jane's office for one of his gossips.

'Well Mrs Lewis,' he said. 'I hear you've been seeing Miles Mihash on social territory?'

'With David, David's wife, my husband and the woman you two were ogling on the stairs, yes,' said Jane. She knew that Tony's interest was vicarious. He never visited people at their homes but he liked to hear all about it.

'And you didn't tell me,' Tony said, doing his disappointed little boy face.

'I would have invited you to join us if I'd've thought you'd come,' Jane teased him.

'Oh no,' said Tony. 'No thank you. But Miles didn't tell me either. Is there something going on between you two?'

'No.'

'Yet isn't it interesting that neither of you told me? I shall have to keep an eye on you two in Swansea.'

You old letch, thought Jane.

'And how is poor Duncan?' Tony asked. 'How is he coping?'

*　　*　　*

When Jane got home that evening Ellen was very full of this brilliant new friend she'd made over at Buddug's, and could she invite her round to meet Alice on Friday?

'Ask your Dad,' said Jane. 'I'm going to be away till Saturday.'

Duncan looked up from where he was trimming the carbonised crust off a semi-successful loaf of bread. 'Oh I thought you were staying over Saturday night. For a breakfast meeting.'

'We've just been going through everything and it's quite likely we'll finish about four on Saturday.'

'Oh,' said Duncan.

Jane asked if there was a problem. Duncan looked rather confused for a moment and then explained that actually he'd said he'd go to the meal evening with Holly.

Jane looked surprised.

'You see she was keen to go, and sad she couldn't, and I said that as you were in Swansea . . .' He let Jane deduce the rest.

This time it was her turn to say, 'Oh.' She had slightly expected Duncan to be pleased by the news of her early return. 'Oh, well, look, I'll probably be tired by Saturday evening anyway,' she said. 'You can always go with Holly and I'll baby-sit here.'

Ellen pointed out you can't baby-sit your own child, and Alice added, while they were on the subject, that she objected to being called a baby.

'But . . . what if I'm back late?' Duncan asked out of the blue.

'You've got a key, for heaven's sake!' Jane reminded him. Duncan did have the daftest notions.

Duncan dropped the subject, agreeing that he was indeed quite, quite daft sometimes. Then Jane remembered Kit's visit and told him the full story.

'She wants you to meet some bigshots at a pre-match party. I said I was happy for you to go.'

'Oh God!' moaned Duncan, but Jane noticed he didn't say he wouldn't.

Over supper, Jane took a second look at her husband. 'What is it about you, Duncan?' she asked. 'Holly and Kit want you to take them to parties, Laura borrows your LPs—'

'No she doesn't', Duncan interjected.

'What do all these women see in you?' Jane asked.

Duncan thought for a moment. There wasn't a straight answer to that question. There were probably a series of answers, to do with Laura being, probably, a bit odd, Kit wanting to pose as a radical architectural patron, and Holly benevolently misinterpreting Duncan's attempt at seduction. But the answer Jane wanted, and the answer Duncan wanted to give, was a light-hearted one.

'I don't know' he said, 'I suppose it's just that I'm available.'

Jane looked at him with what might be taken for a very perceptive gaze. 'Only within certain parameters, buster,' she reminded him.

That night they made love, Jane clambering on top of Duncan in a very determined way. It was all very active and, at least in anticipation, very welcome for Duncan. Sex had really become something of a preoccupation for him since Jane went back to work and had other things to preoccupy her. So it was good to be doing it again. But at the same time there was an ineptness about their lovemaking. From Duncan's point of view the best sex they had was always when he felt that he fancied her beforehand or that he loved her very much beforehand. This was just two people, not finding their relationship easy, bouncing around and having sex.

But for Jane, their coupling was a welcome relief from the two overwhelming pressures currently upon her. She was very anxious that she would do her new job well. Even though it was not of her choosing, Jane was determined that this spell of work would be a success. And, even more importantly, she was very anxious that her children should not suffer. Duncan's needs had to come a poor third. In fact, Duncan's needs really did not figure in Jane's equations at the moment. Except on evenings like tonight when she was stirred by the idea of sex. Yes, there was a need in her and that need could give rise to a sense of well-being, a sense of fun and togetherness that bonded them together. At least we're back on this particular track, thought Jane.

Afterwards, she gathered up her nightclothes and went to the bathroom. 'I love you,' she said, kissing him quickly on the cheek.

Duncan lay back on the pillow and realised he was thinking of Holly. He could see her head resting against his shoulder. It was an image that wouldn't leave his mind.

'Oh no,' he thought. 'Don't let me fall in love with Holly Williams.'

8

Hidden Agendas

One of the reasons why Duncan didn't want to fall in love with Holly Williams was that it really did not seem fair on Jane. After all, it was Jane who was going out to work to support the family, and the generally understood quid pro quo was that, while she was away, Duncan would do some housework, look after the children and not get entangled with the baby-sitter.

But there were other reasons. Duncan was scared of falling in love. Finding his friends' wives attractive was fun, flirting was fun, even the odd spot of lusting from afar or a grope under the mutual pretence of being high on Christmas spirit – all that was fun. It could transform the day in the same way that sunshine could make familiar landscapes look different. A glimpse of Holly at the school gate had always added something to life these last two months.

But actually falling in love was different and dangerous. It subtracted from life, it removed reason, order and stability. Love was mythic and preternatural, life-shattering and life giving. Duncan didn't want any of that *Tristan und Isolde* stuff where people get killed and torn apart for love. He didn't even want *La Bohème*, where people languish and die for it. Duncan liked his relationships with other women to remain in the realms of Lerner & Lowe. He had no objection to the odd bit of soft porn being thrown in, *Gigi* with overtones of *Emmanuelle* perhaps, but from an emotional point of view he was going to stay in the shallow end. Others could drown if they wished. Of course Duncan had been greatly in love with Jane eleven years ago, and once or twice since, but those were passing phases. On the whole his relationship with Jane was a stable one and Duncan did not want anything to disturb it. Someone else would have to fall in love with Holly.

On Thursday morning Duncan was most reluctant to see Jane going to Swansea, which she found rather touching.

'I shall miss you,' he said when the taxi arrived.

Jane kissed him on the cheek. 'You've got Laura and Holly and Kit,' she teased. 'I'm sure you can cope for three nights. Just remember to use a condom.'

Duncan didn't seem to find that very funny. They kissed again and the taxi driver beeped his horn.

Tony Morgan-Jones had arranged for the three of them to travel down together first class, but the 125 from London always slowed to the pace of a local train after Cardiff. The fact of the matter was that west of Cardiff the track began to wind and weave, and so high speeds were not possible, but to Big Fat Tony the line to Swansea betokened an assertion of the Welsh way of doing things. 'We have more time,' the countryside told the English railway system. 'We have no need of your frenetic London ways this side of Cardiff.'

Tony ordered the full Welsh breakfast from a steward who had hoped to be going off duty soon, and the Follet contingent camped out in their corner of the buffet car

– the one white tablecloth amid the serried ranks of cleared tables.

David ordered orange juice and coffee and appeared to be hung over. Jane had a mineral water.

'Now, what is important about this trip,' Tony said, as he started on his toast, 'is that we all have fun.'

Jane gave Tony a look of censure. He was getting frisky very early today.

'Fun,' Tony continued. 'Fun is very important in Swansea. If we go in like hard-nosed American lawyers, which I know is your role model, Mrs Lewis, we will achieve nothing. Swansea is a town built for pleasure.'

'You make it sound like Las Vegas,' Jane commented.

'Brighton,' said Tony. 'Dear Brighton is our model. Swansea was a fashionable eighteenth-century watering hole when Cardiff was just a place to get press-ganged. Cardiff believes in making money. Swansea believes in making whoopee.'

'Right,' said David.

'You're making this up,' Jane insisted.

An hour later, Miles met them at the station in a very ostentatious hired car which was too big for the tight little parking bay.

'*Croeso i'Abertawe*,' he announced in mid-Atlantic Welsh, and opened the door for Jane. Despite her self-conscious role as party pooper, Jane couldn't help feeling her spirits lift as she heard the seagulls wheel overhead in the bright winter sky. Like a child she could almost convince herself that she could smell the sea.

Their hotel faced the marina in one direction and the long beach, towards Mumbles, in the other. Tony insisted on looking in all the rooms to decide which was the best for Jane. In the end she and David both got rooms with a view of the beach while Tony took the harbour side because he intended to watch the nightlife unfold beneath him.

'He thinks he's in Las Vegas,' Jane told Miles.

'Sin City, that's us,' said Miles.

Their first meeting was lunch at one o'clock, so Jane locked the door and ran herself a bath. She felt curiously like a pampered object. Tony and Miles were very solicitous about her comfort, but it was as if they were playing a game and she was the prize.

David didn't really understand what was going on. He was in every respect a fellow traveller, away from the office and Bron for a few days. He was game for anything, but Jane was sure he had no agenda. Tony Morgan-Jones, however, was definitely up to something. He always was. Tony's instincts were conspiratorial. Even in the most placid waters Tony would have to find some underhand way of stirring things up, but Jane knew he got his kicks vicariously. Tony was only a threat in as much as he had brought Jane to the lion's den. Miles was the threat. Miles was the lion – or was he just a pussycat? Jane still didn't know what to make of him. Maybe she was giving him too much benefit of the doubt for being American. Maybe she should read him like she would read any middle-aged British lecher. Perhaps the same signals betokened the same kind of rogue.

Boys, thought Jane as she gave herself fifteen well-earned minutes beneath the complimentary bubbles.

On Friday morning Duncan was feeling rather pleased with himself. He had coped for twenty-four hours without Jane and had been hugely reassuring with her when she rang in on Thursday night. He had also managed something of a coup in getting Norman round to do some work at half-past eight that morning so that there was, notionally, someone in the house for Alice when he dropped Ellen at Laura's.

Duncan had decided to call in at Jacobs to get some doughnuts for himself and Ali at coffee time, and he was just walking up Cathedral Road from Laura's when a large white vehicle drew up alongside. The kerbside window rolled down electronically and Duncan realised that the woman leaning across was that Carolyn person he'd met with Richard and Geraint.

'Thought I'd seen you before!' she called.

Duncan dipped his head to the height of the window. 'Oh, hello,' he replied. Of course this was that white Mitsubishi that transported the Snotgob and had nearly run him over last month. 'It's . . .' He tried rapidly to think which Welsh double barrel she was.

'Cari Parry Morris,' said Carolyn. 'You're the one who doesn't want to be an architect.'

'There are lots of people who don't want to be architects,' said Duncan blithely. 'Most of them architects. I'm the one who *used to be* an architect.'

'Duncan,' said Carolyn.

'That's right,' said Duncan.

'You walk your kids to school. I've seen you.'

'I've seen you,' said Duncan. He refrained from adding, 'You've nearly killed me twice.'

'This is Elinor,' she told him, nodding her head towards a fat girl in 1950s school uniform who was strapped into the back of the car.

'Hello Elinor,' said Duncan to the Snotgob. The poor girl must have been five or six. She looked back at him glumly, as if she knew that her sole role in life was to make Carolyn Parry Jones look glamorous by comparison.

'You got my card?' Carolyn asked. This conversation, conducted against the noise of traffic, below head height, and across the empty passenger seat, was getting physically uncomfortable. Duncan was sure he had no recollection of receiving Carolyn's card, so she passed him one from a holder on the dashboard.

'You should come and see me sometime,' said Carolyn, and put the jeep into gear. '*Hwyl!*'

And off she drove.

'And you should look where you're driving,' muttered Duncan.

The card read:

Carolyn Parry Morris
Corporate Hospitality
THE CPM COMPANY

in Welsh and English.

Duncan could hear Jane telling him he had no instinct for the main chance.

At lunchtime Kit rang to ask Duncan to go and buy some fish with her.

'Why do you want me to buy fish with you?' asked Duncan, who felt he knew Kit well enough by now to challenge her occasionally.

'Because you're a mate,' said Kit. 'We could have lunch in town.'

'I've got Alice off school,' Duncan replied. 'There's nothing wrong with her, but the doctors want her at home till Monday.'

Kit offered to send Gabriele round to look after Alice. It would only take an hour and a half, two hours at the most.

'Well, I'd like to,' said Duncan, 'but Norman's here doing the conservatory. I need to keep an eye on him.'

'Oh for Christ's sake,' said Kit. 'It's fish not a fuck, Duncan.' And she put the phone down.

Duncan was still recovering from that when she immediately rang back.

'I'm sorry, I didn't put the phone down because I was angry with you. I put the phone down because I was embarrassed about what I said. You know what I'm like.'

'I'm learning,' said Duncan.

'Don't worry about the fish,' Kit told him. 'I'll get one of the scrubby cows from Barry's work to come with me.'

'Why do you need someone to help you buy fish?' Duncan asked.

'I am a woman of mystery,' said Kit, 'You go and ponce around with a baking tray.'

On Friday evening Tony wanted to take his team out to dinner, but David and Miles had arranged to play squash and this vexed Tony greatly. Jane suggested that she and Tony went to dinner on their own but Tony was very unhappy about that idea and insisted that they waited until David and Miles had showered and changed.

So Jane had another bath in her room and phoned Duncan, who was in the kitchen talking to Holly Williams.

'Holly's just brought Nel back!' Duncan told Jane almost immediately. 'Do you want to speak to her?'

Jane thought this sounded very unnecessary, but she sent Holly her love. 'I don't think I'm going to be back tomorrow night,' she told Duncan.

'Oh, that's a shame,' said Duncan, looking at Holly who was sitting on the work surface, half reading a record sleeve.

'So you and Holly go to the meal evening.'

'*Right!*' said Duncan loudly – and clearly.

'Are you all right?' Jane asked.

'Of course,' said Duncan. 'Do you want to speak to the girls? They're upstairs with Siôn and Bithygig.'

'You two should move in together,' said Jane.

'What do you mean?' Duncan asked in a funny voice.

Jane explained that she meant with Gwyn away and her away the two families would cope better under one roof. She also added that it was a joke.

'*Yes!*' said Duncan with a half laugh.

'You sound very odd,' said Jane.

'I'll get the girls to phone you back.' Duncan told her.

It was obvious to Duncan, even if it wasn't to anyone else, that he was feeling very uncomfortable in Holly's presence at the moment. That blasted dream had left him very susceptible to her, but of course Holly had no idea of the effect she was having on him. That evening was the first time they'd actually met since Holly had leant her head against his shoulder in the breakfast room and told him he was a good man. Duncan was actually feeling quite nervous about being left in his kitchen with this woman. The four children had disappeared off together at speed despite his attempts to offer them fizzy drinks and chocolate.

Alone in the kitchen together, Holly had laid her hand on Duncan's arm and kissed him.

'Duncan,' she'd said, 'I'm sorry I took advantage of you on Wednesday. I shouldn't have said all those things.'

'Nonsense.' Duncan was amazed that Holly still hadn't rumbled him.

'I told Laura all about it,' she'd continued.

'Did you?' Duncan hadn't liked the sound of that.

'She said I had made a wise choice talking to you and she's actually offered to baby-sit for me on Saturday so we can go to the meal evening.'

And it was at that point the phone had rung and Duncan had nearly jumped when he discovered it was Jane. Her call was irritatingly timely because he had been on the point of lying to Holly and telling her that Jane would be back on Saturday afternoon so he couldn't escort her to the meal evening after all. Now he was stuck with it.

On Saturday morning the light broke into Jane Lewis's room very early. The great spotlight of a sun was beaming down the Bristol Channel and, by a ridiculous alignment of reflecting windows, broke into Jane's south-facing room, making it very clear that she hadn't closed the curtains.

She also realised very clearly that she had no recollection of coming back last night. She remembered the meal in a Champers style bodega somewhere off the marina. She remembered Miles taking her and David to a disco, and she remembered challenging David to a game of squash when he had the cheek to congratulate her for still being able to dance at the age of thirty-seven.

No, she *could* remember getting back to the hotel. It had seemed very late when the three of them staggered into the Kingsway and clambered back into Miles' enormous car. Jane remembered that Tony was waiting in there. He'd actually stayed in the limo with a bottle of champagne and spent the evening watching a portable TV while they went to the disco.

Jane had a recollection of being rather rude to Tony when she had found him still waiting for them outside. Fortunately she couldn't remember what she said to him. She did remember being in the hotel lifts with Tony and Miles later on, and she recalled David slipping on to the floor and falling asleep. And she remembered, now that she thought of it, that while Miles and Tony tried to get David out of the lift on reaching their floor, she had walked off to her room and got inside before either Miles or Tony decided to extend the party. Yes, that was how she came to be back.

She was feeling distinctly hung-over, but she was determined to have breakfast. Downstairs, as she might have expected, Tony was sitting waiting for her. He had finished his full Welsh breakfast and looked particularly enormous, even menacing in his outsize golfing pullover.

'Good morning, Mrs Lewis,' he said archly.

'David's not been down?' she asked, taking her seat. Tony shook his head. Jane could sense that Tony was expecting her to say something. She could either brazen it out or capitulate.

'Correct me if I'm wrong,' she began after the waitress had taken her order, 'but was I very rude to you last night?'

Tony took a deep breath. 'I would say you cast certain aspersions on my character. Aspersions that young David was too intoxicated to understand and aspersions that would probably not have shocked Miles Mihash.'

'Good,' said Jane, wishing like hell she could remember what she'd said.

'Nevertheless, aspersions that would be considered in many quarters libellous. Aspersions that, were they repeated in front of clients or in the office, would make my position or yours untenable.'

'I see,' said Jane.

'Aspersions that I should not wish to hear from your lips again.'

'Of course,' said Jane.

'No matter how canny and accurate your observations might be,' Tony added with only the merest hint of a smile. 'Now. How is dear Duncan? How is he coping?'

On Saturday evening Holly had a very hot bath before the meal evening and drifted away so completely that she didn't notice Buddug had stopped talking to her and actually left the bathroom.

Duncan had a bath too, and spent a long time cleaning his teeth as he used to in the days when he was setting out in the hope of participating in a seduction. He didn't want to get involved with Holly Williams, he really didn't, but at the same time he didn't want to end up entwined with her and worrying that his breath smelt. To be unprepared for who knows what was even worse than going to the meal evening *prepared* for who knows what.

In Swansea, Jane Lewis wasn't having a bath. She had finished her last session with the corporation at seven-thirty and was tempted actually to hire a car and drive back up to Cardiff for the night but, of course, she had foolishly agreed to play squash with David, hadn't she? Tony and Miles had asked if they could come along to watch and were told to bugger off by Jane. However Miles, the butt of so many rebuffs, did gain himself the concession that Jane *would* have dinner with him afterwards.

When David asked if he and Tony could come and watch the dinner, Jane and Miles had both told him to bugger off.

Jane had had to buy some shorts from the hotel shop, and she rang Duncan from the lobby. It was a difficult call. Both of them seemed to take the view that the other was probably having a very good time, and each resented the other's implication that *they* were the one with a good evening ahead of them. Jane asked after a while if she could speak to the girls and Duncan said they were upstairs watching TV.

'Have they been watching TV all day?' Jane asked.

'No,' said Duncan defensively. It was a difficult conversation.

When the baby-sitter, a big jolly woman whom Duncan didn't know, arrived with her bag of ironing, Duncan showed her round the house and then walked to Holly's with the tortilla dish he had prepared and a bottle of wine. Holly was supposed to have ordered a taxi as soon as she got Duncan's call to say he was on his way, but she was still on the phone when Duncan got there.

'They'll be quarter of an hour,' she said, giving Duncan his usual kiss. 'Laura's on her way too.'

Duncan had tried not to smell the soap on her neck but at the last moment he couldn't resist. The effect of breathing in Holly's wholesome scent was absurd. He actually felt one of his knees buckle momentarily beneath him and he only just avoided dropping the tortillas.

Holly poured him a glass of whisky and he drank it rather too quickly. Buddug passed through, grumbling about having Laura Davis to baby-sit. The gist of her complaint was that if you got up and came downstairs while Laura was sitting she virtually got you doing your homework. But neither Duncan nor Holly was listening. She was applying her make-up in the breakfast room mirror and he was watching, transfixed. The secret ceremonials of cosmetics had always fascinated Duncan, who had been brought up without sisters and had never forgotten being enthralled when watching his first girlfriend apply mascara.

With Holly the transfixion was doublefold, because he had no idea that she actually wore make-up, and triplefold because Gwyn's whisky was having its usual effect of slowing down his mental processes. Holly was wearing what was for her a very unbaggy, non-ethnic, really rather glamorous dress, and when she leant forward and lifted her face closer to the mirror the material tightened over her bosom. Duncan stared. He had no choice but to stare if he was to make the most of this rare opportunity to ascertain the shape and exact curve of Holly's right breast, which was, at the moment, the most fascinating thing in the world. Like an astronomer seeing visible proof for the first time of a constellation he had always believed must exist, Duncan stared with a mixture of awe and delight. Suddenly he threw aside his earlier entreaties for Fate not to entwine him with Holly Williams and surrendered entirely to lust. He wanted to caress Holly's right breast; it was such a simple, wonderful thing to do and nothing else mattered in the world. Except that the door bell went and it was Laura, and even Duncan's sex drive could not survive the sight of Laura Leighton Davis in peaked cap and corduroy trousers.

*　　*　　*

Bang! Jane Lewis had taken the view that running two or three miles once a week probably kept her in sufficient trim for playing squash with David, who seemed to drink too much to be a real athlete. But David, overindulged as his body was, was nevertheless practised at the game and more than capable of placing the ball wherever he wanted it. Jane found herself crashing from one side of the court to the other. When she managed to get into a rally he tired sooner than she, but his was definitely the skill, whereas she was slugging it out with determination and aggression.

Seven points each. It was like running, Jane thought. You set yourself targets. Never mind about winning the game. Just win this point. Everything for this point. It was painful at times, but pain could be ignored. Pain was transitory. She knew that from running. Never mind running – she knew that from childbirth! And the difference was with childbirth the pain was inevitable. You couldn't stop it. But the pain of something like this didn't matter because you *could* stop it. You could always stop it. Not that she was going to. The thing that mattered more than anything was defeating David on this one point.

David flicked the ball back lightly and it ricocheted around the court. Jane was too far forward; she retreated, the ball bounced down in front of her but too near, she swerved, unable to move back in time, and just managed to bring her racket under it. Her shot looped vulnerably high through the air. Bugger, thought Jane. The little sod can flatten that. *Bang!* David's racket swatted the ball, sending it ricocheting around three sides of the squash court only two feet above the ground. Jane leapt, desperate to get her racket to the flying ball. She crashed across the floor, missing by inches but hitting herself on the ground harder than she expected.

*   *   *

Holly and Duncan were being a success at the meal evening, which was in Vinny and Col's house. The twenty or so people assembled seemed to think it was great fun – Holly arriving with Duncan – and wanted to know where Jane and Gwyn had gone that night. Vinny (Mott) the hostess was not to be confused with Binny (Barnes), who was there without Flyn, nor with Minnie (Lucey), who was there with Stephen. Several people already well into the Chilean wine found it very amusing that tonight they had a Vinny, Binny and Minnie 'You could have come with me,' said Binny, kissing Holly. 'If only I'd known you were on your own.'

Thank you, thought Duncan. He didn't understand why Binny took such a dim view of him, unless Jane really was complaining about him as fulsomely and comprehensively as was Binny to Jane about Flyn. Jane had always maintained that Binny wanted solidarity, and you didn't have to hate men to give her that. The daft thing was that Binny was fine if she was sitting next to you – as she had been last month with Duncan – or if she was wielding a gong with you – as she had been with old Nick. It was *en masse* that she seemed to tribalise. Girls good; boys bad. And after all, Binny had absolutely no reason to suspect that Duncan had, only half an hour ago, been poised to grope Holly in front of the mirror.

Duncan left Holly in the front room with several women and a few ageing new men who were trying to talk about their emotions, and went in search of the boys who would be with the booze. It was reassuringly quaint that, although none of the people at Vinny and Col's that night could have been students within the last fifteen years, the meal evening polarised like a college party. Girls did the food, men hung around the drink. Somebody called Mike, Steve or Pete asked Duncan what he was having and what he thought of the match. Duncan was equipped to answer only one of those questions properly, but it hardly mattered anyway because in the event he ended up with red rather than white. He sipped slowly and unenthusiatically. After that whisky he was taking it gently tonight. Don't fall asleep now, he told himself.

'Duncan, where's Jane?' asked Stephen Lucey, who was passing through with four glasses.

'She's in Swansea,' said Duncan. 'I came with Holly Williams.'

'Is this something we should know about?' asked Stephen roguishly, but having seen a gap in the crowd he didn't hang around for an answer.

Duncan couldn't help taking a certain pride in this proffered image of a roué, however inappropriate it might seem. Though of course playing up to it was a useful double bluff. He was not going to deny that there was something between him and Holly. Because if there genuinely wasn't, he would be expected to play up to the idea that there was for general amusement. Therefore, as there possibly *was* something between him and Holly, Duncan played up to the fact that there was. He pretended the truth, in fact, so that people would think that it wasn't true.

'You subtle dog, you,' he said to himself.

Eight-Seven. David to serve. Jane pushed the hair away from her temple and tried not to think about how it was working loose. When you ran, the concentration was transcendental. You focused away from what you were doing. In squash you had to focus exactly on the ball, on the moment; you didn't think about what you were going to do with Alice or Ellen or Duncan, or with your sodding hair working loose. God, she hated David. *Bang*! The ball shot past her and on to the back wall. Jane stood to one side to let it bounce forward. The ball dropped down vertically from just below the red. She swung wildly and just managed to scrape the ball up before it bounced a second time – but something stretched alarmingly at her side. David hadn't expected Jane to get that shot, and now he raced forward and across court to where her shot had serendipitously hurled the ball. This time it was his turn to let fly with the racket and he got the ball away a moment before crashing into the wall. *Got you!* thought Jane – now if she could just intercept his shot before David was back in the centre of the court.

The ball flew back high and Jane leapt up, intending to swat it down. Everything was just a matter of effort, she was telling herself, of caring more than the other person, of going the extra mile. God, she should have been in litigation. She hurled herself further into the air. Her racket was within an inch of the ball – she just had to stretch that other inch, it was all that mattered. Stupid, stupid Duncan! thought Jane, and with a great yell she brought the full force of her anger down on David's ball. *Bang!* It seemed to hit every wall and then bounce, bounce, bounce cheekily past David. Jane was concentrating on the ball so much she actually didn't remember landing back on the floor.

'Played,' said David, sniffing and breathless. He offered Jane his hand to help her up. 'Seven/Eight,' he said. Jane didn't reply but nodded in agreement as he handed her the ball.

'Boy, girl, boy, girl!' cried someone called Inge who appeared to be in charge of the meal evening. Although Vinny was actually the hostess that night, Inge Lermoos co-ordinated meal evenings throughout the year, borrowing spoons, glasses and chairs and helping people reclaim their serving dishes for weeks afterwards. Duncan found a place next to Siân Roberts on the long table and, seeing that Holly was standing with Minnie Lucey and two other women at the other end, called her over.

'Holly can't sit by you!' said Binny, who was choosing a seat opposite Duncan.

'We're just good friends,' said Duncan.

'Why can't Holly sit by Duncan?' asked Inge from somewhere in the mêlée.

'Holly *came* with Duncan,' said Binny.

'That he did,' said Stephen Lucey with a wink at Duncan.

'I don't mind,' said Holly.

'I promise we won't even hold hands,' said Duncan specifically to Binny. Somebody laughed.

'Do *you* want to sit by Duncan?' Holly asked Binny in all innocence.

'That isn't the point,' said Binny, and a few more people laughed.

'What's going on? I want some food,' said Big Mike/Steve/Pete from the kitchen doorway.

'Binny wants to sit next to Duncan,' Stephen Lucey explained mischievously.

'No I don't!'

'Sit down and shut up, Binny, there's a love,' shouted Big Mike/Steve from the back.

Now everyone laughed. Binny plonked herself down, red-faced and defeated. Meal evenings were always harmonious. There was nowhere that she could take this argument now without endangering the ambience. It had got as serious as things were ever allowed to get. Holly settled herself by Duncan and Stephen Lucey slid in beside Binny, opposite Duncan.

'We'll keep an eye on them from here, shall we?' he asked.

Duncan wondered about Stephen Lucey. He had an air of always knowing what was going on, which must be a very useful aura to cultivate in the business community. But what did Stephen really think was going on here? And what, if anything, was?

'How's Gwyn getting on in Llandudno?' Duncan asked Holly, passing her someone else's tortilla dish. It was a good question. It observed the social proprieties, it showed proper respect for the rigid coupledom of meal evenings, and yet it made oblique reference to that one intimate conversation that Duncan and Holly had had.

'Subtle dog,' thought Duncan.

Gwyn Williams was on a six-minute rest now. He kept up the count but rested as best he could. The pit in Llandudno was so deep it could have been dug by miners. No chance of the audience seeing what the horns or brass section were getting up to. More importantly, the conductor was at a safe distance too. It was one of Howie's regular jokes when asked who had conducted a particular performance to reply, 'No idea, I never looked.'

Of course, Puccini kept the horns busy. The end of Act One had been a real smack in the teeth. Now they were coming up to the bit where Turandot poses her riddles to Calaf. Bloody odd things, women, Gwyn thought, putting down his mute. Three riddles: if he guessed them right she would give him the kingdom of China and herself. Guess them wrong and he's a gonner. Why? Gwyn didn't usually find himself wondering about opera plots, but good old *Turdandot* nagged at him. Why did the woman offer so much when she didn't actually have to offer anything at all? And why did he accept the challenge? Why did Calaf risk his life for a woman he didn't even know? It was odd, Gwyn thought, but then why was he tearing round Wales and Oxford and Plymouth playing this thing night after night if not for Holly and the children? The things we do.

Ping, Pang and Pong were singing away up above about the homes they missed while working for Turandot. Bloody stupid names. Keep counting. Four minutes. The thing that really got Gwyn about *Turdandot* was when Calaf had guessed all the riddles and won, and Turandot and the kingdom were his, what does she say, this woman? 'I don't like this game, I'm not playing any more.' And what does he say? If she can guess his name he'll release her from her debt to him. Why does he do that? And what does she do, this woman? She doesn't say, 'What a noble gesture, thanks Calaf!' No, she sets about torturing everyone until someone tells her his name. And that's the woman he wants to marry, is it?

What is the point of stories like that? Does anyone live like that? Gwyn thought about Holly. Sometimes when he couldn't sleep he would sit up in bed watching her and wondering where she went when she slept.

Howie was emptying his slides. Ooops. Time for the Emperor of China's entrance already. Gwyn wondered whether he'd paced himself properly. He'd overdone the end of Act One. Hell of a blast up. He should have known better. It was all right for the brass, they'd had a ten-minute holiday. Not like the horns. Emperor of bloody China's entrance. Right! Gwyn wished he'd had ten minutes off before playing this. Riddles and torture, riddles and bloody torture. Puccini knew a thing or two about women.

'You sure you're OK?' David asked Jane. She was about to serve but that muscle at her side was beginning to tug. Ignore it, she told herself. Just keep the serve. She felt the ball in one hand, the grip of her racket in the other. Winning didn't count. What counted was not being defeated. Duncan didn't understand that. She should have done litigation. She could have sued her way across South Wales and the South of England all the way up to the High Court. That would have shown her stupid mother something.

Bang! Jane served and retreated to the centre of court. David intercepted the shot and returned it low, only just clearing the bottom line. Jane ran forward and pitched the ball up so that it floated almost vertically in front of the wall before bouncing gracefully off and landing in front of David, who had had plenty of time to place it. *Bang!* He sent the ball ricocheting round three sides of the court. Jane tore after it. How can you say it's not personal? she thought. Fifteen years later your mother blames you for the break-up of her marriage. Isn't that personal? Jane flung herself into the far corner in order to get behind the ball. And after ten years using up all Duncan's best ideas Howard kicks him out. Isn't that personal? Isn't it? Come on Duncan, how much more personal do you want it to bloody get? Jane had the ball in range now and she fired it straight at David who ducked; the ball hit a side wall and bounced across court. He recovered and lunged after it but he was too late.

Eight-all.

Don't tell me it isn't personal, thought Jane.

'The thing is,' said Mervyn the microbiologist, 'in the West we've addressed most of the basic problems of existence — war, disease, famine. We've even got rid of God, and what remains is sex.'

It was getting to that time of the evening, thought Duncan. All the tostadas and Peruvian salads had been cleared away, all the tortilla dishes (of which there had been far too many) had been half eaten, and now Vinny's table was a mass of South American cheeses, ice creams, lagers and wine, and people were talking about sex.

'Freud began it, and now we can't stop,' Mervyn continued. 'It's an obsession for the late twentieth century because we have nothing truly worth being anxious about any more. You wouldn't get mediaeval man, or eighteenth-century man talking and writing about sex all the time. He just got on and did it.'

'But are you saying it isn't *worth* being preoccupied with sex?' asked someone from further down the table.

'What do you think?' Duncan asked Holly. It was a reasonable question to ask someone after whom you weren't lusting, or even someone you were pretending not to be lusting after, or indeed someone whom you were pretending to lust after as a way of pretending to the likes of Stephen Lucey that you weren't really lusting after them at all.

'Yes . . .' said Holly quietly. 'It is difficult, isn't it?'

'Is it?' asked Duncan.

'Depends how you do it, Hol,' said Big Mike/Pete who wasn't supposed to be part of this conversation at all.

'Duncan,' said Mervyn and with some volume. 'Am I right?'

'Well,' said Duncan. 'Of course I'm the only one here whose wife's staying in a Swansea hotel tonight. So I suppose I'm not in a very good position to get the subject in any kind of objective perspective.'

'Watch out, Hol!' roared Big Mike. 'Dunc isn't getting it in perspective tonight!'

Where do arseholes like you come from? Duncan thought.

Act Three really bothered Gwyn. It started well with *Nessun Dorma*. Sometimes you could hear the stir in the audience as newcomers recognised the World Cup theme song. Gwyn could identify with Calaf at the beginning of Act Three. '*Vincero, Vincero.*' I shall win. You've got to be determined in this life. But then he wins and he throws it away. Never do that. Keep it to yourself. Gwyn thought about Holly again.

Bloody opera. Twenty-nine's coming up, Gwyn remembered. Up there Ping, Pang and Pong want to torture Liu because she gets up and says 'I know his name and I will never tell you.' Now that's a daft thing to do. She sacrifices herself, gets tortured to death for refusing to reveal his name, says do it to me because she loves Calaf that much. She wants to take his secret to the grave with her.

Opera is full of people suffering for no good reason. As if there isn't enough pain in the world already. Get ready now; this bit is never the same, thought Gwyn. Liu's got that beggar of a top note and you've got to keep with her. The horns could make a real mess of this. Of course Puccini uses us when Liu's going to be dragged off to her painful death. We're the mean bastards, thought Gwyn, preparing to blow. When someone dies, we're the ones who get a good tune to play.

The whole band was playing now. Hell of a sound. Death, and fear, and pain, that's us. That's all they ever expect of us.

Ouch! David had opted to go to ten. Was he trying to kill her?

It's not imagining what it'll be like to win that can distract you into fantasy, Jane reminded herself. It's imagining how you'll cope with losing. You mustn't *have* a fall back position. That's fatal. You've got to fight as if your life depends on it. Jane prepared to serve. That's why she didn't litigate, to be honest. A good litigator fights as if there is no compromise, but always has one in mind. Jane's strategy would be never to lose. Jane's strategy would be to kill.

Bang!

She copied bodyline David's serve, which took the ball directly into the back wall. The sod recognised the shot and stood back to be ready to return when it dropped down. Jane moved to the centre, ready.

Bang!

David brought the ball in low, across court, and she just had time to dive into position to catch it on its return.

Bang!

The bugger could predict where the ball was going to go,

that was the problem! Jane told herself to shut up and to stop explaining why she'd lost the game.

Bang!

His shot was heading for the back wall. David had got her running all over the court. I hate you, Jane thought as she scooped up the ball, just, and ran forward till she could whack it into a corner.

Bang!

The ball hit straight into the nick and died, dropping down directly. David was easily seven feet away.

'Shot!' he said, wiping the sweat off his brow. Nine-eight. She just needed one point and the strange thing was he seemed not to care. What is it with these men? thought Jane. Is life so easy for them they don't mind losing?

'Match point,' said David, getting into position.

Duncan was making his way up the stairs in Vinny's house. He knew that Holly had gone up to the loo and she'd been gone so long she must have got talking to someone. The meal evening had now reached its penultimate stage with chairs and people scattered everywhere and relays of coffee being brought through the various rooms in which the guests had sprawled themselves. Mervyn the micro-something-scientist had been told by his wife that he was talking too much; Ceri, a houseman from the Heath Hospital, was singing duets with a children's karaoke set; and Siân Roberts was being boozily flirtatious and explaining to Big Mike how you went about changing locks.

When Duncan reached the landing, Holly was lying on the stairs that led up to Vinny's attic and staring at the ceiling.

'You OK?' asked Duncan.

He watched her rise and cross the landing so that she was by the stairs and capable, therefore, of escape. 'Just thinking,' she said and leant against the wall next to him. 'I was talking to Katharine and then . . . I just got thinking.' Her voice dropped.

'What about?' Duncan asked, dropping his voice too. In the past he'd done this unconsciously with Holly, but this time he was isolating the two of them in a softly spoken inner world, away from the meal evening proper.

'I don't know if I was actually thinking about anything . . .' Holly murmured to herself. 'Often I don't.'

Duncan had his hands in his pockets, and he could sense Holly's hand flat against the wall, within inches of his own. How easy it would be to slip his hand out of his pocket and take hers. And yet, now he had thought about it, how difficult. He should have done it without thinking of the ramifications, the complications, the explanations and excuses. Duncan took both his hands out of his pockets and let them fall on to his thighs in a simple chappish sort of gesture. That would do for a start.

One of the nice things about Holly was that her silences were quite companionable. It didn't seem necessary to speak at all. You could just *be* with Holly. And yet Duncan was aware now that, if he was going to make a move to take Holly's hand, it would seem a much more natural gesture if it was covered by speech. God, this was like being fifteen all over again.

'You're very different, aren't you?' Duncan started to say. He had no idea if this was the right thing to say to Holly Williams. At this stage he was just trying to say something, anything. A burst of shivering, schoolboy nerves, overcame him as he reached down the wall for Holly's hand. She became aware of this and moved to put her arms around him.

'You're cold, Duncan,' she said, and hugged him to her. Duncan felt foolish, very foolish, his hand flapping around on the dado, failing to find its target. But he also felt the warmth and softness of Holly's body pulled against him. It was wonderful and he hugged her back. There was no longer any doubt about it in Duncan's mind. He fancied Holly Williams. Yes he most certainly did, and it was only a small movement now to bring their faces together, to touch their cheeks together and seal it, as the poet said, with a kiss.

Tu che tremi se ti sfioro,	You who tremble at my embrace,
Tu che sbianchi se ti bacio,	You who grow pale at my kiss,

This was the bit that really got to Gwyn

Il mio nome e la vita insiem ti dono.	I give to you my name together with my life.

Calaf was in the clear. He'd got the girl he wanted. God knows why he'd wanted her, but he did. And then he'd thrown her the challenge that if she found out his name by daybreak he'd surrender all that he'd won and she could have him tortured to death. But now the sun was on its way – and what does he do, this prize prick? He tells her his name!

Gwyn almost missed his cue. In come the horns again, big heavy stuff now, death and destruction. Why does he do that? Opera is so stupid, so bloody stupid. He's got everything, this man, he's seized the kingdom and the girl, and yet he throws it back at her and says give it to me again, *but only when you love me.*

Gwyn almost split a note but he just managed to suck it back in. He'd gone cold.

That's what he does, the fool, he gives it back because it's not enough that she's his, she's got to *want* to be his. She's got to want to stay with him.

Someone hissed 'Four bars before Fifty,' frantically in his direction and Howie came in automatically, covering the fact that Gwyn had absolutely no idea where he was. He'd gone. He couldn't move. Christ almighty, that's what it *is*, he thought. Calaf would rather die if she doesn't want him. Four before Fifty? What does that mean? Four what before Fifty? Hell of a noise now, all around him. Christ! Top B flat's coming up. Big crescendo now. The whole band belting out the voice of doom. Where am I? Enter the Emperor of China and judgement. That's it, Christ almighty! Enter the voice of judgement.

Jane wasn't nervous. She had only one thing in mind now. The elimination of David was all that mattered. Her own repertoire of shots was limited. She could hit it hard and alarm him or simply lob it to land halfway down. Jane decided on a sneakily simple shot that would drop the ball at his feet. The ball flew to the wall, Jane ducked and moved back to the T, the ball arched over her head, caught off his guard David ran forward, Jane saw the ball dropping not two feet away from her and heard David cry 'Let!'. Bugger. She looked round. Yes he would have hit her if he'd gone for that. Play let. David handed her the ball blandly, not a reproach nor any note of triumph in his face.

Jane aimed again. She daren't try that trick a second time. But David would probably *expect* something different now, he'd assume a change of tactics wouldn't he? So she could always surprise him by not changing. Then again if he was expecting her to bluff him in that way maybe she could get him on a double bluff.

Bang!

The ball got everything Jane could give it, and she felt a stabbing pain all the way down her side. David stopped her shot in mid flight. Sod! Jane was heading to the mid-court position. She had to stop herself, rush forward and recover the shot.

Bang!

She hit the ball and it floated back over David's head, briefly going out. 'Play on!' yelled David who was in reach of it.

Bang!

The ball whistled past Jane and she span round 180 degrees to be ready on the rebound.

Bang!

She returned it forcefully and unimaginatively into the front wall, but so powerfully it rebounded back at her almost before it had left her racket. She dropped to the floor to avoid obstructing David and felt something definitely give in her back. Bugger and blast! David rushed across court, nearly cannoning into her, and stretched for the shot. She wasn't going to see this one off. No, this was it. But he must have been short. He missed. Jane, looking up, ready to rise, was suddenly aware of the silence. No return.

'Well done!' said David, breathless. She'd won. She'd won. Jane breathed out. The pain in her back was suddenly intense and she cried out as it stabbed all the way up to her collarbone.

Duncan was quite intoxicated by the smell of Holly and the way in which she stroked his back. Jane was a good strong hug person, but Holly had a wonderful touch. Duncan was aware of how different she felt. It was years since he had embraced another woman in this way. He realised that his senses had formed their own hologram of Jane, and into this expected pattern Holly Williams just didn't fit. She wasn't as tall as Jane, but she was, surprisingly, wider. She pressed against him in different places. Duncan felt his trembling subside, thankfully. Surely that must have been a complete give-away to her. She must have guessed what his feelings were for her. His physical feelings, anyway. So, he thought, if she's shocked, why doesn't she withdraw? And if she's going to reciprocate, why doesn't she respond to my subtle attempt to get our lips closer?

Of course, what Duncan didn't know was that Holly believed in the Cosmic Embrace. After all, why should he have any idea about the mind of the woman of whose body he was trying to avail himself? Though transported by the touch of Holly, Duncan was wondering why this initial phase of seduction was taking so long. But the truth of the matter was that Holly would cuddle people all day if time and propriety allowed. She was not aware that this was the first stage in anything. To Holly, she and Duncan were in touch with each other, rediscovering the infinite need we all had as children to be loved and caressed for hours on end.

But Duncan felt that they ought to do something, get to a point where some kind of commitment to something of some sort was in the offing, even if it was just that he'd walk her home later. Other people would be coming upstairs soon.

Padre augusto, conosco il nome dello straniero.	Noble father, I know the name of the stranger.

Turandot was singing. Gwyn's heart was in his throat. He felt as though he'd never *heard* this bloody thing before. All the months he'd been playing it! He'd never heard anything but thirds and sevenths and top B flats before. No horns in this passage, just strings. Steady. He'd got to stop thinking about it. Got to count. But Gwyn was in another world. No horns, just ethereal strings. Oh my God. *Father, I know his name.*

If they asked Holly she'd say, 'Well it's Gwyn, isn't it?' '*Conosco il nome.*' – I know his name. *His name is Love.*

Turandot's voice lifted into the major, and what the hell was happening? Gwyn's eyes flooded with tears. Time for the great cheer on stage, quick chorus of *Nessun Dorma* and down the pub. But this time it wasn't like that. Gwyn tried to breathe; he had to take enough in, had to – he was first horn. But it was no good. Turandot had found love in her heart for Calaf. He had given himself to her as a sacrifice and she had returned the gift with her love. Oh God, Holly, where have we been all our lives? 'Oh, Holly!' Gwyn was choked.

'Holly,' murmured Duncan.

Strangely enough, although he would have admitted that his motives were entirely dishonourable, the only thing to say that kept occurring in his mind was, 'I love you.' The words were there, ballistically programmed into his embrace as clearly as the hologram of Jane. Duncan was not too shy to say the words, he just objected to the lie. He fancied Holly something rotten, but that was best left unsaid. And he couldn't say, 'I love you,' so in the end he just said, 'Holly,' very, very quietly.

'Mm,' she said.

'Holly,' he said again.

'Mervyn,' she said, which rather threw Duncan. But when he lifted his head from her ringleted hair he saw that Mervyn the microbiologist had indeed reached the top of the stairs and was being beckoned over to join the embrace, which he did in a slightly unsteady way.

'Binny,' said Mervyn. 'Come and join us.' And within seconds Duncan found he was taking part in a mass middle-aged cuddle at the top of Vinny's stairs. Next up was Big Mike much the worse for the lagers of Chile and Newcastle.

'Is this a private party or can anyone join in?' he roared.

*   *   *

'I don't like getting it in the neck from the likes of him,' said Martin.

Gwyn apologised again.

'What is it, Gwyn? Not like you.' The leader preferred to keep it out of the band room. He preferred to buy people drinks before he bollocked them. Gwyn had already bought Howie his pint for helping out. Fair play to Howie, he'd done his best to cover, but it hadn't stopped the likes of him coming down from the podium far from happy with the horns, and Gwyn was now being told.

'If it happens again we'll have to go to his room,' said Martin.

Gwyn apologised again. They were in the crowded bar of Llandudno's Cottage Loaf.

'Is it family?' Martin asked. He hated it when members of the orchestra had family problems.

'No,' said Gwyn, saving Martin the embarrassment. 'Don't worry. Won't happen again, Martin.'

'You're definitely telling me it won't happen again?'

Gwyn assured him this was so.

Martin let up a bit. 'Problem with this one, he will keep looking for positive feedback. He likes the eye contact. I spend all my time smiling up at him.'

'Mind if I make a phone call?' Gwyn asked. He really didn't want a heart-to-heart with the leader.

'You go on,' said Martin. Now he had to sort out bloody Merryl and her harp.

Gwyn wasn't expecting to get his own bilingual message on the answerphone, but it gave him time to think what he was going to say. The man on the machine didn't sound like him at all. Matter of fact, it was rather frightening. Very clear spoken, this man who proclaimed the fact he was living with *Holi, Siôn a Buddug*, very full of himself.

'Holly, it's Gwyn. Just want to say . . . Look, I know things aren't quite right but, well, I want to make them better.' God, this was so difficult – but maybe it was better on a machine. He didn't have to pause for her reply and gauge how she was taking it.

'Like I do love you of course, and miss you and, well, maybe things haven't been too right. I don't know, but, well . . . I do love you, see. See you tomorrow.'

Laura Leighton Davis jumped. She had being going through the minutes of the PTA meeting at Holly's kitchen table, and had ignored the telephone when it rang because Holly had told her the machine was on. Laura didn't know much about answerphones. She certainly didn't expect them to broadcast their messages for all the house to hear.

She'd had no idea that things weren't going well between Holly and Gwyn, but that was none of her business. Not at all. No indeed. Laura decided it might be best to finish her annotations in another room.

Fortunately, Jane's hotel had good relations with a local health practice. The doctor who turned out that evening was pleasantly relieved to find it was not another fat businessman who'd eaten too much. She told Jane to have a hot bath and plenty of rest and gave her some pain killers.

'The back is a complicated structure,' she said. 'I can't tell exactly what you've done, but it should get better on its own. If it gets any worse, see your GP in Cardiff. She gave a most undoctorly smile. 'I hope you're not on your honeymoon.'

'No,' winced Jane.

The young woman had noticed three men waiting outside Jane's room; a fat one, a funny little American one, and a young one in sports kit.

'They're my colleagues,' said Jane.

'Well, I suggest you get one of them to drive you home first thing tomorrow,' said the doctor. 'You married?'

Jane admitted she was.

'Well, this is his chance to make a big fuss of you.'

Gabriele the Cheese was driving through Pontcanna at midnight on her way back from a club where the manager always let her in for free if she said something in French to him. Had she not been keeping such a close eye on the wrong side of the road, she might have noticed Micro Mervyn being loaded into a taxi by his wife, and Big Mike setting off down the pavement with Mrs Big Mike and a pile of half-eaten tortilla dishes. She might also have noticed Duncan and Holly and Binny leaving Vinny and Col's house, and Mervyn yelling happily from the taxi that there was room for one more.

'You go, Holly,' said Binny, and Holly, who was feeling the cold, asked Duncan if he'd mind.

Duncan, who was already committed to walking Binny back to Ebenezer Street, felt he had no choice.

But Gabriele saw none of this. She kept her eyes on the road. Unlike the NCT crowd, Gabriele had had no alcohol to drink. She never did on these occasions when she went to the English–Welsh Clubs.

When she got back to Bond-Kyle Avenue, she saw the lights were still on. Mrs Kit and Barry were still talking in the dining room. Gabriele found the Brittos very strange. In Neuchâtel husbands usually ate dinner with their wives, but most evenings Mrs Kit drank her gin and tonics while Barry ate his food, and then she went out *on the pissing* in Cardiff with the people she did not like. Then, once every two weeks, she would get someone to take her to buy fish and then cook all day and there would be much *fuckbloodythisthat*, and then she and Barry would sit up till two or three in the morning talking and arguing and laughing. None of this happened in Neuchâtel.

Duncan got back just after twelve-thirty. The baby-sitter called Linda had done all her ironing and was still awake, cheerfully reading a book. Duncan gave her her tokens, looked in on the girls, and went to bed. It had been a very strange and frustrating evening and he had decided that he wasn't going to try it on again with Holly. That was a disaster waiting to happen. Someone else would have to fall in love with Holly Williams. Besides, after a somewhat monosyllabic but not openly hostile walk back to Ebenezer Street, Binny had grabbed hold of Duncan in the porch and kissed him full on the mouth. It was a gesture that bordered on the aggressive, as if Binny had got wind of the fact that Duncan was making himself available and was having her share of the action.

Duncan had given up wanting to be a dog. He had had enough of women.

Holly Williams had had a lovely evening. She had a good talk with Laura when she got back. The two of them talked more and more these days. Holly had told Laura how *good* Duncan was and Laura had agreed with enthusiasm, almost with a touch of pride. Holly had been surprised how quickly Laura seemed to understand when she hinted at some problems with Gwyn. Though she admired Laura greatly, she had never seen her as a sympathetic listener – but this evening Laura had seemed to be completely in tune. Holly would have liked to embrace her in the Cosmic Cuddle before she went, but she didn't feel that was Laura's thing.

Holly had had hardly anything to drink all evening, but she poured herself a glass of whisky now. As she did she noticed the answerphone was flashing. It was probably

Gwyn or Gwyn's mother. She'd listen in the morning. Holly switched off the machine with the wrong button and accidentally wiped all that Gwyn had tried to say to her and now never would. She went upstairs and got into bed fully clothed with her glass of whisky. Then she remembered she hadn't checked on the children so she got out of bed again.

Half-way down the landing she paused by the large built-in cupboard. For no particular reason she remembered that that was where the photos of her as a student had been hidden. Holly's student photos were unusual in that they were mainly nude studies – eight of them, framed, in sepia and black and white.

As an eighteen-year-old at University College, Swansea, Holly Trewidden had felt no particular inhibition about taking off her clothes, and two observant fine art students had asked if they could photograph her. The pictures resulting from their giggly studio session were homages to the nude in Renaissance, Pastoral and PreRaphaelite paintings, and mainly featured Holly discreetly but stunningly viewed from the side or back, usually draped on a chaise longue or resting against a pillar. Here they were. The glass was broken in one of the frames. Holly could hear the shards clicking as she lifted them past three of her own paintings that Gwyn had never liked.

She looked at the photos across the gap of twenty-four years that separated her from Holly Trewidden. That girl had a very slim, very white figure, her hair wild and whiter still against the black chaise longue and darkened studio floor. Amazing, thought Holly. Amazing that this young woman was once her. Amazing that she was so beautiful – and that she couldn't have felt the cold at all in those days. Gwyn had seen these photos up in her room the first time he came to visit her. To Holly Trewidden the only thing unusual about her pictures was that they were framed. In those days lots of students had photos of beautiful nude women in their rooms. Hers just happened to be in aluminium frames because that's how they'd been given to her.

But young Gwyn Williams had seen it all differently and turned very red. Young Gwyn Williams was persistent and very sweet. He would come to see her every night and they would sit and listen to music and drink coffee until someone came to call for Holly, when Gwyn would always get up very politely, shake hands with whoever it was and quickly go. Sometimes when they were listening to the music he would cautiously put his arm round her shoulder. She'd liked that. Most of the boys Holly knew had made it fairly clear, fairly soon, that they hoped to be sleeping with her, so it was nice to have Gwyn. They used to lean against each other in a very companionable way, until one of the boys came to call for Holly.

But there was one night when nobody came, and at midnight Holly had said she was going to bed and did he want to stay? It was a long way back to where Gwyn was lodging with some relatives.

He had looked terribly embarrassed. Holly had never seen him so red. This was the first time she'd ever asked a boy to share her bed (normally she had never got the chance), and Holly wondered if she'd made some terrible social gaffe.

'I'm sorry,' she'd said, but having pulled off her sweatshirt she could hardly pretend she wasn't planning to undress.

Gwyn had looked incandescent. 'It's not that . . . I'd love to very much . . .' he told her with almost formal politeness. 'Only I don't have . . . I mean I haven't brought any protection with me.'

Holly had understood. She'd also understood that this was not the time to explain that her parents had decided she ought to be on the pill when she was only seventeen.

'That's all right,' she said. 'We can just have a cuddle.'

'Oh,' said Gwyn, looking both relieved and happily expectant. 'That would be very nice.'

And indeed it was. Holly had taken off her clothes and got into bed but, in deference to Gwyn's red cheeks, she'd pulled on a T-shirt. Gwyn kept his underpants on that night. It had been so nice. He had been so nice to her, and she to him. It had gone on for hours. Whereas sex . . . Well, sex was always over so quickly really. Even with the ones who tried to make it last longer, all they did was keep delaying the time when someone took the batteries out.

Holly looked at the photos fondly. Twenty-four years ago. What was that girl hoping to do with her life twenty-four years ago? After that night Gwyn had started moving in, gradually taking over, excluding the bad influences as he saw them. By the time he'd got her to agree to marry him he had also got her to agree not to display nude studies of herself on the walls any more. There was always a danger one of Gwyn's aunties might call, it seemed.

Of course he had been terribly sweet in those days. He had always been very concerned for her. Once he said that any man married to a woman like Holly was obliged to try and make something of himself. Silly. That wasn't how she'd seen it, that girl. She'd just wanted to lie in bed till twelve o'clock, cuddling and eating honey and chocolates for breakfast, and looking at pictures and maybe painting or drawing in the afternoon. But something happened after Buddug was born. Gwyn joined every orchestra he could find, doubled the number of pupils he taught and became very sure and stout and noisy. And Holly got too cold to lie around naked on dodgy sofas.

She put the pictures back. She had agreed to them being hidden now because it wasn't really fair on Buddug, who was never going to look like that girl and already minded. Holly went back to bed. She had completely forgotten about checking on the children.

It had been a lovely evening.

9

A Woman of Mystery

The following week was not easy in Katrin Street.

Duncan's routine was simpler with Alice back in school, but Jane was still in a considerable amount of discomfort. Despite Big Fat Tony's insistence on rest, she decided to go in to work and let Duncan drive her to and fro. Alice and Ellen took advantage of this arrangement to let Duncan drive them as well. This meant that he was in the car, passing very slowly through various parts of Cardiff, from 8.20 to 9.30 in the morning and from 5.00 to 6.20 in the evening. If the girls had had their way he would have been driving between 3.15 and 3.45 as well, but Duncan absolutely put his foot down about that.

'Why can't you take some time off?' he nagged as they sat in the Tuesday-morning traffic jam.

'Because it was my own silly fault,' said Jane. They had got this argument down to its basics now: Jane could take time off/Jane wouldn't take time off/Jane believed that Follets shouldn't suffer/Jane believed that Jane should suffer/Jane didn't seem to mind if Duncan suffered too. Duncan would much rather have spent two and a half hours a day carrying cups of tea to his wife on her sick bed than pass the time nudging their car round the Cardiff streets, but Jane refused to take to her bed.

'We might as well be living in London!' Duncan grumbled.

Mair Lloyd was solicitous but resentful. There was, in her view, room for only one martyr in Tony's team. So she joined the chorus of Tony, Miles and David telling Jane she should stay at home and rest. By the end of the week Jane felt comfortable enough to drive herself in, and the articled clerk who had been using her designated parking space had, resentfully, to start using the NCP again.

The week wasn't easy in Pontcanna Terrace either.

Gwyn Williams returned from Llandudno hoping that things would be different, but Holly seemed the same. Still the same limp way she let him kiss her, still the same way she discreetly withdrew from rooms when he came in. Once or twice he came into the kitchen when she was vaguely doing something to the soup, and said, 'Well, Mrs Williams?' in a hopeful sort of way, but the most he ever got from Holly was a smile, a hug and a 'Later'.

On Wednesday morning Holly spotted Laura at the school gate. She hadn't seen Duncan or Laura since Saturday night and had no idea how she was going to bring up the subject, but Gwyn was at home for *two weeks now* and he kept following her round the house. She really didn't like it.

'What have you arranged for half term?' Laura asked.

Holly had had only the vaguest idea that half term was upon them. 'Oh, I suppose we'll all be in the house together,' she said weakly.

'You don't want that, do you?' Laura asked. In her view boys needed to be kept occupied.

'No,' said Holly, who was thinking more about Gwyn than Siôn and Buddug.

'There are some very good courses at Llanover Hall,' said Laura, getting out the brochure from her shoulderbag. 'I've got Gawain and Arthur building a puppet show and Tris is doing raffia and pottery. They can't take Mordred because he's too young which is a pity. Gerald was going to take a day off so we could go to Bath but Mawmaw will just have to come with us. Holly, are you all right?' Laura squinted up into Holly's face.

Holly had just seen Duncan and Jane in their car dropping off Alice and Ellen. Duncan and Jane are so lucky to have each other, thought Holly. She, realised Laura was talking to her. 'Oh yes,' she replied without enthusiasm. 'I was just thinking that I ought to get a job.'

Laura sighed. 'Money is such a worry isn't it?'

'No, just something to get me out of the house.'

'But you've got a lovely house.' Laura thought 27 Pontcanna Terrace very artistic, if not quite her thing.

'It's *very* full,' said Holly.

Kit Sinclair was not having a good week either. Geegee had gone back to Switzerland for two weeks – or, as the Britto Boys put it amid great hilarity, the Cheese had gone off. Kit could not abide having temporary help in the house, so on Sunday evening Barry had been told that he had to take the boys to school until half term began.

'You sent them to that bastard School,' Kit said. 'You can go down and stand around in the rain with a load of scrubby tarts!'

'Christine . . .' Barry said. Only when he thought his wife was getting overwrought did he call her this but it earnt him a mouthful of abuse that culminated in the assertion that however much the University of Wales thought the sun shone out of Barry's arse he would always be a jumped-up little Welsh spiv in her eyes.

Barry put his arms round her. 'Calm down,' he said.

Kit yelped and jumped out of his embrace. It was now eleven o'clock on Sunday evening. Barry suggested that he could get one of the other medics' wives to drive down to school with her. The new Professor of Cardiology's wife wanted to be friends, but Kit didn't like her. She didn't like any of them. Barry could see that his wife was panicking. There was only one thing to do when Kit boxed herself into an emotional corner like this.

'OK,' he said. 'I'll take them in and we'll see if they can go and play at a friend's house till I can collect them.'

So later that evening than he would have wished Barry got on the telephone to his secretary and put all his appointments back an hour till lunchtime. He made a mental note to buy Lyn a box of chocolates for dropping her in it so late in the day.

It was on Wednesday morning that Duncan, opening the car door for Alice and Ellen, noticed the Britto boys being dropped off by an unusually tall, swarthy man, but he didn't actually meet Barry until the Thursday when Jane was driving herself into work again.

Duncan was very interested to see the famous Bastard at closer quarters, but at closer quarters he realised that Barry was built on an alarming scale. Not for nothing had Barry Britto played at No.8 for the London Welsh first team. He was one of those men who always wore short-sleeved shirts, even in winter, and watching him get his sons out of the car, Duncan was aware that the Britto forearms were about the same circumference as the Lewis calves. The combination of Kit Sinclair, dangerously thin, and Barry Britto, dangerously big, was obviously what had produced the lean, dark, athletic Britto Boys.

'Hi, I'm Duncan Lewis.' Duncan joined Barry as he walked back from the school gate. 'You brought us some wine.'

'Sure,' said Barry. 'Nice to meet you, Duncan,' and he offered a large hand which Duncan shook cautiously.

'How's Kit?' Duncan asked.

'Fine,' said Barry. 'The au pair's had to go home, that's why I'm doing the school run.'

Barry hadn't altered his stride as he returned to the car, he just seemed to have swept Duncan alongside him.

'Look, if I can help . . .' Duncan said, having to speed up to keep pace.

'Great idea,' said Barry. 'Give Kit a ring after ten-thirty. She'd appreciate it. Nice to meet you, Dunc. Any time you need more wine give us a bell.'

And with that Barry, much later than he had intended, swung into the large white sportscar Kit had bought for him and drove off.

Holly was watching Duncan, wondering whether they could speak to him, but he turned up Fulwood Road and had gone before she'd even thought of what to say.

Kit sounded very relieved when Duncan rang.

'Oh Sweetie,' she said. 'I've got so much on and the tart's walked out on me.'

'I thought she was on holiday,' Duncan replied.

'Well it's still the absolute worst time to go with half term next week.'

'Is it?' Duncan asked. This was not the kind of thing a house father likes to find out as the week draws to its close.

Kit gave one of her laughs. 'Oh Dunky,' she said. 'You ring up to try and scrape me off the ceiling and now I've got to sort you out.'

'I'm fine,' said Duncan, who most certainly wasn't.

'You sound as if you're pissing yourself,' said Kit. 'Come and have lunch with me at Garlands and we'll see what we can do.'

*   *   *

Jane Lewis wasn't too pleased to get a panicky phone call from Duncan in the middle of Thursday morning asking if she knew that half term started next week and had she done anything about it?

'Find out about Playcare,' was all she could suggest because she had a client waiting and her back still wasn't ideal.

'You might have told me,' Duncan reproached her.

'Well you're in charge,' she reproached him back. 'Don't you read the newsletters?'

Rather than get into an argument, Duncan walked up to Kit's house and let himself be taken out to lunch. Kit drove them into the city centre in Gabriele's car, giving a foul-mouthed running commentary all the way. 'Look at that silly bugger, *shit* what an idiot; look at that arsehole; what a stupid, stupid cow, serve her right if she did get a lorry up her fanny; what a fucking moron, Christ almighty . . .' The only other time Duncan had been assailed by so much scatology and obscenity was when, as a student, he had been stuck in a bus shelter with a wino.

By the time they reached Garlands mock-Viennese coffee house, Kit was all smiles. 'Darling,' she said to the portly young man who pointed them to a corner table over the stairs. 'How wonderful.'

'This is what they call the Legover Table,' she told Duncan mischievously as they studied their menus. 'The staff, I mean. Blokes ring up and ask for this table when they're trying it on with somebody.'

Duncan was thrown for a moment by the thought that he was a bloke who had recently tried it on, only last weekend in fact.

Kit registered the introspection. 'Don't worry,' she said. 'You're safe with me. I gave all that up ages ago. What about the other mums? How you getting on with those?'

Duncan was alarmed. 'What other mums?'

'That lot down at the school gate. Jane told me they think the sun shines out of you.'

Duncan wasn't aware that Jane had ever talked to Kit about Laura and Holly.

'You've got to be careful, Dunc,' said Kit. 'Available man, sensitive type. Lot of frustrated housewives go for that. Tell 'em you bake your own bread as well and they'll be wetting their knickers.'

'I haven't had any offers,' said Duncan, trying to sound droll.

Kit ordered a salad which she didn't eat and Duncan had a club sandwich. They were supposed to be working out how they could share the childcare over half term and how Duncan could help Kit for the rest of this week, but she decided to tell him one of her life stories.

Kit Sinclair had various versions of her life that depended on how she felt. Today she was buoyed up by the expedition and so Duncan didn't get the mad stepfather, the sexual abuse as a child and the abortions. Today Duncan got the brilliant, rebellious schoolgirl who had been seduced on her sixteenth birthday by a French man who'd taken her with him to New York where he'd tried to put her on the game. Kit had refused to co-operate so he threw her out and she supported herself, first helping out in a fashion store that Duncan had never heard of and then as a fashion journalist.

Travelling round North Africa, she had picked up some rare disease which, the first time Kit told the story seemed to have been sexually transmitted but, the second time around, sounded more to do with the digestive tract. She spent some months in a London hospital that specialised in rare diseases, paid for by her mad stepfather (who was getting only the briefest of walk-on roles in today's version of her life). It was while she was in hospital defying medical science that Kit decided to start writing about medicine, and she had a brief but prodigious career as a medical cum fashion journalist until she met this brilliant young medic who turned out to be Barry.

'When I met him he'd just come back from New York where they were pioneering Cardiology. He actually worked in the first British team, at Barts, and he could have gone anywhere. 'Course he had no money in those days, but I used to support him. Cost me, I can tell you. Then what happens? We're all set to go off to the States to make a mint, or for him to get a consultancy in *any* of the big London hospitals, and what does he do? He gets the call of the wild, this *hiraeth* thing, and has to come back and help Wales. Complete fucking disaster. Wrecked my career. He doesn't even do private practice down here. Turns out he believes in the welfare state and state education. Bastard. I said to him, "OK, you can send them to the local flea pit. But I'm not picking them up and standing out in the rain with a load of scrubby tarts—"'

'Which is where I come in,' said Duncan who, though fascinated by Kit's narrative powers, was aware that they had completely wandered off the point.

Kit was thrown, then highly amused by this prompt. 'I suppose you are a bit of a tart, Duncan,' she giggled.

'No I'm not,' he replied. Duncan had never been called a tart before and he was, to his surprise, rather hurt by it.

'Are you entirely faithful to Jane?' Kit asked.

'Yes,' said Duncan, simplifying.

'Do you want to be?' Kit asked. Duncan hesitated.

'Told you,' said Kit smugly. 'Don't worry, a lot of men are tarts. Barry isn't. Barry's a latter-day saint working for his boys and the salvation of mankind. Barry also knows that if he even thought about it I'd cut off his bollocks. But a lot of men are.' She toyed with an olive and gave him her knowing smile.

Duncan was annoyed. When he wasn't with Kit he thought of her fondly as his ridiculously eccentric friend, but when he was actually in her company he was always struck by these unexpected flashes of insight. OK, maybe she wasn't as clever as she *thought* she was, but she'd got him uncomfortably sized up.

'What about you?' he asked. 'Are you a tart?' He wanted to strike back in some way.

'Nah,' said Kit, as irritatingly blasé as an eight-year-old. 'I've done all that. Believe me, there isn't anything I haven't tried – and I can tell you I know when I'm better off.'

They squabbled over her paying the bill for both of them when she hadn't even touched her salad.

'It was lovely, thanks,' said Kit, handing her plate to the stout young waiter with a smile. It seemed to Duncan that Kit was patronising him, buying him lunch, making sweeping assertions about his character, and inadvertently suggesting that she had given up on sex as passé at about the age that Duncan had been just getting into it.

'If it makes you feel any better it's not my money, it's the Bastard's,' she said when they got up to go.

'It's not that,' said Duncan.

As they walked along the wrought-iron Victorian arcades back to the NCP, Duncan was feeling got at by Kit and by Barry's salary. He had actually been sitting in Garlands wondering whether, as Jane was working and he wasn't, he might suggest splitting the bill instead of offering to pay for it all. But all that time Kit was graciously buying him lunch. And, what was more annoying still, they had hardly discussed next week beyond Kit's idea that the girls could join her sons on a swimming course.

'Is it because I called you a tart?' Kit asked out of the blue as they passed the practical joke shop with its window display of gorilla suits.

'No, for goodness sake!' said Duncan rather too loudly.

An old lady jumped. The arcade acoustics always picked up anything above a mutter, which could be unfortunate.

Kit looked rather crestfallen, which was a look Duncan had never expected to see. He could imagine her turning round and telling him very loudly to fuck off if they disagreed, but he would never have imagined Kit Sinclair having the wind blown out of her sails.

'I'm sorry,' he said.

Kit tried unsuccessfully not to look hurt. 'We're mates,' she said with a shrug. 'You can say anything to mates, can't you?'

'Sure,' he replied. 'I'm sorry.'

'Don't have to apologise to mates either,' said Kit, regaining some of her poise.

'Sure,' said Duncan, taking her arm affectionately.

'Duncan, don't do that,' Kit said as they set off back down the arcade.

'Why?' Duncan asked.

'It's a long story,' she said, releasing her arm. 'I told you I'm a woman of mystery didn't I?'

'Yes.'

'Well, women of mystery have got a thing about people touching them.'

Duncan was asked to stay in the car with her until she parked back in Bond-Kyle Avenue, which he did even though it meant having to walk back down the hill to Pontcanna. It seemed that as well as not wanting to be touched, women of mystery couldn't drive a car on their own. Or maybe Kit just liked having someone to listen to her swear.

Duncan walked back to Katrin Street, did some jobs, and found out that the local Playcare scheme was, of course, fully booked.

On the journey up Cathedral Road Kit had asked Duncan if he would mind collecting her sons that day, as she didn't like the woman from Barry's work who had offered to have them for the afternoon. The quid pro quo was that Kit would have Alice and Ellen to tea. So when Duncan arrived at the school gate his daughters were immodestly delighted to find that they were walking the Britto Boys back to Llandaff.

'We haven't got a car,' Alice said pointedly, 'or we'd give you a lift.'

'We have got a car,' said Duncan from behind. 'Your mother's taken it to work.'

'Our Mum's got a car,' said the big Britto Boy, whom Duncan half remembered as Ben, 'but she won't drive it.'

'In case she swears at someone,' added Little Britto.

Kit had made lots of preparations, which had included ringing the school to say that Duncan Lewis was collecting her sons and setting out a table tennis table, trampoline, paints and overalls in the pristine playroom, part of the house Duncan hadn't seen before.

'Right, you go and back some bread,' she said to Duncan. 'Barry will drop your girls off about six-thirty.'

Duncan was rather disappointed that he wasn't being invited in. He was intrigued to see what Kit the Mum was like, but he had a sneaky suspicion that she had already decided that he would not see Kit the Mum at work. And he was right.

When it was time to pick up the boys Laura Davis was disconcerted to find Duncan waiting at the school gate with a rather gaunt young woman. Laura had thought she knew all the Fulwood mothers from her PTA campaigning. This one, in her opinion, looked rather ill. Although Laura was small in stature, she was pleased that over the years she had developed a shape to her. But this woman who, now Laura drew closer, seemed to be in her early thirties – well, she was simply *thin*, and judging by her pallor not very well.

Duncan had noticed Laura's approach out of the corner of his eye. He half hoped that she would be distracted by Holly or the Iranian widow or someone else. Having coaxed Kit to come down to the school that Friday, he really didn't want her frightened off by Laura or, to be honest, for Laura to be alarmed by Kit. Of all Duncan's friends Laura and Kit were probably the most dissimilar, and Duncan felt the kind of embarrassment about their meeting that he used to feel about college friends meeting his parents.

'Ah, hello Laura!' he said, seeing her squinting up at Kit. 'Kit, this is Laura Davis; Laura, this is—'

'Mrs Britto.' Kit took off her dark glasses and gave a dazzlingly artificial smile.

Don't say anything, *please*, Duncan thought.

'Kit, isn't it?' said Laura, holding out her hand. 'Duncan's told me so much about you.'

Have I? thought Duncan.

'And you're the one with all those sons with wonderful Wagnerian names,' said Kit, ignoring Laura's hand. *Stop it*, thought Duncan. She was sounding like a well-informed member of the Royal Family come to open something dull and charm the locals.

'Arthurian,' Laura replied. 'We had Gawain and Tristram and then we got rather stuck. We hadn't really intended to have four, so it became rather difficult to think of other names.'

'There's Launcelot, I suppose,' said Kit helpfully.

Duncan wondered whether Kit was actually sending Laura up or just playing the part of a Laura kind of woman to make her feel at home.

'Yes,' said Laura. 'And there's Percival – but then they get shortened to Lance and Percy, don't they?'

Kit gave a sudden laugh. Duncan winced, but then he realised that Laura was joining in the laugh. In fact, the two women seemed to be getting on. Opting out of the conversation while he was ahead, Duncan looked around to see if he could catch a glimpse of Holly. He had been wondering all week whether she had re-evaluated his behaviour on Saturday, realised she had been the object of a bungled seduction, and taken offence.

But Holly was not to be seen around the school gate. Then, across the road, Duncan spotted Gwyn waiting by the door of his car. So Holly hadn't come today. Duncan nodded at Gwyn but there was a considerable distance between the two men and Duncan assumed that Gwyn hadn't seen him.

In fact Gwyn had seen him. Gwyn had been watching the way Duncan Lewis was chatting up two of the mothers, and he was getting fed up with how marvellous all these women seemed to think this architect fellow to be. In the one conversation – the only conversation – he'd managed with Holly since getting back, she had made a point of telling him how nice Duncan Lewis had been to her while he was away. When Gwyn asked her what she meant by that, she had laughed at what sounded like suspicion in his voice. Duncan was just someone she could talk to, and so was his wife, Jane, and that was something that she liked.

'We could talk,' Gwyn had said.

'We do talk,' Holly had said, wishing to heaven that he'd stop talking.

'Well then . . .'

Holly had kissed him. 'Well then nothing,' she'd said simply, and stroked his cheek. Gwyn had been just about to follow this up with a kiss of his own when Holly had to go downstairs to look at the lasagne.

Gwyn felt like two men these days. Outside the house he was still principal horn, a member of many committees, a prime mover in the musical life of Cardiff. But inside 27 Pontcanna Terrace he was beginning to feel like Young

Gwyn Williams again, Young Gwyn Williams the trainee music teacher from Swansea who had decided to keep up with his horn lessons, to do something heroic in the teeth of family pressure to get a secure job, because of his love for the unobtainable Holly Trewidden.

Gwyn had been greatly in awe of Holly twenty years ago, but very determined. He had never told his parents about Holly's other lovers, but his view had been that he would see them all off eventually – and he had. Gwyn's mother moved with the times and probably thought to herself that Holly and Gwyn had 'done it' before marriage – as young people did in those days, 'just to make sure' – but she would have been mortified had Holly admitted to her, as she had to Gwyn, that she had lost count of the number of men she'd had before him. To tell the truth Gwyn had been pretty mortified too.

'But who's counting?' Holly had asked him when he had pursued the subject.

'Well, not you for a start,' he'd said.

But then sex had always been more important to Gwyn. One of the reasons he had done it so little by the time they met was that sex mattered to him, whereas Holly had done it so much because it wasn't really something that affected her greatly. Once they became engaged, Gwyn set about becoming a really good lover spurred on by his relative lack of experience, which was one of life's great ironies because Holly had always assumed that once she married sex would become less adventurous. Gwyn Williams sought to perfect himself in the one aspect of human relationships from which his new wife was really quite happy to take a rest.

Twenty years later, Gwyn still found himself wondering how women like Holly could tell that this Duncan was so marvellous in bed. After twenty years of marriage, Young Gwyn Williams was still getting the wrong answers, and it still hadn't occurred to him he might be asking the wrong questions.

Jane had called in to see Binny on her way back from work that Friday night because she was feeling an acute need to talk to someone who wasn't Duncan, or Tony, or Miles or David.

When she finally got back to Katrin Street two glasses of wine and a lot of female solidarity later, the girls were watching TV in their pyjamas and Duncan was cooking. 'How did you get on at Playcare?' she asked. Duncan was offering what would be her third glass of wine, and she decided to justify it on the basis that it was the weekend, it was half term, and it was probably a good way of relaxing her muscles too. 'Fully booked,' said Duncan. 'But I've fixed up something with Kit and Laura.' 'What about Holly?' Jane asked. 'What about Holly?' Duncan replied jumpily.

Jane explained that she thought Holly had been very good to him – she'd had Ellen for three days while Alice was in hospital. Perhaps she needed some time off next week too. 'Besides,' she said. 'You've got to treat all your women fairly.'

'They are not my women.' Duncan was getting tired of this joke.

'Binny says you and Holly were inseparable at the meal evening,' Jane said with mock significance. She had picked up on something that Binny had been half saying not two hours ago in Ebenezer Street.

'Binny!' said Duncan. 'Binny tried to kiss me at the meal evening.' He felt the need to deflect Jane's attention away from Holly. 'Actually Binny *did* kiss me when I walked her back. Did she tell you that?'

'No,' said Jane, laughing at the idea.

'Bloody cheek. Do you know where she kissed me?'

'I'm agog.'

'In the porch.'

Jane roared with laughter. 'Oh, poor Duncan! Didn't you even get invited up to her room for coffee?'

'All I'm saying is that Binny's a fine one to talk. Holly behaved like a gentleman throughout Saturday evening, which is more than can be said for Binny Barnes.'

Jane decided to telephone Holly, but she got through to Gwyn who told her straight away that Holly was out baby-sitting that night. In fact, Gwyn had noticed, Holly was doing a lot of baby-sitting in the next two weeks. His voice seemed to suggest that he hoped Jane wasn't another one looking for sitters.

'Would you tell her I rang to see if she and Duncan can arrange anything for next week,' Jane asked.

'I'm afraid she's got the children off school next week,' Gwyn said unhelpfully.

'That's what I mean.' Jane was thinking what a difficult man Gwyn Williams could be. He always sounded polite, but there never seemed to be a simple 'Yes'.

If Gwyn Williams was feeling any sense of grievance against Duncan that Friday night, it would have been greatly magnified had he known that Duncan had a ticket for the match the following Saturday afternoon. This wasn't any old rugby match or even any International that was being played at the Arms Park; this was *the* Match between England and Wales. For weeks now tickets had been changing hands for sums that Gwyn would not have paid for a new dinner jacket, or even for a weekend away with his wife. Duncan's ticket, which had come to him via Kit and therefore via Barry, cost someone who was keen to impress Barry Britto £450.

'*How* much?' Jane and Duncan asked Kit as she stood in their kitchen dressed for the races.

'Of course we get lunch and drinkies,' said Kit. 'But on the other hand we've got to talk to a load of old farts as well.'

Jane was staggered at the cost. She felt she shouldn't have been, but she was. 'And why can't Barry go?' she asked.

'He's on call,' said Kit. 'But to tell the truth I think he'd rather watch it on telly with the boys. It's what he's used to. The sod's a terrible peasant. And in any case, he knows we've only been given the tickets because some drug company wants to nobble him at the lunch.'

'Well, won't they be disappointed when I turn up?' Duncan asked.

'Yes, but they won't dare show it,' said Kit, laughing. 'That's part of the fun. Besides, I've told them you're high up at Barts.'

'What!'

Kit looked at Duncan and Jane in amusement. 'Only joking,' she said.

You never knew with Kit.

'*Don't*,' said Duncan.

Kit told him to hurry up put on a coat – they had a rendezvous with a lot of cheap champagne. While Duncan was upstairs looking through his jackets Jane thanked Kit for having the girls for part of last week and some of next.

'They really enjoyed coming to you on Thursday,' she said.

'It was nothing,' said Kit. 'Hardly knew they were there.'

Jane didn't believe this. 'Alice said you played games with them all afternoon and somehow got them reading as well. She said it was like being in a "real home". That was a dig at me,' Jane admitted. 'But I think they both genuinely thought you were the original Supermum.'

Kit looked embarrassed. 'Yeah, well,' she said, stubbing out her cigarette. 'You've got to make an effort.'

'It's all right,' said Jane. 'I won't tell Duncan.'

Kit smiled. She liked Jane more each time she saw her.

'No, don't. He thinks I'm some dreadful old scrubby kind of tart. Don't want to disillusion him, do we?'

It was midday, and the pubs were already full as Duncan and Kit took a taxi down Cathedral Road. Duncan sat in the front as he had found the custom to be in South Wales – besides, for all he knew Kit might have a touching-by-accident-in-the-back-seat taboo as well. He really didn't want any embarrassment in front of the driver.

As they turned towards the Arms Park even Duncan felt a sense of occasion. There was very bad singing coming out of the Westgate and some fat lads in red shirts were climbing in and out of a window. Although the match wouldn't start for another three hours people were walking hither and thither in groups across Castle Street. 'Milling' was what they called it. Backwards and forwards, purposefully but with no real purpose except obstructing the traffic. As for Westgate Street, where the Arms Park lay, the police had closed it off already. There was a sense that Cardiff was being colonised by an invading pedestrian army who would patrol the streets relentlessly, and pointlessly, until the gates were open.

Their driver had a very clear idea of what kind of function Duncan and Kit were heading to.

'We dropped a few there already,' he told Duncan. 'Champagne and canapés is it, I suppose?'

'So I'm told,' said Duncan.

'Pricing the honest fan out of the game,' the driver told him. 'How much you pay for your ticket?'

Duncan felt he might not enjoy this conversation so he told the driver that he'd been given it. The driver wanted to know who by.

'Me,' said Kit, leaning forward.

'Oh. No offence,' the driver said over his shoulder.

The taxi slowed down as it encountered the first drifting groups of spectators.

'Don't suppose you could get me one, could you?' the driver asked.

'I dunno . . .' said Kit. 'You're not really my type.'

Duncan looked at her anxiously.

'And he is?' The driver looked at Duncan.

'I like 'em tall,' Kit said, getting into her stride.

'My friend is joking,' said Duncan.

'And nervous,' said Kit. 'I like 'em tall and nervous.'

'S'pose you like 'em *sensitive* an' all.'

Duncan couldn't tell whether the driver was joking on Kit's wavelength or simply getting riled by her.

'Oh no,' said Kit, changing tack, 'I like 'em *rough*.'

'Nearly there,' sang Duncan, his eyes on the road.

'And *tough*,' Kit added.

'I was in the Marines,' said the driver.

Duncan kept his eyes on the road. 'You must excuse my friend, she hasn't had enough to drink.'

The car was drawing up, mercifully, outside a tall block of buildings.

'Tell you what,' said Kit, putting her head between the two front seats, 'you wait here and keep your engine running and if I get fed up with this one I'll be back out.' And with that she bounded out of the cab leaving Duncan to pay.

'Sorry about that,' he said.

'She ought to be careful,' said the driver, nodding after Kit.

'Yes.'

'I mean, I can take a joke but some of the people . . . well, they might take all that the wrong way. Mightn't they?'

'Yes,' said Duncan. 'How much is it?'

Gwyn had taken Siôn round to the house of one of his friends from the National Orchestra who had three boys. Stiffin was divorced, and his ex wife took a vindictive pleasure in making sure it was his turn to have the boys any weekend of an International, thus depriving him the opportunity of going down to the Arms Park. So the two men and four boys would spend the afternoon in red shirts glued to the television and discussing what Wales might have managed if most of the conditions had been different.

Gwyn noticed that Siôn had brought his blasted toys with him, which was disappointing, but Gwyn wasn't going to say anything in front of Stiffin. Besides there was a lot of natter to be got through before the game itself. Pundits, ex pros, natter natter natter. Tired old face after tired old face coming up on screen to talk about the thirty young men who would decide whether or not it was going to be a great day for Wales.

Gwyn liked Stiffin, but he felt that visiting his flat on Penarth Marina was a foreshadowing of what life without Holly would be like. God, he'd got to get her sorted somehow.

The pre-match reception was in a private club up several flights of stairs. Its ground-floor entrance was clean but unprepossessing, a small door in a tall grimy block of what looked like Victorian shipping offices. But upstairs there was a large new reception room, brightly lit and half full of the new money and their mistresses, the Welsh glitterati and – as Kit put it – titterati.

Someone took Duncan's Barbour, somebody else gave him a glass of champagne, and someone else said, 'Have a can*ape*, love.'

Kit looked round the room. 'God, this looks pretty crappy,' she said. 'I'm going off to the bog for half an hour; maybe it'll pick up.' She downed her champagne, returned the glass and disappeared.

Duncan was left suddenly and rather spectacularly on his

own. An immediate fear gripped him. He was convinced he would see the happy smiling faces of Howard Losen and Dic coming up the stairs, and he in turn would have to behave in a friendly, prosperous and happy manner. But a different face presented itself before him.

'It's the architect, isn't it?'

For a moment Duncan didn't recognise Carolyn Parry Morris. When he'd seen her before it was in a badly lit bodega or a cramped Mitsubishi cockpit. But here she looked as bright as the decor. Her hair was backcombed into synthetic perfection, the blonde colour so artificial that Duncan found a rather perverse liking for it. But the real triumph was her outfit in white and gold, proclaiming money and the fact that somebody else was looking after Elinor – not a smear, not a wrinkle, never before worn.

'And you're the lady with the card,' said Duncan as jovially as he could manage.

'Carolyn,' said Carolyn.

'I know,' said Duncan,' I read it.'

Duncan thought that *anyone* done up like that would look wonderful, but he admitted to himself that he was willing to revise his opinion of Carolyn Parry Morris. Although she was a bit concertinaed together, the actual elements, in isolation, were fine.

'*Duncan*—' said the Jane in his head.

'Do you know everyone?' Carolyn was saying, which was another way of asking, 'What the hell are *you* doing here?'

'No one,' said Duncan. 'I've been brought along as a wealthy lady's toy-boy.' He was determined not to impress Carolyn. Or – more honestly – he was determined to impress her with his nonchalance, his very refusal to impress.

'Well, well,' said Carolyn. 'You must tell me which one. Some girls have the strangest taste.'

'You should see the clothes she wears,' Duncan replied. He rather resented having got into this banter. It was substandard, rather cheap: I'll be insouciant with you, you can play at being rude to me. Still, he'd started it. It was his fault.

'I'll introduce you to some people,' said Carolyn.

'I'll be fine,' said Duncan, hoping she wouldn't.

'It's my party,' Carolyn told him. Duncan didn't understand what she meant. 'This is one of Caed's functions. I'm his Director of Corporate Hospitality.'

'Oh I see,' Duncan said.

'I thought you read my card?'

'It was in Welsh,' said Duncan.

Carolyn laughed as if to say, 'Silly boy'. She seemed all fond and proprietorial, especially when she took his arm. Duncan really didn't like it.

Gerald Davis was planning to watch the match on television, and he was rather hoping that Laura might take the opportunity to go out or even retire to bed with the *TES*. Gerald loved his wife deeply; he had been amazed twenty years ago that this young girl devoted herself to him, and more surprised still to find that, as each year passed, he was able to love her more than the last, to find more and more admirable qualities in her – but Laura would treat any televised sporting event as an educational opportunity. Her habit was to sit among all her boys and talk through the entire match, asking questions either for her own information or to draw out the boys and gauge their understanding of competitive sport.

Gerald was in the back room checking the channel against that morning's paper. It would be perverse to have the impartial English commentary on a day like today, so he was struggling to identify where BBC Wales was on the dial. It was at this moment that Laura arrived from the kitchen with a tray of drinks.

'I thought lager for you,' she said, placing the bottle down on an old Bavarian beer mat. 'Or would you prefer a can? Gerry?'

'I really don't mind,' said Gerald.

'I suppose cans are more authentic,' said Laura.

'Mm . . .' said Gerald.

'But the cans are only three hundred millilitres,' said Laura. 'Whereas the bottles are five hundred. So would you want two cans? Gerald? I can chill two cans if you'd prefer.'

Gerald had knelt down and lifted his spectacles, and was now peering at the numbers on the dial; activities which, when accompanied by silence on his part, gave Laura Leighton Davis the distinct impression that she was not being listened to.

'Gerald? One can or two?'

'Oh for heaven's sake!' Gerald exclaimed.

Laura went very still, and calm, and cold. Laura and Gerald Davis tended not to have arguments. They certainly never raised their voices at each other. Gerald got up slowly from the television like a stiff old elephant, for his long legs took some unbending, then he looked at Laura a little shamefaced.

'Gerald.' Laura took a deep breath. 'Are you having an affair?'

'No!' said Gerald in some consternation.

'Because this is not the first time you've been short with me.'

'I am most dreadfully sorry,' said Gerald, opening his arms.

Laura took a moment before accepting the embrace, but once in his arms she knew she would be unable to resist forgiving him.

'How could you ever think that?' Gerald asked her fondly. From long years of practice Gerald Davis knew when his wife wanted a kiss from him, because she would first circle his neck with her wrist and then pull his face down the fourteen inches that separated them.

Some things never lose their wonder, Laura thought. It was worth these upsets to resolve them in an unscheduled kiss.

'Oh,' said Arthur from the doorway, all innocence, 'Sunday, is it?'

Duncan had been talking to a bald senior commissioning editor from Channel 4 in London who was wondering why he had been invited.

'I presume someone wants to bribe me,' said the man, looking round the room, 'but so far everyone's just been very polite and attentive as if getting work was the last thing on their minds.'

'They do things differently down here,' said Duncan.

'Where have you come from?' asked the editor.

Duncan explained that he was local, and that like a lot of people he knew, he'd started off as a student in Cardiff and never got round to leaving.

'You don't find it too Welsh?' asked the bald man, feeling that he'd found an ally.

'No,' said Duncan. 'This is mild. You do get the odd shock to the system when you can't read a roadsign in the morning, or you go into a pub where they're singing "Anglo-Saxons are illegitimate, Bastards all are they". But it sort of wakes you up a bit.'

'Like a national astringent?' suggested the editor.

'Yes, but I don't usually venture any further west,' said Duncan. 'It's more like acid than aftershave once you get past Carmarthen.'

Carolyn heaved her shoulder neatly between Duncan and his new friend. 'Ah David, don't let Duncan monopolise you,' she said. 'There's someone over here dying to meet you.'

'Bye,' said David, affecting helplessness.

'Watch out for the aftershave,' said Duncan. God, he hated Carolyn Parry Morris. What had she ever done with her life to justify swanning around as if all these people were pawns in her game? To tell the truth he had no idea. He had assumed the obvious: that Carolyn had traded relentlessly on her brother's name ever since a very expensive divorce, and that she made a small but tidy income of her own appearing as a celebrity panellist on some Welsh language quiz show. But then again he didn't know. Maybe she had received the Nobel Peace Prize. She certainly behaved as if she thought she had.

'God, this is tacky,' said a woman with two glasses of champagne. Duncan was very pleased to see that Kit was back. 'The bog is full of old prozzies trying to keep their tits in place.'

'What are we *doing* here?' Duncan asked, accepting his glass.

'Making a good impression,' Kit told him.

'Don't bank on it.'

Kit looked round. 'He'll do,' she said, signalling that Duncan should follow her into the growing mêlée.

'Who?' asked Duncan.

'Some old fart that Barry knows. He'll tell us who to suck up to. Come on!'

Jane found it rather odd to be in the house without Duncan. Usually on a Saturday morning she was quite keen to have some time to herself, but now that the girls had gone to play with this new friend that Ellen had taken off Buddug Williams, and Duncan had gone off to play silly buggers with Kit, Jane felt rather at a loss to know what to do with herself. So she got out the washing that Duncan had let stew in the machine and unpacked the dishwasher, bending very carefully at all times.

She wasn't worried about Duncan spending time with Kit Sinclair. It might be good for his work, and Kit had gone out of her way to give off all the signals that she wasn't after Duncan. It was Laura Davis that bothered Jane more. Laura was devoted to Gerald – there was no doubt about that – but she had also very definitely befriended Duncan, and befriended him not as his wife's friend, which Jane found unusual. She had actually said to Binny that she could imagine catching Duncan and Laura *in flagrante* and Laura getting on her high horse about the fact that it meant nothing at all because she was absolutely devoted to Gerald. Then she had changed her mind and said that to be honest she really couldn't imagine catching them at it.

'No, it's not Laura I'd be worried about,' Binny had said in that way of hers.

Of course Duncan was moving at liberty in a primarily female world at the moment, Jane reflected. And that was fine because she trusted him. But Duncan knew Jane's views on adultery. She'd suffered its consequences as a child. Duncan knew there were parameters.

At that moment sex, marital or extra-marital, was the last thing on Duncan's mind. He had run the full gamut of dull, unwelcome emotions that lunchtime. Embarrassment, awkwardness, resentment, a brief moment of hating Cari Parry, and now boredom as Kit was absolutely super to a distinguished looking man in his fifties who, on the strength of a splendid rugby career, had been given overall responsibility for the planning and conservation issues affecting Cardiff and the Bay.

As far as Duncan could see Kit was going in with a very English, fairly New York kind of selling pitch which was leaving the poor bugger no fig leaf of ambiguity with which he could cloak these discussions. She was nobbling in the most blatant manner. Kit was also on her fifth or sixth glass of champagne and starting to make expansive gestures. Duncan could foresee that in the next few minutes the odd reference to 'piles of fucking UPVC' would start slipping in and the poor old bugger would start casting round for someone to rescue him. It was at this moment that Duncan decided he really was not Mrs Britto's keeper and excused himself because he was desperate to go to the lavatory.

'Sure!' said Kit. As Duncan made his way to the gents he could hear her singing his praises, almost literally, across the room. 'He's bloody talented, you know,' she told the Planning Chairman, 'But he can't hold his liquor, poor little ponce.'

In the gents Duncan decided that he would take some time over this pee. It would be good for his digestive system, and there was a fair chance that Kit would have moved on, or passed out, by the time he got back outside.

An unusually tall man with unusually white hair joined him at an adjacent stall. Duncan could only make out his profile and neither man chose to acknowledge the other. Duncan had had enough to drink now to feel a philosophic frame of mind coming upon him, and he reflected how strange it was that both men stared forward observing the decorous fiction that neither was there.

The man finished before Duncan, but was still wiping his hands on a towel from the lavish supply when Duncan joined him at the washbasins. The tall man's reflection spoke to Duncan's.

'Enjoying it?' he said in a splendid clear voice that had all the resonance of a professional Welsh broadcaster. Duncan's reflection looked into the eyes of his inquisitor. The man was younger than his hair suggested, no more than ten years older than Duncan in fact.

'Not really,' said Duncan. 'I'm here under false pretences.'

'Who isn't?' said the man. 'What are you after?'

'I'm an architect,' said Duncan, wiping his hands. 'I'm probably not the best in Cardiff, let alone England and Wales, but I'm a lot better than many of those working in this city – and someone suggested that if I came along today it might help me get work.'

'It might,' said the man. He seemed to have taken an interest in Duncan and rested his backside on the washbasins while taking a better look at him. 'Where do you live?' he asked.

'Pontcanna,' said Duncan. 'Does that matter?'

'It matters if you walk into Wales saying give me a job, yes. There's a difference. If you live here and want to contribute, then you may get help, – but if you just walk in—'

'Well I didn't just walk in,' Duncan interrupted, feeling suddenly irritated. 'I was a student here, I trained here, and I've lived here for twenty years on and off. My children were born here, they go to school here and my wife goes out to work here because I haven't got a job. Is that Welsh enough for you?' He had grown angry while he was saying that. He didn't know why, but suddenly he felt the frustration of an outsider, even the paranoia. Why *should* he be an outsider in this city when he'd paid his dues, and his rates, for so long?

'No one who is halfway good should be out of work,' the man said, in the calm tones of someone who had had less to drink than Duncan. 'It's bad for us as well as you.'

'Well, I'm more than halfway good,' said Duncan challengingly.

The man nodded. He could see that this conversation would be better finished on another occasion.

'You should come and see me sometime,' he said, taking out a card.

'Oh no,' said Duncan. 'I'm getting fed up with people saying that.' He was feeling dangerous now. Who knew where this conversation was going? 'I'm sorry, I don't go and see people *sometime*.'

'All right, come and see me at nine-thirty on Monday,' came back the challenge. 'OK? You'll have to excuse me but the match is starting in half an hour and this is my party.' He was still holding out his card.

Duncan was growing curious. 'Who are you?' he asked, taking the card.

'I thought you didn't know,' said the man with a hint of grave smugness. 'See you at nine-thirty.'

Even before Duncan looked at the card he knew it read Caedfael Parry Morris, Managing Director, CPM.

Wales lost, which was a shame. Gwyn was angry, Stiffin was depressed, even Gerald, whose Pembrokeshire family considered themselves English in exile, was saddened. Barry Britto and his sons threw their empty cartons of orange juice at the television. Even Duncan was sorry. He had never been to an International before but he had been caught up in the atmosphere. The roar whenever the Welsh pack broke towards English lines was like being at Agincourt or Waterloo (but on the winning side) – and the singing! All the years that Duncan had listened to discussions about what was and what was not Welsh, and whether Wales was indeed Welsh at all – and yet all you had to do was go to one of these events and hear all the people who thought they were Welsh sing together in raucous harmony, to believe that they were right, and to believe that Wales was very Welsh indeed. If the English knew how much it meant to us, thought Duncan, they really ought to let us win.

Holly, Jane, and Binny Barnes in their various homes were unaware that Wales had lost or that the match had ended or even begun. Jane and Binny were on the phone discussing weekends away and Holly was rolling out the same piece of pastry over and over again while Buddug grumbled away to her about Gwyn taking Siôn to watch the match and not her when Siôn really couldn't care less and she actually liked rugby.

'Mm,' said Holly when she heard Buddug stop.

Kit Sinclair had remained detached throughout the game, having hidden behind her dark glasses as soon as play began. Duncan got the feeling she was either drunk or exceedingly cheesed off by her lack of success at the pre-match binge.

When the game was over Duncan felt her grip his arm. 'Don't get up,' she said. 'Just stay here.'

'Are you all right?' Duncan asked.

'I'll be all right,' said Kit. 'I've just got to keep still, then maybe I can get to a lav and throw up.'

Duncan said that if she wasn't feeling well perhaps they should get out straight away.

'No, I can wait,' said Kit, her voice grown very quiet. 'Just hold on to me.'

They sat in the cold for half an hour while the vast terraces emptied and the afternoon light dimmed, then Duncan helped Kit to the nearest ladies lavatory and she stayed inside for a long time, emerging as white as a sheet.

'Well, that was fun,' she said, almost losing her footing and Duncan had to support her.

'I'm OK,' she said. 'Now let's see if that randy little sod of a taxi driver's still waiting for us.'

10

Disruptions to the Schedule

By one of those ironies that beset all parents, Duncan Lewis's big career break coincided with the start of half term. At nine-thirty on Monday morning when he might well have been expecting Caedfael Parry Morris to provide a boost to his professional fortunes, Duncan found his daughters were expecting him to provide breakfast in front of the TV while they lazed around in their pyjamas.

Over the weekend Jane and Duncan had spent more time discussing what was to be done with the girls than working on Duncan's strategy for the meeting with Mr Big. Kit was clearly out of it, having taken to her bed on Saturday night and not even responded to solicitous phone calls since. Laura was locked into her own schedule of Arts and Crafts at Llanover Hall, Holly had not rung back, and Binny's Josh was on a different half term because he went to The Abbey, and they didn't break up until everyone else was back at school.

'That leaves Elaine,' said Jane. 'But it's short notice for her. Or Siân. Or Mrs R.'

'Siân,' said Duncan decisively. But Siân had gone away.

'Elaine,' said Duncan. But Elaine couldn't be a brick until the end of the week.

'Holly,' said Jane. 'I'll try her again.'

'No don't,' said Duncan. 'You don't want to push it. She hasn't rung back. She might be offended with us.'

Jane asked Duncan why Holly, possibly the most obliging person they knew, should be offended with them.

'Well, you said yourself we've used her a lot recently,' Duncan explained. 'Maybe she's taken offence.'

Jane could not believe Holly Williams would take offence.

'She hasn't rung back,' Duncan said.

'She's disorganised,' said Jane. 'Dunc, what have you got against Holly?'

Duncan insisted he had nothing against Holly.

Jane pointed out that he was always trying to avoid her. 'Is it because I said she thought you looked sweet when you fell asleep?'

Duncan hated her cross-examining him like this.

'Duncan, you can't hold it against Holly for finding you attractive. If indeed she does. It was only a guess on my part. It's certainly no reason to go around avoiding her.'

'I am not avoiding her!'

Jane picked up the phone. 'Then ring her,' she said.

'Mrs R.' said Duncan.

So on Monday morning Louisa R. came early and reminded Duncan that she didn't know what he and Jane would do without her, and Duncan crept into his suit and out of the house while the girls watched hyperactive programmes on TV in their dressing gowns.

Caedfael Parry Morris' office was in one of the tall Victorian arcades that snaked between the main streets of Cardiff centre creating a pedestrian warren. Up above the shop level ran a gantry of offices, and CPM had taken several of these to create an unusual suite of rooms, designed, so the plaque said, by an obscure-sounding Italian and opened by a famous-sounding Welshman.

The waiting room was plain, but very expensively plain with large empty grey walls, a potted silver birch tree, and a desk carved out of highly polished slate behind which sat a trilingual secretary – English, Welsh and Japanese. That Caedfael Parry Morris had found himself the only Welsh-speaking Japanese secretary was living testimony to the number of pies in which he dipped his well-connected fingers. Local wits held that if life were discovered on Mars, Caedfael Parry Morris would probably be the first to make contact with Welsh-speaking craters.

The secretary gave the impression that she was extremely pleased to be of service, and hung Duncan's coat on the silver birch tree which he realised was actually a cleverly disguised hatstand. Then when a large button on her desk glowed red she led him through. Half-past nine prompt.

Caedfael's office was much more what Duncan had expected. What had once been those same ostentatiously austere grey walls were now colonised by signed photos of Caedfael with just about everyone who had ever been anyone in Wales. This was probably not the Italian designer's intention, but he was long gone back to Turin. Duncan doubted if Columbini would have approved the signed rugby ball on the windowsill either, or the large, dark oil painting which had captured the essence of North Walian sheep-farming in a miasma of muddy green brush strokes.

Caed emerged from the bathroom, tall and distinguished and wiping his hands on a towel. He kept Duncan waiting until they were absolutely dry and then threw the towel away behind him.

'I've been finding out about you,' he said, shaking hands.

Duncan was alarmed. Not only was this man extremely

tall and preternaturally white-haired, but he had been talking to Holly Williams.

'Word is you're pretty good.'

'That's my view too.' Duncan tried a quip as Caedfael indicated they should sit.

Caedfael took time over easing himself into the padded chair behind his desk.

'So, why aren't you working?' he asked at last in his impressive deep voice.

Duncan and Jane had discussed his CV the night before. There were all manner of answers to that question. He could complain that when things got tough the likes of Howard and Dic looked after their own. He could say that he wasn't sure he wanted to be an architect any more. He could admit, as Jane had pointed out, that he'd done bugger all about getting another job so far. Then again, he could inveigh against the way work in Cardiff was sewn up amongst the big boys or parcelled out to prestigious Europeans. Or he could stop complaining and put a more positive gloss on his current predicament.

'I haven't yet found what I really want I to do, and I suspect that what I want to do isn't open to me.'

Caedfael thought about this. In anything other than social situations it was his customary manner to take time before replying, but this was the first time Duncan had come across one of these famous silences.

'You mean Barrage House?' he asked at last. Duncan didn't, but he saw no benefit in denying that he was after Barrage House, whatever that was, so he nodded.

'You know that the competition was my idea, I suppose?'

Once again Duncan nodded. If Caedfael was going to tell him he was a smooth operator Duncan wasn't going to go out of his way to deny it.

'Lewis,' said Caedfael. 'That's a Welsh name . . .'

Duncan hated this kind of question dressed up as a statement. A great temptation welled up in him to say he'd adopted it to escape the ethnic cleansing that had ravaged Pontcanna in the early days of Welsh Nationalism, but he held himself back. 'I think a few generations back my family moved to Manchester . . .' he replied, modestly but not apologetically.

'So did Lloyd George's,' said Caedfael warmly. Duncan got the impression that he was not completely beyond the pale. He was still within. So far so good.

'How much do you know about Barrage House?'

Not so good.

'Not a lot,' Duncan improvised. 'I know that it's not the kind of thing people like me usually get a shot at; I know that you set up the competition, of course . . .' Help, thought Duncan. He had now told Caedfael everything that Caedfael had told him.

'Well, let me tell you the usual stuff,' Caedfael began. 'It's RIBA guidelines. The West Regional rep is advising and there are currently four architects in the frame. I presume you knew all that.'

'No,' said Duncan, warming to the idea of this bluff,' I, er, thought it was more than four.'

Caedfael looked at him, his eyes narrowed. 'It was going to be,' he conceded.

You sly old dog, thought Duncan.

'But there might still be room for other entrants,' said Caedfael. 'I can't guarantee that. The lay members are willing to look at others. It really depends on whether they think it's worth funding you.'

Funding? thought Duncan. This was beginning to come back to him now. He had heard of an idea to build an art gallery, leisure complex or innovative public lavatory overlooking the new Taff barrage, and various bodies were contributing to fund a competition so that a number of young Welsh architects could be financed to come up with something truly adventurous.

'How old are you?' Caedfael asked.

Bugger! Bugger! thought Duncan. It had been going so well. He decided to go on the offensive. 'Can I ask a question?' he asked.

Caedfael considered this for a moment. Then, after more than due consideration, he nodded.

'Why is it that the main concern has to be whether I'm Welsh enough or young enough or lesbian enough? Can't you just look at my work and decide whether there's a good chance I might come up with something you, and your committee, and the people of Cardiff who'll have to live with this building, might like?'

Oops. He'd enjoyed the rush of adrenaline while he was saying that, but now he wondered if he might have been laying it on the line just a bit too much.

Caedfael was quiet for a long time thinking over that one. So long that Duncan began to feel uncomfortable, but he was determined not to start blabbering out of embarrassment.

'Right,' said Caedfael finally, pursing his lips. 'Right, we'll have a look at your stuff. If it looks encouraging I'll talk to Aneurin and the committee. That's the best I can offer.' He stood up, which took a while given the altitude from which his head normally looked down on the world. 'I'm due at the WDA now. Drop us some drawings, whatever – this afternoon, will you?'

'Here?' Duncan asked.

'No. Give Cari a ring, will you? This is her area.'

Bugger, double bugger, thought Duncan as he was shown the inner door.

'Swan, will you give Mr Lewis Cari's card?' Caedfael asked in his booming voice when they reached the outer office.

'I've got it. Thanks,' said Duncan.

When he got home it seemed the girls had been invited to play with Buddug. Evidently Jane had decided to ring Holly from work and Holly had automatically said that Duncan should bring them round before Jane had even asked.

'You're sure they won't be a nuisance?' Jane had asked.

'They'll be company,' Holly had said. 'Gwyn's here as well.'

'Sounds as if you've got your house full.'

'Yes . . .'

Half term wasn't going very well for the Williams family. Holly felt Gwyn was bullying Siôn about annoying Mr Harper in school and never doing anything but building bloody Lego at home, and Buddug had been complaining loudly to her mother that she never, ever listened to her.

'Oh I do,' said Holly.

'Yesterday I came in and spoke to you in Welsh for twenty minutes and you never even noticed!' said Buddug.

'Did you really?' said Holly, amazed. 'What did I say?'

'You just said *Yes* that stupid way you do,' cried Buddug.

'Oh dear,' said Holly, who had no recollection of this at all.

'This family is just *awful!*' shouted Buddug and ran off to her room.

When Jane Lewis had rung Holly that morning it seemed like a good idea to have Alice and Ellen round to play but, of course, Holly had forgotten that Ellen had actually stolen one of Buddug's friends off her two weeks before.

'Oh dear,' said Holly as Buddug flung herself down on the bed again. The news had not received the welcome Holly had expected. But by then it was too late. Even if Holly was the kind of person who could ring up Duncan and cancel, it was all too late now that she could hear him arriving downstairs.

'Oh dear,' said Holly. She really ought to answer the front door.

She met Gwyn on the landing. 'That Duncan Lewis is here,' he said pointedly. 'Siôn's let him in.'

'Yes,' said Holly brightly, thinking this was good news at last.

Gwyn looked at Holly angrily. 'Well, you'd better go and speak to him, hadn't you?' said Gwyn in that same pointed manner.

'Yes . . .' said Holly, who was beginning to wonder what was happening to everyone.

Downstairs she was pleased to see Duncan although she didn't know how she was going to talk to him with everyone around. 'Hello Duncan,' she said with a kiss.

'I've got to go and get some prints of drawings to take to a client, well a prospective client, if that's all right,' said Duncan somewhat stiffly. 'Sorry to be a nuisance.'

'Not at all,' said Holly. 'It's nice to see you, especially you two,' she said to the girls. 'I'm sure Buddug's very pleased you've come.' From upstairs they could hear the sounds of Buddug telling Gwyn in Welsh to leave her alone.

'I'll be back,' said Duncan, looking keen to go.

What is the matter with the world? wondered Holly.

Duncan had hoped that Carolyn Parry Morris would be able to send a PA round to collect the portfolio of photos and drawings he'd put together, but when he rang her mobile she told him she'd be at home that afternoon and to call round before three.

Bugger, multiple bugger and buggeration, thought Duncan. He hadn't minded being interviewed by Caedfael, because whatever you thought of the masonic way in which his kind of people ran things Parry Morris would at least be putting his head on the block if he advocated spending money on Duncan, but the sister . . . ! No one would listen to her. Her influence was entirely based on his influence. She was nothing more than the courier, and yet Duncan just knew she was going to swank around with this opportunity. So he had resisted kowtowing to her in Champers when Richard and Geraint were rushing around trying to satisfy this dreadful woman's need for garnishes, so he'd been flippant on the day of the match but now he had to turn up in Cyn Coed for her to look over his homework. She'd got him. Bugger, many times bugger and bum.

Duncan decided to time his taxi so that he arrived just before three, but of course Metro sent someone early for once.

'Can't you take the scenic route?' Duncan asked the driver, but he either didn't hear or thought Duncan was being sarcastic.

The skies were cold and dark over Cardiff as the taxi lurched over the motorway and up the hill to Cyn Coed, but at least it wasn't raining. The area where Carolyn lived was dense with trees and big cars. In the summer Ty Pica wouldn't have been visible from the road because of the foliage, but in March Duncan could make out the bungalow's huge roof and circular drive through the bare hedging. He didn't like houses like this and he didn't usually like the people who lived in them, and he certainly didn't like Carolyn Parry Morris.

She was in a loose trouser-suit with her hair tied back in expensive informality. She also had on a tight white T-shirt which set off her tan and drew Duncan's attention, inevitably, to her chest. Duncan really wished she hadn't worn that. He objected to fancying women he didn't like, and with Carolyn Parry Morris he didn't even want to consider the possibility of allure.

'Come through,' she said, taking him into a low ceiling-inged kitchen diner where a number of short dumpy women who were all chief executives of this and that were finishing lunch. Duncan didn't remember any of their names as he was introduced but he got an overall impression of jewellery and self congratulation. Someone was saying wasn't it wonderful the way Cari always collected Elinor?

Aha, thought Duncan. That's why she said before three. Got to get off and pick up the little Snotgobberina. Good, no supplementary interview.

'I'll give you a lift back down,' Carolyn said after she had locked Duncan's prints in her office.

'It's all right, I've got a taxi waiting,' Duncan replied.

'Don't be *twp*,' she said. 'Send him off. We can talk on the way.'

Her attitude to him seemed less formal now, as if his meeting with Caedfael had admitted Duncan to a club, albeit at a very junior level.

As it happened, when Duncan got outside he found his taxi had been commandeered by two chief executives who seemed far too under the influence to build their companies' fortunes that afternoon, but who nevertheless were insisting on being taken back into work.

The journey down to Pontcanna was not one that Duncan was looking forward to, but Carolyn was less condescending than he'd expected.

'Caed thinks well of you,' she told him. Duncan realised that she must have reapplied her lip gloss while he was waiting, because that information was delivered with a smile from a very brightly shining mouth. Carolyn's whole demeanour signalled to him that in terms of glad tidings Caed's good opinion came somewhere between receiving a bardic chair and a knighthood.

'I think well of him,' Duncan said. He was slipping into this banter on automatic pilot again and wished he wouldn't. There was no humour in that retort. He and

Carolyn just didn't spark each other off in that way. But Carolyn laughed. To her the idea that someone might judge Caedfael was inherently funny.

'Is your wife recovered from Saturday?' she asked.

'That wasn't my wife,' Duncan replied.

'Oh yes, I forgot,' Carolyn laughed again. 'You're the toy-boy.'

Hoist on your own facetiousness, my boy. What Duncan found strange about this conversation was that, although Carolyn was clearly behaving as if it was necessary for them to talk, she never mentioned work or architecture all the way down. Mainly she seemed keen to know who else Duncan knew. She was impressed that he was intimate in Barry Britto's circle.

'Very sound, Barry Britto,' she commented. It sounded like a quote to Duncan. Something she had heard others say. Carolyn Parry Morris probably knew as much about medicine as she did about architecture. 'So Barry's wife gets around, does she?' she asked with a slow smile.

'I don't know,' said Duncan.

'Or are you her only toy-boy?' she giggled.

'I really don't know,' Duncan replied. Hoping to get Carolyn off the subject of Kit's perceived promiscuity, he asked what happened now in terms of Barrage House.

'You're keen,' she said.

I'm not in this car because I enjoy your company, thought Duncan.

'Give me a few days, eh?' Carolyn wrinkled her nose at him.

They were in Cathedral Road by now. 'Where shall I drop you?' she asked. Duncan tried to think. The last thing he wanted was Carolyn driving the Mitsubishi jeep into Katrin Street.

'Oh, anywhere round here,' he replied. 'I've got to, er, visit a friend.'

'What's *her* name?' teased Carolyn with exaggerated frivolity.

'She's married,' said Duncan.

'Seems most of your women are.' Carolyn pulled in. With a great sense of relief Duncan realised they were outside Jacobs.

'Your stop, I think,' said Carolyn. 'Ring me Wednesday. Ciao!'

Duncan got out. Of all things it was starting to snow, huge great daft flakes floating down and melting on impact. Duncan wondered whether he'd made a career breakthrough, sold his soul, or just wasted his time that day. He bought some tulips from the deli and took them round to Holly's as a thank you.

Seeing Holly Williams after Carolyn was such pure joy that Duncan's heart leapt and he quite forgot that he suspected that Holly suspected him of trying to seduce her, and he kissed her before she even kissed him.

'Oh, hello Duncan,' said Gwyn, walking in and looking very embarrassed at the lips and flowers. 'Don't you bother about me, boy.' And he walked straight out again.

Holly looked at Duncan as if to say, 'You see?' but Duncan was not aware what it was that Gwyn's behaviour was supposed to betoken. It had elements of farce more than anything else. The front door slammed.

'Is everything all right?' Duncan asked.

'Oh, Duncan,' Holly said, and he could see there were tears in her eyes. Duncan would have embraced her at that moment out of sheer compassion and affection had not Alice and Ellen come running in pursued by Siôn wearing a Roman Soldier breastplate and swimming trunks. The girls screamed, said 'Hi Dad', and resumed screaming as they ran off upstairs.

'Can I come and see you and Jane?' Holly asked.

'Of course,' said Duncan. Poor Holly.

*　　　*　　　*

Holly was out baby-sitting that evening, so she didn't turn up until Tuesday evening. It seemed Gwyn had been funny about her going out at all.

'He seems to want something from me but I don't know what it is,' said Holly, idly picking at the fluff Mrs R. had allowed to accumulate on the Lewises' sofa. Duncan had lit a fire in the upstairs drawing room and left Jane and Holly alone together, although Holly had said she loved them both very much and was quite happy if Duncan stayed.

'Have you asked him what it is?' Jane asked from where she was kneeling on the hearth.

'What what is?' asked Holly.

'The thing you think it is he wants from you.'

Holly thought about this. 'No,' she said. 'I don't think I have. I presume he'd tell me.'

'I think you need to talk,' said Jane.

'Oh I *do*,' said Holly.

'I mean to Gwyn,' Jane told her.

'Oh . . .' said Holly. She didn't like to disagree with Jane. It was such a negative thing to do, but really she knew that if she talked to Gwyn there'd just be more of him about the place. 'Yes, I suppose so,' she said in a distant sort of way. The fire crackled and the room glowed and the Lewises' sofa was very comfortable, and Holly just felt herself drifting away.

The Lewis girls were supposed to be in bed but it was half term. Duncan found them listening at the drawing room door and wanting to know what was going on.

'Holly's come to talk to Jane,' Duncan said, marching them downstairs.

'Why?'

'Because they're friends and Holly's got things she wants to talk about.'

'Is Mum a lestian?' Ellen asked out of the blue as they reached the kitchen.

'*What*?'

Ellen looked rather surprised at the force of Duncan's reaction.

'They're women who sex other women,' Alice explained.

'The word is lesbian and, no, as far as I know Jane isn't,' said Duncan. 'What do they teach you at that school?'

On Wednesday Duncan took Jane into work and then drove to pick up Mordred. He had offered to have Laura's youngest for most of the day (while the other Davis boys were locked into their raffia and puppet-building courses) so that she and Gerald could go to Bath. It had snowed again overnight and this time the mountaintops had stayed white, so Duncan suggested to Laura that he'd take Mordred and the girls sledging on the Wenallt.

'Well . . .' said Laura. 'I'm sure Mawmaw would love to . . .' They were standing in the back room of Meirion Street and Laura was dressed for lunch in the Pump Room. Gerald was propped up against the breakfast table reading the paper.

'Yes, yes I would,' chimed Mordred.

'Particularly as, with Gerald being so much older than other fathers, the boys don't get enough of that kind of exercise.'

Duncan glanced at Gerald who seemed to have no objection to having his frailties discussed in this way. Presumably he was used to it.

'I'm going to get my scarf and glubs!' said Mordred, setting off for the stairs.

'No, no, Mawmaw. Mummy needs to think.' Laura caught hold of him.

Duncan sat down at the table. He knew these deliberations could take some time. Laura had to be scrupulously fair to all her boys, even if that meant most of them spent most of their time being denied things. On this occasion Laura's moral maze was a matter of deciding whether Mordred's being allowed to toboggan, as Laura called it, compensated for not being old enough to go to Llanover Hall with the big boys, or whether it over-compensated for it.

'You did have that truck on Monday, didn't you Mawmaw?' Laura reminded him.

'I don't want that truck,' said Mordred. 'I want my scarf and glubs.'

'I know what Tris and Arthur and even big Gaga are going to say when they hear that you had a truck *and* went tobogganing with Duncan,' Laura told him sadly.

'I don't want my truck!' Mawmaw began to cry.

Gerald put down the *Guardian*. 'Time to go, I think,' he said, standing up.

'But Gerald—' said Laura. She really couldn't be rushed into a decision about this kind of matter.

Gerald got down on his haunches and took Mordred by the shoulders. 'Now listen, little man,' he said. 'Your Mummy is worried that if you go tobogganing with Duncan you'll have so much fun that Tris and Arthur and Gawain will be jealous . . .'

'No they won't!' howled Mordred.

'So, listen here. I want you to promise me something.' Gerald's eye twinkled. 'You can go tobogganing with Duncan and Alice and Ellen, but on one condition. If you start to enjoy yourself *too much*, you'll come home straight away. All right? Now do you promise me that?'

Mordred couldn't quite get his mind around all the codicils, but he seemed to have got the gist. 'Can I go tobogganing with Duncan?' he asked, to be quite sure.

Gerald looked up at Laura, who was smiling with great love and pride at her two lovely men. 'Yes,' she said, and off ran Mordred to get his hat and gloves.

Gerald stood up in his slow creaking way, but his head was immediately pulled down again to receive a kiss from Laura.

'Isn't he wonderful?' she asked Duncan.

Of course, when they got to the Wenallt Alice and Ellen became very superior. They had been all for sledging first thing, but listening to Mordred's high-pitched enthusiasm as they drove up the hills left them feeling that it was actually a very babyish activity, and now they wanted to do something else. So it was Duncan and Mordred who tobogganed across the common while Alice and Ellen discovered there was nothing much else to do on a snowy hillside. After a while they dragged their plastic sledge away, beyond another family, and began screaming down the slopes on their own. And, of course, when it was time to go, they wouldn't.

Duncan eventually lured everyone down with a promise of lunch in McDonald's, which was absolutely heaving with parents wondering what to do at half term. Mordred had never been to a McDonald's before, and took to fast food with enthusiasm. The girls simply couldn't believe any four-year-old would have missed out on such a seminal influence as Happy Meals with extra fries, so they insisted on showing him round, pointing out facilities like the rumpus room, the party area, the lavatories, serviettes and cutlery.

'Mordred has eaten before,' Duncan reminded them.

'But not a MacDonners,' said Mordred, his face covered with ketchup.

On the way back to Pontcanna, Mawmaw explained to everyone that when he was older his grandfather was going to die and then he would go to The Abbey.

'Why do you want to go there?' Ellen asked.

'Because the classes are smaller,' said Mordred, quoting his mother.

'But if the classes are smaller you might not be able to stand up!' Alice said, trying to be clever.

'That's classrooms,' Duncan corrected her, feeling someone must stand up for Mordred and give the Leighton Davis' values a chance.

'Besides, they're all Snotgobs at The Abbey,' added Alice.

'That's enough,' said Duncan.

The day was a great success, and Duncan enjoyed having a surrogate son to share the fun with. Unfortunately, when he took Mordred back, it immediately became clear that he had completely failed to uphold the Leighton Davis values. The McDonald's Happy Meal box looked rather conspicuous on Gerald's mother's old oak kitchen table, and the complimentary plastic toy – a harmless-looking aircraft – did seem to have inspired Mordred to run around the house shouting 'Bang Bang you're dead!' at his brothers.

To make matters worse, it turned out that the three other Davis boys had only ever been to McDonald's for their friends' parties, and they were now muttering darkly about jacking in their courses at Llanover Hall if this was the alternative.

It took all Laura's dignity, authority and reason to quieten Tris, Arthur and Gawain into submission.

'Oh *Duncan*,' she said, entirely in sorrow.

Jane said the same in less elegiac tones when she found out that Duncan hadn't rung Carolyn Parry Morris.

'She said ring her Wednesday!' she complained.

'I'm sorry, I forgot,' said Duncan, who had only half forgotten. He had remembered from time to time during the day but let the memory slip away again as soon as possible.

'This could be a big break for you,' Jane reminded him.

'I don't need to be reminded of that,' Duncan reminded her.

'Well, do something about it then!'

Jane's back was playing up again and she felt particularly unsympathetic towards his pose as someone for whom work is not a consideration. *She* had to go out to keep *him* while he lumbered around impressing other women with what a wonderful father he was. Ever since Kit had suggested that Duncan's other-worldliness might in fact be posturing, Jane had been growing more and more suspicious of him.

'I've got to read a pile of papers tonight,' she announced. 'The least you can do is ring this woman!'

Seeing Jane wince, Duncan asked her if she was all right. She replied that she might have to take some time off soon if her back didn't get any better.

'So please, Duncan, just do it.'

'I'll do it,' said Duncan. 'But if I ring this dreadful woman, will you promise to take some time off?'

'Dunc, if you will get a job I will give up altogether,' Jane replied. She was being hard on him, but maybe he needed it. Certainly this was becoming a subject of increasing tension between them, and the last thing she needed was more tension.

Duncan took the portable phone upstairs to ring. He didn't want to talk to Carolyn in front of Jane. In fact he would have called from a phone box if he'd had half the chance. He really didn't want Cari Parry's world seeping into his own.

He got through to her answerphone, which greeted him first in Welsh then in English.

'Hi, this is Cari. Please leave a message after the beep.'

Duncan started to speak but the recording was intercepted by Carolyn herself. 'You work late, Mr Architect,' she said.

'I'm sorry, I've been busy,' said Duncan, leaving the conversational ball in her court.

'Buying more flowers for other people's wives?' Carolyn was in a frisky mood tonight.

'Different wife this time,' said Duncan, but he didn't want to get into this silly banter again. 'You asked me to ring,' he said.

'Yes . . .' said Carolyn, sounding busily preoccupied – deliberately, Duncan thought. 'Let's see. Can you meet me tomorrow?'

'Yes,' Duncan said. If he had to, he could.

'Let's say seven at Le Monde.'

'Why Le Monde?' Duncan asked. He had no intention of going on a date with this woman.

'Would you prefer somewhere else?' She clearly thought they were going to go somewhere.

Duncan considered this for a moment. He really didn't want to go back downstairs and tell Jane he'd just stood up Carolyn Parry Morris. 'Who are we meeting?' he asked. May as well make it clear he considered this work.

'A few colleagues and some people,' Carolyn explained.

'Le Monde is fine,' said Duncan. 'Seven o'clock.'

'That's my boy,' said Carolyn.

'Bitch,' Duncan wanted to say, but he simply signed off, 'I'll see you there.'

On Thursday morning the light was flashing on Duncan's answering-machine when he came back from dropping the girls at the home of the new friend Ellen had stolen off Buddug.

Duncan wound back the tape, fearing the voice of Carolyn telling him to pick her up from Cyn Coed, or reminding him to dress smartly – but it was Kit.

'Hi Duncan, it's that dreadful Mrs Britto telling you I'm back in the land of the living. Sorry I screwed up all the half term arrangements. Everyone at Barry's work thinks I'm a complete and utter—Oh Christ, your kids may be listening to this. Gimme a ring, OK?'

Duncan rang her straight away and agreed to take her to buy some fish while the boys were off swimming.

'But why do you need me to help you buy fish?' he asked as Kit blasphemed her way through the traffic. The last time he'd asked her that, it had been a way of getting out of helping her, and she'd sworn at him and slammed down the phone. So today he didn't ask the question until they were well on their way to Ashtons in the market.

'Because I'm a woman of mystery with terrible secrets,' said Kit.

'Oh come on,' Duncan reproached her. He felt he and Kit knew each other well enough now.

'Fuck you, buster. What a pillock, honestly!' A car in front of her had had the temerity to turn right. After a respectful silence, Duncan reiterated that he wanted to know the real answer.

The car slowed at the traffic lights in front of the Angel Hotel. 'I panic,' said Kit. 'Sometimes.'

She left it at that, and then, because the lights were slow to change, she said, 'Never in the house – just when I'm out, in the daytime. That's why I like to have someone with me.'

'But why?' asked Duncan.

The lights had changed and Kit released the handbrake with a jolt. 'Why? Because people fuck you up. As the poet said. Christ almighty what a total tosser!'

And with a further eruption of expletives Kit declared the subject closed. She and Duncan had a very harmonious time shopping in the covered market, then went to the New York Deli for a bagel lunch.

'Have you got an empty plate so my friend can pretend

to eat?' Duncan asked the American proprietor. 'It's much cheaper and stops us wasting the Earth's resources.'

Perched on stools in the Deli window, Duncan told Kit about Carolyn Parry Morris.

'She probably likes you,' said Kit. 'You've got to have an interest in people to do her sort of job. Have you thought of that?'

Duncan hadn't.

'I don't mean she's after you, like Laura and – what's the other one?'

'They are not after me,' said Duncan. 'Holly. Her name's Holly. She's going through a bad patch with her husband at the moment, but she is not after me. Anything but.'

'Oh. Did you try it on with her, then?' Kit took a swig from her seltzer.

Duncan looked up at her. How did she have these instincts? Was he so obvious or was she unusually bright? The fact that he had paused like that was, of course, enough to convict him in Kit's eyes.

'Oh, Dunky!' she laughed, putting down the can.

'Don't say it,' said Duncan. He really did like Kit, but he drew the line at being called a tart.

'I'm not going to say it,' she said. 'But you *are*.'

'I'm under a lot of pressure,' said Duncan. God, that sounded pathetic.

'You don't have to explain to me,' said Kit. 'You're a mate. Christ, some of my mates are inside. Doesn't stop them being mates. In any case, nothing you could do is going to shock me. I've done the lot.'

'You won't tell Jane?'

'Nah – and I won't tell you what Jane gets up to, either.'

He wanted to ask Kit why she had given up on her allegedly wild life, but she announced that, it was time she picked up her boys from the National Sports Centre.

Duncan was shocked to realise the time. Alice and Ellen were in danger of overstaying their welcome at the house of Buddug's former friend.

'What a pair of lazy tarts we are,' Kit said as they got up to go.

On Thursday evening Holly was going out baby-sitting for Binny Barnes. Gwyn ate his supper in silence, as did Buddug. Gwyn knew that Binny was a friend of Jane Lewis, and an imprecise suspicion was forming in his mind.

'We ought to do something tomorrow,' said Holly.

'What had you in mind?' Gwyn asked.

'Well, it's the last day of the holiday,' said Holly.

'Yes, but what had you in mind?' Gwyn repeated himself cruelly for effect.

'Oh, it doesn't matter,' said Holly, affecting a sudden loss of interest.

Gwyn stood up abruptly. 'You've got to decide,' he said.

She looked at him and then at the children, trying to work out what this was about. 'Decide what?' she asked in genuine puzzlement.

Gwyn was embarrassed. He would have sat down again but he'd made the gesture now, he was up. 'Whether – whether we're going on like this,' he declared.

Holly looked at him. Buddug started to cry. Siôn kept his head down over the car he had built.

'I'm going out,' Gwyn said. 'What time are you going to this Binny?'

'Eight o'clock.' Holly was almost whispering. She was still looking up at Gwyn in bewilderment.

'Right. I'll be back at ten to.'

Holly put her arms round Buddug.

The last image Gwyn had of his family was Holly holding

on to Buddug and Siôn running his Lego slowly up and down the tabletop.

Duncan was very bored. The people that Carolyn had introduced to him seemed as cheerful and brainlessly self-important as her. And their relevance to his work and Caedfael Parry Jones seemed nonexistent. Something in the Welsh Development Agency, someone in publicity at the New Theatre, a senior commissioning something-or-other with the Welsh Fourth Channel – they hung around the bar very happy to be sharing a few bottles and a lot of gossip. Duncan ostentatiously made his one glass of Muscadet last.

Carolyn seemed to be having a good time. She was dressed in a tight black skirt with a loose gold top and black jacket that effectively obscured her plumpness. It was only the expensive cut of these clothes that distinguished her from the crowd of jolly secretaries who were out for the night further down the bar. What on earth was Duncan doing here with her?

At one point a red-faced young man with a broad North Walian accent came up to Duncan and told him that there was a lot of building work coming up in Swansea. Duncan tried to point out that he was an architect, not a builder, but the young man had had a few drinks and insisted on talking over the top of him.

'Don't think you know everything about Swansea, because you don't,' he said, giving Duncan an exaggeratedly meaningful look that betokened great wisdom.

'I'm sure there's a lot you could teach me about Swansea,' said Duncan, hoping that the words alone would carry his disdainful import.

'That's right,' said the young man. 'You're damn right there.' He fished in his wallet for a card. 'You should come and see me some time.'

'Thank you,' said Duncan.

After an hour and a half of this charade, those who were staying to eat were told that their food was ready and they lurched off to a long table somewhere in the darkness and sawdust. Carolyn said she and Duncan had better go and collect his portfolio.

'I'm parked across the road,' Duncan said as they hit the cold night air. 'Do you want me to give you a lift?'

'Absolutely,' said Carolyn, who had presumably arrived by taxi. She hadn't had a lot to drink but she was on a different plane from Duncan. The alcohol and chat had clearly created the sense of being out for the evening. She had that buzz about her.

Duncan unlocked the Lewis Volvo with a certain reluctance. This was part of his territory, his family. His daughters visited their friends in this car. Laura Davis' four-year-old son had enthused about MacDonners in this car. Most days Jane Lewis went out to work in this car in order to keep Duncan. Well, some sacrifices have to be made. Carolyn slid her tight black bottom into the passenger seat and shrieked when she discovered a sachet of McDonald's tomato ketchup.

'Thank God it wasn't opened,' she laughed. 'Who's got your girls tonight?' she asked as they set off.

'Their mother,' said Duncan, turning the ignition.

'Elinor's with her father,' said Carolyn. 'He has her at the weekends and occasionally during the week.'

'You're divorced?' It was obvious that she was, but Duncan was simply curious to confirm his suspicions.

'Twice,' said Carolyn. 'You'd think I'd learn!' She seemed to be intent on establishing some kind of personal rapport which Duncan resented. What he wanted was his prints and photos back with a tick from teacher so he could go on to whatever the next stage was that Caedfael had in mind. Still, it was interesting that Carolyn was a double divorcee.

'You men . . .' she said with some significance.

At Ty Pica she sent him into the lounge. This was another of these low-ceilinged rooms, this time with a number of black leather settees designed for sprawling on.

'Fix yourself a drink,' Carolyn said. Duncan looked around the room, unable – and not particularly willing – to locate the drinks cabinet. On one table he saw a cluster of silver-framed photos. Elinor as a baby and Elinor as a fat little bridesmaid. He could also make out a wedding photo of Carolyn taken many many years ago. She must've been married very young the first time. She looked quite pretty, if a little too pleased with herself. She had a pleasant enough face, Duncan thought, an ordinary farm-girl's face. The problem was that she would try and pass herself off as a glamour puss. Duncan looked closer at the photo, and was trying to work out which was the groom and whether a younger Caedfael Parry Morris was visible when Carolyn came in with his portfolio.

'Now, Mr Architect,' she said, sitting down in a business-like manner and placing the folder on an adjacent sofa. 'Oh, you haven't got a drink.'

'Couldn't find any,' said Duncan.

Carolyn gave him her 'Silly Boy' look and marched smartly over to the book case, where she pulled down a dummy shelf decorated with gold-leaf spines from books which, now Duncan thought about it, the Cari Parry he knew was unlikely to have possessed. He should have guessed.

Carolyn spent a while in the drinks cabinet and came back with a whisky for him and something else for herself.

'Cheerio,' she said, handing him the glass at arm's length. 'Well, drink it!' she laughed, and sat down.

Duncan realised he was behaving like Snow White in the presence of the wicked queen, so he took a generous gulp and sat down too. The whisky hit him almost immediately.

Carolyn watched, amused. 'It's Special Reserve. Twelve years old. Caed's a director of the distillery.'

It was bloody good, Duncan was thinking, but it was reminiscent of having your scalp set on fire. Carolyn was looking at him strangely. She took a sip of her drink and then came over. The next thing Duncan was aware of was Carolyn Parry Morris bending down and kissing him. The kiss took a while as she explored his lips.

'I like the taste of whisky on a man,' she said.

Duncan was simultaneously aroused and angry about the kiss. He wasn't her toy. He put down his glass, pulled Carolyn on top of him, and kissed her back. He felt her mouth fight for a moment against opening to him, but after a series of little struggles she yielded. Duncan didn't know what he was doing. Was he fighting her or making love to her? In the end he gave up thinking and simply went for the physical moment. When they stopped and drew breath he realised that Carolyn was sitting astride him in her short black skirt. Her hair was collapsed in disarray and she was breathing furiously, as indeed was he. Carolyn swept back her hair several times, still breathing heavily. It was as if they'd had a skirmish and were regrouping. Maybe the thing to do was to get out now.

'Well,' Carolyn said, finding her voice. 'This is a bit ahead of schedule.'

Her gold blouse had come loose in their tussle, and Duncan could see enough cleavage to intrigue him. He placed his hand on her left breast and undid one of the remaining buttons with his finger and thumb. It was an outrageous act but they were fighting a different war now. The way Duncan felt at that moment he didn't care if he was kicked out of Wales and the Royal Institute of British Architects, he was going to feel one of Caedfael Parry Morris' sister's tits.

But Carolyn seemed to welcome the intrusion, and she

rubbed her free hand around Duncan's groin. Each of them stared into the eyes of the other, breathing hard. Can't she tell that I don't even like her? Duncan wondered, but another part of him was wondering how Carolyn Parry Morris got to be so good with her hands.

'Well, this *is* ahead of schedule,' Carolyn said again.' You are a keen boy aren't you?' She swooped forward and they kissed again, intrusively, violently, and Duncan unbuttoned as much of Carolyn as he could get to. He hated being called a boy. He hated her. He wanted to get some of those expensive clothes off her back, make her vulnerable.

By the time they'd finished that kiss Carolyn was pretty dishevelled, her small white breasts dislodged from the black lace bra. She stood up to sort herself out. 'You wait here,' she said, her chest heaving, 'I'll just change into something . . . more comfortable.'

'No,' said Duncan, still feeling the anger in him fuelling this lust. He'd spent too much time recently being told by people that he should come and see them sometime. He wasn't going to be put off any more. 'We do it here, *now*,' he said. He meant it too. That was the alarming thing about this new sensation. He wasn't ironic when he said that, he wasn't putting it in inverted commas and standing back inside himself, detached. He meant it.

Carolyn gave him a look of anger, her breathing rapid now, rapid and shallow, and her face seemed to glow. 'You've torn my blouse,' she said, looking at the sleeve distractedly, but then she slowly hitched up her skirt and lay back on the coffee table.

'OK then,' she said opening her legs, 'come on.'

Duncan had never done anything like this before. He had had wild sex with Jane – but this wasn't wild. It was rough, it was vicious. It was as if he had to push his hate into her harder and harder until he'd broken her, although, of course, it was he who broke first in the end. They were on the floor by this stage and in complete disarray. Duncan was exhausted, but Carolyn kept moving beneath him. When he tried to withdraw she held on to him, thrusting her body on to his until he was actually in pain. It developed into a fight, but finally Duncan pushed her away and rolled till he hit the side of the sofa, his open mouth making contact with the black leather upholstery. Behind him he could hear the sounds of Carolyn jerking herself to a final climax.

Duncan sat in the car outside Katrin Street for a long time, wondering how to go in. It wasn't that he felt he couldn't face Jane. Considerations like fidelity seemed like icing sugar after what he'd just done. He had discovered a side of himself so violent that he was unsure he was the same person. What right had he, somebody who behaved like that to another human being – what right had he to go into that big cluttered house with its warm smell of things growing mouldy underneath the fridge, and its bags of schoolgirls' homework lined up in the hallway, and its list of NCT coffee mornings pinned up on the cork notice board? There was part of him that was alien to all that. Completely alien and antipathetic to their world of parenthood and social comedy. He hadn't realised. Did he belong here any more? And would he now destroy everything if he resumed his old place within it?

It was one o'clock when Kit Sinclair took a phone call in her office. She was writing an 8,000-word essay for a national magazine which she didn't intend to send off, but it would be good to know that she could still do it, and that they couldn't have it.

Duncan sounded strange. He was ringing from a call box. 'Kit, we're mates OK?'

'What's the matter?'

'I need to talk,' the voice said

'What've you done?' Kit asked. She was suddenly worried about having this voice in the same house as her boys.

'You said I could tell you anything.'

The voice gave up and went silent.

'Duncan,' said Kit. 'Get a taxi, don't walk.' Now she felt calm, very calm.

'I've got the car with me.'

'Oh, for fuck's sake don't drive!' said Kit. The pips began to go. 'Where are you?'

'Outside the launderette in Pontcanna Street,' said the voice, sounding more like Duncan now.

'Stay there!' Kit said, feeling that she had to shout in the remaining few seconds before Duncan's money ran out. 'I'll get the car. Stay there whatever you do.'

The line went dead. Kit pulled on her boots. She'd been putting off going for a pee for over an hour now but that would just have to wait.

'Bastard Duncan Lewis!' she muttered, hopping to the door in great discomfort.

Jane Lewis woke at five in the morning, suddenly very aware of Duncan's absence. She went downstairs in case he had come home and fallen asleep in front of the TV. No sign of him, but she noticed a sheet of A4 paper stuck through the letter box. Scrawled in capitals it read:

JANE – DON'T WORRY. DUNCAN PISSED BUT SAFE WITH US. YOUR CAR IN PONTCANNA STREET OUTSIDE POST OFFICE. ASSUME YOU'RE WORKING FRIDAY. BARRY WILL COME AND TAKE YOUR GIRLS TO THE SPORTS CENTRE AT 8.30. IS THAT OK? RING ME IF NOT BUT PREF NOT BEFORE 8 AM. KIT.

At eight thirty-five Jane Lewis met Barry Britto for the first time under rather unusual circumstances.

'Is Duncan OK?' she asked this enormous man.

'Still sleeping it off,' said Barry.

Jane asked Barry if he knew what had happened, but Barry was good-naturedly discreet. He never asked Kit about what she got up to because he knew she'd tell him if it was important. He and Kit went back a long way and they'd been through a lot together. If his wife crawled into his bed at three o'clock in the morning and told him another man was sleeping in her office, and that he was to go and pick up this man's children by eight-thirty next morning and take them to the sports centre, there was probably a good reason for it. He also knew that questioning Kit before she was ready to tell him any more was counterproductive.

Alice and Ellen had read the note for themselves and had already got their swimming costumes ready for a day out with the Brittos.

'Have a good day,' Jane said to her family.

'I guess Duncan will pick them up,' said Barry. 'Don't worry, Kit will sort something.'

Duncan woke up to find Kit's house quiet and empty, which was just what he needed. There was a towelling robe on the camp bed with a note from Kit.

IF YOU WANT A BATH/SHOWER USE DOWNSTAIRS OR TOP FLOOR, NOT MINE. COFFEE IN KITCHEN.

When Duncan made his way into the kitchen Kit was sitting reading the paper and wearing her white track suit.

'We look like an ad for breakfast cereal.' Duncan gestured to her outfit and his towelling robe.

'I've rung Jane. She knows you're OK,' said Kit. 'And Barry's sorted your girls.'

Duncan nodded his thanks.

'You don't have to tell me anything,' said Kit. 'Or you can tell me the lot.'

'Nothing shocks you, does it?' Duncan checked, helping himself to coffee. So he told her. It all came out very easily once he started. Strangely, he was able to talk about the force of his emotions without feeling them at all. Normally when discussing sex he selected his vocabulary carefully, depending on the company, but now he found he had explained exactly what he and Carolyn had done without even having been aware of choosing terminology.

After Kit was up to date he sat down. 'Well, do I shock you after all?'

Kit shook her head. 'I thought it would be someone but I didn't think it would be her. My money was on the hippy or perhaps Julie Andrews.'

Duncan wondered if the unpleasantness of it all had surprised her.

'Christ, no,' Kit replied. 'You're talking to someone who's done far worse.'

'But I didn't know I could feel like that about someone,' said Duncan. 'I wanted to hurt her.'

'Listen,' Kit told him. 'As you might have guessed I'm not the best person round here to tell anyone what's normal but . . . these things happen. The mistake is to believe that somehow you're a completely different person now. For my money that's the important thing. It's just a bit of you that you didn't know was there. Next week you may discover you're a Muslim, I don't know.'

'What do I do now?'

Kit asked him not to ask her that. 'You've got to decide but, take my advice, don't do anything too drastic.'

'I don't want to tell Jane. I wouldn't know how to.'

Kit thought that Duncan would have to tell Jane sometime, but that didn't mean it had to be now.

'There are still things I haven't told Bazza. I will one day, but I'm not ready yet,' she said.

'And you won't tell her?'

'I've told her you turned up here pissed,' said Kit. 'Whatever else happened is none of my business.'

'And what about Carolyn?'

'Well, that's something you ought to think about,' Kit agreed.

'She might accuse me of rape,' Duncan said in sudden shock.

'Was it rape?'

'Mutual rape,' Duncan admitted. 'I feel as if I've been sand-papered.'

'Well,' said Kit. 'You're talking to the all-time emotional disaster area here, but if I were you I'd go and see her. And if it's over—'

'Of course it's over,' said Duncan.

'Then tell her,' said Kit. 'It's as simple as that. If you're lucky.'

11

Something that Was Never Going to Happen

Duncan did feel he was lucky, at least at first.

When he rang Carolyn that afternoon her answering-machine was on, so he was able to leave a simple message: 'It's Duncan Lewis, I'll ring back.' He really didn't want to speak to Carolyn if he could avoid it, so ringing her home and not her mobile, at a time when he knew she would be picking up Elinor, was a safe bet.

As he walked down to collect the girls from what had become their all-day swimming lesson with the Brittos, he realised that in any case he didn't know what to say to Carolyn. It had been a long time since Duncan had had sex with someone he wasn't married to. In fact, the night before his wedding was the last time. And that was with Jane. There had been one or two amorous entanglements since, but nothing that would count as sex – in the way that last night counted as sex – nothing that needed to be spoken of the next day, in the way he was going to have to speak to Carolyn.

Duncan picked up the girls on automatic pilot. A number

of new concerns were going through his head. Firstly, when he'd made a hasty and monosyllabic retreat from Carolyn Parry Morris' bungalow, he'd left his portfolio behind! Second, he hadn't worn a condom. What an extraordinarily silly mistake – which proved how out of practice he was. Third, he had actually stuck his address and telephone number on some of those drawings when he'd made prints. Bugger, damn and bugger it. What if Carolyn chose to ring him? Or worse, to turn up at the house and denounce him in front of Jane and the girls?

So it was very reassuring to hear Jane responding as if they were still living in the realms of social comedy.

'Whisky, I suppose?' she said when she got back that evening. Duncan admitted it had indeed been whisky that had occasioned his downfall.

'Honestly Dunc, this is beginning to be a pattern with you. You're just lucky Kit found you, I suppose.'

'Yes,' said Duncan.

He wanted to tell Jane. He wanted to tell her very much, but where to begin? Certainly not in the kitchen while the girls were regaling their mother with what a great day they'd had with the Britto boys. Nor over supper, when Jane started telling Duncan what a dreadful old letch Miles Mihash was.

'He's still keeping me to that dinner I promised him in Swansea. He said he'd wait till my back was better. I said I was quite capable of eating with a sore back.' Jane laughed and was surprised to see Duncan wasn't amused. Of course she was still in the land where sex outside marriage was comic territory. He was in his own little world of Strindberg.

The phone rang. Duncan jumped up and got to it with an alacrity that would have been transparent had Jane harboured any suspicions at all.

'Duncan, it's Binny.'

Phew, it was Binny. Duncan was just about to automatically hand over the phone to Jane, when he remembered that Binny's Josh went to The Abbey with Elinor Parry-Fat-Thing. What if Carolyn had been in the car park today telling all the other Mitsubishi Mums that she'd been all but raped by this unemployed architect from Pontcanna?

'Jane's eating at the moment,' he said pathetically. 'Can I take a message?'

'Who is it?' Jane asked.

'Oh, ask her to call me, will you?' said Binny. Duncan tried very hard to discern Binny's attitude from her tone. Was this her usual 'I know you, Duncan, you're no better than Flyn' tone? Or a new level of disapproval? 'Oh Duncan, however could you have done it? You terrible, terrible man.'

'Who is it?' Jane asked again.

'Binny,' said Duncan, his back against the wall.

'Binny,' Jane cooed into the receiver.

Duncan fortified himself with a glass of wine, but the expected look of sadness mixed with angry accusation never came in to Jane's eyes. She and Jane were involved in fixing up something about a girls' weekend in Llanthony Abbey in a few weeks' time.

They talked for ages while Duncan cleared away, and Jane made a joke about Duncan doing penance for the excesses of last night.

'He went out supposedly making contacts and came back plastered with a friend,' Jane laughed. Seeing Duncan's face, she held out a hand to him. She did love him for his weaknesses. She didn't want him to think he was being denounced to Binny.

Duncan looked morose but he didn't mind the tease; he dearly wished it was as funny as all that.

It wasn't the right time to tell Jane in bed either. He very much wanted to make love to his wife, but when he curled his body round hers she reminded him that her back still hurt like hell. She did turn round for a cuddle, but when he started to kiss her through her pyjamas she was adamant. For Duncan to have said at that point: 'Last night I had violent sex with a woman I don't even like,' would have seemed like crude provocation. Not to mention dangerous provocation. Not to mention suicidal folly. Bad back or no, Duncan knew Jane would not respond calmly to what he had to say.

But by the weekend Duncan had decided he was being silly. As Kit had said, he didn't have to tell Jane for years. Perhaps he could even pretend it hadn't happened. In fact, by Sunday morning he was beginning to believe that maybe it *hadn't* happened, when Ellen walked into the bathroom and pointed out that he had four large scratch marks down his back. Duncan disappeared under the bubbles and told Ellen that he'd hurt himself helping Norman put up struts for the new conservatory roof. His heart was pounding. What if Jane hadn't been in bed with Alice, listening to her read? What if it had been *Jane* who walked in to the bathroom?

By Sunday afternoon the weather had turned dull and moist again, with warnings of gales on the coast. This weekend had been one of those cruel foretastes of spring that get people like Holly Williams moving their geraniums outside too soon.

Duncan and Jane took the girls for a walk with David and Bronagh, who lived in a cottage out near Southerndown. As they were coming back along the clifftops, David ran on to try and light the log fire and Duncan noticed that Bronagh was talking with the girls. This, he thought, might be the moment to get Jane on her own and tell her that something had happened which was a mistake and which meant nothing and which wouldn't happen again – but it suddenly started to rain heavily and Jane ran ahead to round everyone up. And so Jane never knew until it was too late.

On Monday morning Duncan had taken the girls in to school and was walking back to the top of Meirion Street with Laura Davis. Laura had been looking into the nutritional content of Happy Meals, and was explaining to Duncan her decision that it should be possible henceforth for McDonald's to be a treat for her boys, but only individually, and only if Gerald was up to driving them that far, when she broke off and pointed out that a white Jeep, parked by Jacobs opposite, was flashing its lights at them.

'Oh, it's . . . someone from my work. Excuse me,' said Duncan, his throat going dry.

He crossed the road, glad to have left Laura behind. If he had been embarrassed about putting Kit and Laura together he could imagine nothing worse than introducing Mrs Dr Davis and Ms Parry Morris.

Carolyn pressed a button to wind down the window. She was wearing sunglasses and her face gave nothing away. 'Another one?' she asked.

'A friend,' said Duncan, keeping it simple.

'You left your stuff behind,' she said. Duncan noticed that she was wearing an expensive track suit like the one Kit breakfasted in, though Carolyn dressed for athletics with all her jewellery on.

'Yes, I did,' he replied, hoping that this meant she had brought his portfolio over with her.

Carolyn pressed another button and the passenger door unlocked.

'Get in.'

Duncan had great reservations about journeying to Cyn Coed with Carolyn. He had no idea if she was going to turn on him for what had happened or ask for more. 'I tried to ring,' he said to break the silence. But it froze over again.

Then, as they reached the long stretch of Cathedral Road, Carolyn began to speak. 'What happened on Thursday . . . shouldn't have happened,' she said.

Duncan felt so relieved. 'Yes,' he said.

'We got carried away,' Carolyn continued in a cool, mature, sophisticated voice, her eyes on the road.

'Yes.' Duncan relaxed.

'It was too soon,' said Carolyn.

Oh no! thought Duncan, suddenly far from relaxed.

'You've got to sort things out,' Carolyn said. 'You can't be chasing after all these housewives all the time.'

He didn't know what to say. Somehow the rules of hospitality seemed to dictate that, while being driven round by her, he shouldn't launch into disabusing Carolyn of this belief that he was some kind of Pontcanna Lothario or, more importantly, that he and she were involved in some sort of courtship that had run ahead of itself.

'What about the Barrage House project?' he asked after a pause. He really wanted to get off the subject of his sex life.

She gave him a cool look. 'I've had your stuff looked at. My contact has endorsed it, so I've told Caed that we think you're sound.'

Duncan was pleased that Carolyn hadn't relied on her own judgement, but he found himself wondering who her 'contact' was. One of those daffy businesswomen? The arsehole who knew a lot about Swansea? The man who cleaned her swimming pool? 'And what happens now?' he asked.

'Don't exploit people, Mr Architect' she told him archly. She was sounding more like her old self now, but there was an edge to her voice as if she was ready to believe the worst of him.

When they got inside Ty Pica, Carolyn left Duncan in the leather-clad lounge while she went to her office. The house was cold. She didn't offer to make coffee, or invite him to fix himself a drink or even to sit down. He felt that he was on the borders of being *persona non grata* here. Carolyn returned with his file and put it down on the settee behind her just as she had on Thursday.

'Caed said that you'll have to write in to the committee with a CV, asking to be considered.' She handed Duncan the address which was on a piece of paper. They were standing so far apart that Duncan had to walk over to reach it.

He suddenly felt sorry for Carolyn Parry Moris. She must have been getting the message from his silence over the weekend, plus the fact that today he hadn't talked about anything other than work, that Thursday night had been nothing more than a move to further his career.

Carolyn was holding out the paper and making a point of retaining her dignity and looking censorious. She seemed a sad thing despite her expensive clothes and jewellery, a little country girl tending to the round, who might have aimed to be PA to someone interesting one day but who, because of her famous brother, was having to try very hard to impress the world with her wheeler-dealing.

'Thank you,' Duncan said, and as her took the paper he squeezed her hand. 'I am grateful.'

Carolyn adopted a more offhand approach. 'Just don't foul up,' she said. 'Caed doesn't like sticking his neck out for the wrong people.'

They had moved closer to each other, and as Duncan passed to get his file he felt drawn to kiss her. Their very physical proximity made it seem right, and nothing made it seem wrong. A kiss on the cheek. A way of saying 'Thank you' and 'I'm not just here for my job'. Carolyn must have sensed his intentions because she moved too – perhaps to avoid him, who knows? – and in the resulting flurried mis-direction of heads it was their lips that ended up not missing but touching and kissing. And then kissing for longer.

Carolyn broke the kiss and, to his surprise, held on to Duncan. 'We were so stupid on Thursday,' she said, taking a deep breath.

'Yes,' Duncan agreed. He was being pretty stupid now. You didn't get much more stupid than this, but thank goodness someone had noticed.

Carolyn stepped back and pointed a finger at him. 'You didn't use any protection,' she said.

Duncan admitted that he was sorry about that, that it had all happened so quickly, that he hadn't gone to her house intending that they would do what they had done.

'I'm glad to hear it,' said Carolyn with a secret smile, and she moved slowly back towards him. He was aroused by the touch of her body against him and particularly aroused when her hands started exploring his trousers again. She did that so well. Before he could stop himself, Duncan had pushed his hands up under the waistband of her track suit and found to his surprise that she wasn't wearing anything underneath, top or bottom. The shock of all that unrestricted skin made him forget all his resolutions and even the fact that he didn't find her attractive. The sheer prepared availability of Carolyn Parry Morris was irresistible.

They crashed on to one of the settees, Carolyn tugging at the belt of Duncan's trousers.

'What about Elinor?' he asked, remembering The Abbey's idiosyncratic half term as he pulled off her track suit bottoms.

'With her father,' Carolyn gasped as she wrenched his trousers down.

'What about—'

'Behind the clock on the mantelpiece,' said Carolyn, pulling off her top and shaking her hair free. Duncan kicked off his shoes and crumpled trousers while he dug behind the imitation carriage clock to find an unopened packet of condoms. As he struggled with the cellophane, Carolyn turned on the flame-effect gas fire, and by the time he had finished with the wrapping there she was, stretched out naked on the white hearth rug.

'Come and get it,' she said.

Duncan hadn't realised until now that Carolyn had assumed from Thursday night's excesses that he liked violent sex. It was a reasonable misinterpretation on her part but it came as a shock to him to be quite so mauled and bitten. She was a strong girl, and although the fight was fun it was also quite painful at times.

When Carolyn had finished bouncing and grinding to what was a very noisy climax, Duncan was quite relieved. Jane had a few sounds that she'd made in the days when they used to have sex, code noises which he recognised: 'More of this please', 'That's enough of that', 'I'm enjoying this', 'Oh *yes*. Thanks, I've finished now'. But Carolyn seemed to have taken her cue from films she'd seen on TV, and she kept up a soundtrack of aggressive vocal uninhibitedness. Of course, Duncan and Jane had always made love in student rooms or terraced houses. Perhaps their sex life had been circumscribed by the proximity of neighbours, he wondered. Carolyn on the other hand seemed to believe that it was her job to scare off the wildstock as well as batter and bruise her partner to the point of sexual exhaustion.

'Well?' she said afterwards.

Duncan didn't know what to say. He felt loath to commit himself to words. Last time they'd had sex he had left almost without saying anything. If he spoke now he feared that he would end up making some horrible kind of commitment or protestation. 'Very good,' he said as warmly as he could. It *had* been very good, but it had also been worryingly like making love. Still more aggressive than anything he had done with Jane, but something basically positive, something fuelled by enjoyment rather than hatred.

Carolyn had fetched them a bottle of champagne from the fridge, and now she was dipping her finger into the glass and drawing patterns on his stomach.

'I mean,' she said warmly, pausing to lick off some of the champagne. 'I mean, how do I compare with your other women? All those Cardiff mams you "walk home" with.'

Duncan thought of Laura, and Holly and Kit, and even Jane, and he felt rather sad. What was he doing here with Carolyn Parry Morris?

'*Well?*' said Carolyn archly, pouring a little champagne into Duncan's groin.

'Well,' said Duncan, 'you're a lot more energetic.'

Carolyn liked that. 'And . . . ?' she said, licking after the champagne.

'And uninhibited,' said Duncan, running out of things he could say.

'And . . . ?' said Carolyn again, looking up from Duncan's pubic hair.

'And rounder, I suppose,' said Duncan. He got a champagne bottle in the groin for that. Its flat bottom spread the impact but he was still in considerable discomfort. Carolyn was genuinely angry, and when Duncan tried to make her feel special by explaining that he'd never had a plump girlfriend before, she ordered him out of the house.

Gwyn Williams was in Bristol for most of the week. It was an odd venue, because WNO would pay for you to stay over, and yet the journey back was less than an hour door-to-door. In the past Gwyn had come home more often than not, but given the way things were with Holly he'd decided that he would stay this time. It wasn't easy. He liked his family and his home. It was Holly, Buddug and Siôn he had problems with, although he loved them very much still.

Thank God someone had decided that the Bristolians didn't deserve *Turdandot* this season. Mozart came as a great relief to Gwyn. Just a question of not letting your attention wander.

But by the end of the evening Gwyn felt played-out but not emotionally involved, used but still very awake. No problem driving back to Cardiff after a show like *The Marriage of Figaro*, no danger of driving west up the Severn Bridge's east-facing slip road (when everyone else was coming down), as he had done once after *Tristan*. But as he wasn't driving back tonight he went for a drink with some of those who were staying in Clifton.

Merryll the harpist was always one of those who stayed over wherever they were. Merryll wasn't married. Merryll, so she claimed, didn't even have cats. Merryll made a point of travelling light through life which, as Howie had once pointed out, might have been a reaction to lugging that bloody great harp around everywhere she went.

Merryll had come over early for a workshop she was giving in St George's the next day. Gwyn knew she was already to be found in her corner of the bar with an orange juice and a book. This made her admirably accessible for his purposes, although the book – which seemed to be an astrological guide for women – put him off. Fortunately she seemed unembarrassed about Gwyn seeking her out for advice, which was good because he could muster enough embarrassment for both of them. Merryll listened to the complete story as best Gwyn could tell it then she batted her big dark eyelids before replying. 'Are you sure your wife got the message?' she asked.

Gwyn told her that Holly must have because he checked the machine when he'd got back and it wasn't on the tape.

'Maybe one of your kids intercepted it,' Merryll suggested.

Gwyn hadn't thought of that.

'Or maybe the tape jammed and the message was never recorded.'

Gwyn hadn't thought of that either.

'Or maybe there was a power surge . . .'

'Hang on,' he said. 'Are you saying there's no way you can be sure someone gets the message you recorded?' Gwyn didn't have much of an understanding of technology, but he had faith in it.

Merryll leant forward. 'I read in a magazine about a man in New York who was waiting for a message to say he hadn't got cancer, and when there was nothing on the tape . . . he tops himself.' She leant in further still. Her white face was as thin as a vampire's. 'And, do you know, there was nothing wrong with him.' She sat up straight again and gave Gwyn a significant look.

'But what do I do?' said Gwyn, horrified at the story he had just been told.

'I think if you really want to know whether she got your message, Gwyn *bach*, you ask her.'

Gwyn spent the next day being annoyed with Holly and Merryll. Women, in his eyes, made life very complicated.

When he rang Holly that night, she told him that if he rang later she'd be out sitting for Inge Lermoos, so not to worry. It had come up suddenly.

'What about Buddug and Siôn?' Gwyn asked.

'They're coming with me. They're going to sleep over at Inge's.'

'I see.'

Holly must have detected something in his voice because she added, 'I only told you in case you rang later.'

'Well I'm hardly going to ring later if I've rung now am I?' said Gwyn.

'No . . .' Holly said in vague agreement.

'This is all very sudden isn't it?'

'Yes,' Holly said.

Gwyn was beginning to hate speaking to her on the phone. 'And after all, I mean, if I had rung I could have left a message couldn't I?' he asked significantly. 'You do pick up the messages, don't you?' Now that was a hint if ever there was one.

'Oh yes,' said Holly, glad to be finding something to agree on, 'always.'

'Well then,' said Gwyn, and they pretty well left it at that.

Gwyn missed an entry in Act Two, which could have been embarrassing but Howie covered for him.

'What's the matter, Gwyno?' Howie asked as they packed up later that night.

'Tell you the truth,' said Gwyn, 'I'm a bit bothered about some of the windows at home. Holly's away and I'm not sure if I locked up properly. Came to me in the middle of that chorus, it did. Bloody offputting.'

Howie asked Gwyn if he wanted him to go round to Pontcanna Terrace and check. He was good-natured like that, Howie – stroppy at Union meetings, but nothing was too much trouble on the personal front. Gwyn said he didn't want to trouble him, but if Howie was driving back that evening could he bum a lift?

'No problem,' said Howie.

So at ten-thirty Gwyn set off towards the M4 with Howie and a violinist called Jayne who was complaining that Mozart wrote for repetitive strain injury in the string section. They crossed the Severn Bridge in silence. Jayne was all but asleep by the time the A48(M) ran out of steam as it crossed the Taff and stalled at a series of traffic lights, despite the fact there was never anything to stop for at this time of night.

Gwyn was the first to be dropped off. He found it odd to be back in his own house under this subterfuge. Siôn's Lego cracked underfoot in the hall. Gwyn turned a light on. The house felt empty. It also looked more than usually untidy, as if Holly had disappeared with the children suddenly. Gwyn checked all the rooms, although he hardly expected them to be occupied. Paranoid as some of his imaginings were, he hadn't really expected that Holly had sent the kids away so she and Duncan could have free libidinous run of Pontcanna Terrace. He went into the breakfast room and saw the unblinking light of the answering-machine, but rather than replay all its stored messages again he went to the notice board and looked up 'Lermoos, Inge' on the baby-sitting list. Then he sat down and dialled. If Inge answered he would ask to speak to Holly; if Holly answered he would put the phone down. But it was Inge's answering-machine, with some American man saying leave a message for Bill or Inge after the tone.

Gwyn swore and clicked off the handset. What did he do now? He had proved nothing except that Holly was, as she had told him, not home. It was nearly midnight; he could hardly go round and bang on the Lermoos door and demand to be shown his wife. Gwyn decided that he would try trapping her the other way around. He looked up 'Lewis, Jane', although he wasn't certain what on earth he was going to do next. It was unlikely that Holly would answer Duncan's telephone even if she was there. On the other hand there was nothing to lose, and doubt was gnawing him into an obsessive need to do something.

This was his house . . . They were his family . . . and something was going on that he did not understand.

As he dialled, his heart began to race. He could of course pretend to Duncan that he was ringing home from Bristol and had got the wrong number. The Lewises' phone began to ring. No, that was daft. No one would believe that he couldn't remember his own bloody number!

Ring, ring. Or of course he could say that Holly had said

she was babysitting for Duncan and Jane and he had to speak to her urgently: 'Oh – sorry, sure she'd said sitting for Duncan and Jane.' *Ring, ring*. No, that was *twp*.

And what if she *was* there, what would he say then? The realisation that he didn't know what he was going to do paralysed him. *Ring, ring*. Silence.

'Hello?' said a voice on the other end.

Gwyn thought rapidly. What did he say?

'Hello?'

Gwyn tried to make himself think. Was it Holly's voice? No. So what did he do? Did he ask for Holly?

'Hello, who is this?'

It was Jane Lewis' voice, Gwyn realised in his panic. Surely that meant that there couldn't be anything going on between Duncan and Holly that night. Unless Jane was involved too . . .

What?

No. She might be English but she was a solicitor after all!

'Hello, who's there?'

Suddenly the whole thing seemed completely ludicrous and Gwyn slammed down the receiver as if it were red hot.

Recovering, he rang Inge's answering-machine again.

'Hello, Inge,' he said, aware that he sounded artificially good-hearted now. 'This is Gwyn Williams. I think Holly's sitting for you. This is just a message to say I found I'd left some things behind, love, and I've come back to the house. Don't be surprised if you find me there in the morning.'

Phone down. Gwyn breathed out. He'd been a bloody fool but he'd acquitted himself like a nice reasonable husband, not wanting to give his wife a shock in the morning. Gwyn poured himself a large glass of whisky and took it to bed with him. And as long as Holly *had* received that message from Inge by the morning her story would be confirmed and all would be fine.

What a relief.

Unfortunately Gwyn had rather stirred things up in Katrin Street.

Since Monday's tumble with Carolyn, Duncan had kept his head down. He had changed his route to and from school. On Wednesday morning he had even taken the girls to school in the car (much to their delight), and then dropped Jane off at Follets because of a spurious out-of-town meeting that he concocted. He had done his best always to answer the phone first, to intercept all messages on the answering-machine and keep an eye on the post. He'd been careful not to undress in front of Jane in case she saw the scratch marks on his back or that very obvious new bite on his arm.

He wasn't sure what mood he had left Carolyn in on Monday. She had marched off to the shower after he had been less than gallant about her waistline, but not before she had thrown his clothes at him and told him to fuck off out of her house. Whether Carolyn now believed that their affair was over or whether she was waiting for him to come crawling back, Duncan was unsure.

He was unsure about himself as well. What was happening to him? Last week he had all but attacked a woman. Yes, he had been provoked, but the level of anger he had discovered inside himself had been alarming. Then on Monday he had spent the morning making love to this same self-important little woman whose physical attributes and personality were not to his taste. Why? He had been attracted to a number of women since his marriage, but it had never gone beyond a discreet kiss, the occasional hug or a mild bit of flirting. But with Carolyn the taboos seem to have been broken down. They had

done it once, they could do it again. Maybe they would
. . . No!

Duncan was worried about what he was finding within
himself. Where was all this anger and violence and lust
(if that was the right word) coming from? But more
immediately, he was worried that Carolyn Parry Morris
might retaliate in some way – and to Duncan the worst
form of retaliation would be if Carolyn told Jane before
he did.

But things had been fine for the last two days. Duncan
was beginning to believe he might be in the clear. He had
his drawings back. He even had the opportunity to apply
for Barrage House funding, unless Carolyn was going to tell
Caedfael that she'd changed her mind. But even if she did,
what did it matter? All that really mattered was Jane and
the girls and keeping them out of all this.

Then on Thursday came that midnight phone call, and
someone at the other end who wouldn't speak and then
put the receiver down.

It was classic and it was obvious. Carolyn was going to
strike back.

Duncan had been in a deep sleep when the bedside
phone had rung, so it was Jane who answered. She seemed
unnerved by the experience.

'There was somebody there,' she told Duncan, going over
and over what it might mean.

He was annoyed that Carolyn was doing this to Jane, but
he also knew that it was now only a matter of time before
she found out. Therefore, regardless of what Kit had very
sensibly said about biding his time, Duncan decided that he
had got to be the first to tell Jane – and so he did.

Jane Lewis had particular views on marriage and adultery.
Indeed, one of the reasons that as a career-orientated law
student she had nevertheless married Duncan Lewis was

that he was so unlike her own parents. Wing Commander Ronnie Beale had been a glamorous man who had never expected to have sprogs. And his wife was basically a glamorous woman who never intended to have them either. But at some stage, between postings, Mrs Beale had Jane, and then her sisters, and thereafter Mrs Beale, as she often put it, found herself confined to barracks. Wing Commander Beale was an attentive father for all of six months, but after that he had started getting himself unaccompanied tours and detachments to places where his family couldn't visit him.

Mrs Beale soon became resentful and frustrated, stuck as she was on RAF Scampton and Northolt and bloody Biggin Hill. Not surprisingly, the Beale girls grew up acutely aware that Mummy was trapped in the kitchen while Daddy was off having a high old time (which Jane initially understood to be something to do with the altitude at which he flew).

By the time Jane and her middle sister were being sent off to boarding school it had become obvious that the Beales were divorcing. Jane, tall and determined like her father, had already decided that she was never going to marry. She had seen too much of her mother's self-pity, her mild but persistent addiction to infidelity and alcohol. Jane saw no point in putting oneself through all that.

But when she met Duncan Lewis in her final year at University, Jane was surprised that he didn't seem to notice what a hard-nosed-lawyer-in-the-making she was. She responded very warmly to this rather dozy trainee architect with unkempt hair who listened to her with his head on one side. She grew to trust him and to believe that *he* was the one who could really achieve things if she got behind him and gave the push he so obviously needed.

Duncan Lewis seemed to attract women because he was interested in them, and because he listened to them, and because, although no oil painting, he was physically comfortable to be with. In Duncan, Jane saw absolutely nothing of her father, a tall, athletic, exciting, invariably absent man. Duncan by contrast was always around. He was reliable, funny and lazy – of course, that was the irritating thing about him, his lack of ambition – but he was a good man to have at the centre of a family. Someone you could really trust. Even when he was sent off to London for six weeks and got romantically entangled with some silly woman he was working with, Jane knew she could trust him. He told her all about his enthusiasm for, and then his disillusionment with, this young German associate, and although Jane got very bored with Duncan's phone calls she knew that she was not excluded, that Duncan was keeping faith, that she genuinely could trust him.

And now he was telling her that last week he had had sex with this woman who claimed to be furthering his career.

Well, she could handle that. She wasn't pleased, but Duncan had been drunk on whisky and there were women out there who would take advantage of someone like Dunc who couldn't hold his liquor. It had been an accident waiting to happen.

'And was that the only time?' Jane asked in the quietness of their bedroom. They were now both sitting up on the bed, like children at prayer. The room was dark, just a crack of light breaking in from the street lamp. Jane had slowly tightened her grip round a pillow which she was now holding in front of her.

Duncan very much wanted to say yes, that had been the only time. He looked around their bedroom at all the things that he and Jane had bought together and bought for each other over the years. And he had a horrible feeling that they had reached some dreadful kind of watershed. In front of him was his wife, whom he loved so much, and her face was very pale.

He didn't associate Jane's face with vulnerability. Why was he doing this to her? He could lie. What was it Kit had said? Things that have to be told don't have to be told straight away. He could tell her the rest once she had got over the first shock.

But Jane could read Duncan's face too well. 'It's not the only time is it?'

'No . . . We did it twice.'

'When?'

'The second time was on Monday.'

'This Monday?'

'Yes, after I had taken the girls into school.'

Duncan was going to say that he didn't know what else to say except that he was so sorry. But that was when Jane attacked him with her hands and her nails and the pillow and her feet and anything that she could find to hit him with. Duncan tried to absorb the blows, to hold her in the hope that her anger would peter out and then he could nurse her, nurse them both. But Jane wouldn't be comforted. Jane wanted to destroy him. She kicked and kicked until she got him off the bed. He grabbed a pillow to try and protect himself but she had taken hold of a reproduction Victorian coatstand in her anger and now she toppled it so it crashed down within inches of his head.

'What are you doing!' Duncan shouted. He was so shocked by the violence of Jane's reaction that he was, incongruously, in danger of laughing. He mustn't laugh. He knew he must not laugh.

'You took our daughters to school . . .' Jane hissed, almost unable to get the words out, 'you took our daughters to school and then you went off and had sex with this woman!'

Duncan scrambled to his feet and tried to hold her. She was kicking and lunging at him again. 'Ju Ju,' he began.

'Don't call me that!' she screamed at him, and she turned

round to sweep the mantelpiece clear of all its photo frames and souvenirs. They crashed down, all the bits and pieces of their life together, making an awful noise.

'Stop it!' shouted Duncan, stepping back. 'Please!'

'Get out!' Jane screeched with a horrible, terrible finality.

The next morning being Friday, Kit Sinclair drove her sons into school in what was for her an unprecedented act of bravery. The Cheese was coming back on Saturday, which meant there was just one day of fetching and carrying left, and as Barry was in surgery that morning it was a question of asking favours of the scrubby tarts or doing it herself. Not even Kit would expect the Bastard to postpone a cardiology operation.

So with strict instructions to her sons to keep quiet in the back unless they wanted her to hit something, Kit set off. Her youngest put his fingers in his ears in case he heard words that he shouldn't, but Kit found that she could actually manage the quarter of a mile. As long as she concentrated on her breathing it was OK. Breathe, relax. Breathe, relax. She even relaxed enough to notice Duncan and the Lewis girls crossing Cathedral Road, but they didn't respond to her beeping the horn.

Kit was pleased with herself when they had got to the school, especially when she had parked without reversing into anything. She was good on spacial concepts, but she had once panicked while trying to park in a multi-storey car park and ended up shunting back and forth in a frenzy until she got clear, but not before damaging four other cars in the process. But today she squeezed Gabriele's little car neatly in opposite Fulwood Road Infants & Juniors, and felt on top of the world. She saw the boys in, then got talking to Laura Davis who, it seemed, shared her views on The Abbey.

'I'm afraid we just can't afford it, not on an academic's salary,' Laura said wistfully.

'Oh, we can afford it,' said Kit blithely, remembering to put her dark glasses back on. 'It's just the sod, I mean my husband. Barry. He's very committed to the state sector. Won't send the boys anywhere else. What a— Oh look, there's Dunky.'

Duncan had just arrived looking very subdued, as did Alice and Ellen.

'He doesn't look well,' said Laura.

'No,' said Kit with a sudden horrible feeling that she knew what was the root of that look.

Gwyn was sitting in the Williamses' Volkswagen a little way down Fulwood Road. He had offered to take Buddug and Siôn in that morning, and had been about to drive back home when he saw that Duncan Lewis on his way down. He wanted to take a look at Duncan Lewis.

Holly had come back that morning very chirpy.

'Well, Inge certainly cheered you up,' Gwyn had said when he met her in the kitchen.

He could hear her humming as he came down stairs.

'Yes,' Holly had said, kissing him. 'We had a lovely talk.'

But the question remained: Gwyn was in Pontcanna Terrace, Jane Lewis was definitely in Katrin Street, Inge Lermoos was in her house, but where were Duncan and Holly last night? And why had she come back so happy? If Gwyn saw Duncan looking equally buoyant this morning he would know that his worst suspicions were confirmed.

But as Duncan drew closer Gwyn could see that he was anything but. He looked tired and distracted. He did not look as if he had spent the night making love to Gwyn's wife while Inge had minded the children. Gwyn was almost disappointed.

*   *   *

Duncan had actually spent the night in one of the attic bedrooms in Katrin Street which was where he slept on Friday night too.

There was very little communication between him and Jane, but on Saturday morning she insisted that they told the girls what was going on. She was their age when she had worked out what was happening between her own awful parents, and she wasn't going to put Alice and Ellen through all that agonising guesswork.

'And what *is* going on?' Duncan asked.

'You are having an affair,' Jane told him venomously. They were laying out the breakfast things and a number of cereal bowls were going down with a bang.

'I am not having an affair,' Duncan replied. 'I had sex with another woman. I don't know why I did. It was a mistake.'

Jane pointed out that it was a mistake that had happened twice, once in broad daylight when Duncan hadn't even had anything to drink. 'How many more *mistakes* are there going to be?'

'It won't happen again,' said Duncan, keeping his voice down. 'I don't even like her. I just can't explain what happened. Maybe it was simply because sex was possible with her.'

Jane banged down another bowl. She always thought he had more discrimination than that. 'Don't you blame me!'

Duncan tried to explain that he wasn't blaming or even trying to justify himself (which he was), he was just trying to explain why something which was a total aberration had happened. But Jane was already telling Duncan a bit more about what she thought of him.

'I go out to work because you can't get a job, and all you're supposed to do is look after the children—'

'I do look after the children!' Duncan interjected.

'But what do you do all day? You swan around being

admired by that silly coven of self-satisfied witches, and fucking other women instead of trying to get yourself some work!'

Duncan started to tell Jane that the only reason he had even spoken to Carolyn Parry Morris was because he was trying to get himself a job.

'Well, try application forms and interviews instead of screwing next time,' Jane replied. 'You might have more luck that way!'

Duncan was angry. Whatever he said Jane was just going to escalate matters. He seemed to have two choices: to hit her or to get out. He chose the latter.

'What about the girls?' Jane demanded as Duncan took down his jacket from a peg in the hallway. 'You ought at least to be here when we tell them.'

'I think they'll have a pretty good idea what's going on,' said Duncan. 'I'd imagine the whole bloody street knows by now.'

Jane came after him and threw one of the girls' school bags. 'Where are you going?' she shouted as he opened the door.

'I don't know!' he yelled back.

Jane told him if he was going to that woman he needn't bother coming back. Duncan tried telling her not to be absurd, but she threw two coats and a thing made out of egg boxes at him.

Once he had slammed the door, Duncan wondered where he would go. He couldn't go to any of their friends. That wouldn't be fair on them. And he didn't really have any friends of his own, only his horrible former colleagues. He didn't have any money with him either. He kicked the gate twice and decided to go for a walk in the park. It always did wonders for Jane.

Back inside number 11, Jane was in tears at the bottom of the stairs. She felt so completely humiliated. All this violence wasn't doing her back any good either, but the worst of it was she had sounded just like her own mother used to. Young Jane Beale was never, ever going to let that happen to her. And what had happened? And *how* had it happened?

The girls crept downstairs. They weren't used to hearing Jane cry. Alice put her arms round her. Ellen picked up her egg-box structure and looked resentful.

The house was silent apart from the noise of Jane trying hard not to cry, unable to draw her breath.

'I'll make some toast,' said Ellen. 'Somebody's got to.'

Holly Williams was having a very nice time. She felt a lot happier with Gwyn over in Bristol, and even when he'd come back unexpectedly he'd been considerate enough to warn her with that message to Inge. Holly was beginning to hope that things might well settle down again, providing Gwyn wasn't around too much.

It had been particularly nice of him to take the children to school on Friday morning. This meant that Holly could go straight up and have a nice long hot bath to soak away the rigours of sitting up so late talking to Inge.

When Gwyn got back from the school run he had come and sat in the bathroom without saying anything. Holly quite liked that. It reminded her of when they were first together in Swansea, the companionable silence of Gwyn just sitting there. Holly remembered he'd sat and watched her take a bath the morning after they'd first slept together. She had enjoyed those days, the way that Gwyn was always around. That was until she realised that after a while nobody else was. It had become just Gwyn.

For Gwyn Williams, the experience of sitting watching his wife humming to herself in the hot bath was not such a tranquil one. He had thought of a hundred ways to ask Holly if she was having an affair with Duncan, or of asking her if she had ever heard his message on the answering-machine. These days he was beginning to feel increasingly like the tongue-tied student he used to be when they first met. Eventually he got up in frustration and said he'd better go back to Bristol.

'Yes . . .' said Holly, almost to herself.

'I'll be back over Saturday morning. See Siôn and Buddug, is it?'

'Yes . . .' Holly smiled up at him.

Gwyn looked at his wife's beautiful face and at her white breasts floating in the water, and he felt so sorry and so angry to think that maybe she loved another man. 'Look,' he said suddenly. 'We'll . . . we'll make it work, won't we?'

'Oh *yes* . . .' said Holly after a moment's thought. She didn't know what Gwyn was talking about, but it sounded basically positive and certainly the kind of thing she could agree with.

On Saturday morning Holly woke up bright and early as she often did when Gwyn was away. Buddug was sleeping with her, which she had done once or twice since Gwyn had shouted at them over half term.

'Let's go and pick mushrooms in the dew!' said Holly, and so they did although Siôn was very reluctant to stir. Fortunately he always kept his school bag stuffed with Lego, so while Holly and Buddug took off their shoes and danced around in Pontcanna Fields, Siôn sat in the Volkswagen making rockets.

Holly was shocked at how cold dew felt underfoot. As a teenager she and some friends actually used to bathe in it (until Holly's parents found out). How on earth Holly Trewidden could have stripped off in temperatures like this Holly Williams had no idea.

They were just getting back into the car when Buddug noticed Duncan Lewis walking on the embankment. He looked angry and was striding along at quite a speed. Although Holly and Buddug waved, he didn't respond.

'Perhaps he's late for a meeting,' Buddug said, a very practical girl.

'Yes . . .' said Holly. But she was worried. Duncan hadn't looked right. Laura had said something similar on Friday, about Duncan not looking right. It seemed a shame to Holly, because Duncan and Jane had been so nice to her over Gwyn.

When Gwyn arrived back from Bristol, Holly asked if he'd keep an eye on the children while she rang Jane Lewis. 'I'm worried about Duncan,' she explained.

'What's the matter with him now?' grumbled Gwyn.

'We saw him this morning; he didn't look happy.'

Gwyn despaired inwardly. Why was it so important that Duncan Lewis was happy? Look at him. He wasn't happy. Nobody was making phone calls to cheer him up!

'So, Duncan was here this morning, was he?' Gwyn asked, expecting the worst.

'No, in Pontcanna Fields,' Holly explained, picking up the phone.

'What were you doing in Pontcanna Fields?'

Holly was dialling by now.

'I said, what were you doing in Pontcanna Fields?' Gwyn insisted. His wife's flagrant behaviour was beginning to gnaw at him again.

'Picking mushrooms,' Holly replied, as if it was the most natural thing in the world.

'You were picking mushrooms with Duncan Lewis? Where were Siôn and Buddug?'

Holly covered the receiver and looked at Gwyn as if he was *twp*, one of the few Welsh words she had mastered. 'I wasn't picking mushrooms with Duncan, I was picking mushrooms with Buddug.'

'And where was Siôn?'

'In the car.'

'With Duncan Lewis?'

'No!' said Holly, almost laughing.

Gwyn was getting het up now. He had been looking forward to getting home to his family, and what had he walked into? The usual, plus Holly laughing at him. Of course, he was acutely aware that musicians never know what is going on when they are away, and this fear of his own ignorance was really getting to him now.

'Look, I want to know what's going on!' he demanded.

'Nothing's going on,' Holly replied, wondering what on earth was going on.

'I want to talk to you, Holly!'

'We are talking,' said Holly.

'Just put that, that, that *telephone* down until we've sorted this out!' said Gwyn in his firmest voice.

In Katrin Street, Jane Lewis had half hoped the call might be from Duncan. Half hoped because she wanted to know where he was and that he was safe, although she knew that the sound of his voice was bound to annoy her again.

'Hello?' she said. But there was no answer. The line wasn't dead, she could hear some muffled noises as if somebody had their hand over the mouthpiece and the phone was moving across the caller's palm.

'Hello, who is this?' she asked. Still no reply.

'Look,' said Jane. 'This isn't going to achieve anything. If you try this again I shall have these calls traced.'

And she put the receiver down.

When Duncan came back at about eleven Jane was upstairs lying down. The girls ran to meet him and he felt undeserving of their obvious delight. He hugged them both for a long time. Jane appeared at the top of the stairs. Duncan looked up at her.

'I . . . don't seem to have any friends,' he said, trying a joke.

'We're your friends,' said Alice in her 'Poor Daddikins' voice. She seemed determined to see all this as a silly tiff.

'Will you come up? Jane asked. 'We've got to talk.'

The girls agreed to tidy their room while Duncan and Jane talked, but only on the condition that neither Duncan nor Jane started shouting again. Duncan sat one side of the drawing room fireplace while Jane paced slowly up and down on the other. She looked very unlike her normal self. Her eyes were red and her hair was unwashed, which was unusual for a Saturday morning. Duncan was sorry she looked like this. He wanted to apologise again but he thought that he had better let Jane say her piece.

'Duncan, I don't recognise you as the person I married,' she said. Duncan wanted to interject straight away, but he knew he shouldn't.

Jane, having begun, now found her feet. 'Our marriage was based, and I mean *was*, on trust. I trusted you. You were someone I could trust. Now I don't know who you are and I don't know if we should stay married.'

Duncan was horrified, but Jane ploughed on deliberately.

'That is not an easy thing for me to say, but I have got to decide whether I still want to be married to the person you've become.'

'You're punishing me,' said Duncan, looking up at her.

'I'm trying not to,' Jane replied. 'I don't know, maybe I do want to punish you, but this is more important than that. We need to take time to decide . . . what happens next. The girls need to get used to what's going on. When you first told me I felt I never wanted to see you again, but now I think you should stay at least until we've worked out what has happened and why, and what is left.'

'I want to stay,' said Duncan, looking into the empty

fireplace. The dead embers of their cozy weekends seemed horribly symbolic of what was happening now.

'But you'll move your stuff upstairs,' said Jane.

'Oh really . . .' Duncan began, but he could see Jane was adamant.

'There's more,' she said. 'You will continue to look after the girls—'

'Of course,' said Duncan.

'And I don't care what you do during the day, but you're not to fuck any of your women in this house.'

'Oh, this is ridiculous!' said Duncan, but Jane was absolute.

'I mean it, Duncan! If I found you've had any of them, just one of them, in this house . . .' Jane drew breath. Duncan wondered what was coming next. 'Just remember, I'm supporting you financially at the moment. But I'll contact the bank and stop you drawing money on my salary cheques if you even so much as *dare*!'

Duncan wondered how on earth they had come to this.

'Can I say something?' he asked.

'There's more,' Jane replied. 'I've had another of those silent phone calls from your, your *mistress* I suppose I should call her.'

'She's not my mistress,' he insisted.

'All right,' said Jane. 'Whatever she is. I want you to ring her or go and see her and make sure these phone calls stop.'

Duncan agreed this.

'As to what we tell our friends, Binny and Flyn, Elaine and—'

Here Duncan interrupted. 'Look, I don't think we tell our friends anything until we know what's happening. I don't know what's happening, do you? All I know is that I had sex twice with a woman I hardly know and certainly don't like—'

Now it was Jane's turn to interrupt. 'I'm not interested,' she said with cutting finality.

'Then *how* are we going to work anything out?' Duncan asked her pointedly.

'I don't know,' said Jane, in all honesty. 'Maybe we won't.'

Gerald Davis saw Duncan in the Post Office on Saturday afternoon. Of all things, Duncan had realised it was Mothering Sunday tomorrow and he'd taken the girls to buy a card while Jane had a sleep.

'We've made cards in school,' Alice had complained, but Duncan thought they ought at least to buy a present.

'We've made presents too,' Ellen had added as they walked up Cathedral Road. 'Pencil holders and table mats. Mum's getting two of each.' Alice had suggested they should perhaps give Duncan one of the pencil holders for his new room upstairs – which the girls were, fortunately, pretending to find a rather fun development in the house. Duncan had replied that he felt that Jane should have some flowers or chocolates.

'Let's get her something she'll like,' he'd declared.

'She'll like my pencil holder,' Ellen had said in an injured tone. Both girls had looked at Duncan as if he'd said something truly awful.

'Yes, of course she will,' said Duncan.

It was while the patient Asian proprietor was listening to an argument about which pencil holder would be Duncan's and which Jane's that Gerald arrived in the Post Office with poor Arthur. Arthur it seemed had actually bought Laura a big Mother's Day card because he was rather ashamed of what he had produced in school. However, knowing that Laura liked to assess the cards that her sons made her, Arthur's nerve had failed him before he had even undone the cellophane, and he had confessed all to Gerald.

'Oh dear,' said Gerald, who had promised to redesign the train track with Tris that afternoon. Gerald knew, as Arthur did, that tomorrow would be an extra-special day for Laura, combining as it did tributes from her lovely boys and a chance to compare the development of their hand/eye co-ordination.

Duncan let Gerald take his place at the counter while the girls debated which chocolates they would most want their mother to be sharing with them on Sunday night.

The nice proprietor was rather shocked at being asked to take back Arthur's enormous flowery card, but when he had examined it he agreed to an exchange, and both families joined in an assessment of the chocolate counter.

How very good Gerald is, thought Duncan after Gerald had explained Arthur's *faux pas*. What a good and conscientious father. Gerald Davis looked very worn and tired to be nipping out in the cold afternoon with his son. But such matters had to be sorted.

'Wonderful things, mothers,' Gerald said, hopping from foot to foot in the hope of improving his circulation.

'Yes,' said Duncan. Why had he put so much at risk? And could he ever put it right again?

12

Taps, Tails & Subterfuge

Poor Gerald Davis was having a difficult day. The Dean had called a meeting to discuss the latest report she'd commissioned from the University's external assessors.

It was Gerald's belief that the German department had got off lightly this time.

Philips, the new accountant whose main role in life seemed to be making Gerald's life thoroughly miserable on a day-to-day basis, had nevertheless balanced the books. Teaching units were looking positive, modules were looking healthy, applications were actually up, and he had even been commended for his scheme to further the teaching of German through the medium of Welsh. But the Dean had a new bee in her academic bonnet. They were sitting in one of the new business unit conference rooms: Philips, Gerald and the Dean. Gerald could smell the freshly laid carpets.

'I refer to page twenty-six, paragraph four, Gerry. Have you seen your department's ethnic profile?'

'Yes, yes, I'm sure I have. Aren't we doing rather well on that?' Gerald asked.

'Bad racial mix,' said the Dean.

Philips hummed as if he might have to agree on this one.

'But forty per cent of last year's intake was Welsh,' Gerald checked. 'And forty-five per cent English. I thought that was rather good racial mix myself.'

The Dean wondered whether Gerald was being deliberately obtuse. 'What about the other fifteen per cent?' she asked.

Gerald ran his big cumbersome hand down the figures. 'Asian . . . American . . . and Chinese,' he said, tracing his finger along the columns. 'Oh and Miss Labinovicz from Israel!' He gave a little laugh. He had always thought the recruitment of this student rather unusual, and he did have a particular soft spot for Miss Labinovicz.

'What about the Afro-Caribbeans?' asked the Dean.

Gerald had another look at the ethnic profile. 'We don't seem to have any,' he conceded.

Philips hummed again. This could be bad news.

'Precisely,' said the Dean. 'Do you know there are no Afro-Caribbeans studying German in the entire University of Wales?'

'Well, well,' said Gerald.

The Dean was a woman in her mid-forties who exercised deliberate patience when dealing with the university's old guard. She asked Dr Davis how he thought this glaring omission might have come about.

'Perhaps Afro-Caribbeans don't want to learn German?' he suggested.

'*That*, Gerry, is not the kind of generalisation you should repeat outside this meeting,' the Dean admonished.

Gerald saw Philips making eye contact with her. He was beginning to find these faculty inquisitions more and more irritating. 'All right,' he said. 'You tell me.'

'I think,' said the Dean, 'that rather than blaming Britons of Afro-Caribbean extraction for not applying to study

German in Cardiff, we should be looking at making the course more attractive to them.'

Gerald asked her how 'we' might do this.

The Dean, with studied politeness, pointed out that it was not her role to tell Gerald how to run his department.

It was another of those days when Gerald Davis thought about resigning or taking early retirement. He believed himsef to be a flexible man and a realist. He had never expected university life to be all about teaching a subject he loved to interested students. He had in his time adjusted departmental policy to embrace student militancy, feminism, the Welsh language and the business ethic. He had even accepted the notion that German literature might be better taught without requiring students to learn the German language. In his heart he believed he really ought to be capable of reinventing the department to accommodate racial monitoring and affirmative action, but the mental agility was gone.

It was time to make way for younger men and women (of whatever racial origin the Dean chose to stipulate). But the Davis boys had fourteen more years of schooling and a further three years of University education ahead of them. Gerald knew that this was not the time to jump ship. He had watched his wife make her calculations in bed most nights, and he had seen how often Laura drew a circle and wrote inside it *Grandpa Leighton's Money?* Gerald wouldn't bring his wife to that.

Until recently Gerald used to walk home through the Park and over Blackweir, the volatile suspended pedestrian bridge that spanned the Taff and bounced alarmingly if you were overtaken by joggers. But increasingly these days he waited for the bus on North Road. It was while he was standing here lost in his own thoughts that Gerald all but didn't notice Duncan Lewis also lost in his on the opposite side of the road. Duncan was dressed for some track event but he looked rather down, thought Gerald. There was no point in trying to attract Duncan's attention over the roar of commuter traffic but Gerald made a point of remembering to tell Laura. She had been quite concerned about Duncan of late and had even suggested that he might be avoiding her.

Duncan Lewis *was* avoiding Laura. He was avoiding most people at the moment. But Kit Sinclair had kidnapped him that afternoon. It had started with a phone call.

'Duncan, listen to me.'

Duncan had been relieved to hear Kit's voice rather than Carolyn's. There was an archness in the way both of them spoke and for a moment Duncan had thought it was Carolyn Parry Morris but the voice was unmistakably English. Unmistakably Kit.

'Dunks, listen. The boys have invited your girls to tea and Gabriele's picking them up. Is that OK?'

Duncan had said it was fine. Perhaps he should ring the school to confirm the arrangements.

'Absolutely,' said Kit. 'And then we're going for a run.'

'Where?' Duncan asked, assuming she wanted chauffeuring into the country.

'Round and round, that out of breath sort of stuff', said Kit. 'You know how keen I am on keep fit.'

This was news to Duncan. As far as he could tell Kit was keen on drinking a great deal and falling over, but if this was what she wanted to believe about herself he was not going to argue. He had had enough arguing with women at the moment.

So Gabriele dropped Kit off at three o'clock and drove on to collect the boys and the girls, and Duncan reported for duty in an old track suit that dated from the 1980s jogging craze, and dated badly.

Kit on the other hand was in lycra with a loose silver top which was made out of something that had been invented for astronauts.

If Duncan was a touch anxious about setting off across Pontcanna Fields with Kit Sinclair, he soon found she was no Jane. By the time they had crossed the rugby pitches to the Taff Embankment, Kit was virtually walking.

'Let's sit down,' she said, plonking herself on a tree trunk and taking out two packets of glucose tablets.

Duncan studied the view while Kit got her breath back.

'How's it going?' she asked, squinting up at the late winter sun which was bearing down over Duncan's shoulder.

'How's what going?' Duncan asked.

'That's up to you,' said Kit, chewing a mouthful of tablets.

After a moment checking the view, the park and the distant university, Duncan admitted, 'I told Jane.'

'I guessed you had,' said Kit.

He then explained that he hadn't wanted to tell her but Carolyn had started to make these silent phone calls.

'Oh God,' said Kit. 'She's serious then.'

'Yes. But what about?' Duncan asked. 'What does she want?'

'Duncan, if a woman has it off with you once and immediately starts ringing up and not speaking, she's serious about you. I mean, about getting you off Jane.'

Duncan was very alarmed by that thought. But he found time to correct her. 'Actually, we did it more than once . . .'

'Oh *Duncan*!' Kit rocked backwards as she offered him another glucose tablet. 'You really are an old tart aren't you?'

Duncan was riled by this, but he felt he deserved no better. 'It's all right for you, you probably have a sex life!'

• We Think the World of Him

'Yeah,' replied Kit noncommittally. 'But this isn't going to help you get back inside Jane's knickers is it?'

Duncan looked down into the chill inky stillness of the half-empty Taff with its weary dark trickle of water. When the barrage was built this river would cease to be tidal. All the milk crates and the rubbish, all the jagged edges would be covered up. Duncan had been discovering some pretty unattractive things at his own personal low tide-mark recently. He rather wished for a barrage in the life of Duncan Lewis: something to cover everything nasty up again.

'Can we walk a bit further?' he asked.

They half-ran north up the embankment as far as Blackweir pedestrian bridge, by which time Duncan wanted to talk again. As they started on Kit's second packet of glucose, Duncan leant against a stile and asked what Kit thought he should do. Kit was being sphinx-like now. She told Duncan that only he could decide what it was he wanted, but he had better be careful because it was more than likely neither Jane nor Carolyn was going to wait around for him to make up his mind.

'They may well decide for you,' she warned him, climbing on to the gate. 'If Jane's anything like me you're already busted and out and it's only a matter of time before you find out.'

Duncan looked worried.

'Then again,' said Kit, 'Jane probably isn't much like me. It's probably Carolyn you've got to watch.'

'How do you see that?' Duncan asked. So Kit gave Duncan her thumbnail sketch of Carolyn Parry Morris, which was based partly on hearsay and partly on watching her at Caedfael's party, and mainly on Kit's own sense of the dramatic, – but which was unusually accurate for Kit Sinclair, novelist.

'Imagine you're the little sister of some Welsh Mr Fixit. Everyone thinks the sun shines out of his arse. He's the man with the golden touch. Whereas you, you've got two failed marriages behind you. You've kept the house, the car and the kids—'

'Kid,' said Duncan.

'OK, kid. And you've got Hubby Number Two paying the school fees, but you've got to pay the mortgage. So you've got to earn a bit and you've got to keep up appearances. That's the difficult bit. How old d'you reckon she is?'

'Thirty-five, I'm almost certain, 'Duncan replied.

'OK. So she's been moving in these circles for fifteen years. Two husbands have let her down Now her only entrée to this world is through Big Brother. Only everyone knows she's just an expensive bit of set dressing. No real use and not that glamorous these days. Let's face it, the body's beginning to go . . .' Kit looked at Duncan.

'My lips are sealed,' he replied.

'So what's she got? She's got some influence but she's never even going to land Commissioning Editor for This and That at S4C, not even if her precious brother pulls every string he's got. And anyway, he's not going to set himself up for a fall is he? So she needs to find someone with marketable talent but who needs her influence to get on – and that, I guess, is where you come in.' Duncan clutched discreetly at the bridge supports. 'Me?'

'Well, not just you. I imagine she's running a few career-stalled architects, producers, minor politicians, you know. To see who is going to be the one who makes it. Don't look so worried. This is only my idea. I'm probably talking cobblers.'

'But you think she is looking for a husband then?'

'Something serious, I reckon: long-term, live-in, matrimonial. You know what I mean . . .'

'Buggeration,' said Duncan.

Kit drew her legs up so that she looked for all the world like a silver-clad pixie perched on the metal gate. 'And you thought it was just a quickie?' she asked. 'Women are complicated things, Duncan. Christ, you've been married to one for ten years.'

Duncan felt cold. He felt frightened. Depth of emotion was not something he had either sought or found over the years. Marriage to Jane had had its moments of great contentment, even profundity, but Duncan had always been content to splash around in the shallow end of human relationships. He had just unleashed something pretty awful in Jane. He had discovered some disturbing things about himself. The last thing he wanted now was to stir up yet more depths with Carolyn Parry Morris.

'I've got to talk to her,' he said. 'Tell her it's all over.' He had been putting off ringing Carolyn, despite his promise to Jane. It had seemed difficult to ring someone up out of the blue and demand that they stop making silent phone calls to your wife. Duncan had hoped that he might intercept one of these mystery calls, thereby making the contact and putting Carolyn at a disadvantage, but there had been no more since the weekend.

They walked to North Road, and while Kit looked out for a taxi Duncan found a phone box. Carolyn's mobile told him, 'The number you are calling may be switched off,' which Duncan felt was just typical of her.

He tried the home number, which was engaged, and then he tried the mobile again. By this time Kit had got hold of a taxi and was gesticulating at him, but Duncan indicated that she should go on ahead without him and resumed his continuous dialling. He felt that every minute he did not speak to Carolyn was endangering his marriage and even the way he wanted to live his life.

'Cari Parry,' said a voice.

Duncan jumped. He had lost count of the number of times he'd pressed redial. It had become an almost unconscious act. Dial/*Click* Engaged/*Click* Redial/*Click* Engaged. But now, instead of that dumb and relentless tone telling him that the phone was in use, or more likely left off the hook by little fat Elinor, here was Carolyn Parry Morris in person.

Duncan's voice almost deserted him at the sound of her professional, friendly tone. It didn't sound like any of the Carolyns he knew, and yet it was her – he was in live, dangerous contact. 'This is Duncan Lewis. I'm sorry I haven't rung.'

Duncan was going to wait for her to reply. He wanted to gauge her response before saying anything else, but nerves overcame him. 'Could we meet?' he asked.

'Just a minute,' Carolyn said, neither friendly nor unfriendly. Duncan heard her talking in Welsh to a child. Of course, it was nearly half-past four. Elinor would be at home.

He heard the sounds of Carolyn lifting the receiver back to her ear. He had had time to prepare some kind of apology if she decided to have a go at him, but in fact she was very calm.

'I'm busy this week,' she said, as if talking to a client in whom she took a friendly interest when work allowed.

'I'd prefer to meet,' said Duncan. Suddenly he wondered whether Kit had been completely wrong. Was Carolyn no keener on a relationship with him than he with her?

'I've got meetings till three each day and then I'm picking up Elinor.'

No, there was something about the way she was treating him, the specific unavailability, the forced calm. This was someone who was telling him in quiet but very large capital letters that she was not always going to be available when the likes of him deigned to get in touch. 'Do you have a lunchtime free?' he asked. It seemed a good move not to suggest evenings. Nothing too presumptuous.

'It's a busy week,' Carolyn repeated. Duncan felt himself

getting annoyed. He hadn't rung her so that she could demonstrate how insignificant he was in her life.

And, he realised, he was down to his last 10p.

'But Elinor does have ballet on Thursday,' she announced. 'I suppose I could meet you for an hour then. Say three o'clock?'

'That would be fine,' Duncan agreed. 'Where would suit you?' He just hoped she wasn't going to say Caedfael's office.

'Do you know Garlands?' she asked.

Perfect, thought Duncan. Nice civilised little coffee house. The arcades were a public place. Good venue to talk over the mistakes we've made; no real danger of either of us seducing the other or throwing things. 'I'll see you there at three,' he said.

It had all seemed so calm, so straightforward. Duncan thought everything might be OK after all. He couldn't believe that any woman in Carolyn's position, being phoned a week later and agreeing to an hour's meeting in a town-centre coffee house, could believe that this affair was still on.

Duncan came out of the phone box feeling a lot happier than when he went in, but then he remembered something: *this* Carolyn Parry Morris sounded sensible and dignified, but there was another one who made silent phone calls to Jane and drove around in a Mitsubishi with nothing under her track suit. Which would Duncan get on Thursday? And worse still, solving the problem with Carolyn didn't necessarily solve the problem with Jane.

By Wednesday morning Jane Lewis decided she had had enough of people asking her if she was all right. Big Fat Tony had tiptoed in several times in the last week and asked how things were. In response to these intrusions she had made a point of briefing him very thoroughly on each of her cases. Serve him right. Even David had taken her on one side at the drinks machine and asked her how things were. Jane was annoyed with these men and annoyed with herself.

For Jane Beale had never been the kind of girl who went to pieces when life got tough. Or so she thought. She had coped perfectly well when she had been sent away to school, and she had helped her sisters through that stupid messy time when her parents divorced. Her mother had even accused her of coping too well when, several years later, she had turned on her.

Jane Beale had been a rock of certainty to her fellow students and a reliable member of any firm she had worked for, regardless of her private life. Now that Duncan had behaved so badly towards her and the girls, Jane felt that she was coping very well with that too.

But what galled her was that people seemed to notice that she was coping so well, which must prove that really she wasn't. First Tony, then David, now Miles had called in to suggest that it would do her good if they took her out to dinner.

'Do I look as if I need doing good?' Jane asked him pointedly.

Miles looked back at her with his big dark European Jewish eyes. They were eyes that seemed to have seen a continent of suffering. 'Jane, you're not happy,' he said in his slow, compassionately American tones.

Jane felt her lower lip slip out of control. 'Fuck off, Miles,' she replied, got up and walked to the window. She was trying to make absolutely nothing of it, but she could feel the light from the horizon stinging her eyes. She knew she was going to cry.

'Jane,' said Miles. His voice was nearer. He must have crossed the room towards her.

'Get out of my office, Miles,' she said between gritted

teeth. Sensing no movement behind her she swung round viciously.

'Just get out!' she yelled.

Jane could see registering in his face the fact that Miles had recognised something wild and desperate in her. He lifted his hands as if to say, 'It's OK. I'm backing off,' and he did just that, backing towards the door.

Jane realised her hands were shaking. She placed her palms flat on the desk. She would be all right in a few minutes. There was a client who needed a discreet rocket. She could channel all her anger and emotion into that phone call. The discipline would help. Jane was never rude to clients.

Mair Lloyd looked in, for Miles had not closed Jane's outer door. 'Oh Jane,' she said, 'I heard the shouting, and Miles Mihash has left in a terrible state . . .' She left this report hanging in the air. It was Mair's style to cloak in tones of great concern her rampant curiosity and her desire for dreadful things to befall other people. She lifted her head expectantly for an answer, like a dog begging innocently for titbits, except that the titbits Mair Lloyd wanted were bits of Jane Lewis.

'Go away!' Jane snapped, not looking at her.

'Well, Jane—' Mair began in injured tones. She was pleased to see that something was genuinely wrong, but the force of Jane's response had surprised her.

'Get out! Get out! Get out!' shouted Jane, and she picked up a copy of Halsbury's *Law & Precedents*, which she threw hard but deliberately wide of Mair Lloyd.

Jane didn't remember Mair going but she heard the outer door slam, and then she collapsed in tears over her desk. She thought she was going to be sick, but eventually the nausea and the tears passed. After a time which could have been minutes or hours, Jane found herself sitting on the floor by the window. The warm radiator was easing the pain in her back and helping her drift off almost to sleep.

The next thing she remembered was Tony Morgan-Jones with a tray of tea. He was sitting in her office chair with the folds of his suit and stomach spilling out over it. She looked up at him, aware that her face must appear blotched and tearful. She was not a vain woman, but she knew that tears did not become her in the slightest.

'Well, Mrs Lewis, *fach*,' said Tony, using the Welsh endearment.

'I'm sorry, Tony,' said Jane.

'I'm sending you home, Mrs Lewis.'

Jane tried to say it was all right, she could cope, but even she didn't believe that any more.

'Sort it out,' said Tony kindly but firmly. 'There are enough problems in this firm without you and Duncan adding to them. I presume it is dear Duncan who is at the root of all this?'

Jane sniffed and nodded.

'Sort it out,' he said again. 'I've looked at your diary. You're in the Newport office for the rest of this week, then I want you to take some time off.'

Jane shook her head.

'*And* I'm keeping you on full pay until you have sorted things out. Then I want you back and bushy-tailed or I don't want you back at all. Is that understood?'

She nodded again.

'Right, now, get your coat,' Tony said, prising himself with difficulty out of the chair. 'David will drive you back.'

It was not a good night for Duncan to talk to Jane. He could tell that as soon as she arrived, but that Wednesday evening he had had the meeting with Mr Harper that they had set up last half term. Holly had taken the girls back with her while

Duncan had been in to check up on whether the process of segregation was going to be continued.

Jeremy Bear had been grave faced, something that Duncan really had not expected. 'I'm afraid they're being quite impossible at the moment,' he'd explained.

'In what way?' Duncan had asked, sitting down, just as he had when last term's bombshell had burst.

'Totally disruptive,' said Jeremy Harper. 'Last half term they were resentful at first, but I really did feel they were accepting the idea of being kept apart in lessons. But now . . .'

Mr Harper was not normally a man to let sentences hang in the air unnecessarily. Duncan could see that he really was at a loss to describe the behaviour of Alice and Ellen. 'It is as if the whole idea of school is hostile to them. That's the only way I can describe it. It's only been happening for a week or so. Have you noticed anything of this at home?'

Duncan hadn't. When he and Jane had noticed the girls at all, they seemed to be the ones who were coping best. 'I'll see what I can do,' he had assured Jeremy Harper.

He had collected Alice and Ellen from Holly's, where he had been too preoccupied to notice Gwyn's remark: 'Oh, hello Duncan, you here again is it?'

Nor had he noticed the way Gwyn had got up and simply left the house.

For as soon as he saw Holly, he had remembered that on top of sorting things with the girls tonight he was supposed to be sorting things with Carolyn at three tomorrow.

'Would you mind having the girls again?' he asked. 'I've – er – got a business meeting. Tomorrow. It's just come up. Two of the lads from my old company are setting up together.'

'No, that's fine,' Holly whispered. She still had half a mind on Gwyn's rapid disappearance and the banging front door.

'I am sorry to trouble you,' said Duncan.

So when Jane came home that Wednesday evening Duncan felt he had got things reasonably under control. He had told Alice and Ellen that he and Jane wanted to talk to them, and he had made tea for Jane. This was a ritual they still kept up, though in the last week it had occurred mostly in silence.

Duncan explained the upshot of his interview with Jeremy Harper, although he modified the man's sudden pessimism. 'I suppose it's to be expected,' he said. 'I've told the girls we want to speak to them. I think it's best we do that together.'

'Yes,' said Jane. She seemed to be looking at him as if this was all his fault.

'It isn't going to help if you just assume this is all my doing,' he told her. 'Jane, please, we've got to think of the girls.'

'You don't have to tell me that,' she said.

Duncan asked if they could try and keep this non-partisan. 'We're not helping with all this anger,' he added.

'Don't you blame me,' Jane warned him.

He didn't feel he should get into arguing about blame as he wasn't on strong ground, so he changed the subject and told Jane that he had arranged to see Carolyn tomorrow. 'To sort things out.'

'I don't even want to hear her name,' Jane said.

'All right,' said Duncan. 'But I thought you'd want to know that I've arranged to sort things.'

Jane replied with quiet venom that she wasn't interested in his arrangements to see his mistress. In her eyes all this was a result of Duncan wantonly destroying everything they had built up together. How dare he posture as the firefighter when he had flung lighted matches everywhere.

'She is *not* my mistress,' Duncan repeated yet again. 'It was all a mistake and that's what I'm going to get sorted tomorrow.'

Jane glared at him. 'It was a mistake that happened twice, Duncan. How many more times is this going to happen?'

'It's over!' That came out more loudly than he intended.

Jane stood up. 'Don't you raise your voice to me. You sort this mess and maybe when it's over we'll talk.'

Duncan stood up too. 'You're not even trying!' he said, feeling genuinely distressed.

'I don't have to.' She turned on her heel. She was chilling, but Duncan was getting angry.

'Listen,' he said. 'I *am* sorting things. *Tomorrow*. And then we have to try and get back to a normal life. We have to try. That's what people do.'

'Do they?' Jane asked as she made to leave the kitchen.

Duncan grabbed her arm. 'Yes they do if they're grown up! They certainly don't expect their husbands to sleep on a camp bed in some underheated attic. They try and behave in a civilised way.'

Jane broke free of Duncan's grasp. 'If you don't like it you are welcome to go and sleep somewhere else. I'm sure she'll have you back!'

'I told you I'm finishing it!' Duncan shouted. 'Tomorrow. You silly, silly woman!'

'Well don't come back expecting a medal,' said Jane, and with that she walked out of the kitchen.

They were supposed to be talking to Alice and Ellen, but both had forgotten. It seemed impossible at this stage for Duncan and Jane to begin speaking without one of these recrimination sessions setting in. Duncan felt he had to get out, so he grabbed his jacket and marched round to Jacobs, which was one place that was always open.

'Do you deliver flowers?' he asked the girl behind the counter.

'Not at this time of night,' she replied in surprise.

'But tomorrow. First thing.'

'Eight's the earliest we can guarantee,' she told him.

'Right,' said Duncan. 'I want a big bunch sent to this address.'

And with that expensive gesture, Duncan Lewis sent carnations, irises and chrysanthemums to arrive at Ty Pica before Carolyn Parry Morris set out the next morning. He wrote the card himself. It was signed, 'The Architect'. She could take it as an amorous gesture or a gesture of thanks for the help with his career. Duncan didn't particularly mind how she took it. It was a way of getting back at Jane that didn't involve another scene in Katrin Street.

Meanwhile Jane Lewis was in the girls' bedroom, explaining that Dad had had to go out but that Alice and Ellen had to understand that when big arguments like this happened it didn't mean that Mum and Dad loved them less, or that Mum and Dad loved each other less. Things like this had happened in Mum's family when she was young.

'But Grandma didn't stay married to Grandpa Beale, did she?' Ellen asked.

'No,' said Jane. 'But it wasn't inevitable.'

'What's inevitable?' murmured Alice from Jane's lap.

'It means that Mum and Dad need to keep trying. It doesn't mean anything's over.'

The girls cuddled up to her.

'And while we're being silly and shouting, you must try and be a bit nicer to Mr Harper ... is that agreed?' Jane asked.

Alice nodded and Ellen passed Jane a tissue from the big box on their bunk bed.

Things weren't much better in Pontcanna Terrace. Gwyn had come back from his walk around the block to find that Duncan Lewis and his cocky little daughters had gone. Gwyn was developing a real aversion to Duncan now. Everywhere he went Duncan and Duncan's childcare arrangements seemed to be the main topics of conversation.

'Oh he's gone, has he?' he asked.

Holly smiled. Sarcasm was wasted on Holly Williams. 'He had to get back to see Jane,' she replied as she set the table for supper.

'*Jane*. Oh that's the one he's married to, isn't it?' Gwyn asked.

Holly gave him a puzzled look. To anyone unconscious of irony, Gwyn simply sounded thick.

'Duncan and Jane,' she said, and went to do a last-minute thing to the soup.

'Oh yes and what's the name of those girls who are always here?' Gwyn continued pointedly.

'Alice and Ellen,' Holly said from the kitchen. 'Alice is the slightly taller one. I think she looks rather like Jane.'

Gwyn wasn't at all interested such opinions, but having embarked on his ironic attack he felt he had to keep up with it until Holly noticed. 'And I suppose the other one looks like Duncan,' he continued, pitching his voice so Holly could hear in the kitchen.

She put her head round the door. 'Do you think so?' she asked.

'I don't know. You're the one who spends all your time gazing into his eyes.'

Holly's head appeared in the doorway again. She looked at Gwyn and then she laughed. It was a laugh of confusion, but it angered Gwyn. This was the second time she had laughed at him.

He strode into the kitchen where Holly was just dishing up. 'Holly, what is there between you and Duncan Lewis?' he demanded.

Holly stopped her ladling and thought for a moment.

Then she looked at Gwyn. She really couldn't get her mind round that question.

'I said, what is there between you and Duncan Lewis!'

Holly was still looking for all the world as if she no longer spoke the language. For a moment Gwyn wondered whether he'd accidentally addressed her in Welsh. For all the effect he was having he might as well have used Swahili.

'He's . . . a . . . friend,' Holly said very quietly and in such a simple way it seemed to throw the question back at Gwyn.

'Yes, but why's he always here?'

Holly thought about this one too. She put down her ladle and arranged the soup bowls slowly on the tray while she considered her answer. 'Because he's a friend?' she replied, hoping that this would make enough sense.

Gwyn could see from her eyes that, although Holly was being as co-operative as possible, she clearly thought he had gone cuckoo.

Well, now he had had absolutely *enough*. 'Are you having an affair with Duncan Lewis?' he roared.

Holly's reactions were always slow, but this time she blinked twice at him. Then she looked away. Then she looked back and blinked again, and then she coloured very red. For a moment Gwyn thought he had caught her out, and that the blood was rushing to Holly's cheeks in a flood of guilt. But it wasn't guilt Holly was trying to suppress. It was hilarity.

Her shoulders started to rock silently and her eyes watered, and then she was unable to hold back the laughter any more and she simply brayed with laughter.

'Holly, stop it,' said Gwyn.

But she had already slipped on to the floor and was sitting there, her many layers of clothing flowing in all directions, paralysed with laughter.

'Stop it!' Gwyn demanded. But she couldn't. Gwyn turned and walked out of the kitchen.

'Where are you going?' Holly shouted after him between gulps of laughter.

'Out!' he retorted.

'But you've only just come back!!' cried Holly, and then she collapsed in laughter again.

Siôn and Buddug found their mother sitting red-faced on the kitchen floor and assumed unkindly that she was drunk. A bowl of soup was left on the kitchen table for Gwyn Williams, but he didn't come back till late, smelling of the place where he had been drinking with Stiffin.

The next day the Williams family breakfasted in silence, and Holly tactfully avoided mentioning in front of Gwyn that Duncan's daughters would be coming to play after school.

Gwyn had teaching most of the day, for which he was profoundly grateful, but in the early afternoon he had to go into Cranes for some valve oil, and it was while he was walking back to the NCP that he spotted Duncan Lewis, looking quite smart, entering the Castle Arcade from the High Street. On an impulse that was in no way honourable but certainly irresistible, Gwyn changed his route and followed Duncan. It was nearly three o'clock. Duncan and Holly ought to be picking up their children soon. So where was this Duncan Lewis going?

Gwyn followed as best he could. He found it surprisingly easy, because Duncan always walked slowly and was, of course, making no effort to shake off anyone tailing him. Duncan Lewis had his problems, but he did not live in Gwyn's paranoid world of suspected treachery and agonising jealousy.

Halfway down the gaudy arcade and just opposite the joke shop, Duncan forked left and Gwyn caught up in time to see him enter Garlands coffee shop. A coffee shop! Gwyn's granny had never approved of coffee shops, believing they were where housewives gossiped, idled and spent their husband's money. Coffee shops were not in Gwyn's cultural make up. He was a thermos-in-the-car man. Duncan Lewis entering a coffee shop was therefore doubly suspicious.

Gwyn walked slowly past the dark window but saw nothing. A few couples at the nearest tables, but none of them Duncan and Holly. Nor even just Duncan. Gwyn stopped outside Jothams, the gentleman's tailor, once he was well out of sight of anyone sitting in the window, and wondered what to do next. Did he risk passing by again and being spotted? Yes. If his wife was in there he had to know. He chose a closer trajectory past the large dark window, so that there would be no reflection to dazzle him, and passed by more slowly this time. He still couldn't see Duncan, but then he noticed a man in a light-coloured suit sitting himself down in the furthest corner. Of course, if Duncan Lewis had taken off that silly waxed jacket he might well be wearing a light-coloured suit underneath.

Gwyn decided that the time had come for a quick and decisive strike. He had observed that there was a small wooden vestibule just inside the door. He would go into Garlands and linger there, unobserved by the rest of the café. Then on an instant he would put his head round the vestibule, take a quick look and be out before anyone had even noticed him.

Gwyn would see who was with Duncan Lewis.

After a count of three, he opened the glass outer door quitely and slid into the vestibule. He was just about to peep round the corner when it became apparent that a rather stout young waiter, currently extracting a cake from the carousel cabinet, was looking up at him. The young man was clearly wondering what was going on.

'Surprise,' whispered Gwyn with a wink. The young

man nodded. They got all sorts in on a Thursday afternoon.

No longer needing to behave like a normal human being in front of this witness, Gwyn peered round the corner with great stealth and saw Duncan Lewis for sure sitting at a table over the stairs. He was on his own.

Dammo, thought Gwyn and he left, smiling foolishly at his co-conspirator. But then again, he thought as he stopped by the joke shop, That Duncan Lewis might be *waiting* for someone. He might be waiting for *Holly*. So Gwyn positioned himself on the opposite side of the arcade in order that he could window-shop along the thoroughfare while keeping an eye on Garlands' door.

After fifteen minutes, he realised that Duncan hadn't come out and Holly hadn't gone in and he had seen all he ever wanted to of ethnic goods and bespoke tailoring.

Gwyn Williams was about to leave Duncan's private life in peace, but a final burst of curiosity overcame him and he strolled past the window a third time, fixing his eyes hard on the corner where he knew Duncan to be. And there, to his surprise, he saw that Duncan had been joined by a woman who was not Holly, but a very attractive professional-looking woman who turned herself out well.

Had Gwyn but known it, Duncan was sharing the Legover Table with Carolyn Parry Morris. It was not the kind of meeting either of them had expected, but then when they had arranged it Duncan hadn't just sent Carolyn a very large, very expensive bunch of flowers. Moreover, he didn't know that she hadn't been in receipt of such a tribute for some time (except in official thank-yous for her underpaid work). Nor had Duncan calculated the effect on Carolyn Parry Morris of believing herself appreciated. She had come to reproach and reproof, but she had arrived convinced of her own attractiveness – and Carolyn's conviction was in itself convincing.

When Duncan repeated his apology for not having been in touch, and when he tactfully alluded to the unfortunate cause of his departure last time they met, he did not do so in the way in which he had rehearsed these words. Carolyn's breathy proximity definitely had an effect on him, which was probably something to do with his body sensing it had unfinished business with her body. But more than that, for the first time he could see something genuinely attractive in her. She breezed sex appeal that afternoon, and he was caught on that breeze. Sex appeal was something that the women Duncan knew had very little time or energy for. Holly was too sad; Kit too kooky; Binny probably had it but she was too mixed up about men; Jane used to have it but she was too busy these days. Only Laura Davis still radiated a bit of it, but then only on Sunday afternoons. However, Carolyn Parry Morris definitely had it in Garlands coffee house, and Duncan was definitely within its range.

Not that Carolyn was going to be a pushover again. Besides which, she had to pick up Elinor in three quarters of an hour's time – but she did want to tell Duncan that she had arranged for him to go to a reception for the opening of a new University Business Centre a week on Saturday, where three lay members of the Barrage House committee would be. She knew them by name, knew their foibles and prejudices. She also knew the positive and negative sides of Duncan's candidature and the kind of design that was going to win. This was what Carolyn was good at, and it showed.

'If you can convince them you're what they're looking for you could be home and dry,' she said, and her lipstick seemed to glisten like her eyes.

Duncan responded to her energy. He was thinking that if this woman was his mistress at least she might be able to do something for his career, and as for sex with her — well, he did concede that he might be able to develop a liking for it. So she wasn't his ideal? He probably wasn't hers. But he was getting the feeling they could have some fun together.

He must have said something that hinted at a presumption of this, because Carolyn laid one of her hot round hands on his and said: '*Don't* jump to conclusions.' Then she added: 'We'll see how you get on next Saturday, *Mr Architect*. Maybe if the stakes are that high you'll make the extra effort.' She smiled at him.

What Duncan found quite thrilling was that, despite all her reservations about him as a person, he got the distinct impression Carolyn was actually tempted to do it there and then. As was he. Now that would be a first at the Legover Table. What did it matter if they didn't really like each other? Some things are more basic and immediate than that.

Carolyn had to go. 'Make sure you've done some preparation for next week,' she said. 'Go and survey the site, sketch something . . .'

Duncan was amused by her ignorance but he knew what to do. 'I'll be prepared,' he said, getting up to help with her coat. 'Will you be?'

Carolyn turned round to kiss him goodbye. 'Elinor's probably staying with her father,' she said, unable to resist a smile, and when they kissed goodbye she briefly slipped her tongue between his lips.

Gwyn Williams got back home early. While he was tailing Duncan he had completely forgotten about an appointment to teach at Howell's Girls School. When eventually he rang in three quarters of an hour late, it had been suggested with a certain stuffiness that he didn't bother to turn up this week. Gwyn felt aggrieved that the afternoon had cost him, but it hadn't been entirely wasted. Trying to teach two sixth-formers to produce a reasonable noise out of the French horn was difficult enough at the best of times. But to do so while your mind is speculating on the likelihood of your wife having an assignation with Duncan Lewis in Garlands coffee house would be well nigh impossible.

When he got home Gwyn was quite pleased to see Holly again, although she looked somewhat alarmed to see him. She was ironing in the breakfast room when he arrived, but she immediately abandoned her work and walked into the kitchen to put on the kettle.

'You're home early,' she said.

Gwyn lied to the effect that his afternoon teaching session had been cancelled.

'Oh, that's a shame,' said Holly. She was being unusually communicative.

Gwyn, who was of a highly suspicious disposition at the moment, became immediately suspicious again. 'Anything the matter?' he asked.

'No, everything's fine,' said Holly, brightly bringing in the tea pot. 'Hasn't it gone warm all of a sudden?'

At that moment there came a shriek from upstairs and a lot of girlish laughter. Gwyn saw Holly looking embarrassed.

'Gwyn, you mustn't say anything in front of them,' she said, almost entreating him.

'What?' said Gwyn, wondering what was going on.

'Duncan's girls.'

'Oh, not again!' He sat down, half in anger and half in despair. Why was it that Duncan's social life couldn't operate without the Holly Williams Crêche?

'It's not their fault,' said Holly. Now that yesterday's hilarity had died away she was obviously scared of Gwyn's reaction to any mention of Duncan.

'No, I know it's not their fault,' said Gwyn wearily.

'It's not even Duncan's fault,' she continued. 'Something came up suddenly yesterday. A meeting with two men he used to work with, and they could only make three o'clock today.'

Holly stopped talking as she saw the strange expression on Gwyn's face. 'It's something that might help him get another job . . .' she added falteringly. 'Why are you looking at me like that?'

Got him, thought Gwyn. I've *got* the little bugger. Got him good and proper. 'Meeting two men he used to work with, is it?' Gwyn asked. Holly nodded.

'At three o'clock?'

Holly looked as if she might make a run for the door.

Gwyn was grinning strangely. 'I've just seen Duncan,' said Gwyn. 'Saw him at three o'clock this afternoon in Garlands coffee house. Having tea with a woman. Very glamorous, she was. I don't think she was two men he used to work with.'

Holly retreated across the breakfast room as Gwyn continued. 'You ask him, Holly. You ask him, love. I think you'll find he's lying to you.'

Kit Sinclair was in a bad mood and threatening to go out and spend the evening with her so-called friends from the *Western Mail*.

'What's the matter?' Barry asked from his seat in front of the TV. He had entertained no expectation that Kit the Superfit would remain on the agenda for long, but he was surprised that his wife was lapsing again so soon. The Britto boys were about to come down from their bath; in days gone by that would have meant that Kit would be on her way up for her biggie and her ciggie in the Batcave before changing into her secret identity. But for the last two weeks at this time of day she had exercised in the playroom while Barry was being a good father. She had even sat with him while he ate whatever Gabriele had prepared, knocking back the mineral water at an alarming rate.

But tonight Kit was threatening to go out and fritter away her husband's money on some scrubby tarts who laughed at her jokes.

'You go if you want to,' said Barry, suppressing his surprise. 'I'll only be working.'

'You don't care, do you?' she asked, slinging herself into one of the deep leather chairs alongside him like a disgruntled teenager.

Barry was aware that the boys were about to come downstairs, so he put it in shorthand. 'Kit, if I didn't care like hell I wouldn't be married to you.'

Kit leaned forward towards him so there was no chance the boys would overhear. 'They're after me again, Bazza. Rang this afternoon at five o'clock. They want me to do another one.'

Barry used the remote control to turn down the TV. 'Then they must've liked the last one,' he replied simply.

'But it's crap,' said Kit, leaning in even closer. She could see her sons watching them from the top of the stairs. The scene must have looked as if she and Barry were drawing closer in the expectation of a kiss.

'Don't do it then,' whispered Barry.

'But it's money,' said Kit. 'You know what a dreadful old whore I am.'

Barry knew his wife pretty well. 'You mean they've asked you to write another and you've already said yes?'

'Yes,' said Kit. 'Bastards.'

'And now you want to get drunk because you're just too embarrassed and ashamed?'

'Bazza, you can read me like a dirty little book,' she said.

'Look,' said Barry, putting his arm round her. 'Really we ought to be celebrating. Give me half an hour with the boys and an hour to catch up on my work and then how about we *both* go out?'

Kit kissed him on the nose.

'Cor,' said the Britto boys from the stair.

'Not every day your mother gets commissioned for another Mills & Boon,' Barry explained.

'Bastard! Bastard! Bastard!' said Kit.

It was at this point that the phone rang. Barry answered it to avoid a blow that was definitely coming his way. Kit had just finished swearing her sons to utter secrecy on pain of having all their teeth extracted, when Barry announced that there was a Laura Leighton Davis on the telephone.

'Kit, it's Laura,' came the clear ringing tones. 'Holly has just rung me. I want us to meet tomorrow. All of Duncan's friends. Would you come to coffee here after we've all taken the children in?'

'Sure,' said Kit, sounding surprised but ultra-reasonable. She could always get Gabriele to drop her off after the boys had been left at the school.

'I'm sorry not to say more on the telephone,' said Laura, who sounded in quite a state.

'No, that's OK,' Kit replied. Besides, she had a good idea what this was all about.

On Friday morning Duncan was driving over to Penarth for a meeting with Richard and Geraint. Penarth's marina, with its few expensive boats and its unfulfilled but grandiose plans, lay a mile across the bay at the opposite end of what would one day be the Taff Barrage. Duncan wanted to get a perspective on the Barrage House site from the seaward end, but he was also interested in picking Richard and Geraint's brains on the subject.

He had dropped the girls at school, a concession they now took for granted, and then dropped Jane at the station for Newport. During the journey down Cathedral Road the two of them only spoke of the girls and Mr Harper. Jane's plans and Duncan's plans they avoided discussing.

In the silence that ensued Jane did quietly mention that Norman seemed to have lost interest in their conservatory since two large girders arrived in the garden.

'At least we don't have to pay him anything,' said Duncan, and they left it at that.

Duncan was thinking of the night of their last dinner party, when Alice had been ill and the conservatory had looked so ethereal in that light blue painted glow, and Miles had paid court to Jane, and she had put on that dress with the slit skirt and refused to wear Miles' rose in her hair.

Jane was thinking very much the same thoughts. It was something that the two of them did out of long habit. Now they talked so little, both had forgotten how often a stray remark would set them both thinking in the same direction.

But Jane was thinking much darker thoughts too. Thoughts of cruel deception and the suppressed desire for revenge. She almost wished Duncan would crash the car and kill them both. Except for the girls of course. It was just a fantasy, an extreme reaction to news she had received of Duncan's most recent betrayal.

Fortunately Jane couldn't read Duncan's mind, but if she could it would only have confirmed what she believed of him. As he took the back route through Riverside, Duncan was thinking of Carolyn Parry Morris, about the time she'd worn nothing under her track suit, about the time she'd lain back on the coffee table and hoisted up her skirt, about the frustratingly prim cleavage she had displayed when they met in Garlands and how cleverly that dress had been designed to emphasise her bust and minimise her waist. He was thinking that next time they met he wanted to have sex with her wearing that dress.

Jane didn't know what had transpired at Duncan's meeting with Carolyn yesterday, because that was one of the many things they did not discuss. But she now knew *far worse* about her husband, and she just wished they could get to the station sooner so she didn't have to see any more of him that day.

Coffee at Laura's house was not an elaborate thing, although Holly arrived bearing flowers and kissing Laura rather as if she had come to a funeral. Coffee at Laura's house was instant and in mugs with a plate of digestive biscuits on Gerald's mother's table.

Kit had decided that she was there as a spectator. She had come to observe how big a harem Duncan had mustered, but in fact the gathering was just her, Laura and the hippy woman, run to seed, whom Kit had often thought might be Holly.

Laura spoke first, very much in the way she would have spoken had she fulfilled her parents' ambitions and become Berkshire's youngest headmistress. 'I'm afraid Holly has discovered that Duncan has been seeing a woman while Holly has been looking after his children. We think she is someone from outside the area . . .'

You mean not one of Us, thought Kit to herself.

'I don't know if you were aware of this, Kit . . . ?' Laura asked.

'It . . . makes sense,' Kit said. The last thing she wanted to do at this stage was upset Holly or Laura by saying that Duncan had told her everything. There was a sense of hurt pride about these two women. It was as if they were both thinking, If he has to have an affair, why does it have to be someone so *unsuitable*? Kit didn't want to rub salt into that wound.

'The question now facing those of us who are Duncan's friends, but who also value Jane of course, is,' and here

Laura paused, 'is should we consider this none of our business or should we do what we can to help?'

Holly looked blank and rather sad. Laura looked resolute, yet with no purpose, as if the saving of Duncan's marriage might become one of her great causes but she didn't know how to go about it.

Kit felt it was up to her to say something. 'Men, eh?' she muttered. She was dying for a cigarette.

Laura took this remark as her cue. 'We can't expect them to be anything but what they are,' she announced compassionately. 'My own husband was married when we met . . .'

Kit was intrigued by this but, sensing her curiosity, Laura quickly added that Gerald was of course in the throes of a divorce.

Kit felt mischievous and inclined to play the innocent. 'Look, do we know for certain that there's anything in it? She might be one of these career consultants that people like Duncan go to.'

Holly shook her head and Laura spoke.

'No, I wish that were so, Kit, but Duncan has lied to Holly. Why else would he do that?'

'There's more,' said Holly, regarding the table with great sadness. Then she looked up and spoke. 'Last night, after I rang you Laura, I . . . I . . . rang Duncan and Jane . . . at about half-past ten.' Holly's voice, normally so quiet, was gaining in strength. She told how, unable to believe what Gwyn had said, she finally got up and rang the Lewises, not knowing what she was going to say. The phone had been answered by Duncan. Holly had stood rooted to the spot for a few seconds, terrified, and then when she was about to put the receiver down, Duncan had started talking. He had called her Carolyn and asked her to stop ringing and said that it only made matters more difficult, but added that he was looking forward to seeing her next Saturday.

The three women sat in silence digesting Holly's terrible story.

'He's not himself,' said Laura after a while. 'But I am at a loss to know what to do.'

Jane Lewis was at a loss too. She spent that Friday in Newport, detached from what was going on. She knew that things really were falling apart now, completely falling apart, because last night she had picked up the bedroom handset after she heard the downstairs phone being answered. And she had heard Duncan talking to his mistress. His tone wasn't as harsh as Jane wished to hear, but at least he was telling this silent woman not to make any more of her phone calls. And then she heard him telling this Carolyn woman that she was making things more difficult for him by ringing.

And that he was looking forward to seeing her next Saturday.

Jane had wanted to drop the phone. She had been coming round to the belief that Duncan had erred but that he was redeemable. One day he would have been punished enough. But not this Duncan. She hated this Duncan more than ever. She hated herself too for giving in to eavesdropping on a telephone conversation – but now she knew. And now she hated Duncan more than she had ever hated anyone in her life.

The real Jane Lewis, who was now in Newport, felt she had switched off from the Jane Lewis everyone saw outside. Part of her continued being a mother and a solicitor, and even a wife. But inside she was cold and she could not believe that she would ever trust anyone again. When Duncan had gone to bed this last week, sometimes her bedroom door had been open and he had stood in the doorway and said goodnight. He hadn't presumed to cross the threshold to what used to be his own bedroom, but he would speak from the theshold and Jane would reply. But not last night. When Duncan had made his way to the attic, her bedroom door was firmly closed.

At lunchtime on Friday Jane got her messages through from the Cardiff office. Among them was a note to say that Miles Milhash had called. Without more thought, she picked up a phone on the desk she was borrowing and dialled Miles' answering-machine.

'Miles. It's Jane Lewis. I'll be happy to have dinner with you next Saturday,' she said calmly. 'Oh, sorry for my behaviour.'

Why not have dinner with Miles? She wouldn't really be there at the time.

Duncan had had a useful meeting with Richard and Geraint, who had rented a sumptuous office at a knock-down price overlooking the main harbour lock. Richard had even got a nearby flat thrown in as part of the deal. The only problem, he admitted, was at weekends when all the divorced fathers had their kids to stay. Richard had found that most of his neighbours were not bachelors enjoying the marina *dolce vita*, but sad-faced men between marriages who didn't have the money to live the lifestyle that a dockland flat demanded.

Oh God, thought Duncan. Is this where I'm heading? Weekends with Alice and Ellen walking round the marina, looking at the few plush boats he would never be able to afford and hoping that neither of his daughters fell in. Suddenly he felt very anxious. He didn't want to lose Jane and the girls. Maybe he'd just use Carolyn to get the job and go back to Jane with everything sorted. After he and Carolyn had had a few more nights together, of course.

Duncan was remembering how Carolyn had pulled off her track suit top and laid back in front of the flame-effect fire, and about how adept her hands were at infiltrating his trousers. He wanted very much to take hold of the folds of skin at her waist and turn her over, and—

'Have you seen this?' Richard asked, showing Duncan some PR in *The Journal* about a firm Duncan had spent some weeks with in London.

'No,' Duncan said absent-mindedly, taking it to look at. It was impossible to think of work and saving his marriage and what he wanted to do to the Parry Morris body all at the same time.

As he left Penarth, winds sprang up from the sea. It seemed a beautiful but nevertheless desolate little haven, where young men could move into unoccupied palatial offices and the flotsam of married life washed up in isolated comfort.

Duncan thought he had got to sort his life out but, at the same time, he was remembering Kit's warning that Jane and Carolyn would be sorting things out too. He had to decide what he wanted before they did.

If it wasn't already too late.

13

Duncan, This Is Wrong!

Because there was no curtain over the skylight in the Lewises' attic, Duncan tended to wake up early, sometimes to the glare of uncommon sunshine but more often to the incessant patter of rain. As he stared up at the grey wet nothingness that was the sky above Cardiff, he realised that some things had to change. He loved his wife. He had loved his wife. But his wife was now impossible. Ever since the day he had met with Carolyn to tell her it was all off, Jane had reached a pitch of hostility that now went beyond words. It was as if she could actually tell, just by looking at him, that off it wasn't.

And there was definitely something about the way in which she informed him that she was having dinner with Miles on Saturday evening that suggested she knew about what Duncan and Carolyn had arranged for the afternoon.

Duncan was deeply depressed, but he was also aggrieved that Jane assumed any career move on his part to be simply the cover for another tumble with Cari Parry. And yet, of course, Carolyn *had* promised that if he made a good enough impression on Saturday, Elinor might well be spending the weekend with her father. To Duncan, the prospect of coffee tables and flame-effect gas fires and condoms behind the carriage clock was at least as alluring in the short term as full-time employment in the long term. In fact, he thought, sex was the *greatest* short-term pleasure. The problem was its long-term consequences. But in those cold, empty early mornings with the rain snaking down the window panes, he positively yearned for some short-term pleasure. The long term could wait.

And if all else fails, he thought, turning over, at least by getting out of this room and this house it will be a clean break, and then Jane and I can renegotiate. Maybe if I spend a few weeks in Cyn Coed or Penarth Jane will decide she wants me around. Maybe she'll miss me. Then again . . . maybe I'm kidding myself.

Maybe I'm making the biggest mistake of my life.

But, as he tried to get back to sleep and listened reluctantly to the wetness buffeting Katrin Street, Duncan couldn't see what else to do. If it all fell apart, perhaps it was always going to.

Holly Williams was on standby to baby-sit on Saturday. The official fiction was that if Duncan was late back from his business lunch and Jane had to go out to her business dinner, Holly would be on hand to look after the girls. This was what Duncan had arranged. This was what Holly had agreed to believe, responding quietly to Duncan's phone call and hiding her disappointment.

But the unofficial, almost unspoken consensus between Jane and Duncan was that there was no chance he would be back in time to look after the girls. Jane knew – and Duncan had a good idea that Jane knew – that Duncan was probably going off with Carolyn after this official opening thing.

The unofficial consensus about Jane was that she would

be back, but back when she chose to be back. Jane was going out with Miles to prove a number of things, but she wouldn't be taking coffee in his hotel room. She would be there for Alice and Ellen on Sunday morning. Which is, when you come down to it, why Duncan took the means of contraception with him on Saturday and Jane didn't.

When Duncan met Alice and Ellen in the hall just before he set out, the presence of a threepack in his jacket pocket made him feel even more ashamed than he felt already.

'Are you going to work?' Alice asked.

'Yes,' said Duncan. The girls would soon be nine, but Duncan still crouched down when he talked to them.

He put an arm round each. 'I love you very much, you know,' he said.

Ellen looked squarely at him. 'You never used to say that when you went to work,' she pointed out reproachfully.

'I didn't used to feel it as strongly as I do now,' said Duncan, and his eyes swam with tears. He hugged them both close to him so they wouldn't see.

'You don't have to go to work,' said Ellen into his shoulder. 'Mum can go to work and you can collect us from school. We don't mind.'

Duncan felt so unworthy he thought he might really cry. 'But that's been the problem,' he explained. 'We've tried it and it hasn't worked out. That's why Mum and I have been shouting at each other. I think I've got to get back to work so we can all be a happy family again.'

'Promise?' Alice asked.

Duncan stood up. 'Look,' he said. 'I know what I'm going to do. I'm going to write to some people I know, people I used to work for in London who are expanding—'

'People who are expanding?' Alice interrupted, trying to be clever.

Duncan explained that he'd read how a firm who used to like him were taking on more work now, and if Alice and Ellen would help him he'd write them a letter, so that if today didn't get him a job maybe their letter would. The girls liked this idea. It seemed to bear out the line that Duncan and Jane had been spinning them. They ran as a trio up to Duncan's attic, and Alice dictated a letter while Ellen did the envelope.

Duncan used Ellen's envelope but while Alice popped downstairs to the loo he substituted his own quickly handwritten note and sealed down the envelope. Duncan's contact was one of Alice's far from conscientious godfathers who would forgive and even understand the envelope. It might even prompt the bugger to remember the twins' birthday for once.

Jane met Duncan and the girls going out to catch the twelve o'clock post. 'I thought you were going to this thing at the university,' she said with patent heaviness of heart. Much of what Duncan and Jane said these days was couched in terms that meant one thing to each other but something more innocent to the girls.

'We're going to post a letter that's going to get Dad a job!' Ellen stated.

'I wrote it,' said Alice proudly.

'And I did the envelope,' added Ellen.

'That's nice,' said Jane. But the look she gave Duncan was signalling that he should not be trifling with his daughters' hopes in this way.

'Look at the envelope,' said Duncan.

Alice showed Jane while Ellen insisted on reminding everyone that it was she who had written the address.

'Very nice,' said Jane, looking mainly at Duncan. It seemed to her that he was now setting out to make a complete mockery of the whole business of getting a job. It was like an act of defiance that he had flung in her face and, worse, one that he had co-opted her daughters into.

Duncan said he'd bring Alice and Ellen back before walking to the university.

'I'll see you when I see you,' Jane replied, wishing that he wasn't going but if he was he could go to hell.

'Yes,' said Duncan, wishing he wasn't going now but what was there to stay for? 'Have a nice dinner,' he added.

Jane glared at him as if to say, 'What I do with my private life is no longer any concern of yours.'

And Duncan gave her a half-smile as if to reply, 'Did I say it was?'

Duncan Lewis did not know that Dr and Mrs Dr Britto were also going to be at the reception, but it might have been audibly obvious to anyone passing down Bond-Kyle Avenue that Saturday morning. Kit Sinclair was not happy, and no number of pre-emptive swearing exercises could reassure her that she wasn't going to let Barry down.

'Why can't you take someone else?' she was shouting from her bathroom and banging cupboard doors.

'Because I'm not married to someone else,' Barry replied from the landing outside.

'Take one of those scrubby nurses who fancy you!' Kit yelled.

'It's not that kind of party!' Barry called back, and he sat down to wait for more.

Barry Britto believed he and Kit had been through a lot together. They weren't out of the trees yet, but as the years passed life was getting more and more like that thing which other people did. There had been a time, after Ben was born, when Kit had been unable to go anywhere or even look after the baby on her own. Things were better now than they had ever been.

Barry had always known his own mind, and it had never bothered him if it took a while to get what he wanted. His certainty about marrying this daffy fashion journalist nine years ago had come as a great shock to his friends, to the many nurses who had high hopes of him, and to Kit herself. What Kit Sinclair wanted nine years ago was not a husband and family. Kit wanted an abortion. Kit had never ever intended to have children, or even Barry for that matter.

But Barry had calmed her fears and eventually convinced her that all would be well. And when it became clear, after the baby was born, that things weren't going at all well Barry set about changing their life so that Kit got as much support as she needed. He knew that it was going to be a long haul, but Barry's motto had always been that some things were worth working at, and Kit was definitely one of those things.

She was now a hugely conscientious mother (even if she refused to pick up the boys from school), she was slowly rebuilding her career, and she was – despite everything she claimed – a highly conscientious wife (to the extent of letting him come back to Wales, and even making herself absent from official gatherings if she felt that she couldn't behave any longer). But Barry Britto believed that if Kit was ever going to get back on board with the rest of the world she had to do it as herself, and if that meant she was going to tell the Professor of Pharmacology to fuck off over the profiteroles, then so be it.

'You'll be fine,' he told the bathroom door.

'There'll be nobody there I know,' Kit shouted. But of course she was wrong.

Duncan had arrived without Carolyn, but he met her in the brass and polished slate entrance lobby. The University of Wales Business Centre was an impressive tribute to the money that was expected to roll in. It reminded Duncan of a bridegroom decked out in all his glory, convinced that with this much finery on show any number of brides would soon be trotting up the aisle.

He accepted a name badge from a woman in a blazer who looked remarkably like the person who'd encouraged him to 'have a can*ape*, love' at Caedfael's pre-match do. Then he took a drink and wandered round to look at the bronzes. Were these notable Welshmen, distinguished academics, prominent local councillors or valued customers of the University of Wales Business PLC?

The first was a rugby player and, unless he was mistaken, it was a duplicate cast from a bust he'd seen at the New Theatre or St David's Hall or the National Museum. Instant Pantheon, thought Duncan. Two rugby players, a poet, a Hollywood actor and a dead politician – it was the Welsh civic equivalent of flying ducks. Every home should have them.

Carolyn slipped her arm through his. He knew it was her by the touch. 'You've got work to do.'

When he turned round he saw that Carolyn was also in a blazer, a very expensive blazer with a tight white shirt that had buttons. From the age of fourteen Duncan had been interested in the buttons on girls' shirts, but he had no time to savour them today. He had to meet someone. As she led him across the lobby, Carolyn told him not to try to be too clever. Caedfael thought he had tried to be too clever.

Oh God, thought Duncan, I don't want to go through life with Caedfael Parry Morris grooming me by remote control.

'I don't try to be too clever,' he muttered. 'I try to be funny.'

'Why try to be funny?' Carolyn asked, not altering her pace. 'You're an architect.'

Duncan realised they had never found anything funny together. Why was he thinking of temporarily sharing his life with a woman with whom he had never even shared a laugh? Couldn't they forget all this networking and career development and just have sex somewhere? Get to the bit that was definitely worthwhile? Go for the short term and stop debating the long-term consequences of trying to be too clever vs. sucking up to influential halfwits?

But Sir Aneurin Fitzwater was not a halfwit, indeed the old man seemed to have more wits about him than Duncan could muster on a Saturday lunchtime. He was a small man, small in a way that would be remarkable in England but which just about passed muster in Wales. Duncan had missed the celebrated return of this grizzled expatriate who had anchored his yacht in the Bristol Channel and ostentatiously announced his intention to bring in millions of pounds in investment to his home town.

Sir Aneurin Fitzwater had, with that gesture, got up the maximum number of local noses possible, but the money had followed, much to the disappointment of those who would have dearly liked to see him fall flat on his well-tanned, white haired face.

Now Fitz, as he liked to be known, was chairman of the university's Inward Investment Committee, and he had badgered his way on to various architectural initiatives including the Opera House and the New Architects Committee.

'You're a bit old to be a New Architect, aren't you boy?' he growled.

Caedfael had already given Duncan the answer to this one via Carolyn. Duncan had worked all his professional life in Cardiff, but now he was setting up on his own in a new kind of architectural practice which would be doing things that hadn't been attempted before.

'Such as?'

Duncan had patiently explained to Carolyn that anyone with any sense at all was bound to follow up with that question, but fortunately he knew enough about what was new to be able to busk. Carolyn left them alone. She looked relieved that Duncan was coping.

Jane had gone to see Binny, much to the annoyance of her daughters who disliked being palmed off with mad Josh while Jane talked to someone who wasn't Duncan.

The irony had not been lost on Jane that, now Duncan was no longer Duncan, this actually made it more difficult for her to talk about her marriage to the likes of Binny Barnes. The two women had always shared confidences about the awfulness of men on the basis that Duncan and Flyn were basically sound, depite everything. But now that Duncan *wasn't*, Jane had no idea what to say.

They were sitting next to an oil heater in Binny's under-restored kitchen when Josh came in complaining that Alice and Ellen had locked themselves into his bedroom and wouldn't play with him.

'Never mind,' said Binny, hoisting up her large five-year-old and placing him on her lap. 'Are you going to tell Jane what you're going to be?'

'A page boy,' said Josh.

'That's nice,' said Jane.

Binny, alert to the fact that Jane wasn't cottoning on, added, 'Flyn and I are getting married. He asked me last weekend. It took me three days to decide. Can you believe that?'

Jane still wasn't replying. She felt she had to say something but she couldn't think what.

'Aren't you pleased?' Binny asked, giving Josh a cuddle.

'Yes,' said Jane, unable to gauge her own feelings at all.

'And we were thinking,' Binny continued. 'You know this trip to Llanthony? We were thinking, Flyn and me, whether we might all go? You, me, Duncan, Flyn and the children. You know, to celebrate – a sort of stag and hen – and chickens – weekend.'

'Oh,' said Jane, wondering how many people she was going to have this kind of converstaion with in the next few months. 'I'll, er, have to check with Duncan. What was the date?'

Duncan was doing well. Sir Aneurin Fitzwater had clapped him on the back and told him that age was a matter of attitude, and when Carolyn guided him to Stella Loomis-Bryce, Duncan found that he and Councillor Bryce shared similar views on the design of the new Opera House.

Carolyn returned when the regal lady was just about to move off. 'You're definitely doing well,' she said squeezing his arm.

'Who was she?' Duncan asked as they threaded through the crowd.

'Chairwoman of the Barrage House committee. I thought you'd hit it off with her. I shall have to *watch* you, won't I?'

The next person on Carolyn's agenda was a tall man immersed in much hilarity with two jolly women from HTV, so Carolyn suggested they got some food.

'Oh look,' she said, pulling Duncan by the arm. 'There's another of your women.' And indeed as Duncan turned round he saw Kit and Barry Britto. Barry was dressed in a good tweed jacket that Duncan remembered Kit buying him, while his wife was standing to one side 'showing the teeth', which was her expression for the fixed smile she adopted when hugely bored but determined not to show it.

'Come on,' said Carolyn as if Duncan needed mild reproaches for lingering over the prospect of one of his former conquests.

As they browsed the buffet Duncan began to piece together Carolyn's picture of him. And much of it was as Kit Sinclair had suggested: here was a talented man who could make a good impression if he put his mind to it, but who had simply wasted his creative energies by making facetious jokes to the people who mattered and shagging the people who didn't. Carolyn clearly saw the role she was taking on as channelling the primal forces in Duncan Lewis. Henceforth he would say the right things to the right people and, presumably, she would also make sure he also shagged the right people too (which, so it seemed, was her).

And, hey presto, he would be a success.

Well, why the hell not, thought Duncan.

Then again, Carolyn's petty possessiveness alarmed him. Jane had always found it rather amusing if Duncan found an admirer. But Carolyn was clearly going to police that area of his life very rigorously. Of course she did labour under the misapprehension that he was the Lothario of Pontcanna. Would she be disappointed or relieved to learn that she was his only conquest, particularly when really he had been hers?

'I think Councillor Talbot's coming free,' Carolyn murmured, turning Duncan round.

'*Super*,' said Duncan.

Carolyn looked at him.

'The vol-au-vents,' said Duncan. 'They really are quite super.'

Across the lobby Kit saw Duncan being piloted round by Carolyn Parry Morris, and she allowed herself a wry smile inside her perfectly poised persona, only to notice a newly arrived couple standing on the raised slate platform upon which all invitees got temporarily marooned until someone rescued them with a badge, a drink and a smile.

Dr Gerald Davis and Mrs Dr Davis did not look comfortable. Gerald's tweed jacket, unlike Barry's, gave the impression that it was used for walking in the country, and Laura was dressed as if she was being taken out to tea in the Home Counties.

This is going to be fun, thought Kit.

'Darling,' she said with a big big smile to Barry, 'I must have a word with the Head of German and his sweet wife, they've just arrived. Will you excuse me?' she asked Professor Arsebender or whatever his name was.

Duncan was just being introduced to Councillor Talbot when out of the corner of his eye he caught a glimpse of Kit, sneaking stealthily round the back of the lobby like a big game hunter, and wondered what she was up to.

Carolyn was patting his shoulder and telling this Talbot man that Duncan had some very new ideas on architecture in the Bay.

'Of course, I liked it as it was,' said Talbot, shaking Duncan's hand in a huge grasp. 'I grew up and worked in the Bay, *unlike* Aneurin Fitzwater, who got out when he was fifteen and never saw the place again till now.'

The man seemed friendly enough, but Duncan wondered if this was some kind of challenge. Was he expected to comment, to come down on one side or the other?

'I bet you think all architects are poofs,' was what he wanted to say, but he started to talk about the need to preserve what little was left of the old Cardiff Bay without turning what was genuine into pastiche: the dilemma of the conscientious architect. It wasn't difficult to trot out.

'How do you stand on Community Housing, then?' asked Councillor Talbot.

'Very important,' said Duncan, who thought he recognised the person Kit was talking to, a tall old man with sloping shoulders whose face was turned frustratingly away.

'Duncan's done a lot of inner-city work,' Carolyn lied, placing her hand on his arm again.

Duncan had had time to reflect that, as the reception had worn on, Carolyn had made physical contact more and more often, more and more ostentatiously. He was obviously doing well; in all likelihood Elinor was already with her father.

Then Duncan, in the very moment that he recognised Gerald Davis, saw Laura. She was standing with a glass in her hand, staring at him as she had the first time they met. Laura Leighton Davis did not believe her eyes.

'Bugger me,' said Duncan, audibly.

Councillor Talbot stopped in mid-sentence. Carolyn looked up at Duncan, who quickly regained some composure.

'I'm sorry,' he said.

'No,' said Councillor Talbot. 'I quite agree. It's an outrage, shifting out good people to make way for some six-lane yuppie boulevard, but what I want to know from *you*, Mr Lewis, is will your indignation translate into action?'

Laura was still staring at Duncan, her cheeks flushed.

'Will you excuse me?' he asked. 'I'm very pleased to meet you, but something's come up.'

Duncan left the lobby by ducking under the main staircase. He was unsure of where he was going but found himself in a low, dark corridor that seemed to lead past a series of meeting rooms. Here he felt safe. Never had he been so alarmed since his mother died. Her disapproval was relentless but half-hearted, whereas Laura's was all the more alarming for the obvious shock that was manifest in her face.

Meanwhile, back in the lobby, Carolyn was doing very good service on Duncan's behalf and Kit was being charming to Gerald Davis who had resigned himself to making small talk to his colleagues that lunchtime and rather felt he had landed on his feet.

'No, actually Fashion and Medicine,' said Kit. 'Rather an odd combination, but there you go. I do the odd book as well. Are you all right, Laura?'

Laura Leighton Davis was no longer staring at Duncan

Lewis but at the woman who had been caressing him in public. Then she put down her glass and walked off.

'Preoccupied,' said Kit to Gerald with her best smile. 'Now. Tell me, haven't you got all those sons with wonderful Wagnerian names?'

Duncan wasn't sure what to do now. Was he running away from Laura or was he going to brazen it out and pretend she wasn't there? The sound of a voice from the crowded lobby asking if a man in a light-coloured suit had come this way decided him: he was running away. Immediately to hand there was no obvious exit from the building, but there was one place where not even Laura Leighton Davis would follow him. Duncan slipped into the gents.

'And this is my husband,' said Kit, knocking back her champagne. She was beginning to enjoy the party after all. Barry and Gerald shook hands while Kit commandeered another drink.

'My wife was here a moment ago but she's just disappeared,' said Gerald by way of nothing in particular.

'Gerald's wife wants to send her sons to The Abbey,' said Kit out of the blue. 'Only they can't afford it. Unlike some people I know,' she added pointedly and tactlessly.

Gerald began to explain that with four sons he and Laura would have to make a very large financial commitment over a period of some fourteen years, during which time he would be retiring, otherwise of course he and Laura would not hesitate.

'D'you hear that, *Darling*?' asked Kit.

'Yes, Christine,' said Barry.

'My husband,' said Kit, 'is a man of very high principles out of whose arse—' At this point she mid-sentence, coughed, and started again. 'Out of whose department remarkable work is being done. Will you excuse me?' she asked.

She had felt it then, the rush of adrenaline, the launch-pad into who knows what, and she had checked herself. Good. Get out of it while you're still in one piece. Go to the lav and throw up.

Duncan was emerging from the gents at about the same time that Kit was making her way to the ladies. There was no obvious sign of Laura, so he made his way back towards the lobby only to spot Laura talking in a firm but friendly way to a woman he did not know but who was in fact the Dean of Gerald's faculty. The Dean and Laura were in different camps over the Gerald issue, but they always got on better than Laura expected because the two women shared an interest in education policy. The Dean had even been known to murmur that *Mrs* Davis would be a lot more use to the university than her husband.

Duncan slipped past, pretending to admire an oil painting of North Walian sheep farming. He could sense Laura's eyes on his back, but her clear bell-like voice continued to ring out in conversation. There was no dread maternal summons: 'Duncan, come here.'

On the other side of the main staircase Duncan cast a glance over his shoulder to check he was in the clear, and whilst doing so he virtually walked into Carolyn.

'Sorry about that,' he said.

Carolyn regarded him drily. 'One of your women?' she asked with a raised eyebrow.

'In a manner of speaking,' Duncan replied. 'Look, I've met all the old farts, can we go now?'

'You're in a hurry,' she said, savouring what she took to be rampant lust on Duncan's part. 'You know I can't *possibly* go until the presentation.'

'Well,' said Duncan. 'How about I nip back and turn on the gas fire?'

He liked the way Carolyn looked tempted by that. Her lip gloss sparkled.

'You'd never switch off the security system,' she said with a smile. 'If you've had enough of this, go and wait for me in the car park. My keys are with the porter.'

So saying, she popped one of her cards into Duncan's breast pocket, tapped him on the chest, and moved off.

Duncan felt he was in the clear. He had his escape route set up, without wrecking all the spadework they'd just put in; he even had an escape vehicle in which to hide out!

On his way to the main door, he paused to speak to good old Barry and good old Gerald who seemed to be running out of things to say to each other.

'Kit not around?' he asked.

'Not feeling too good,' said Barry with a matter-of-fact smile.

'And Laura?'

'Looking for you, I think,' said Gerald, with another matter-of-fact smile.

'Ah,' said Duncan. 'Well . . . tell her I'll catch up with her next week.'

'Right,' said Gerald in a very agreeable way.

Duncan wondered how much Gerald knew. There was more to good old Gerry than met the eye, but how much more? Duncan made straight for the porter's desk, Carolyn's keys and freedom. Except that at that moment in through the sliding outer doors came Howard Losen and Dic Prosser, – of all the laughing, self-congratulatory men in the world, possibly the two Duncan least wanted to meet.

Bugger-double-buggeration, he thought, and diverted his course to send him back round the side of the lobby again and under the main staircase. There must be some other way out of this building, he thought. What about fire regulations, for Chrissake!

He was faced with two dark tunnel-like passages, one on this side of the lobby and one on the other. Although the nearest one seemed to have no external exits he knew, at the very least, that it had a gents lavatory in which he could hide again if the worst came to the worst. So he set in the direction of a source of light at the far end, only to find a fire door which aggressively advertised. THIS DOOR IS ALARMED. The last thing Duncan wanted was to be caught breaking out of a university reception while klaxons wailed.

He crept along the corridor, feeling the handles of the various rooms in case one was unlocked and had a window out of which he could escape from his past and into his future – and indeed one handle did give. Duncan slipped into the darkness inside and switched on the low lighting. The room had a large central table surrounded by comfortable chairs. Duncan skirted these as he made for the window opposite. He had just inspected the catch and worked out what was involved in releasing it when he heard the door close behind him very firmly. Someone had come in.

Duncan spun round to see Laura Leighton Davis with her back against the door and a very dangerous look on her face.

Duncan had always enjoyed the company of women, but he had a healthy fear of their emotions. Jane's anger, Carolyn's possessive passion, Kit's helter-skelter waywardness, his own mother's routine censure – all alarmed him in different degrees. But Laura made him quake.

Laura's look was one that Duncan couldn't fathom, partly because he avoided her eyes but also because the mixture of disapproval and love was such a heady one that he didn't know where to look.

'Duncan, this has got to stop,' she said.

They looked at each other across the room. 'It's too late,' said Duncan, knowing exactly what they were talking about.

'No it's not,' said Laura.

Duncan didn't want to argue, but Laura had her back to his escape route.

'Jane and I have reached a stage when it's best that I get out, and maybe we can rebuild things after a cooling-off period,' he told her.

'No,' said Laura, shaking her head. 'If you leave Jane now you won't be going back, you know that.'

He hated to tell Laura to mind her own business, but that was what he knew he must say. She was behaving as if his life *was* her business, and if he didn't prevent her that might well become the case. Unless he argued back, Laura was going to gain a stake in his life by default.

'Listen, Laura,' he said, 'I'm very fond of you, but—'

'Some things are *wrong*, Duncan,' said Laura. 'You know this is wrong.'

Duncan saw how her dark eyes shone, and how the high colour in her cheeks spread all the way down her throat.

'It's easy to say that—' he began.

'It's no easier for me than you,' Laura interrupted him.

He really felt that Laura was trespassing on the respect that he always accorded her. She was pushing him too far.

'Look,' he said.

Again Laura interrupted. 'We are all tempted!' she declared with the fervour of that lithograph missionary he had once seen in her. 'It isn't any easier for me than you, but what matters is that you make the right choice now.'

'Oh for God's sake!' Duncan raised his voice.

'Whom do you love, Duncan?'

'Don't ask me that!'

'Is it Jane or is it that woman out there?'

Duncan was about to tell her not to refer to Carolyn in such a way, when the simple force of that question hit him.

'Jane,' he said.

It was as if he'd only just noticed.

And then something yet more powerful swept over him. A wave of emotion that was virtually palpable. That awful, dangerous wave of simplicity that causes people to sacrifice everything for a simple burning truth. That *Tristan and Isolde* realisation that nothing else matters but the thing which is gone.

'I love Jane and Alice and Ellen,' he said, and he started to cry.

He started to cry.

'Then you must go back to them,' said Laura. 'Nothing else matters.'

'I love Jane,' said Duncan, sitting down and sobbing uncontrollably. He hadn't cried in years and he could feel the pressure of those years coming out in his tears.

After a moment Laura walked up to him and put one hand on his head and the other on his shoulders and drew him to her. It was the first and only time they touched, and it was for her a communion. She was bringing Duncan back. Her lost boy, her friend and . . . many other things that need never be spoken.

Kit was outside the committee room, having come out of the ladies to see Laura going in after Duncan. In the last five or ten minutes she had seen something and heard something of what was going on through the frosted glass, but not a lot. Just a bit. Kit Sinclair enjoyed living vicariously, but she didn't need to know everything. She stayed out in the dark corridor guessing what the distorted figures the other side of that glass door were doing. She was a novelist after all; she could make it up.

Kit was still there when Carolyn Parry Morris came bustling up, having found that her car keys were still with the porter.

'Have you seen Duncan Lewis?' she asked Kit in exasperation.

'Sorry Sweetie,' Kit said, leaning back against the frosted glass. 'Is it your turn next? I thought it was mine.'

Carolyn looked angry at Kit's impertinence and really would have said something, but instead she stalked off. When the coast seemed clear, Kit returned to the lobby, sniggering. Sighting the broad shoulders of Barry the Beloved Bastard, she threw her arms around his back and begged to be rescued.

'Darling,' she said, 'I have been so good. So fucking, fucking good. Please take me home before I start swearing at all these arseholes and cocksuckers.'

Barry moved slightly to one side in the merest show of embarrassment. 'This is the Secretary of State for Wales, darling,' he told her.

When he was sure there was no white Mitsubishi Jeep in the car park, Duncan went back with Laura and Gerald in the Davises' ancient Volvo estate. Laura had said that if he had nowhere to go he should stay with them, but that the price of hiding out with her was talking to Jane.

Duncan agreed. 'It won't be easy,' he said, sitting on Gerald's mother's sofa where once before he had talked to Laura. The sun, for no reason but perversity, had late in the day chosen to emerge from behind the grey Cardiff clouds, and it shone through the French windows like a golden blessing on the calm of Laura's household.

Gerald had gone to pick up the boys from Jane's friend Elaine, who had been booked well in advance and was earning many tokens that day. Laura had thought it only right to pay double the hourly rate for looking after non-sleeping boys. Which meant that Laura and Duncan had another chance to talk. They no longer touched, that was already in the past. For Laura it had been a special moment made all the more special by being unique.

She gave Duncan a whisky and sat down opposite. 'These

things aren't easy,' she said. 'When Gerald didn't get the chair he was so difficult, so unlike himself, – but we kept at it. You have to. And there was a time when I was seriously worried about his relationship with one of his students. But you have to keep trying, Duncan.'

Duncan wanted to ask Laura about her feelings. Had she never been tempted, disillusioned, envious of what others had, angry about what she lacked? But already they were drawing away from each other. The intimacy of two hours ago was over, he realised – and in any case, if he was ever to have Jane again he couldn't allow himself to be distracted by Laura. She wouldn't allow him to either. The subject under discussion was *Duncan and Jane*.

'Every time we talk we end up arguing,' Duncan confessed. 'I want to write to her.'

'You could always try ringing her and telling her you want to talk,' said Laura.

With a shock Duncan realised that by not returning home he must have encouraged Jane to believe he *had* gone off with Carolyn. And she was going out with Miles that evening! He rushed to Laura's phone, but got through to the baby-sitter.

'Hello?' said Holly.

Damn, though Duncan, she's already gone. Having just been told by Laura that Holly also knew his secret, Duncan could think of nothing to say to her so he put the receiver back down quietly.

'It's gone dead,' said Holly, who had answered the phone while Jane was struggling into her third choice of dress.

'That *bloody* woman!' Jane growled. At which point the doorbell rang to announce the arrival of Miles Mihash. 'Put the answer-phone on will you, Holly?'

And Jane was gone.

*   *   *

When Duncan told her that Jane must already have gone because Holly had picked up the phone, Laura rang his house and spoke firmly to the answering-machine until Holly came on the line.

'Duncan's safe. He's with me,' she said.

'Oh, bless you,' said Holly.

'Has Jane gone?' Laura asked.

'Just,' said Holly. 'She's out with a man from her work.'

Laura asked Holly if she knew where Jane was going, but Duncan intervened. He was not having Laura turning herself into a marital snatch squad.

'I'm going to write her a letter,' he declared.

Miles Mihash was excellent company for a woman in her late thirties who wanted to feel attractive. As it happened, Jane was unable to decide how attractive she wanted to feel that night, but Miles seemed able to adjust to that as well. They had been going to Le Monde but Jane changed her mind *en route*. Le Monde had memories of Duncan, both with her and with That Bloody Woman. So they went to the Riverside, a wonderful Cantonese restaurant where the wonderful Cardiff Cantonese ate and where the dark, exotic, down-at-heel atmosphere made the food seem doubly authentic.

Miles behaved as if he knew the staff personally, and they behaved as if they knew him.

'I should warn you I may become lachrymose after a few,' Jane said as Miles filled her wine glass.

'My shoulder is free and available,' he assured her.

'Tell me about divorce,' Jane asked.

'Not my area of the law.'

'Tell me about *being* divorced,' Jane persisted. 'As a friend. Are you my friend, Miles?'

'I am your friend,' he replied.

'Were you friends with all your wives before you divorced them?'

He took a sip from his glass and brushed his moustache. 'If you are asking me to talk to you about the human consequences of breaking up a marriage, Jane, then you are asking an unfair question of a man who has worked for three months to get you to this table.'

Jane had not intended to outwit Miles; she was simply dwelling on her own maudlin obsessions. 'OK. Tell me the plus sides,' she suggested.

'The plus side is that I am here with you now and you are here with me. That is a plus side of my many, many divorces.' He smiled and took another sip. His gestures were very small gestures, Jane thought. Small and precise. He never wasted a movement.

'Now,' she said, 'Tell me the truth, the whole truth.'

Miles shook his head.

'Miles,' she said. 'Do you think I'm ever again having anything to do with a man I can't trust?'

Miles sighed. 'OK,' he said. 'Let me put it like this. Divorce is probably the worst of all self-inflicted wounds. And it's worse because you have no idea what it's going to be like. That I can tell you from experience. Think of . . . of what it was like when you were a kid. You must have discussed death with your girls? A kid thinks she knows what death is going to be like. Am I right? She thinks death is an absence of life, and that's a sad thing because life is on the whole a nice thing. Well, that's nothing like the whole story. If you have been close to death – and this happened to me once – you know that death isn't just an *absence* of something nice, you are filled with something terrible.' He was warming to his subject. 'Well, being divorced is like that. Someone who is married might think that being divorced is like an absence of those things you value in your marriage. But it's not. Being divorced is like a whole new thing that invades you. And it doesn't leave you. It's a state you enter, not a process. You may stop being married, but you remain divorced even when you marry someone else. It becomes part of you.'

'You make it sound frightening,' Jane said.

Miles picked up his wine glass in a small, significant gesture. 'Then again, being frightened is no reason not to do the right thing, Jane.'

Before Jane could ask Miles what he meant by that the Peking Duck arrived.

Duncan was sitting in Tristram's room as the sun went down. He had his letter to write. Laura had put Tris in with Arthur for the night. Duncan was enjoying having the boy's toys around him and he was amused by the list of positive adjectives that Laura had pinned to Tristram's door. These were affirmative images for his idiosyncrasies. All the Davis boys had them. Halfway down Duncan noticed where Laura had obliterated the word *Dopey*, which was presumably Gawain's contribution to Tristram's personality profile.

Duncan looked at the sheet of paper Laura had provided, and wrote 'Dear Jane.' Where to start? There was no form for this kind of letter, so Duncan just wrote the obvious.

Dear Jane

I am staying with Laura and Gerald because I want to come back to you, and Alice and Ellen, but I do not think you want me back. I know you will be even less happy to see me again when I tell you that I had made an arrangement today to see Carolyn. The reason I am with Laura and Gerald is that I broke that arrangement.

I cannot begin to excuse my behaviour, but I hope that one day I will be able to explain it to you and that you will want to hear my explanation. Mine is not an original story of course. I am the man who has realised very late that his wife is the person he loves above all others. That is why I want to come back to you and that is my only hope of coming back to you. I am not asking you to take me back because I believe my behaviour can be condoned, but because I love you and want to be with you and I hope that part of you still loves me and wants to be with me.

Why isn't life this simple when you're living it, Duncan wondered. Suddenly he remembered that in all the months Jane had been going out to work he'd never actually thanked her for stepping into the breach like that. But no, this wasn't the time. He could say that face-to-face if they met again under more favourable circumstances. Duncan thought of Jane's face.

I can reasonably ask very little of you after what I have put you and the girls through these last three months, but I hope that you will let me come home. I know now that I would rather live in our attic, knowing that you and Alice and Ellen are near, than in a palace with anyone else.

Duncan paused. He had been quite moved by what he had written, but the realisation that Carolyn had never actually invited him to live with her, as his letter suggested, brought Duncan up with a jolt.

I can only hope this letter and my apologies do not arrive too late for us to try and rebuild things.

Duncan was tempted to add that he also hoped that if Jane let him come back she would at least talk to him, but this was not the time for recrimination. This was the time for being abject or nothing. At the bottom of the page he slowly added:

I shan't pester you further, but please ring me at Laura's,
With love, and my regret,
Duncan

Now, he thought, I'd better write to Carolyn too. Tell her the truth, or as much of it as possible without humiliating her.

Gawain wandered in. He seemed so simple and straightforward. 'Mum says you want a letter taken round,' he pointed out.

'Yes,' said Duncan, folding the missive and wishing that he was eleven years old again. 'Good luck.'

Jane and Miles were on to their second bottle of wine which had, fortunately, not produced the threatened tears. She was hearing the story of Miles Mihash and the many Mrs Mihashes, and she was enjoying the company of the man himself. Miles knew how to open up in these situations. Jane found herself responding to a man who would talk about his emotions. And yet, he reminded her of Duncan for that very reason.

'And whose fault was it?' she asked, sweeping back her long dark hair.

'Whose fault was what?' Miles asked.

'The first divorce, the second divorce,' said Jane. 'Whose fault?'

'Well, I'm the common factor,' Miles admitted, offering his glass up to the waiter.

'Ah,' said Jane, waving her chopsticks at him.

Miles pushed his bowl just an inch forward and thought for a few moments. 'Jane,' he said. 'This is not what I intended to say to you. But I will say it because, among the other feelings I have for you, I do respect you.'

He wiped his moustache and began. 'If I am honest with you I do not believe that divorce is usually any one person's fault. You might say it takes two. And what I'd say to you is this: if your marriage is only halfway gone to the bad, if you can see any way of saving it, then *I'd save it* if I were you. This is foolish of me, but I'm going to finish . . . I can't tell you how to save your marriage, Jane, but I can tell you that if you break things with Duncan then part of you will always regret it.'

Jane picked up her hot flannel and wiped her hands and mouth. 'Maybe,' she said, showing how tough she could be.

'However,' Miles continued, 'if you do decide to divorce then remember I'm first in the queue.'

Jane threw her flannel affectionately at him.

'I mean it, Jane. America's a good country to bring up kids,' he said. 'Your girls would love it.'

'Yes,' said Jane. 'I'm sure they would.'

Miles gave her hand an affectionate squeeze. 'And I reckon I've said enough on Duncan's behalf. Christ, the guy can't even get a decent haircut.'

Duncan looked at the sheet of paper in front of him.

Dear Carolyn,

This is not an easy letter to write, it said and, as if to prove it, Duncan had not written anything else for the last twenty minutes.

What was this truth he was supposed to be telling her? The emotional truth he now understood, albeit perhaps too late – but what *had* happened and why had it happened? And even if he could work it out, would Carolyn be interested?

You have every reason to be angry with me, he wrote.

Well, that was certainly true.

When Jane got home, Holly told her that the girls had been exemplary, then asked about her evening, and then she gave her a kind, compassionate look and a hug before they kissed goodnight.

Jane put her remaining baby-sitting tokens back in the jug and looked at the empty kitchen, wondering what to do next with her life. She thought about Duncan's hair, that silly mop that gave him his deceptive schoolboy charm. Jane wasn't immune to the charm yet. But Duncan wasn't here, was he?

The doorbell rang and it was Holly with a letter she'd forgotten to hand over.

∫

The End

The weeks that followed were what Duncan and Jane later referred to as *That Time*, when they felt they were being pushed in a direction that they both wanted to travel, but that neither of them could have gone without Laura and Gerald and Alice and Ellen and Holly and Big Fat Tony. Even Kit played a not insignificant part, sending Barry round with two bottles of champagne.

During those weeks, Duncan returned to living in the attic and Alice and Ellen used to take notes from him to Jane and from Jane to him.

Would Dad like to come down for coffee?

Would Mum like Dad to make a fire in the drawing room?

And Duncan used to pause for longer and longer on the threshold of Jane's bedroom, talking before going up to his room. Jane still had moments when her anger resurfaced, but Duncan warned her that however they felt about each other the last thing they wanted was to ring any alarm bells with Laura, the girls or Holly. Laura was a frequent enough visitor as it was, dropping off notices about concerts and offering to take the girls out on Saturday afternoons.

Alice was reluctant to go to Laura's, but Ellen was a great fan of Gerald's train set, and of Gerald himself, so a visit was agreed. That afternoon Duncan was fixing a Swedish blind to the skylight in his attic bedroom when Jane came up with one of Kit's bottles of champagne and two glasses.

It was the first time Jane had visited Duncan's flat, and she was both impressed and peeved at how nice he'd made it. They sat in the little student sitting room which Duncan had turned into an office.

'We've been very lucky,' she said.

'Yes.'

'Having the girls and Holly and even Laura making such a fuss of us.'

Duncan said he felt they didn't deserve it. Jane agreed that certainly *he* didn't, but she retracted what she said with a world-weary smile.

'And Tony's been very good too,' she added in order to be positive.

'Yes,' said Duncan.

'And Miles.'

Duncan was surprised. He didn't dislike Miles Mihash, but Miles was clearly a roué of the old school. 'I don't blame him for trying it on with you,' Duncan said, 'but I'd hardly say he was on our side.'

'No, he said something that Saturday,' Jane explained 'And it was funny, really. We'd talked a lot about the pros and cons of divorce, and Miles had been very fair, but then he mentioned your hair.'

'What?' said Duncan.

'He said you were a nice guy but you couldn't even get a decent haircut.'

Jane looked at Duncan's hair while Duncan wondered what the hell was so wonderful about Miles saying that. And Jane stroked Duncan's hair as she had wanted to ever since the night of that Saturday. They put down their glasses and hugged each other very very tight.

'Oh God,' said Jane. 'Please can we go to bed?'

When they realised the time and came downstairs, Laura had already brought the girls back and was getting them tea in the kitchen.

'Laura, I'm so sorry,' said Jane, struggling to find the proper way to keep her towelling robe together.

'Not at all,' said Laura with a very happy glow on her face.

'It would have to be Laura,' Jane told Binny. 'I sometimes feel I've got Duncan back by the grace of Laura.'

'Oh well,' said Binny, who had an American cousin helping to draw up her marriage contract, 'at least you'll both have someone to blame if it goes wrong again.'

While Duncan and Jane were getting back together again, and telling each other that it would never happen again, they lost all interest in the lives of other people, with the exception of Alice and Ellen. Fortunately the outside world reciprocated and hardly impinged upon them. To Duncan's great relief there was no dread reply to the letter he had sent Carolyn. No ominous envelope waiting there for him on the mat, its handwriting struggling to contain the unspeakable Parry Morris rage. And, an even greater relief, those silent phone calls stopped too. Duncan thankfully assumed Carolyn had lost all interest in him now.

When that special time was over and the Lewises emerged, blinking into the light of everyday life, Jane was very sorry to find that things between Holly and Gwyn were no better. Indeed, they were distinctly worse.

'You've been so supportive to us,' Jane said as she and

Holly sat by the drawing room fireplace together. 'I just wish there was something we could do for you.'

'But you wanted to stay with Duncan, didn't you?' Holly asked.

Jane nodded.

'That's the thing,' said Holly, looking hopeless.

Jane put her arms round Holly, which was what Holly so much wanted and so much needed.

'I think they're having a snog,' Alice said to Ellen at the doorway.

'Downstairs!' said Duncan.

Most things continued evenly as spring gave way to summer. The conservatory remained unfinished because Norman had found some more lucrative work to go to down the Bay and, although Alice and Ellen settled down in school, it did become apparent that Ellen's work was above average while Alice's remained below. That was going to be a long-term problem.

Then, in May, Jane realised very belatedly that she must be pregnant. It could only have been from that time she and Duncan drank champagne in the attic. Thereafter they had been careful.

Duncan was delighted but Jane was appalled. 'I can't go to work and leave you to bring up a baby,' she cried. 'Two nine-year-olds who can look after themselves, yes – but not a baby.'

When Duncan thought about it that did sound way beyond his capabilities. 'I'll get a job,' he said.

'You're an architect,' Jane reminded him. 'Architects can't go out and get a job just like that.'

But Duncan did. With the firm that he and Alice and Ellen had written to. Alice's godfather came up trumps both for her birthday and his career. It wasn't something deeply creative, but Duncan didn't tell Jane that. It was a good routine job in a big well-run company. It suited Duncan nicely. It meant commuting to Bristol on a daily basis but it was, in the circumstances, quite well paid.

Of course, Duncan had been intending for some time to write a polite note to Caedfael, explaining his decision not to enter the Barrage House competition, but he hadn't. Unfortunately to do so now that he had another job fixed up seemed far less noble than to do so when he had no source of income whatsoever – but Duncan no longer lived in the world of heroics. He had returned, thankfully, to the realms of social comedy, although these were not the terms that he used in his letter to Caedfael Parry Morris.

Remarkably, Duncan didn't see Carolyn for months, and then only briefly at St David's Hall when he glimpsed a VIP reception in the Celebrity Lounge. There she was with her arm resting approvingly on a rather pleasant but worried looking chap who, Duncan guessed, was working very hard. Carolyn didn't seem to see Duncan, and he didn't seem to see her either.

Jane told Binny that she was pregnant when they went to Llanthony in May, and Flyn used this as an excuse to get Duncan very drunk and very ill. But they kept the news back from everyone else till they threw a conservatory party at the beginning of June. Norman had finished the job very quickly when Duncan simply refused to make any interim payments.

Duncan and Jane's 'Thank God the conservatory is finished' party was slightly overshadowed by Gerald's illness. It had happened one Sunday afternoon, a strange turn and a dreadful pain in the chest, and the people at the hospital seemed uncertain as to whether this was or was not a heart attack. Laura was very brave and didn't tell anyone, but Gawain sent Tristram round to tell Duncan.

'Gawain says Dad's been ill and Mum won't tell anyone,'

recited Tristram as if he wasn't really aware of what these words meant.

Duncan went down to the CRI that afternoon and found Gerald looking very grey but cheerful.

'She'll be here soon, I should imagine,' said Gerald. 'But I'm very glad you've come.'

And then he explained that as far as he could see he'd been lucky this time but one day he wouldn't be, and if that happened when Duncan was around he wanted Duncan to help out. 'In any way you can, old boy. Will you do that for me?'

'Of course,' said Duncan.

'You see, she won't ask,' said Gerald. 'She's so brave.'

And here Gerald looked as if he was going to cry. Duncan took his big hand in his own.

'You see, she's very fond of you,' Gerald continued.

'I know,' said Duncan. 'I don't know why.'

Gerald breathed out with a big release of emotion. 'Ah well, that's Laura,' he said. 'Never really knew what she saw in me either.'

But Laura did come to Jane and Duncan's conservatory party, as did Norman, which was a bit of a cheek.

He was soon recruited by Kit who had come without the Bastard. 'My husband? He's attending some conference in Carmarthen to control the extent of venereal disease amongst sheep shaggers,' she said to anyone who was listening. Then she began to explain to Norman this idea she'd had for a revolutionary new conservatory. 'Not just a load of UPVC doors stuck on top of each other but a whole new concept,' she said as Norman took out a pencil and old envelope.

Holly came to the party but without Gwyn, which was going to be the pattern from now on – until there was no longer any expectation of the two of them.

And Binny and Flyn came (but left separately), and David and Bronagh who was, to her deep regret and David's, pregnant. Given the black looks between them, Jane said nothing to them of her own news.

And Siân Roberts came with Roger, to no one's surprise; and Elaine came, having said she couldn't, but only at the last moment. Big Fat Tony didn't come of course, and Miles left a message on the answer-phone saying he was the Big Bad Wolf and he'd huffed and puffed but he could see that nothing was going to blow their house down, so good luck and come and see him in Seattle some time.

Duncan and Jane felt a warm and unrealistic sense of support from all their friends, most of whom had come for a drink and a gossip with hardly any inkling that they were relaunching the marriage of Duncan and Jane.

Duncan had had it in mind to announce that they were having a baby at the party, but Jane thought this was gross. Besides, Kit had already guessed and the girls had found out that morning, It was only a matter of time before everyone knew.

'We've got to tell Holly and Laura,' Duncan said as he made more highly alcoholic punch.

So Holly and Laura were brought in separately, once Mrs R. had been eased out of the kitchen. Duncan had invited her as a guest but she insisted on making him feel guilty by collecting glasses from the garden. 'You knew what you were doing when you invited me,' she grumbled happily.

By rights it should have been Laura who was the first to be told, as she was, in Jane's words, 'Duncan's Number One Fan.' But Laura was engrossed in discussing The Abbey with Kit in the garden. So Holly was the first to be told the news and she gave them both a big hug and cried a bit in the kitchen.

Then Laura responded to Duncan's entreaty and came inside. Kit winked at him as Laura went to see Jane.

Laura took the news very graciously, behaving as if she was the first to be informed. Images of death and sadness had so clouded her life recently that new life seemed just what was needed.

'I'm sure it will be a boy,' she said with enthusiasm.

You would say that, thought Jane, but 'Duncan would like a son,' was what she said.

'This is *such* good news,' said Laura, for Gerald had been spared this time. Not this time, the Fates had said – not yet, but one day. 'I'm so happy.'

She kissed Jane and shook Duncan's hand.

'You know,' she said, taking the most optimistic view, for what was the point of any other? 'You know, we think the world of both of you.'